BOUND BY THE SLEEPER'S HARP

THE ARCANE ARTIFACTS 1

MELISSA MITCHELL

For all the book girlies who fell in love with Ruhn Danaan and craved another tattooed, pierced protector with a heart of gold.

CONTENT NOTE

This book contains on-page depictions of domestic violence including physical assault, choking, and bone breaking. Sexual assault is referenced and discussed in detail but occurs off-page. Additional content includes explicit consensual sexual scenes, on-page violence and murder, supernatural mind control/compulsion, kidnapping, stalking, and detailed discussions of past trauma and abuse recovery.

The story centers around healing from domestic violence and features a survivor's journey toward reclaiming her life and dreams. While these themes are handled with care, readers should be aware of the content before proceeding.

For a more detailed content warning list, please visit: https://www.authormelissamitchell.com/bbtsh

1

———

The scent of coffee eased some of the tension bracketing my body. I took a deep inhale and got in line, letting the atmosphere of Awake Coffee wash over me. The background jazz music, the din of voices, the loud noises from the grinder and espresso machine. It was pure comfort, the single indulgence I allowed myself these days.

I flexed my aching shoulders and glanced down at my raw knuckles. Today's MMA class had been brutal in the best way. I suppressed a smile at the sight of my inflamed skin. Every bruise was chosen, not inflicted, not anymore.

My routine was the same every Monday, Wednesday, and Friday. I went to my MMA class at 2:00pm, then dropped by Awake on my way home. Grabbing my favorite drink was the best reward for pushing myself outside my comfort zone, one I frequently reminded myself not to feel guilty about. Especially if it meant getting a few minutes inside my favorite coffee shop.

Awake Coffee was located in the heart of one of Walton's quieter neighborhoods. I loved West Cross for its clean streets and walkable establishments—a human neighborhood that supernaturals largely ignored, unlike the high-rise chaos of Midtown just a few miles away. Making it safer, too.

A burst of raucous laughter had me glancing over my shoulder as a group of locals entered. I turned away before anyone had the chance to greet me or make small talk, fixing my gaze on the hand-decorated chalk menu, pretending to contemplate my choices, even though I had the entire thing memorized.

There were times I missed the girl I once was. But that girl had died at the hands of Luke Portman. Died and come back stronger, albeit not without scars.

The changes had been gradual. The slow death of my confidence. The retreat into myself. The loss of my friends—all except one. Everything leading up to the night that both stripped me bare and gave me my life back.

It had taken the better part of two years to heal. To forge me into the woman I was today. But there were some things I might never get back because of how I was forced to live now. The secrets I was forced to keep.

The line shifted again. It was busier than usual today. I zipped my two pendant necklaces along their gold chains, fiddling with them as I waited. The patron in front of me placed an order then moved out of the way. It was my turn to order.

"Rose!" the woman behind the counter greeted me. "Hey, girl."

"Hey, Tara." I plastered a grin on my face, wearing a facade I'd mastered.

"Sorry about the wait. No Vivi today?" Tara glanced past me toward the door. Her hopeful expression dimmed when I shook my head.

Tara and Vivi had been playing a game of cat and mouse for years; Tara was the cat. I wished they would give it a chance, this thing between them. My helpless heart couldn't take much more of it.

"Just me today," I answered. "She's busy packing."

"She's…wait, packing? Does that mean we have to cancel girls night tomorrow?" Her expression dimmed even more.

"Yeah. Long story." I didn't want to admit I was relieved about the cancelation of our monthly get together. Vivi said it was good to spend time with our friends. If it weren't for her, I'd literally have zero. But honestly, it was probably better that way. "There was some family drama with her sister and her fiancé—"

Behind me, an impatient throat cleared. I glanced over my shoulder at a middle-aged woman waiting with her arms crossed. Her eyes were fixed on my hair, her expression turning sour with judgment.

"Sorry," I muttered—mostly out of reflex. Some of my old scars peeking through.

I turned back to the cute blonde behind the counter. Tara had a short bob, blue eyes, and a smattering of freckles across her nose and cheeks. Her style could mostly be described as retro, anything that ranged from seventies to nineties. She always wore something fun. Today's dress was a salmon-colored number with bell sleeves and bright flowers. Her black apron was cinched at the waist showing off her curves.

If that wasn't enough to recommend her, the fact that she co-owned Awake Coffee didn't hurt. Vivi was an idiot for not locking her down *immediately*.

Tara chewed on the inside of her cheek. "All right. Well, what can I get you? Dirty chai latte, venti?"

"Yep." I fished my wallet from my purse.

"And a white chocolate mocha for Vivi?"

"Also venti. Extra shot. Actually, can you make that two?"

"*Wow*…" Tara's brows shot up. "All right."

"She's got a late night."

Tara worried her lower lip. "Should I call her?"

"She'll probably be on a plane by the time you close up here. But you should definitely text her. I think she'd like that."

"Right. Okay." Tara gave a soft smile as her fingers flew

over the touch screen console, logging my order. "Seven-forty-two," she said, adding, "family discount."

Even though we weren't family.

"Thanks," I mumbled as my cheeks flushed. She was trying to be nice, and I wasn't one to turn down a discount. My finances couldn't afford that and Tara knew it. But still, I hated the embarrassment that followed.

My burner phone buzzed with incoming texts as I pulled cash from my wallet. I threw the extra bills into the tip jar.

I thanked Tara and pressed my wallet under my arm before unlocking my phone and stepping away.

Vivi had sent two images, each with her holding a different outfit in front of the mirror. A string of messages followed.

> VIVI
>
> Which outfit says I'm going to kill my sister's ex fiancé?
>
> VIVI
>
> The black one, right?
>
> VIVI
>
> That way I'll blend in, just in case there are any witnesses.

I snorted, typing out a reply—

And collided with a wall of muscle in the form of a broad chest. A rush of warm liquid poured down my hands and the front of my clothes and I gasped, jumping backward. My purse, phone, and wallet dropped to the floor as I regained my footing. A massive coffee spill covered the front of my lavender T-shirt. It was one of my favorites, too, with a picture of a Ragdoll cat wearing fairy wings. "What the *hell*—?!" My words cut off as I locked gazes with a simmering pair of green eyes.

My lips parted as I took him in.

It wasn't just that he was tall, with layers of muscle beneath his black T-shirt. He was also covered in tattoos and piercings. His black hair was long on one side and shaved on the other, with tribal patterns etched in. Everything about him screamed *danger!*

A rush of warmth dumped into my stomach. A sensation I was surprised to feel when I'd felt absolutely nothing for the past two years.

I forced my breaths to calm, a technique my therapist had coached me on.

When I blinked, the male's glamor wavered and I no longer saw a human, but a goblin. His skin changed from golden to gunmetal gray. His ears turned to points. His piercings and tattoos multiplied. A piercing appeared in his septum, another in his lip and eyebrow. I sucked in a breath.

"Maybe watch where you're going, yeah?" he gritted out.

The moment the words were spoken, the spell was broken. I blinked and his glamor snapped back into place, making him appear human again.

"I'm—sorry! It was an accident," I sputtered.

Wait…

Why was I apologizing?! That wasn't who I was anymore. I wasn't a scared, cowering girl.

"Someone grab her a towel," Tara called to one of her employees as another rushed forward with a mop to clean the bit that had landed on the floor.

"Thanks, Tara," I managed, regaining my composure.

"I'd like another coffee," the male told Tara, never taking his eyes off me. I felt his stare caress my skin as he looked me up and down.

That same, almost foreign feeling welled up inside me again. Attraction. He wasn't even my type.

"Uhm." Tara hesitated, like she wanted to argue. "Another refill. Sure. Mark will take care of that if you head over to the barista counter."

I ripped my gaze away, turning my eyes downward. Most of my belongings had spilled out of my purse. I wiped my hands on my yoga pants then crouched and swept everything

—including my unmentionables—back inside, then grabbed my phone and stood, only to find the goblin holding my wallet, examining it.

Every nerve ending went on full alert. "What are you doing?!" I accused. I didn't carry identification anymore. Something I'd stopped doing after Luke destroyed any hope at a normal life.

"I'm just looking for your license, you know, to make sure it doesn't indicate your need for corrective lenses, since you obviously couldn't see where you were going—"

I snatched my wallet from him and shouldered past, heading for the drinks counter. Instead of taking the hint, he stalked after me. I gritted my teeth, ignoring him as he set his mug down for his refill, crowding me.

"You okay?" Mark asked, handing over a towel before glaring at my new shadow. Mark had asked me out a few times, but I'd always firmly declined. I didn't date—not anymore.

"I'm fine," I managed, blotting up what I could so my shirt was no longer dripping. I tossed the towel onto the counter.

Mark hesitated before nodding. "I'll have your drinks out in just a moment."

"Thanks." I took a steadying breath, trying to calm my nerves. A hint of musk and something woodsy met my nose. I couldn't resist another inhale until I realized it was the goblin. I took a step to the side, putting more distance between us. He mirrored my actions, stepping closer—too close.

I flinched. The reaction was followed by embarrassment as I reminded myself that I was okay. That he wasn't going to hurt me. That no one would ever hurt me again.

The goblin immediately took two large steps back—which only furthered my humiliation. "Just waiting for my refill," he said, his voice quieter than before, like he was trying to reassure me. Funny, since he hadn't cared before.

"There's literally a million other places you could wait," I said under my breath, finally finding my backbone.

"I wouldn't say a *million*. Realistically, there's more like—"

"Are you always this much of an asshole?!" I rounded on him.

The corner of his mouth twitched. "Usually, I'm worse. But you're right. I'll tone it down a notch—for now."

I trapped my bottom lip between my teeth, fighting a smile. A real, genuine smile, as Mark finished up my drinks.

"I didn't mean to make you uncomfortable," the goblin added after a long stretch of silence. He kept his voice low. I noticed that he didn't move any closer, either.

"Yeah, well," I gestured to my shirt, trying to keep my tone light. "Kinda failed from the start."

"You should pay better attention to your surroundings." There wasn't any censure in his tone, just calm concern.

My shoulders went tight anyway. I wanted to argue, but he was right. I'd been careless letting myself get distracted by my phone. I knew better. Or, I should have. Maybe enough time had passed that I'd grown complacent. I wasn't sure if that was a good thing. "Thanks for the tip."

"Anytime." His gaze remained fixed on me, a physical sensation that was impossible to ignore.

"Drinks are ready, Rose," Mark said, offering me a nod as he slid them onto the counter.

I moved forward to collect them and caught another delicious inhale of that woodsy musk.

"Take care of yourself," the goblin said as I strode away.

I said nothing in return.

It didn't matter that I could feel him watching me as I made a beeline for the exit. I didn't look back.

2

____

"Rose? Is that you?" Vivi's head popped into the hallway as my keys plunked into the bowl just inside the door to our apartment. Her gaze landed on our drinks, because she was *that* obsessed with caffeine that she failed to notice the massive stain on my favorite cat shirt.

"You're a life saver." She flew forward, all five-foot-three of her, snatching the mocha from my hand. Then she froze, the drink halfway to her mouth. Her jaw went slack. "What… What the hell happened to you?!"

"Oh, you know, just bumped into a goblin before he spilled his coffee down the front of my shirt."

"A goblin?" Vivi was curvy with bronze skin, dressed in an elegant black top and designer boots that screamed 'art curator.' Her job at Origin, a museum downtown, paid well enough to afford our West Cross apartment.

"Yep. A six-foot-something goblin. Pointed ears and all."

Her gaze roved over my features until her expression morphed into something suspicious. "And…did this goblin happen to be good looking?"

"That's… How could that possibly matter?" I sputtered.

"Because you're breathing hard and flushed. Look at you."

"If I'm *anything*, it's because there was a goblin at Awake."

"So? You deal with supernaturals all the time. One lone goblin is nothing."

"Need I remind you that this is a human neighborhood? We don't get supernaturals here."

She knew about the supernatural community because I'd told her. It was illegal for supernaturals to tell humans about their existence, but there was no law against *me* doing it. Hopefully.

"He was probably just passing through," she assured me, lifting a shoulder.

"Right. Passing through."

"Did you make him replace your shirt?"

"My shirt? I… Well… No. I mean… It was kind of my fault. What? You were texting me about your outfits. And yeah, I kind of wasn't watching where I was going. So—this." I gestured to my poor shirt.

"Well, if he was a true gentleman, he would have offered to replace it."

"He didn't. Besides, I hardly think he fits into the gentlemen category." My thoughts immediately went back to his appearance.

"Oh my *gawd*!" Vivi nudged my shoulder. "You *are* into him."

"I am not! Besides, it doesn't matter."

"Uh-huh." She made a humming noise, growing smugger by the moment. "Didn't I tell you you'd get it back eventually?"

"Look. Just drop it. Let's get you packed so you don't miss your flight." I took a fortifying sip of my latte, prompting her to do the same.

She took a drink. "*God*, this is so good."

"I bet Tara would keep you plied full of those things if you started dating."

She snorted. "You know I see through your attempts at matchmaking, right?"

"As long as you notice the effort I put in." I lifted a

shoulder.

"Come on. I need your help figuring out what else to pack."

I followed her down the hallway to her room, asking, "Do you think Cameron will be okay?"

Vivi's shoulders sagged. "I'll make sure she is. Right after I get the full story."

"And you'll text me when you find out?"

"Of course!"

"If you need me to fly out so we can kill her fiancé together, just say the word. You know I'll help you bury the body." Vivi had been there for me when everything happened with Luke. She'd stuck with me during the darkest time in my life. There was no way I wouldn't walk through fire for her.

"Who says there will be a body left after I'm done with him?" Her grin was malicious.

I cackled with glee. "I'll be your alibi then."

"Deal!"

God, I loved her.

I looked over her outfit choices and pointed out my favorites before settling on her bed as she finished packing. "At least she found out before the wedding and not after," I said.

"I suppose there's that," Vivi muttered, attempting to cram everything in. "I swear, this is why I don't do love."

"I thought it was because you're 'too busy' for a relationship?" I added air quotes.

"That, too! Besides, I'll put myself out there again when *you* do."

"Touché."

Vivi stood, tugging her suitcase up onto its rollers. "I think that's everything."

"You sure you don't want me to go with you to the airport?"

"I'll be fine." She pulled her phone from her pocket and ordered a ride share. A few moments later, it chimed. "Five minutes. Perfect."

"I guess this is goodbye then." I stood, setting my latte on the dresser to give her a hug.

"Take care of yourself while I'm away, yeah?" She eyed me. "Be careful at work. Don't let those supernatural assholes give you grief. Text me every day."

"You know I will." I wrapped my arms around her, squeezing her tight. She smelled like the citrus body wash from the luxury bath shop she loved.

"Okay, I better go before I get all emotional." We pulled apart and my throat tightened. It's not like she'd be gone for long. Still, it had me missing her already.

"Text me when you get to the airport." I grabbed my drink and followed her out into the living room.

"Will do. See you later alligator." She grabbed her purse and threw open the door, rolling her suitcase out with her. I watched her go before turning the deadbolt and locking myself in.

Only then did I let my thoughts return to the goblin. I leaned against the door, taking slow breaths as my mind raced back over our encounter. The way his gaze felt on my skin. The way my stomach warmed under his perusal.

My decision to remain single was a necessary one. I couldn't afford to get tangled up with anyone. Up until today, that hadn't felt like a problem.

Wrangling my emotions, I pushed off the door and set off down the hallway.

My shift at Vortex started at eight, which left just enough time to get ready and eat a quick dinner.

My bedroom was my little slice of heaven. It was decorated to suit my style with bright neon pastel colors. There was a plush chaise lounge perfect for reading, a queen bed piled with throw pillows, and a desk—all of it thrifted. The shag rug was a lovely shade of neon blue, and the art on the wall practically glowed with depictions of illuminated cityscapes and neon signs. Vivi had gifted the art to me right after moving in. I didn't want to know what it cost. The only reason I hadn't forced her to return it was because they'd been final sale.

I changed into my work clothes, a pair of black, form-fitting slacks, a black long sleeve button down, and stylish dark purple blazer that had the club's symbol embroidered on the front. The contacts I wore made my eyes dark brown instead of their natural hazel. Then I did my makeup and curled my hair until my cotton candy waves pooled around my head and flowed to the middle of my back, thick and flawless. There was no sign of my honey blonde roots. I paid enough to keep it that way. To keep it perfect. Anyone who had known me from my old life wouldn't recognize me now.

My phone buzzed.

Seconds later, she sent me a thumbs-up emoji.

In the living room, I put on the TV. It powered on to a random news channel, whatever Vivi had been watching. Then I set about reheating lasagna leftovers.

Vivi's lasagna was a drug. I thanked my lucky stars that she'd made an entire casserole dish just yesterday. Now I'd have leftovers through tomorrow. I carried my plate toward the table, absentmindedly listening to the newscaster in the background.

"Authorities have publicly released the identity of the body found in her home late last week as Professor Jane Miller—"

I froze midstep, my eyes fixing on the flatscreen, on the grainy photograph beside the newscaster. My vision tunneled and I blinked to clear it.

"Details are still under investigation as to the motive behind her murder. Let's head over to WN's Doreen Morris for more."

The plate slipped from my hand and clattered to the floor. I barely heard it drop as footage flashed onto the screen. Professor Jane Miller's house, surrounded by yellow caution tape, was a buzz of activity. The dark night accentuated the flicker of blue and red lights as authorities swarmed about.

The camera zoomed in on Doreen Morris. "Yes, thank you, Tania. Authorities have been tight-lipped about what happened last week, but additional evidence leads us to believe Professor Miller's death was a premeditated act of violence. Evidence of a physical altercation and knife wounds indicate a struggle. A full autopsy is still underway, with no idea when or if the details will be released to the public. Witnesses say Professor Miller was seen leaving Walton University late last Monday afternoon but reported nothing unusual about her behavior. When she didn't appear for her evening lecture, worried students noted her absence to the authorities. The WBI is still looking into the details, but the question remains: What was the motivation behind such a gruesome attack? And is the university community safe?"

The footage flashed back to the newsroom before going to commercial. A small whimper escaped my lips. I reached for the remote, frantically fumbling before finding the power button. A roar sounded as blood pumped past my ears.

I took in the scene around me. The floor was a mess of broken stoneware and lasagna, almost like blood and guts. Some of it had splattered onto my black boots.

My fingers twitched and my hand unconsciously reached for the medallion pendant at my neck. I clutched it, squeezing tightly—

My phone buzzed and I jerked. It was just Vivi.

VIVI

Just boarded. I'll text you when I land.

An ache built in my throat. I needed to tell her what I'd just seen. She hadn't known Professor Miller like I had. She'd only taken two courses with her. But she still needed to know. I started to type, but stopped, erasing my words before I began again. What was I supposed to say? Especially when she had enough to deal with. Swallowing down the urge, I fired off a message.

Have a safe flight. Love u!

VIVI

Love u too!

I'd tell her later, after she landed.

I glanced down at the mess on the floor, then at the clock. My throat worked, swallowing against the acidic taste of bile. I couldn't eat now. The thought of food made me want to puke. With one final swallow, I rushed into the kitchen and used a paper towel to clean my shoes, then bolted for the door, grabbed my purse and keys, and fled.

3

I balanced a tray of empty glasses above the chaos, weaving through sweaty bodies toward the bar. Vortex pulsed around me—bass thrumming through my bones, supernatural patrons shouting over music that could wake the dead.

"Rose! There you are," a voice yelled, barely loud enough over the noise. Kaylee rushed over, breathing hard, and slammed her tray onto the bar's edge beside mine.

"Kaylee. Hey." I tried to muster my usual level of enthusiasm, but it fell flat.

I took in her rapid breathing and light sheen of sweat on her warm brown skin. She was sporting a deep burgundy lipstick and had straightened her hair to twice its normal length until it was sleek and shiny.

Like me, she was one of the few other humans employed at Vortex.

"I can't wait for tomorrow night," she gasped out, clutching her side and smiling. "I need a break from this shit. Did you guys need me to bring anything?"

"Oh, crap. I almost forgot."

Her face fell. "Did something happen?" Taking my wrist,

she pulled me toward the hallway leading to some of the VIP balcony boxes. It was only mildly quieter. "What's wrong?"

"Vivi had to fly home earlier."

"Wait…*what*? Is everything okay?"

"Things are fine. Cameron's engagement fell through."

"Oh, *damn*! What happened?"

"Her fiancé cheated."

"That asshole! Ugh."

"I know."

"So…no girls night then? Unless… You guys still want to get together, maybe go out instead?"

"Actually, I'm going to pass. I might just pick up an extra shift instead." Or just stay home and wrap my head around what I'd seen on the news.

"What? *Ewww*. Come on! Let's go out. You need to let loose—"

"Ladies!" a voice barked, saving me from coming up with more excuses. Zach, also known as Eaden's right hand, appeared. "Less talking, more working. Rose, boss needs to see you."

Kaylee offered me a rueful smile. "Let me know if you change your mind. I'll text the others."

I nodded, following Zach to the back of the club and up a set of stairs. "What's he want this time?"

"Fuck if I know."

The first time I'd met Zach, all it took was a single blink to see what he was. A shifter. A massive lion's head had replaced his face, the transparent overlay shimmering in my vision before I'd blinked it away. Like the other shifter enforcers that Eaden employed, Zach kept things under control at the club. Vortex was filled with supernaturals. Not just staff, but patrons.

Located in the heart of Walton, it was a popular congregation spot.

We stopped at Eaden's door and Zach knocked. It was quieter here, but the walls still throbbed with the pulse of the music. Eaden's voice was muffled as he called for us. Zach, with his supernatural hearing, heard him perfectly as he opened the door and let me through.

Eaden's office was almost like a study. Plush rugs, a gas fireplace, a wall of books, and nature paintings in gilded frames. When I blinked, his transparent wolf form overlaid his human form, but only briefly. He had dark skin and muscles for days.

Eaden's eyes lingered on his phone a moment before he looked up at me. "Rose," he said, his voice a deep rumble, "there you are. Zach, that'll be all."

"Right." Zach backed out of the room, closing the door behind him.

"Everything good?" Eaden asked, eyeing me. He'd always had a way of seeing past the bullshit straight to the heart of me. It's how he'd known something was up when he met me. How he'd guessed at what I'd been through. And probably why he'd offered me a job.

He'd run into me when I first took up MMA. He taught at the same gym, some of the more advanced classes. I'd known absolutely nothing about self defense when I'd started, and he'd been one of the subs when our instructor was out.

He'd guessed—rightly so—that I was a dancer simply because of how I moved. It just so happened he was short a couple of them. Coincidentally. I'll never know if that was the truth or not.

It was only once I was more comfortable interacting with supernaturals, males in particular, that he'd allowed me to work the floor as a server instead. Something that gave me a much needed pay bump. Something that had helped boost my confidence and harden me—*heal me*, after Luke.

I was forever grateful to him for both opportunities.

Forcing a genuine smile onto my face, I shrugged and said, "I'm good enough, I guess. Did you need something?"

He hesitated. If he saw my lie, he chose not to call me on it. "I need you to dance tonight."

I opened my mouth, then promptly closed it. "I'm on the floor tonight. Don't you dare."

"Micky didn't show up. I'm short a dancer."

I drew in a breath and released it, forcing my voice to calm. "Well, did you call her? She's probably just running late." He gave me a look. Because of course he'd called her. I probably wouldn't be here if he knew where she was. It was unlike Micky to miss work without warning. She was a shifter, and Eaden kept a tighter leash on his people—on everyone who worked at the club. We were like family.

Sighing, he leaned back. "I need you out there tonight, Rose. Just give me this, yeah?"

I was one of his best dancers. Paired with my vibrant pink hair, and my stage name of *Candy*, I was an attraction for all sorts of clientele, especially the inhuman.

"I've gotta make rent next week, Eaden. I can't survive on dancing wages—you know this." Vortex served expensive alcohol and entertained a higher echelon of clientele. They tipped well for their drinks. I needed those tips.

"I'll give you a hundred an hour. Give me two hours and two solos. I've got a couple of high rollers on the balcony. I want you out there."

My shoulders relaxed. "Two hundred?"

"As I said."

"Fine." I could work with that. I'd already made a decent amount of tips over the past two hours, and if I could finish the night out with a few more VIP sections, I'd be solid.

"Good. Go get ready. I want you on in fifteen."

———

After changing into a gold crop-top and thong in the staff locker room, I made my way to the empty cage at the center of the club's floor. There were ten platform cages in total, all gilded in gold and ridiculously lavish, with poles running through their centers. They were filled with scantily clad males and females, most of whom were exotic supernaturals. I supposed I was meant to be the exotic human specimen.

Our DJ, a fae named Tanner, nodded my way. I gave him a quick half-smile. Tanner knew which songs I liked and which to play for my solos. I climbed into my cage, shut the door behind me, and began to prowl. The song died down before the flashing lights zeroed in on me. The rest of the club darkened.

Taking a deep breath, I stepped into my persona of Candy, shedding my worries about Professor Miller and everything else that had happened today. Something about being in the cage had always made me feel safe. Safe from everyone outside. Safe from my life. Safe to be whoever I wanted.

Candy was bold and seductive with her pink hair, gold lipstick, smoky eyes, and shimmer coating her skin—nothing like the cowering Rose who'd fled an abusive relationship, even if she'd healed over the past two years. Even if she'd come back as something stronger.

The transition finished and a new song came on—Candy's song.

I crept around the pole in the center of the platform. There was a lurch and the whole cage lifted off the floor, raising up a few feet to make me more visible to the crowd and balconies above. Somewhere overhead, a machine shot fog into the air. The world around me glowed, like something out of a dream, making the shimmer on my skin come to life.

I let the music flow over me, exhaling and loosening my limbs before sliding into motion. The beat picked up and I reached for the pole, sweeping my body around and dragging myself along it, engaging my core. My stilettos kicked into the air, and I settled into a well-known trance of twisting and spinning and contorting myself.

Losing myself to the music.

I loved how when I danced, I became a thing of fantasy. Someone desirable and unobtainable. Someone who didn't carry scars.

As a child, I'd enjoyed ballet and other traditional forms before quitting those in favor of hip hop and jazz. I'd moved on from there to pole and other exotic forms, which offered the kind of challenge that made me thrive. Dance was one of the reasons I did so well with MMA. I had decades of coordination working in my favor.

The crowd screamed, their arms lifted in the air, swaying with the beat. Cellphones came out, recording videos that would pop up all over social media later with *#cottoncandyvortex* and other various hashtags synonymous with my persona. I tossed my hair, making eye contact with anyone close enough to see, turning up the heat. Every movement was calculated, controlled, sinuous.

My treacherous thoughts went back to the goblin in the coffee shop. What would he see if he were here, watching me? A woman fighting for her confidence? Or someone who had already won?

My solo came to an end, the music settling into a slower rhythm. I continued dancing as the other caged dancers began again, effectively pulling some of the crowd's attention away. Now that I wasn't blasted with spotlights, my eyes roamed the club. It was packed tonight, people swarming the floor, dancing and drinking.

Eaden had mentioned the VIP balcony boxes, which was where most of our important clientele congregated. Those boxes were by reservation only, with a hefty price tag. Vortex was a favorite for supernaturals who wanted privacy. Ideal for the types of deals taking place here tonight.

My eyes slid over the faces of Walton's richest patrons. Most were engaged in hushed conversations. All it took was a blink and a little intense staring to see what they were. Elves, fae, shifters, vampires…and even a few humans.

I faltered as my gaze passed over a head of shaggy blond hair peeking out beneath an all too familiar baseball cap. Walton University's WU logo front and center. I did a double-take, my heart taking off into a gallop. His face was shadowed, so I couldn't make out his features. But I could imagine them. Cold eyes, pointed chin, strong jaw.

My hand slipped, sending me careening down the pole. Recovering, I moved into an intentional dive before pulling up. I was known for my impressive flexibility and athleticism. The surrounding crowd gasped and cheered, then clapped, delighted. I threw them a seductive smile, playing it off, and continued dancing, swinging around for another look.

He was gone—like he'd never even been there.

Because I'd probably imagined him.

He was human. What business did he have in a supernatural club, anyway?

Anger replaced fear. I was so, *so* tired of looking over my shoulder. Imagining Luke's face in every head of blond hair. If he hadn't found me after two years, he wasn't going to. Professor Miller's medallion was supposed to ensure that. My pink hair and contacts merely a secondary safety precaution.

Determined to put this behind me, I continued dancing.

Swinging around, trying not to think of Luke—because he didn't deserve a second of my attention—my eyes landed on a figure hidden in the darkness. This time my breath hitched as a swarm of butterflies took off in my stomach. I blinked, not quite certain what I was seeing. Afraid it was another illusion.

But it wasn't.

The goblin from the coffee shop was watching me, leaning against the far wall of one of the VIP balcony boxes, with his arms crossed. Curious but nonchalant. Maybe he'd tracked me down to replace my shirt?

I huffed because, yeah, fat chance.

Our eyes met and held. His gaze was a dark challenge that had alarm bells ringing. A single encounter could be passed off as coincidence. But twice in one day?

I forced my paranoia to take a back seat. I needed to stop assuming the worst. He was a supernatural, after all. And this was a prime location for his kind.

Pulling my attention away, I focused on my work.

The second hour passed in a blur of bright lights and heightened breaths.

As my cage settled to the floor, I didn't allow myself to look at the balcony boxes, to see if the goblin was still there. Instead, I slipped away, moving through the mass of bodies to the other side of the club. I keyed in the code and slipped into the quiet of the locker room. My shoulders sagged and I collapsed on the bench beside my locker. Every muscle was strung tight and aching, especially after my training earlier. Catching my breath, I ditched my stilettos, then pulled on my black slacks and black boots. I reached for the hem of my metallic gold top—

My phone began buzzing. I fished it out and frowned. Very few people had my number. The one I saw on the screen was one I didn't recognize, with an area code I was unfamiliar with.

I slid the answer button.

"Vivi? Did you forget your charger? Is everything okay?" She should have landed by now.

A muffled female voice answered, too garbled to understand. It *did* kind of sound like her, but the signal was too choppy. I stood and moved around the room.

"Vivi? Can you hear me?"

"Rose?" I managed to make out the sound of my name. Shit. Had something happened to her? My heart began to race.

"Hello? Vivi? Is that you?"

The voice responded again, but it was too indistinct.

"You're breaking up. Sorry, hold on."

Heading for the back door, I pushed it open and kicked the doorstop into place. Darkness and cool spring air greeted my flushed skin as I emerged into the alley behind Vortex.

"Can you hear me?" I asked, staring at the opposite wall. "Vivi?"

The line went dead.

"Damn it!" I pulled my phone from my ear and looked down at the number again. What the hell?

A shoe scuffed beside me. I spun, but a hand clamped over my mouth before I could scream. Arms locked around me like a cage. "Hello, Elle," a voice whispered against my ear. My blood turned to ice as a million horrible memories crashed over me. "Love what you did with your hair by the way. But I still prefer the blonde."

A whimper sounded in the back of my throat, because I'd been completely wrong. It *had* been Luke in the VIP balcony box. He'd finally found me. And I'd walked right into his waiting arms.

Bastian watched from the shadows, keeping his arms crossed. Few of the patrons on the balcony noticed him, and when they did, they gave him a wide-eyed look and scurried away. He'd managed to stay out of sight of Eaden's people—thank fuck for that. His eyes tracked the head of cotton candy pink hair, the color of spun sugar, as it bobbed through the crowd, her gold top glinting in the mass of darkness. In the crowd of bodies, her pert little ass was no longer visible, but he'd certainly gotten a distracting eyeful while she was dancing.

He didn't mix work and play, but fuck, he was starting to rethink that rule, already considering the exceptions that might be made.

She reached the far end of the club, disappearing through a security door. He held his position a few minutes longer, waiting for her to reemerge. Her shift was meant to last another two hours. He hadn't expected to see her in the cage dancing. That had been an unforeseen surprise. An inconvenient one, since he'd hoped to intercept her while she was serving drinks on the floor.

He inhaled, letting his chest rise and fall, remaining alert. Eleanor Rose Kennedy. She'd been a complete wild card on his list of suspects. He hadn't expected a bombshell of a female with intelligent eyes and pink hair. Pink, fucking cotton candy hair. And yet, the longer he'd watched her dance, the more it grew on him.

He'd had a hell of a time tracking her down. It didn't help that she'd been going by her middle name. A red flag, that. Because she didn't want to be found?

If that was the case, what was she hiding from? Or rather...who?

All the more reason to dig deeper into her. If there was one thing he was certain of, she had the answers he needed.

He shifted uncomfortably, running a hand over the shaved side of his scalp, angling his body to better see the club. The minutes ticked by. No head of pink hair emerged.

Closing his eyes, he burrowed into his magic, letting his sense of metals take over. He'd already attuned himself to hers earlier. It was simply a matter of locating the gold around her neck, which had been a lucky find. A flare of recognition reached him. She was still in the room behind the security door, moving around almost erratically. Her direction changed, then she was moving toward the back of the club.

He frowned.

There'd been a moment earlier, just a brief flash before she'd seen him, when she'd spotted someone in the VIP box near his. Whoever it was had made her falter. He'd looked over, but hadn't picked out anyone specific.

His senses tingled. The glint of gold around her neck had stopped moving. Tunneling deeper, becoming one with the metal, he focused on its surroundings. He felt the brush of skin—*her* skin. He ignored the warmth of it, the distracting softness of her chest where the pendants rested. Then he felt something else, something kissing the other side of the necklace. Cool, night air.

"Fuck," he muttered.

He was moving before he realized it, descending the stairs and striding through the club, then through the front door. He was out onto the street in seconds. His street bike was parked just beside the curb. A quick wave of his hand and his helmet appeared.

There were people gathered in small clusters along the curb, chatting, laughing, waiting for ride shares. They scooted out of his way, gaping as he passed. Whether it was his towering stature or the *fuck off* look he usually wore, they stayed out of his way. Most were supernaturals, but a few were humans. His glamor was one of the best in the supernatural world—thanks to his unique brand of magic. So they probably couldn't tell what, exactly, he was. Not unless they had enough magic to see through his disguise.

Had Eleanor? It seemed unlikely, given that she was human. And yet…

Her reaction to him in the coffee shop had been interesting. Her initial response had been one of fear, but she'd quickly reverted. There had been a moment when her eyes lingered on his ears, his teeth, that he worried she could see through his glamor.

He wasn't sure what it was about her. But something made his goblin side roar to the surface and purr with curiosity. He told himself it was purely the hunter in him. Because that was easier than the alternative.

He felt for the gold again, using his goblin senses, his affinity for metals, to pinpoint her location. Grabbing his helmet, he shoved it over his head and climbed onto his bike, revving it to life. With a quick thrust, he set off in search of his quarry.

He ignored the coldness in his fingertips, the sense of rising worry. This was the middle of Walton. One of the largest cities in the country. With a higher-than-normal presence of supernaturals. This particular sector of Midtown held far too many dangers for someone like her to be outside in the middle of the night. Especially in a fucking gold top that shone like a beacon.

She was nothing to him. Nothing but a potential lead. And yet, his fingers grew colder, urging him to hurry.

In all his years, he'd never failed on a job. It had earned him a reputation among supernaturals. Something real fucking hard to do for a goblin, since they were treated like dirt. Not that he cared about his reputation all that much. He didn't give a flying fuck what other people thought about him. But he did like getting paid. Gold, preferably.

Rounding the corner, he put on a burst of speed, searching for Eleanor. She was drawing closer; he felt the gold at her neck. It was time to make his move. He had a job to do, and he'd be damned if he let this little human slip through his fingers.

5

Abject fear made my mind go blank. Two years of self-defense right out the window as my body went rigid with shock. My eyes watered from the hand tangled in my hair, sending pain along my scalp. It fell away, only to wrap me in a chokehold.

"Thought you could hide from me?" Luke's hot breath fanned my ear.

"Luke, *please*," I gasped, immediately falling into old habits, my scars ripped wide open. Dormant instincts screamed at me to submit, to make myself smaller.

Several more bodies materialized, reminding me to *fight*. Keeping my movements small, I slipped my phone into the side pocket of my pants. I needed to get back into the club. To Eaden.

"How'd you find me?" I managed, trying to distract him.

"Tony, you got the car ready?" Luke said, ignoring me. "Let's get her out of here."

He dragged me away from the back door.

Acid bubbled up into my throat. I couldn't let him take me. I couldn't go through this again.

I pressed my chin into his forearm, keeping ahold of it with both hands, then I stepped forward, pulling and shifting my weight. I kicked the heel of my foot up, hitting him in the groin. Just like I'd practiced a thousand times.

Luke grunted, bending forward. "Stupid bitch!"

A shot of triumph burst through me as I broke free, trying to get around him toward the door. For a second, I thought I made it.

"What the fuck?!" he hissed, darting forward. He grabbed my wrist and jerked me off balance. A crack reverberated through my hand. First, there was a moment of nothing, then searing pain shot up my arm. I screamed, stunned.

A loud roar filled my ears. A blur of movement and then a motorcycle skidded to a stop beside us. The rider removed his helmet, giving me an eyeful of black hair, piercings, and tattoos. Our eyes locked. It felt like a million years passed between us in a single heartbeat.

Then my heart took off in a gallop.

"Get on!" the goblin growled.

I pulled against Luke, trying to break free.

A dagger appeared in the goblin's hand. Luke grunted as it sank into his chest. He stumbled back, releasing me. I gasped, blinking, then rushed forward, swinging my leg over the back of the bike. We were moving before I could fully position myself.

All I could do was cling to my rescuer.

Gunshots rang out from the end of the alley—Luke's people. The goblin lifted a hand, waving it through the air. Bullets around us exploded into dust. We skidded out onto the main drag. I cried out, tightening my hold on him, as the pain in my wrist sent knives up my arm.

The goblin slowed, coming to a stop several streetlights down. "Put this on," he shouted over the roar of his bike. A sleek helmet appeared in his hand. He held it over his left shoulder. When I didn't immediately grab it, he shook it to get my attention. I released my uninjured arm and took it, shoving it over my head. It was a perfect fit.

"That's better," came the low voice in my ear. I jerked in surprise. There were mics and speakers in the helmets.

The goblin took off again, melting into traffic.

"Want to tell me what the fuck you were thinking, going outside like that?" His voice had morphed into the same asshole tone he'd used in the coffee shop.

"I…"

Tears clouded my vision. What *had* I been thinking? I knew better than to slip outside alone, even though the alley behind Vortex was—or had been—relatively safe in my experience. My coworkers often stepped back there for a smoke break or for peace and quiet. But most of them were supernaturals.

They didn't have a dangerous ex hunting them. Just earlier, I'd thought it was Luke in the crowd, then chastised myself for being so paranoid. All it took was a panicked call—probably staged. I'd rushed right out into harm's way.

"At least this time you walked into actual danger instead of just me," the goblin muttered, as if reading my thoughts.

A tangled mess of emotions crashed over me. Anger, that after how hard I had worked, I'd barely managed to do anything against Luke. Humiliation, that I *still* needed rescuing. That my body barely responded and hadn't been strong enough. That I had wasted precious moments panicking.

I was so tired of being weak—all because of *him*.

I took in a gulp of air, then another, and another, trying to blink away the tears from my vision. What was the point of the past two years, if I was going to freeze up when it mattered most?

I realized I was trembling, clenching my teeth to keep them from chattering as the adrenaline that flooded my system began to abate.

Traffic thinned and the bike picked up speed, surging forward. Buildings streaked past. We were speeding through the city, weaving in and out of cars. The bike handled the curves with ease, as did the goblin I was practically wrapped around. I felt the bunch of his muscles as his body responded, leaning into each one.

"We have to go back," I finally managed to say. I needed to tell Eaden what had happened, though he probably already knew. There were cameras on the back side of the building. My only hope was that he might protect me from Luke… somehow.

"Is that so?" purred the goblin.

"Please. I need to go back."

"Don't think so, sugar."

"My name's Rose," I bit out.

We took a sharp turn and I tightened my grip on him. Pain shot up my arm and I whimpered. His muscles tensed beneath me, in response to the sound. "Are you hurt?" The question softened his voice.

"My wrist. I think… I think it's broken."

He made a growly sound in the back of his throat but said nothing else.

"Where are you taking me?"

"Somewhere safe. We'll be there soon enough, then we can see to your wrist." He revved the engine and we jumped forward, accelerating as if my admission had spurred him on.

High-rise buildings began to thin, replaced with smaller structures and warehouses.

Trying to distract myself from the pain, I said, "Why were you in the coffee shop today?"

"Hold on tight," was all he said in answer. The road opened up. He put his bike into gear and we shot forward.

I sucked in a breath as my stomach lurched, pain making my nausea rise. "Going a little fast, don't you think?"

"Not fast enough."

"No one's following us," I bit out through clenched teeth. "Not at this speed. You might be a goblin—"

"So you *do* know."

"—but I'm not. So, if we crash—"

"We're not going to crash, sugar."

"You can't promise that."

"No, but I *can* promise that if we did, I would keep you safe."

Safe?

I didn't remember what that felt like—to be safe. Not anymore. Not after Luke. Not after spending the last two years in a heightened state of paranoia.

"Trust me, yeah?"

"Fine," I lied.

Eventually, larger houses dotted the landscape, half hidden by trees, as we passed into Kentwood. A few minutes later the goblin veered off the road and up an asphalt drive. Trees lined both sides, obscuring everything from view. As they thinned, a house appeared, a massive craftsman with a light blue shingled exterior and white accents, a large porch, and huge windows that glowed with warmth.

It was *stunning*. Not like most houses on this street. Not loud and ostentatious, but also not the type of house I would have expected, assuming it was his.

That did all sorts of things to my curiosity, which I didn't want to acknowledge.

We pulled into a sweeping circle drive and he parked in front.

"Off," he barked.

He didn't need to tell me twice. I couldn't get off fast enough. Holding my injured wrist against my chest, I struggled with my other hand to remove the helmet. A pair of hands reached for me, sliding it free. My pink hair fell into place.

My rescuer stared down at me, his expression unreadable. All it took was one blink, and a transparent image of his goblin form overlaid his human one, betraying his glamor. I hated to admit it, but he was positively breathtaking even without glamor, even with skin the shade of gunmetal gray. I blinked once more and his human appearance returned.

Both helmets disappeared into thin air.

"Give me your wrist," he snapped, impatience lacing his tone. I ground my teeth together. "I'm not going to hurt you, little female. Let me see it."

Setting my jaw, I offered it to him, wincing when he reached for it. I needn't have worried. His touch was shockingly gentle. My eyes zeroed in on those beautifully masculine hands, on his ringed fingers as they assessed the swollen area. He pressed near the veins on the underside and I flinched.

"Ow," I breathed.

He hummed, going still. "Broken, I think."

"I think so, yes."

"This will feel hot," he warned right before his thumb stroked over the skin. Searing heat made me flinch. I turned guarded, every muscle locking up tight, but I didn't pull away.

The heat disappeared almost as quickly. He glanced up, gauging my expression. Something in it made his jaw tighten. He looked down again, moving my wrist around, holding my hand with his and lacing our fingers together.

With smooth motions, he rolled my wrist around. I stared transfixed at his rings as they caught the light, the warm metal heating the skin between my fingers. I wanted to ask about them, suddenly curious about everything that had to do with this goblin, but I couldn't form words.

"There." He dropped my hand and stepped back. The loss was so abrupt, it felt like he'd taken my warmth with him. I moved my wrist around, then dropped my hand, looking up at him. He'd healed me. A goblin. I hadn't even known it was possible.

"You going to gape at me all night, or shall we go inside?"

An incredulous huff fell from my lips. "That depends. Where are we?"

"Hm..." He continued looking me over, once again ignoring my question. Which he seemed to do a lot. "Where's your phone?"

"My..." I frowned. "My phone?"

"Your phone—where is it?" He held out his hand, waiting.

Cold realization slipped into my belly. If Luke had gotten ahold of the number to lure me outside, could he be using it to track me? I pulled it from my pocket. The goblin snatched it. A second later, it disappeared, just like the helmets had.

"Wait, you can't just *take* my phone! That's like—"

"Looks like I just did. Now, get inside."

"You expect me to…walk in there?"

"Need me to use smaller words?"

"Not sure. I don't speak asshole."

His gaze hardened. "Then we're going to have communication problems, sugar, because it's my native tongue."

"What happened to toning it down?!" I shot back.

"Let's go." He moved behind me, prodding my back between my shoulder blades, sending me forward involuntarily.

"Excuse me?" I rounded on him. "What. The. Actual. Fuck?!"

He made a sound of annoyance, then reached for me. My training chose that moment to kick in—better late than never. My fist flew through the air and I landed a satisfying right hook to his cheek. I heard a crunch. For a moment, I smugly thought I'd broken his jaw. He stumbled backwards, more from shock than anything as his eyes clouded over with surprise. He swiped away blood where I'd busted his lip—

And then the pain hit.

"Holy…fuck," I screeched, shaking my hand out. "*Owww. Ow, ow, ow.*" It struck all at once, nearly as bad as my broken wrist. I tried to move my fingers, only for it to intensify.

The goblin swore under his breath, eyes darkening at the sight of my injury. "You are so fucking reckless." Then, with a wave of his hand, my entire body seized up and I could no longer move. I screeched in fury as I struggled against the invisible bonds. "Going to have to hog-tie you if you can't stop getting yourself into trouble."

"Let me go," I seethed.

"It's for your own fucking good." Another wave of his hand and I was suddenly floating inches off the ground.

He stalked for the house.

"You can't treat me like this—!" Another invisible bond wrapped around my mouth cutting off the remainder of my tirade. The more I struggled the worse it got. His magic clamped around me so tightly I couldn't do more than jerk my head. My arms were pinned at my side, the fingers of my injured hand screaming.

The front door loomed before us. He punched in a code on the tech security panel before pressing a finger against the pad. There was a zapping sound followed by a dim blue glow that momentarily blanketed the house before disappearing.

If I hadn't been so angry I might have been impressed.

He stepped inside, then used his magic to propel me through the door and into the entryway. The door slammed behind us and the magical leash around me disappeared. My feet dropped two inches, landing with a thud on the wood floor.

"You are such a fucking asshole—" The words ended in a hiss as my hand flared with pain—because I'd tried to clench it.

He whirled around and lifted it, clicking his tongue as he examined my broken bones. "Second time tonight, sugar. Let's not make a habit of this, yeah?" A warm rush flowed beneath my skin and the injury disappeared.

I sagged with relief, my anger dissipating.

"Not going to apologize?" he said, lifting an eyebrow.

"You deserved it."

The corner of his mouth twitched but he merely dropped my hand and walked away.

I took in the interior of the house. Everything was designed with comfort and style in mind. Through an arch on my left, I spotted an elaborately carved dining table and chairs, presided over by a chandelier filled with glittering orbs.

On my right, a spacious sitting room was dominated by a luxurious dark blue sectional. It was covered in knitted blankets and throw pillows. There was a detached ottoman with a wooden tray. It held a vase of fresh cut flowers and an electric candle display.

Soft lights glowed from lamps and wall sconces around the room. Tasteful art hung from the walls, showing black and white images of the city. A giant television screen sat above a gas fireplace, framed in gold. Like it was a fancy painting.

Was this place really his?

The goblin stood at a liquor cabinet that I hadn't spotted until just now. I moved into the living room, then hesitated, glancing back at the door. There was a mat for shoes. I kicked off my boots before making my way into the room. He walked over with two snifters, both filled with amber liquid. He handed me one.

I was surprised by the gesture until he opened his mouth, once again ruining everything. "Sit. Let's talk."

"No."

"Don't make me make you."

"You wouldn't fucking dare."

"I would. You know I would."

"You're insufferable!" I stomped over and sank onto the sofa, taking liberties with his pillows to messily arrange them around me. I grabbed a throw blanket to spread it over me. The goblin lifted an impatient brow while I got comfortable. "Is there a problem?" My voice came out extra sweet.

"Nope." He chose a seat at the other end of the sectional and leaned back, comfortably spreading his muscled thighs while throwing an arm over the back. The moment those green eyes fell on me, a hot flush crept up my neck.

His eyes dropped to my chest as he said, "Interesting necklaces."

Ignoring the statement, I lifted the glass to my lips and took a sip. Warmth and flavor rushed over my tongue, down my throat, immediately dulling some of my irritation. My eyes darted up to him in surprise. I took another sip, savoring it before I swallowed. "This isn't, like, poisoned or anything is it?"

"Unbelievable," he muttered, then took a sip of his own.

"What?" I groused. "You can't blame me for wondering—"

"What happened in that alley?"

"You're joking, right?" He simply stared at me. "I don't even know you! You expect me to just start answering questions after dragging me—?!"

"Oh, pardon me for being so *rude*." With careful movements, he set his drink on the side table and stood, offering me an exaggerated bow before reclaiming his seat. "My name is Bastian Croft. I would say it's a pleasure, Eleanor, but then I'd be lying."

I made a sound of disgust. "Ha ha ha, very cute little act. No one calls me *Eleanor*. It's Elle, or it used to be before I stopped going by that. Do your friends call you Bas? Do you even have friends? Or does your charming personality drive everyone away before they get the chance?"

He stared at me, expression unchanging.

"Fine. Whatever." I looked down at my drink and took a sip to calm my ire. Honestly, I didn't care if it was poisoned. Death would be better than putting up with *Bastian Croft*.

What kind of name was that, anyway?

"You done with the sass, sugar?" I snorted, throwing him a glare. "Great. Fantastic. Glad we cleared that up. Now, tell me what happened in the alley."

I didn't owe him anything—certainly not an explanation—merely because he'd rescued me.

He must have sensed my refusal to talk because he added, "By all means, take your time. You aren't leaving until I get answers."

"Excuse me?" I sputtered, sitting up straighter. "You can't… You can't keep me here. I'll leave when I want." I glanced at the door, then back at him.

"Oh? And how do you plan to get home?"

"I'll walk."

"In the middle of the night? All the way back to West Cross?"

I opened and closed my mouth, because he had a point. "Fine. You win. I was ambushed, all right?"

"Gonna need more than that."

My irritated growl could have rivaled his. But I gave in, telling him how I'd been on the phone. How I'd stepped outside for better reception, only to be ambushed. How I'd broken free, only to have my wrist broken. "And then you showed up, all dark knight and whatnot, and kidnapped me on your bike."

"I see." He shifted on the sofa, which drew my attention—*annoyingly*—to his trim hips, to the way his jeans fit him so perfectly. I couldn't seem to look away, watching shamelessly as he lazily lifted his glass to his lips, as they puckered slightly, as his throat bobbed when he took a swallow.

Then I blinked and snapped the hell out of it. "Great. Cool. Now that I've answered your question, it's only fair that you answer mine."

The grin that spread across his lips was all predator. If I blinked and focused hard enough, those blunted, perfect teeth would turn to narrow points. "Is that what you think, sugar? That I'm in the business of giving mouthy little females exactly what they're asking for?"

I tutted, ignoring the jibe. "Why were you at the coffee shop earlier? And Vortex? Are you—were you following me?"

"Yes."

"Oh-*kay*? Why?"

"To get answers."

"Answers," I repeated, not quite comprehending.

"To a few questions."

I huffed, staring back at him. He didn't blink, didn't even *move*. It was a little unnerving.

"Fine. What do you want to know? I work in a nightclub.

My life is as mundane as it gets. And in case you haven't noticed, I'm quite human. I know what you are. I know goblins do all the dirty work for the fae. Trust me, I've never had anything to do with them. There's nothing I can say that would possibly be of interest."

"That so?"

"Yep." I rolled my lips between my teeth.

"How well do you know Professor Miller?"

My hand froze, glass halfway to my mouth. "What?"

"Jane Miller. How well do you know her?" His eyes flashed back toward my chest, to my necklaces.

My stomach dropped. "I… I don't."

"Oh?"

"Oh."

"That's interesting," he mused, rubbing his jaw.

I scoffed, dismissive. "Why's that?"

"Because Jane Miller died last week, and when her family reviewed her will, they were unhappy to learn that she left everything to you."

"*What?*" The glass slipped from my fingers, whiskey soaking into the plush throw blanket. Professor Miller had left me…*everything*? But that meant—

"Oh, my God!"

"Yep." Bastian grinned like a cat who ate the canary. "So… about those questions."

6

B astian waved his hand and my spilled whiskey vanished from the blanket, the glass reappearing on the side table. "Surely you see how this looks," he continued. "A professor dies. No one knows how it happened. Come to find out, she left everything to you. Someone who supposedly doesn't even *know her*. I find that very *interesting*, don't you?"

My ears were ringing with every word. Because yes, when framed like that…

I licked my lips and said, "You think I did this? That I… That I…" I couldn't even say the words aloud.

"Like I said, how well did you know her?"

I exhaled, all the fight leaving me. "Am I under arrest or something? Are you an undercover cop? Are the Fae trying to bring me in? Do I need to hire a lawyer? Should I—"

"Enough!" Bastian growled. "I'm a bounty hunter…of sorts. All of this is off record—for now. But yes, I'm looking for Professor Miller's killer. I admit, you're at the top of my list." He set his empty glass on the side table and leaned forward, resting his tattooed forearms on his knees.

My skin itched beneath his severe gaze. When I opened my mouth to speak, nothing but a choking sound came out. "I… I didn't do it. This is…" A deranged laugh bubbled up from my chest. "It's ridiculous. I haven't spoken to Jane in two years."

"So you *do* know her."

"I do—did. Years ago."

"Uh-huh. And why haven't you spoken to her since?"

Guilt slipped into my gut, hot and uncomfortable, making my nausea rise. "I… We fell out of touch."

"Right." He leaned back, his gaze showing obvious mistrust. "What was the nature of your relationship? How did you know each other? Why would she leave everything to you?"

"I knew her from the university," I said, my voice faint.

"How so?"

I gave him an idiotic glare. "How do you think? I was a student there."

This was insane. Why would she leave everything to me? I knew she was somewhat estranged from her family—in that she didn't talk to them much. But… Why me?

"Right," Bastian gritted out. "Funny thing about that, when I looked through the university records, there was no trace of Eleanor Rose Kennedy."

"Shit."

"Yeah. Shit." Bastian's expression spoke volumes as his assessing gaze raked over me. Like he'd already made his mind up about me and was merely playing along.

"I can promise you, I was a student there."

"Uh-huh."

"You think I'm lying?" The notion burrowed beneath my skin, making my muscles tighten. I didn't mind being misjudged by people, but I hated, *absolutely hated*, when someone didn't believe me. Luke had never believed me. He'd never taken me seriously.

"I'm sure you look at me and all you see is a party girl with pink hair who has no greater ambition than exotic dancing—"

"Woah, woah, woah, sugar." He held up his hands, placating. "I never said that."

"—but once upon a time I was a master's student at WU, working on my thesis."

Back in those days, I had a passion for art history and archeology—studying what people found beautiful, what survived through the ages. All of it was taken from me.

By Luke.

"A master's student." He lifted an eyebrow.

"Look, asshole," I hissed. "I had no idea Jane successfully removed me from the records. I knew she was going to try. I never followed up."

"That raises plenty of additional questions. But we'll table it, for now." His voice was calm, like my words had no effect. "Let's say I believe you. Let's say you were a student at WU and what, got your master's degree? Then what?"

I swallowed. "I never finished—never got my degree. I left the university."

"To do what?"

"Isn't it obvious?" When his expression didn't change, I tutted, gesturing to my hair and outfit. "You sure you're the right person to track down her killer?"

He didn't rise to my bait. "So you've been working at Vortex ever since?"

"That about sums it up."

"Except it doesn't, sugar. Not really." He crossed his arms. "Like, for example, why did you leave the university? And why didn't you stay in touch with Professor Miller?"

My cheeks heated. "My reasons for leaving are private and have nothing to do with Jane."

"How convenient."

"You're such a fucking asshole, you know that?" I surged to my feet and stalked out of the room, straight for the front door. Shoving my feet into my boots and zipping them up, I decided to take my chances walking home. Better than sitting here accused of murder.

"Where do you think you're going?" His voice exuded a level of patience that rankled.

"Home," I snapped, reaching for the doorknob. It didn't budge. I twisted and yanked, then swore. "Why won't the door open?"

He didn't answer.

A gnawing sensation settled over me. I looked at the nearest window and strode over. Flipping the latch, I pushed upward. It didn't move. Like it was never intended to be opened.

Magic. It had to be. I'd seen the blue glow surrounding his home. This asshole had trapped me.

"Are you fucking serious?" I rounded on Bastian. He stood in the archway watching me, his arms crossed, casually leaning against the frame.

The corner of his lips twitched.

"You think this is funny?" I cried.

"I think it's fucking cute, sure."

I opened and closed my mouth. "Great. I'm glad you get such a kick out of me. I want to go home. I'm done playing your question games. We're through."

"Not going to happen. We're not done here, and it's almost two in the morning. I'm not taking you home right now."

I balked. "Seriously? What the fuck else do you want to know?"

"I want your input. If not you, who do you think could have killed Professor Miller? I want to know how exactly you two knew each other. I want to know how close you were. Close, obviously, if she left you everything. You're my best lead. You think I'll just let you walk through that door?"

I blew out a breath. All the energy I'd mustered for my tantrum drained away. Until this moment, I'd been on the defensive. I cared about Jane, even if we hadn't spoken for years. She was the reason I remained safe from Luke for this long. Now she was dead, and someone deserved justice.

Bastian might have wanted her killer for financial reasons —or whatever it was that hunters received in exchange for finding prey. Me? I wanted the killer to pay. This was personal.

I took a moment to study Bastian, really taking him in. He looked like a mean motherfucker. If anyone could make it happen, he could.

"You really want to catch her killer?"

"That's what I've been paid for, yes."

"But you think it's me, and I take offense with that."

"Sugar, I've seen lambs capable of ripping a person's face off."

A laugh burst from my lips. "I don't know whether to be offended or flattered. That you think I'm a lamb, or that you think I could rip someone's face off. I'd like to rip yours off, for starters. And believe me, if I could, I would have done it already."

The corner of his mouth didn't just twitch this time, it pulled up into a smile—the first I'd seen from him. My stomach flipped, going all fluttery. It was *annoying.*

He isn't even your type, I reminded myself.

"All right," Bastian said, lifting his hands and taking a step back. "What if I rescind my accusation? Treat you like a partner instead of a suspect. Would you be willing to answer my questions, help me get to the bottom of this?"

I chewed on the inside of my cheek. "Do I get another glass of whisky?"

"Sugar, you can have the whole fucking bottle if it means you'll get that cute little ass back on that couch and start talking."

"Fine." A smirk formed on my lips. I all but sashayed past him, flicking my pink locks over my shoulder, right back into the sitting room. "Glad you think I have a cute ass," I purred, then dropped said ass back into my seat. I lifted my feet, pulling my boots off and chucking them at Bastian's dumb face. He caught them effortlessly, lifting his eyebrows before dropping them near the door.

While he poured another two fingers of whisky for me—

this time bringing the whole bottle with him and setting it on the wooden tray—I took a deep breath and got started.

"I met Professor Miller while I was doing my undergrad at WU. She taught my art history classes. I knew I wanted to study historical art and cultures, history of things both known and unknown, stuff like that. Most humans don't know it, but many ancient things have magical qualities—"

"Wait." Bastian halted me, resuming his seat. "You're reminding me of another question. You're human, no? And yet you knew I was a goblin. The same way you know certain things have magic?"

"Not the same, no. I know you're a goblin because I can see through your glamor." My hand went to the charm around my neck before I realized what I'd done.

"Ah. They're both artifacts, aren't they? Your necklaces?"

I held up the charm. "This one lets me see through glamor. It overlays it with an image of the person's true self."

"So, you can see my true form."

"Not all the time. Just if I blink and focus or whatever. I see a flash of it."

He hummed, thoughtful.

"We're getting off topic," I continued. "Professor Miller was head of the university's archeological department. She convinced me to stick around and study there, to get my master's degree. She became something of a mentor to me." He didn't need to know that my relationship with my mom was strained. That we'd had problems ever since my dad had died—even before. That Jane had filled a void my mother failed to. "As time passed, she became something of a good friend, too. I think she loved me like a daughter. We had a shared passion. That brought us together…"

"And then you left the university," he finished when I'd let the silence stretch between us. "Why?"

"Right. Yes. I… Something happened. Not between Jane and I," I clarified, so that he understood there were no hard feelings between us. "Someone…" I awkwardly cleared my throat. "It was something else. So I left. I found a different path in life."

"Just like that? You gave it all up?"

I shrugged. "People change."

Lifting my glass to keep from saying anything else, I drained it.

"I find that hard to believe." He stared at me like he was suddenly desperate to peel back all the layers. I didn't like it.

There was a long stretch of silence, during which I poured myself *another* glass. After a small sip, I looked up at him. My chest tightened with my next words, "I didn't know that she had died until tonight. I saw it on the news, right before I left for the club."

My eyes started to burn. I forced the tears back. The last thing I wanted was to cry in front of a stranger. Especially a sexy stranger who was sort of an asshole.

"I…" Swallowing, I forced my emotions down. "All I could think was that I'd never reconnected with her. I let things go between us. And then she just—died. I didn't even get to say goodbye."

Damn this fucking alcohol. It was making me emotional. I grumbled and set my glass down. "If I have any more of that, I'll turn into a mess. You should probably take it away from me."

He ran a hand over the shaved side of his scalp. "Any idea who could have done this? Did she have enemies? Was there anyone who might have wanted her dead?"

My first instinct was to deny the possibility. Professor Miller was loved by everyone. She was strict with her students, but fair, and she always encouraged them to excel. Her work was her passion. Which was probably why she wasn't very close with the rest of her family. I knew she had at least one sibling, a couple of nieces and nephews.

After her husband died, she threw herself deeper into her work and didn't bother with much else. She'd never had kids, opting to focus entirely on her career. I was a part of her work, which was probably why she spared me the time.

A cold knot formed in the pit of my stomach. A nagging feeling that I couldn't quite form into a coherent theory. I'd left the university because of Luke. He'd known about my closeness with Professor Miller. What if he'd found out what she'd done? How she'd hidden me from him? What if this was his way of taking revenge. What if he'd killed her to get to me—?

"Well?"

"I… I don't know." I wasn't ready to talk about Luke. There was no way in hell I'd share vulnerable parts of my past with him. Not even my friends knew, except Vivi. "I haven't spoken to Jane for years, Bastian. I don't feel qualified to make any assumptions. She could have met any number of people since then."

Assuming it was Luke did feel like a stretch.

"Fine. Perhaps you should sleep on it. See if any new theories come to you."

"Sleep?" I frowned. "Where?"

"I've got a guest bedroom you can use. Come on, I'll get you settled."

"I'm not comfortable with that," I managed.

"Well, sugar, that's too fucking bad."

"Is this because you still don't trust me?" I demanded, rising to my feet. Because the feeling was mutual.

"You're the best lead I have. So I think I'll keep that cotton candy head of yours around a little longer, hmm? Come on."

I clenched my teeth. My feet stayed planted where I stood. I glanced at the windows again. It's not like I was getting out.

"I want to go home."

"Tomorrow, perhaps. I've got some thinking to do first."

"Your *thinking* is what got us into this mess," I called after him as he disappeared through the arch. One second of silence ticked into two, into three—

"Damnit, Eleanor, get that cute ass over here. I'd like to get some sleep sometime tonight."

I was tired too, and trapped. Despite every instinct screaming at me to keep fighting, I recognized defeat when I saw it. I wouldn't be going home tonight—and maybe that scared me less than it should have. Still, I needed to set boundaries. I wasn't some lap dog who jumped on command.

So I planted my feet and crossed my arms, not moving an inch.

Bastian's dumb face reappeared in the doorway. "Looks like we're doing this the hard way, then."

I was fully prepared for him to wave his hand, do some fancy magic, and put me into some kind of invisible binding like he'd done before. Prepared to hate him all the more for his manhandling. What I *wasn't* prepared for, was for him to sling me over his shoulder and march out of the room. Waving a hand to dim the lights as he went.

"What the fuck?!" I screeched, hammering him with my fists. "Put me down, asshole."

His palm came down on my ass—hard. Accompanied by a loud slap and a sting that made my stomach flip. Heat rushed through me—not from anger. "Behave," he growled.

"You did not just—"

"I did. Now then." Suddenly, everything heaved upright and I was placed back on my feet. I stumbled and he reached out an arm to steady me, wrapping it around my waist until we were chest to chest.

My breaths came faster, eyes locked on his. They were so green. So… pretty.

For a moment, it was like before, back in the alley, where everything else disappeared and time seemed to stretch around us. Then my brain snapped back into reality and I gave his chest a hard shove, putting as much distance between us as possible.

Because I was *not* attracted to a goblin bounty hunter.

Especially one who thought I was a useful tool for his latest case. And certainly not one who trapped me inside his house.

7

Bastian took a deep breath, trying to clear Eleanor's scent from his nostrils. He'd forgotten himself for a moment. Throwing her over his shoulder had been the worst idea. And punishing her with a slap to her ass? What the *hell* had he been thinking?

He hadn't.

Because something about her scrambled his thoughts.

Made all his critical thinking fly right out the window.

Fuck.

Thankfully, the guest bedroom was on the first floor, which put plenty of space between them. Even if he had a feeling that being on opposite sides of the same house wasn't nearly enough distance. "There's an extra toothbrush and…other things in the bathroom," he found himself saying. "You should have everything you need."

She glanced down at herself. "What about PJs?"

"PJs?"

"I certainly hope you don't expect me to sleep in this." Her eyes glinted with mischief, voice turning breathy as she added, "Then again, I *could* sleep naked…"

He took a large step back. "Just 'cause I said you were

cute, sugar, doesn't mean I want you throwing yourself at me."
The words came out sharper than necessary.

She reared back. "You think I'm hitting on you? Don't flatter yourself, *goblin*. I don't do fuckboys." Then she sashayed past him into the room and turned, regarding him. She might have been shorter, and yet, it still felt like she was looking down her nose at him.

He bristled, but didn't bother defending himself. Yes, he enjoyed one-night-stands. But his partners always understood what they were getting into. No strings. No repeats.

He didn't do relationships.

"I'll get you something to wear," he bit out, turning on his heel and disappearing. The moment there was space between them, he felt like he could breathe again. His mind got sharper, making him realize just how careless he'd been. He had a job to do and didn't need her distracting him.

Easier said than done.

Taking the stairs two at a time, he swept into his room. He rifled through his drawers and grabbed a pair of lounge pants, then hesitated and dropped them back inside. Instead, he settled on one of his favorite T-shirts. It had nothing to do with him wanting to see her in it, and only it. Nothing at all.

He just wanted her comfortable. Comfortable at the end of a long night. His shoulders dropped at the realization. She'd been through a lot this evening. Learning that someone she cared for was now dead. Working a long shift. Getting assaulted in an alley afterward.

The male he'd stabbed had broken her fucking wrist. He'd *hurt* her. That alone left his blood boiling. He fought the sudden urge to go back to Vortex. To track the fucker down and make him pay—*really* pay.

He took a deep, steadying breath.

Because the thought of leaving Eleanor alone in his house left his throat dry. No, he wouldn't do that. Not when she was in a new place.

He turned and left, heading back downstairs. She wasn't where he'd left her, standing in the middle of the room. Instead, she was snooping, inspecting her surroundings. "Here," he said, announcing himself. He tossed the T-shirt in her direction. She caught it and frowned down at it. "Problem, sugar?"

"Just surprised you didn't give me a potato sack."

He shrugged. "Fresh out."

Without another word, he retreated back to his room.

Sleep was nearly impossible. All he could think about was her downstairs wearing his shirt—his fucking shirt—snuggled up in bed. The insult she'd lobbed at him earlier kept replaying in his head—annoyingly. It made him wonder what kind of partners she *did* enjoy.

To distract himself, he forced himself to go through the information she'd given him. He'd been surprised to hear she'd been a master's student at WU. That she'd given that up. There was a story there, he was certain. But she hadn't been willing to share it, even if he'd wanted to pry it from her.

But he recognized the need to dial it back. If only for tonight. Tomorrow was another day.

He didn't plan on releasing her until he'd wrung every secret from her. Until he'd discovered her deepest, darkest thoughts. Until he'd tasted her lips, perhaps even licked her cunt...

"*Fuck!*" he cursed, rolling over and punching his fucking pillow.

No female should've had this kind of effect on him.

He'd known of her existence a mere three days, run background checks, infiltrated her life to try and track her down, to get information. He'd only set eyes upon her today. That's all it had taken for this little female to burrow right under his skin.

Mother fucking fuck.

No. He wasn't doing this. Instead, he formulated a plan for the morning, then forced himself to stop thinking about her, to stop thinking about how he'd be so much happier if he went downstairs, lifted her sleeping body into his arms, and carried her up to his bed. Like a prize. Like she belonged to him.

He bolted upright and kicked the sheets away, getting to his feet. A growl rumbled in his chest as he started pacing, muscles coiled tight. This wouldn't do. His glamor flickered, then fell away entirely. His frame expanded, shoulders broadening, magic crackling under his skin. Only, his goblin form offered no relief. It just made him more possessive, more dangerous, until his breathing turned ragged.

"Get the fuck ahold of yourself," he commanded.

His hand hovered over the doorknob when he literally forced himself backwards, despite every instinct screaming at him to *go to her*. Clenching his teeth, he made tight fists until his claws broke through the skin of his palms, blood dripping onto the floor. The pain helped him focus, helped him push down the urge and wrestle his magic under control. His glamor settled over him like a second skin.

Then he took himself back into bed, where sleep found him.

8

The smell of coffee and bacon had my gritty eyes peeling open. I inhaled, stomach growling. There came a muffled clatter from the kitchen. I blinked, my thoughts sharpening into something intelligible.

Oh, my God. Was... Was the goblin cooking breakfast? Throwing back the covers, I jumped up, ready to witness the unexpected.

Then I hesitated, common sense taking over.

I stepped into the bathroom and brushed my teeth, finger-combing my pink waves. My mascara had smudged, leaving dark circles under my eyes that enhanced my exhausted, sleep deprived state. I did my best to wipe it off with dampened toilet paper, which unhelpfully disintegrated.

It would have to do, for now.

On my way through the room, I checked the clock. It was eight thirty. I usually let myself sleep until ten. But... bacon.

When I reached the door, I looked over at the clothes I'd tossed onto the lounge in the corner. Then I glanced down at my bare legs and T-shirt. It was oversized on me, falling to mid-thigh. I bet it fit Bastian like a glove. Like the black one he'd worn yesterday.

The decal on the front said *Walton Comets* with a giant

comet overlaying a football. In sub text, it said, *"Streaking into the endzone since 1963."*

I huffed. Either he was a football fan, or it was a shirt he hated and didn't mind giving up. Still, it was soft and comfy. It smelled fresh like his detergent. Maybe I would keep it, just for the hell of it. I wasn't a huge football fan but, why not?

Inhaling again, I pulled the door open. The noise in the kitchen abruptly stopped, then resumed. I trudged barefoot down the hall and right into…the kitchen of my dreams? Rustic wood cabinets, butcher block island, white granite countertops with flecks of smoky gray and silver that glittered. I silenced the groan that threatened to escape.

Because of course this asshole had a gorgeous kitchen.

Bacon sizzled in a frying pan. A coffee maker sat with its pot full. There were ingredients littering the counter for… pancakes? And an open carton of eggs.

But none of that was what stole my attention.

It was the goblin with a towel draped over his shoulder, lounge pants hugging low on his hips, and an entirely bare torso on display. Because… *wow*. His tattoos didn't just cover his arms. One of them went over his right shoulder and crept across his chest, a maze of tribal markings that I could only assume had something to do with his goblin ancestry. He had piercings in *both* nipples. The rest of his torso was golden, human-looking skin, showing off a cut of muscles that had saliva pooling in my mouth.

What the hell?!

"Morning, sugar." His gravelly voice went straight to my core as my body betrayed me, sending heat zinging to the apex of my thighs. It didn't matter that I couldn't stand him. Didn't matter that he was an asshole.

I hid my response with an irritated scoff. "Can't you just call me Rose?"

"Nah." He crossed his arms, his tattooed muscles flexing. The corner of his mouth twisted up in a half-smirk—one I was growing to both love and hate. Green eyes burned tracks over my body, lingering on my bare legs before blackening. "How'd my shirt work out? Looks good on you."

"Fine," I snapped. "Hope you weren't planning on getting it back."

"No?"

"Not a chance."

"Hmm. It's my favorite. Might have to peel it off that cute little body of yours if you refuse."

"You wouldn't dare."

"Oh?" He stalked forward, hands reaching for me.

I sputtered, backing up, until I hit the counter behind me. "Okay! I'll give it back. Just—not right this second, *obviously*."

His grin was wicked "Glad to hear it. Want some coffee?' How'd you sleep?"

He was standing close—too close. I cleared my throat. "Coffee, please. And, I slept fine."

"Just…fine? I paid a lot of money for that mattress."

I huffed and slipped past him, over to the coffee maker. He moved in the same direction, shadowing me as I came to a stop. Goosebumps pebbled my skin as a corded arm reached up. He opened the cabinet and retrieved a mug, setting it in front of me. I swallowed, very aware of the heat pouring off him. Very aware of his front nearly flush to my back.

"You want cream and sugar, *sugar*?" He said my nickname like a purr. His breath against my ear sent a shiver through me.

"Yes. Uhm. Both, please."

"You got it." He moved away, rummaging around the kitchen before he deposited both, along with a spoon. I began measuring out everything exactly how I liked it. His eyes remained fixed on me, garnering that familiar heat I was coming to recognize whenever he stared at me. I threw a questioning glance his way. He merely shrugged, then went back to whatever it was he'd been doing.

"Make yourself comfortable at the island. I'll get you breakfast."

Warmth seeped into my chest at the declaration. Luke had never cooked me breakfast—unless you counted weak coffee and burnt toast.

I did as he said, taking a seat. "You really didn't have to make me breakfast."

The gesture didn't really fit with his whole…persona. Which only left me confused. And made whatever was happening inside my chest all the more confusing.

"You had a rough night. It's the least I could do." There was a long hesitation. I gaped at his back, suddenly wishing I could see his face, his expression. "I wasn't exactly…you know. On my best behavior."

I snorted. "Is that what you call it?"

"Eleanor," he warned, tossing a glare over his shoulder. I pressed my lips between my teeth, forcing my expression clear. "Anyway, figured I should get something in you before we discuss our next steps."

"Next steps…?"

"Yup."

"Right." I looked at my coffee and took a tentative sip. Flavor filled my mouth as warmth shot into my belly. My eyes widened. I took another sip, catching notes of chocolate and…caramel?

"Like I said," he continued, "let's eat first, yeah?"

I had to restrain myself from gulping down the entire mug.

"You with me, sugar?"

"What?"

"I said we'd discuss things after we eat."

"Oh. Right. Yeah, sure. As long as I can have like, three more cups of this?"

His eyes danced with something I couldn't quite place before a plate slid onto the island in front of me. I stared down at it, blinking. A stack of three pancakes, four slices of bacon, and fluffy scrambled eggs done to perfection, with a sprinkle of cheddar cheese on top. The ball of butter on the pancakes was pooling up as it melted. The scent of vanilla and bacon tickled my nose and I inhaled.

A small carafe of syrup landed in front of me. It was heated, a tendril of steam curling up into the air. It was followed by a clink of cutlery as a knife and fork were laid down beside my plate. Finally, a napkin.

My lips parted as I took everything in. "Wow. This looks… There's no way I can eat all this."

"No problem, sugar. Eat what you want."

Our eyes connected across the island as a crackle of sparks flared between us. I was vaguely aware of the plate in his hands, piled high with a mountain of pancakes, bacon, and eggs. At least three times as much as was on my plate. He held my gaze a beat longer, then lifted his eyebrows in challenge.

It's like he was a completely different person today, opposite of how he'd been last night. There wasn't a whole lot of asshole present. Which left me to wonder: why?

Dropping his gaze, I started spreading butter over my pancakes, then doused the stack in syrup. He took the seat beside me, so close that his elbow brushed mine as he prepared his own food. I was far too aware of his proximity. The heat radiating off him.

I cut into my pancakes. They were so fluffy, they sponged up after I pulled the knife through them. Absolute perfection. I lifted the fork to my mouth. The second I took a bite, I moaned.

Bastian completely stilled beside me. When I opened my eyes, I found him angled toward me, watching intently. His lips were parted, his pupils dilated. I quickly chewed and swallowed. "What? They're fucking delicious."

When he said nothing, I turned back to my meal and began devouring it. His eyes lingered for several more bites. I was only vaguely aware of him turning back to his own food.

We were both quiet for a while. I felt his eyes return to me several more times, mostly because when I tried the bacon and eggs, I offered up similar vocal responses. I didn't care. It was *good*. He should take it as a compliment. Maybe he did. Maybe he was just shocked that I enjoyed his cooking this much.

I finished before him, so I rushed to take my plate to the sink and rinse it. "Just leave it," he grumbled, placing a hand on my arm to stop me from standing. "I'll get it later."

"Oh, okay. Sure." I felt compelled to do the dishes since he'd cooked. Even though with Luke, he'd always wanted me to both cook *and* do the dishes.

I refilled my coffee cup before refilling his. He drank his coffee black. Big surprise. It needed to match his soul and all that.

He waited until I sat back down, then said, "After you're ready, I'd like to head over to Professor Miller's house."

I jerked toward him. "After *I'm* ready? *Me?*"

"You." He dragged a forkful of pancakes—his last bite—through the remaining syrup pooled on his plate. I watched as he shoved it into his mouth. His jaw worked as he chewed. His throat bobbed as he swallowed. I didn't bother hiding my fascination.

"I want to see if you notice anything amiss. You've been to her house before, no?"

"Well, yeah. I mean, years ago. But yeah."

"Good. Authorities don't know what all was taken—if anything. But I would not be surprised if something was missing."

"Hmm…" I contemplated.

"All the usual valuable stuff was still there. Desktop computer, laptop, televisions, all that. But there could be other stuff missing."

"I suppose," I hedged. "What about…after?"

"What do you mean, after?"

"After we finish up there. You'll take me home?"

His expression remained unchanged, but his eyes darkened until they were solid black. Then his skin began to change, to turn gray. As if his glamor was weakening. An instant later, he was back to normal—human looking.

"I'll take you home afterward," he decided. "But... I'd like to make a deal with you."

My skin prickled. "A deal..."

Wasn't there some sort of thing against this? Something where you shouldn't make deals with goblins? Or supernaturals in general? There was probably a fairytale, or ten, that advised against it.

"I would like your assistance on this case. Think of it as... an advisory role. In exchange, I'll give you ten percent of the profit."

I gaped at him. "You're joking, right? Why would you need my help? *You're* the professional here."

He held his silence a beat too long, like it pained him to voice the next words. "I'm good at tracking people, sugar, not solving academic mysteries. You knew Professor Miller's world, what she valued, who she worked with. I need that insight. I need someone who can spot what I'm missing."

Ignoring the way his words created a burst of excited pride in my chest, I said, "And you think that's me?"

"I do." He dragged a hand through his hair. "Guess the question is, do you want to help catch Miller's murderer, or not?'"

I gave myself a moment to consider before sitting up straighter. In for a penny, in for a pound. "I deserve thirty percent, at the very least."

He stared at me, those green eyes calculating. "Thirty percent," he agreed slowly. "But you start now. And, sugar?" His voice dropped low. "You're mine for the duration of this case. No backing out."

The way he said 'mine' sent heat pooling low in my belly. When it shouldn't have. Especially if we were about to be working together.

9

———————

Eleanor hesitated outside of Professor Miller's house. The entire place was done up with caution tape. Bastian had received clearance to inspect the premises. He'd done so several times already. On his own, it was unlikely he'd discover anything new, but with Eleanor? He was hoping she'd bring fresh insight.

He gently prodded her between her shoulder blades. She threw him a glare, then walked up to the porch. She was still wearing his damned T-shirt, tied in a knot at her waist. She'd paired it with her pants from the night before.

Seeing her in his clothes did things to him he didn't want to examine. Especially the way she'd looked coming into the kitchen this morning. Bare legs on display.

Cooking breakfast was a win. He hadn't been sure how it would go over. But hearing her make those little sounds as she ate *his* food? He'd wanted to pull her off the damn bar stool and carry her upstairs. Or rather, the goblin in him had.

For now, he recognized his lust for what it was, but he could see exactly where this was heading if he allowed it. The goblin side of him would grow protective. Would start seeing her as his in ways that went far beyond physical. His instincts were already stirring...

61

Fuck.

It was good that he was dropping her off at home after this. He would keep their relationship strictly professional going forward. Consultations over the phone rather than in person.

Eleanor stopped at the front door, hesitating as if to collect herself. He pressed in behind her, close enough that his chest grazed her back. He forced himself to relax and ignore the sensation. "Whenever you're ready, sugar, it's unlocked. Take your time. We can hang out here, if you need."

Just keep standing there, his body demanded. *I don't mind the feel of you against me.*

He didn't want to rush her. Even now, her scent had changed. He could smell the heavy dregs of anxiety rolling off her skin. It raised his hackles when it shouldn't have, pulling at a primal part of him. As soon as this case was solved, they'd have no reason to see each other again—what did he care if this upset her?

When she nodded, the top of her pink ponytail brushed his chin. He glanced down at it and his lips twitched. His free hand lifted, reaching for it, but he stopped himself before he could.

"I..." she sighed and shook her head, opening the door at last before stepping through.

He gave her some space, waiting for her to acclimate. She walked through the entry and into the living room, then began moving around the space, inspecting things. He studied her, noting the way her lips had pressed into a thin line, her expression pinched tight.

The air was stagnant, the scent of death lingering even now. Everything was eerily silent. Something had happened here beyond a simple murder. He felt it the moment he first arrived on the scene, and each time thereafter. A fine trace of malice, almost imperceptible.

It had always been that way for him, which was what made him so good at his job. His ability to sense lingering traces of death. Not that it had done him any good in this case.

"What happened to her after…after she died?" Eleanor stood frozen in the middle of the living room.

"Moved her to the morgue for autopsy."

She shuddered, then nodded. Her throat bobbed. "Where…?"

He pointed. She followed his finger and walked over, head down, studying the area. "Burn marks?" she asked.

"Yes, they found them around the body, and a charred streak across—" He cut himself off, because the graphic details weren't something she needed to hear. "Just focus on the house, sugar. What do you see? Anything missing? Out of place? Anything that makes you suspicious?"

She looked up at him, eyes narrowed, then pointed at the ground. "This. This makes me suspicious."

He sighed. "We can get to that later, if you like."

Her jaw clenched, then she nodded, moving away.

She inspected everything, remaining silent. He stayed out of her way, watched as she moved from room to room. He *should* have used the time to get one more look at everything, even though he'd been over it twice. Instead, he watched her. Fixated on the way her brow furrowed, the way she sucked her lip between her teeth, like she was contemplating.

Once done, they headed back to his truck. He'd left the bike at home, knowing she'd be more comfortable in this. A long silence stretched between them once she was belted in.

"Well?" he asked.

She blew out a breath. "I can't say for sure, but…" She angled toward him and their eyes locked. "Professor Miller had a private collection of…things." His eyes narrowed in question. "Like, artifacts, I mean."

"Artifacts…"

"Things built by humans, you know?"

"When you say humans, you mean *artificers*?"

She nodded.

He made a humming noise in his throat.

Magical objects—artifacts—were well known and regulated among supernaturals. These were objects constructed by humans, and those humans were known as artificers. The why of the matter wasn't fully understood. Humans crafted them and used supernatural blood to imbue power into them. During ancient times, artificers had become blood chemists, learning to mix different supernatural bloods holding different magics to create new recipes of power.

It was the only advantage humans had over supernatural races—that only a human could make such an object. And it had been exploited throughout history. Especially in days long past.

Before the Supernatural Council had been formed, more commonly dubbed the SC, races had no qualms about enslaving humans, forcing them into crafting dangerous objects of power. This made it far more difficult to keep the magical world hidden. Now, only a select few humans became artificers, which made them answerable to the SC, but they also had rights, just like any supernatural.

Eleanor cleared her throat, remaining silent otherwise.

He said, "You mentioned studying art history and other ancient things with Professor Miller. You were really just referring to artifacts, then?" She nodded. "And? The artifacts Professor Miller had in her possession, are they missing?"

"Some of them," she managed, her voice falling to a whisper. "But she could have, I don't know, sold them, or gotten rid of them. Maybe donated them."

"What does your gut tell you?"

"A few of them were really important to her."

He sat up straighter. "How do you know that?"

"Because..." She chewed on her bottom lip, briefly drawing his attention to her plush mouth. "Because I helped her find some of them."

He sat forward. "You?"

"During...like, when I was studying under her."

He huffed. "You guys went out and hunted artifacts or something? Like some modern tomb raider shit?"

"Actually, yes. That's…that's exactly what we did."

He gaped at her, realizing he'd vastly underestimated her, then snapped his mouth shut. "They let you get a master's degree in shit like that?"

"Well, no, not really." Her cheeks flushed. "But…"

Damn. She was a mystery unfolding. He rubbed his chin.

"We did it in secret—Professor Miller and I. My master's was supposed to be in art history, minor in archeological anthropology. When people don't know magic exists, ancient objects are seen as relics of an old time. Humans have no idea that half the things in their museums are, in fact, magical objects. And then there are the allusions to artifacts that spring up in art pieces all over the world, objects of myth and legend depicted in paintings and journals and such. That sort of thing. Those were often what we searched for. Common things like armor, belts, crowns, jewelry, masks, mirrors, musical instruments—that's always a fun one—tools—"

"Okay, okay." He exhaled through his nose. "I get it. *Shit*. This changes things."

The realization was sinking in. If Professor Miller was tangled up in something like this, then it was very likely her death was premeditated and centered around her artifact work.

"Right. Well. So, yeah. That's what we did together. Most of the things we reclaimed were in the name of the university, as part of our research and whatnot. But sometimes we did stuff on the side too. That's how she got her own collection."

"And your necklaces?" He lifted an eyebrow.

She shrank down in her seat. "I mean…well, yeah."

He studied her. Clearly this wasn't something she wanted to discuss. He was tempted to push, but if it didn't have anything to do with the case, then it didn't matter. And yet, it mattered a whole hell of a lot to him, when it shouldn't have.

In fact, nothing about her should have mattered to him.

Nothing. And yet, he found himself wanting to know more. Wanting to know everything.

Wanting to hear stories of the adventures she'd been on. Of the artifacts she'd found.

He pushed that aside and said, "Fine. All right. I want you to make a list of all the artifacts you remember in Professor Miller's house. I want to know what they did, too. I can go through it to see if it explains this. It might be our best lead."

She nodded, her eyes going distant as she gazed out over the quiet suburb street they'd parked along. "I can do it after I get home," she whispered.

"Good. Then let's get you home." He turned the key in the ignition and they set off, all while ignoring the sense of dissatisfaction blooming in his chest over the idea that he would soon be separated from her.

10

I sat silently in the passenger seat of Bastian's truck as the city rose around us. Seeing Professor Miller's house had been difficult. I needed another hot shower, fresh clothes, and my bed, which was why I couldn't wait to get home. There was a part of me that panicked—wondering if Luke had found me at the club, could he find my home too? But the other part of me, the one desperate for comfort, brushed it aside.

I blew out a breath, which earned a glance from Bastian. At least I had the night off. I was almost relieved that we'd canceled girls night—

Oh, shit! My throat tightened. "Bastian," I croaked, "I need my phone back. Where is it?"

Had Vivi tried to contact me? The real Vivi, not some voice that sounded like her from some unknown number. I didn't want her worried.

Bastian sighed. My phone appeared in his hand as he dropped it into my lap. I tapped the screen but nothing happened. "You've got to be kidding me!" I looked up at him, jaw clenched. "You couldn't keep it charged when you put it, *wherever*? It's dead."

He lifted a shoulder. "Not my problem."

I scoffed. "Ridiculous. Whatever. Please, tell me you have a charger in here."

He reached into the center console, keeping his eyes on the road. A charging cord materialized. Exasperated, I plugged my phone in, waiting for enough juice to turn it on.

Another phone rang and I glanced up. The dash screen illuminated with an incoming call and a name. *Christian Morris.* Beneath it, in parenthesis, was *Walton Bureau of Investigation.*

I stared at the contact.

Bastian grabbed his phone from the dock and answered, switching it off bluetooth. Clearly he didn't want me eavesdropping. "What do you have for me? "

I could just barely make out the voice on the other end, but not the words. Bastian stiffened, going rigid. His eyes darted toward me, then back to the road.

"*Fuck.* Right... Right... Okay.... All right."

Another long hesitation and then—

"Yeah, she's actually with me. We're on our way. ETA puts us at ten. Yep... Okay. Hang tight." He hung up and set the phone back on its mount.

His face was a mask. Impossible to read.

Meanwhile, a sour taste filled my mouth. "Who was that?" Silence stretched between us. When he still didn't speak, I glanced over. "Bastian!"

A muscle in his jaw feathered. "Walton PD just called in the WBI for a case. New homicide reported in West Cross. At the Glenneg Apartment Complex."

"But that's..." My fingers turned to ice. I clenched them together and buried them in my lap, phone forgotten, and stared out the windshield, eyes blurring. Around us, the city slid by, but inside my head, every thought went silent except one. Something had happened in my apartment building.

Bastian's exhale was drawn out. "Let's just get there and see what's going on."

"What did they say?" I asked, half afraid to hear it.

"You sure you want to know?"

My swallow was practically audible. No, of course I wasn't sure. "I'd like to be mentally prepared for the shitstorm we're about to walk into."

He nodded. "Your apartment was broken into. Trashed, by the sound of it. They only found out because one of your neighbors didn't show up for work this morning."

"What?!" I gasped. He'd said homicide. "Who?" I whispered.

"Peter Gains? You know him?"

A cold ball of sick dread dropped into my stomach. "Oh, my God."

"I take it that's a yes."

"He... He was this... He was just a sweet old man! How... What... Someone did this? How do they know it has anything to do with my apartment? Wait, do they think it was me, since I was his neighbor? I was with you all night. You can vouch for me, right? Am I going to be arrested? Is that why your—why *Christian*—asked about me? You told him I was with you—"

"Elle, relax." It was the first time he'd called me that and it made me freeze. I'd forgotten how much I missed hearing it. "There aren't a lot of details yet, from the sound of it. WBI got called because the scorch marks around the body look similar to the ones they found around Miller..." He trailed off, then his brow furrowed. "Well, it would seem that this absolves you completely. If both people were killed the same way, and you were with me during one of the incidents, then it's doubtful you killed Professor Miller."

I screeched in fury and punched him in the arm, hard. The wheel jerked. "Are you fucking kidding me?! I told you I didn't kill her!"

"Yes, well, I don't rule out a suspect completely unless I have solid evidence that proves otherwise."

"Ugh. You are so...*Ugh!*"

The corner of his mouth twitched.

"It's not funny!" I roared.

"Good thing you like me, sugar, because that actually hurt."

"I don't like you! And you're lucky I'm not one of those lambs you mentioned. Because then I would absolutely fucking rip your face off right now."

"Good thing."

I pressed my lips together, turning to face forward again, only so I didn't have to look at his dumb stupid ridiculous face anymore. I couldn't believe him—*this*. That he carried even a shred of suspicion toward me after last night and this morning.

My anger quickly abated, though.

Peter Gains was…*dead*. It didn't feel real. I thought about all the cookies I'd baked him. Thought about his cute cat I borrowed when I needed something to cuddle. Oh, shit. I still needed to call Vivi—to tell her.

I picked up my phone. A hand shot out and wrapped around mine, around my phone. "I wouldn't do that right now. This is a federal investigation. You should refrain from contacting anyone, especially on this phone. If it's hacked or tracked, and even if it isn't…"

His words slid right out of my mind. I looked down at his hand, covering mine. Gaped at it like an idiot. At the warmth that seeped through his skin. The way it instantly calmed me to have his touch.

He sighed, then squeezed. When he pulled away, I instantly missed his touch.

"Just hang tight, sugar. We'll figure things out." His voice was softer this time. Maybe he could see the tears blurring my eyes. Or sense my growing distress.

"What did they do to my apartment?" I whispered. Only just now remembering he'd mentioned that it was trashed.

He didn't answer.

———

My breaths were shaky as I climbed out of Bastian's truck. The entire street had been closed off, only letting cleared personnel in or out. Bastian had flashed some sort of identification that got us through. I shut the door behind me and gaped at the swarm of uniformed people going in and out of Glenneg Complex, my six-story apartment flat in the heart of West Cross. Two blocks down, if I squinted, I could make out the sign for Awake Coffee.

"Here, put this on." Bastian draped a heavy leather jacket around my shoulders, probably summoned from thin air. It smelled like him, like the cologne he wore, which immediately comforted my nerves. I pulled it around me and clenched it in my fists, using it as an anchor.

"Rose?" A voice to my right had me spinning. In a huddle of wide-eyed watchers, Candice was staring at me.

The others nearby heard my name and turned. I was acquainted with about half the people in my apartment building. We did mixers on the roof sometimes, that sort of thing. "Thank God you're okay," Candice said, rushing over. She threw her arms around me and pulled me tight.

"Hey, Candice. I'm good," I mumbled into her shoulder. She was on the taller side, and curvy. "Vivi's out of town so she's fine, too," I added.

Candice lived on the floor below ours.

"I heard someone moving around upstairs," she explained. "I thought you'd come home from work—pissed off or something, by the sound of all the destruction happening. Didn't put two and two together. I should have texted you." That wouldn't have made any difference, but I didn't say so. "They're saying Peter was murdered," she whispered, holding my shoulders to inspect me. I felt Bastian hovering nearby, heard the hushed murmur of his voice talking to someone. "Can you believe it? In our own apartment building? I thought West Cross was *supposed* to be safe." Her rich beige skin was pale, dark eyes searching mine. "I wouldn't be surprised if you wanted to move, though. After this, after what happened to your…” She trailed off, eyes darting behind me and widening briefly.

A large, heavy hand fell comfortably on my shoulder.

“Wow…” she whispered as she took in Bastian. A flush rose to her cheeks. “Who’s your friend?”

“Oh, right. Candice, Bastian. Bastian, Candice.” I turned to better see him, dislodging his hand in the process. “Candice lives in the apartment below mine.”

“I see.” Bastian’s eyes narrowed, calculating. “Did you already give your statement?”

“Yep,” she nodded, squaring her shoulders. “Told them what I told Rose. Thought she’d come home pissed, was banging around and making a ruckus upstairs about three in the morning. Woke my ass up. Should have texted her, but figured she’d had a rough night…working at Vortex and all.”

Bastian made a humming noise in the back of his throat, then nodded. Leaning close, *too close*, his lips brushed the shell of my ear and he spoke in a low voice. “You’ve been given clearance to enter. You ready?”

I shivered. But not because I was afraid of what came next. I swallowed against the dryness in my throat. “Right. Let’s go.”

We set off, entering through the front doors and taking the elevator to the sixth floor. I shared this floor with Peter, who was across the hall. I couldn’t help but wonder, was he the intended target, and my apartment merely collateral? Or was my apartment the target all along, and poor Peter had gotten in the way?

When the elevator doors opened, the landing was swarming with activity. I expected to see a bunch of cops in uniform, but most of them were dressed in polos and slacks, business casual, all wearing lanyards and badges. A male stepped forward, a WBI badge clipped to his pants. “Bastian, there you are. I assume you’re Vivian Mora’s roommate?” I hesitated then nodded. He’d probably gotten her name from the rental agreement. His eyes flicked to Bastian. “You’d better show her into the apartment, but—" He turned back to me. "Don't touch anything yet. WBI is working on fingerprints."

"Uhm… Why is WBI involved in a simple break-in?" I managed to ask. Bastian tensed beside me.

"The body found across the hall had—"

"She doesn't need the details, *Christian*."

"Oh, I think I need the details, *Bastian*." I glared at him.

"Later," he said, putting a hand at the base of my spine, guiding me forward. I really should have complained, instead of just letting him lead me away with a low, "Come on."

My heart started to race, palms growing sweaty. Everyone we passed nodded at Bastian. I was too fixated on my open door to notice. It was hanging crooked, like it had been kicked in. We moved through the opening. A whine wrenched from my throat. My feet no longer worked, freezing me in place.

Behind me, Bastian let out a low whistle, then said, "Keep going, sugar." His hand pressed more firmly against my lower back, imparting warmth I didn't realize I needed.

"Hey, Bas," someone said, nodding, walking by with a clip-board in hand, right out of my apartment.

"Oh, my God," I whined. Tears pooled in my eyes. "This… What…?"

"I'm right here," he said, crowding in close, lips brushing my ear. His thumb rubbed circles at the base of my spine. I didn't really notice. "Everything can be fixed, Sweetheart. All this can be cleaned up. You're safe. It's just…stuff."

"Stuff?!" I dragged in a deep breath, released it, took another. My eyes darted everywhere, over to the table, the shattered bowl of pasta still on the floor, amid the mess of my apartment. My chest began to ache.

Everything was trashed—absolutely *destroyed*! The table was broken, the couches had been knifed, with stuffing spilling out, our bookcases were broken, books and trinkets scattered around them, the television screen was shattered. A sob escaped my chest. This wasn't someone looking for something. It was intentional.

"Fucking, *Luke*," I breathed, realization sinking in.

"What's that, sugar?"

I swallowed and shook my head. It *had* to be him. Who else would go to so much effort? Who else would purposefully destroy my things? Especially considering I'd gotten away from him last night.

I reconsidered Candice's words. She said it happened around 3:00am. Luke had cornered me around 12:00am. That meant he'd come here afterward.

So he had known where I lived.

I began trembling. What if Vivi hadn't gone out of town? What if she'd been here? She could be just like Peter—dead.

A sob broke free of my throat. I clamped a hand over my mouth, taking a deep breath, holding it in. Then I counted to ten and released it. "He knows where I live," I managed, knowing that my carefully curated life was over. The notion that I was no longer safe had bile rising in my throat as a sour taste filled my mouth.

Bastian frowned, his gaze darting between me and the mess of my apartment. "Take it this has something to do with that human trash from last night?"

I gulped and nodded.

He scrubbed a hand over his face, his rings catching the light. "Well, this just got a whole lot more complicated."

"Why?" I whispered.

"Stay here while I go check on some things," he said, ignoring my question. "You can have a look around like Christian said. But don't touch anything. WBI needs fingerprints."

Several people were moving around the space, doing exactly that—dusting for fingerprints. I groaned, knowing I needed to see my room. Could I make my legs move me down the hall? Was I prepared to see what I would find?

"You going to be okay for a few minutes?" Bastian's thumb stroked at the base of my spine, but he didn't pull his hand away. It remained tucked beneath the jacket he'd given me, warmth radiating through the fabric of my shirt.

"I... Yes. Go."

I felt his disappearance as cold air rushed in around me. Mustering up my courage, I moved down the hall. My bedroom door hung askew, partly removed from its hinges. I winced but didn't enter. The space was near unrecognizable. Most of the art was torn from the walls. The mattress was cut open, foam and springs exposed. My clothes had been ripped from drawers, some of it shredded.

My stomach roiled and I placed a hand over it.

Turning on my heel, I fled. Straight into Peter's apartment. His space was swarming with investigators. It wasn't in shambles like mine. No one seemed to notice me as I headed for the door to Peter's bedroom.

"Ah-ah-ah!" Warm hands wrapped around my stomach, pulling me against a firm body. "Not a good idea, sugar. You don't want to see that."

Bastian's hands splayed over me, tightening. I held still a moment, let the feel of him ground me. Exhaling, my shoulders fell. "I want to see it, Bastian. I need to. Peter... He was my neighbor. If this is...if this is my fault—"

"Eleanor! None of this is your fault. Did you *ask* someone to kill Peter?"

"What?! No!"

"Then it isn't your fault. Hear me?" He lowered his head until his lips brushed my ear, sending shivers over my skin. "If I hear shit like that out of your mouth again, we're going to have words, understand?"

I swallowed but nodded, then said, "Please, let me go."

He sighed, then released me.

I stepped forward into the chaos. Peter's body was on the floor of his bedroom, limbs splayed. There was blood seeping into the carpet. His night shirt was long, but it didn't fully cover his legs.

My breaths came faster with each second.

A large hand came around my stomach, splaying wide as Bastian crowded in behind me. "Seen enough?" he bit out. "You shouldn't be here."

I didn't answer. My eyes were still fixed on Peter's body, unblinking. There was a bullet hole in his forehead. But it was the darkened markings on the floor and one across his torso paired with the cut of a knife, that had me whispering, "Scorch marks."

"I see that. Why do you think WBI was called in?"

A tremor passed through me. Bastian's hand tightened on my stomach. "Come on, sugar. Out of here. You've seen enough."

He pulled me away and I let him, trying to get Peter's face out of my mind, his open mouth, glassy eyes, wide with fear. What struck me as weird, though, were the scorch marks, both on the floor and his body. The one on his body was paired with a knife, like it had been on fire when it cut him.

I chewed on my bottom lip as Bastian led me from the apartment. At some point, his hand had twined with mine. It was a testament to how rattled I felt that I hadn't even reacted.

"You're not staying here," he growled, turning me to face him, dropping my hand to take my shoulders. "For obvious reasons,"

"I… There are a few friends I can call."

"Nope. Not happening." His grip tightened on my shoul-ders. "Get some clothes, whatever you need for the foreseeable future." I tried to speak, but nothing came out. "I'm taking you home, sugar. With me. End of discussion."

11

Eleanor gaped at Bastian. "With… With you?"

"You heard me. Hurry up."

She opened her mouth—

"Look, sugar, I don't want you here longer than necessary. You've seen enough."

Her expression morphed into a glare, but he didn't back down. In fact, he welcomed that sass. Better that than the alternative, given what happened to her apartment and neighbor.

"I can stay with friends."

"No." He ran a hand over the shaved side of his scalp. Fucking hell. What the fuck was wrong with him? This was *not* how things were supposed to happen.

He was supposed to put more space between them. Not less. But that was before this.

He didn't trust anyone with her safety. Not when someone clearly wanted to harm her. She'd said his name earlier. *Luke.* The piece of shit who'd hurt her.

As far as he was concerned, anyone who harmed women deserved the worst kind of pain, and he was eager to find this asshole—make sure he felt it.

Eleanor finally blew out a breath and nodded. "Okay. Fine."

He deflated, glad this wasn't about to become a battle of wills.

A yowl sounded, followed by a series of hisses. He spun on his heel right as Eleanor dashed forward, pushing past him. "Oh my, God. Teddy?!" She reached for the white cat currently being carried from Peter's apartment. "Stop. That's —*give him to me*," she insisted.

The WBI employee eyed Bastian a moment, as if asking for help. He lifted his eyebrows as if to say, *better listen to the woman*, and the investigator relented.

The cat tumbled into Eleanor's arms, immediately wedging its head beneath her chin. He gawked at her. What the fuck?! She closed his leather jacket around the frightened creature.

Oh, hell fucking no. Now he'd get it back covered in cat fur. Great.

"You poor thing. Poor baby," she cooed, nuzzling it. Her eyes filled with tears and she squeezed them shut. "I'm going to take care of you from now on, okay? Everything's going to be all right," she whispered, bouncing the damn thing like it was a baby.

He grumbled, forcing himself to focus on the sight of her cuddling it. If she wanted something to cuddle, he was standing right fucking here. His jaw ticked. Jealous of a goddamn cat. What the fuck was wrong with him?

All he could think to say was, "Sugar, we are not taking a cat home."

She rounded on him, expression morphing to anger. "Oh yes, we are! Teddy's coming with us. Otherwise, I'm not going."

"Mother fucking fuck," he muttered, rubbing his temples.

She lifted her chin and squared her shoulders, all five foot eight inches of her. Her fierce expression silenced him from further protest. "Fine. Go get your shit. We're leaving."

"I'll need to get Teddy's stuff too, his litter box and whatnot."

His head lolled back, gaze lifting toward the ceiling. This fucking female. She went from cute to irritating at the drop of a hat. "Get whatever you need," he bit out, straightening up, willing patience into his tone. "I need to talk to a few more people before we go."

She nodded, then hesitated. "Bastian?" He turned back. "Are you sure about this? Me staying with you?"

The vulnerability in her voice caught him off guard, softening him. "I'm sure, sugar. Now go pack."

Ten minutes later, Teddy was in his cat carrier. Bastian held the carrier in one hand, a duffle bag of cat things thrown over his shoulder—fucking *cat* things!—while guiding Eleanor by the elbow through the gathered crowd. She wheeled a massive suitcase behind her in one hand and carried an empty litter box in the other.

A few camera crews had been allowed on the scene. Their equipment was already set up to capture whatever they could. Newscasters held mics to their mouths, explaining what had happened. It would be all over TV by the evening.

"Don't talk to anyone," he warned, tipping his head low to her ear. The scent of her shampoo—the stuff he kept in the guest bathroom—swirled around him. It smelled good on her. He'd been doing that a lot lately, putting himself close to her, closer than necessary.

He steered her toward the truck, putting Teddy's carrier into the bed—

"Don't you dare put him back there! Teddy rides with us."

He opened his mouth, then snapped it shut, giving a jerk of his head. Grabbing the carrier, he flung the truck doors open and deposited a yowling Teddy into the back seat, tossing the duffle in after him. Then he hauled up the massive

—unnecessarily massive—suitcase of Eleanor's things. His gaze shot skyward, begging for mercy. What the fuck had she brought? Her entire damn wardrobe?

Once they were situated in the vehicle, she buckled herself in. He reached over and gave her belt a tug, ensuring it was latched, which earned him another glare. Fuck. All right, then.

The engine revved to life. Minutes later, they were driving through the city in silence, punctuated by periodic sighs from a certain female in the passenger seat, and the pathetic mews of an unhappy cat behind him. He had no interest in conversation.

A vibrating phone broke the silence. Eleanor jerked, then pressed her phone to her ear. "Vivi?"

He inhaled sharply. His hand shot out, reaching for her phone. She wrapped her fingers around his wrist. Heat shot up his arm, her touch burning through every rational thought. Their eyes locked, and for a heartbeat neither of them moved. Her pulse hammered against his skin where their bodies connected.

"I won't say anything *sensitive*, Mr. Paranoid," she bit out. "What are you, my bodyguard?"

Bodyguard. It made his chest expand. Protecting her, keeping her safe, being responsible for her body—fuck. He yanked his hand back, out of her grip.

"No, no," she said into the phone. "Sorry, that was…this guy I'm with. *No*, God no! You know, the one I mentioned from the coffee shop? Yes, that one." His head jerked in her direction. "*No, Vivi*. I'm okay. Yes, someone broke into the apartment. I know, I was just there… No, I don't know much yet. No! Of course I'm not staying there. I'm not an idiot." She sank lower in the seat. "I know, I thought about Kaylee… No. He said I can't stay with any friends."

She fell silent, listening to the voice on the other end of the line. She hummed. With his goblin hearing, he could make out Vivi's words, but he wasn't going to tell Eleanor that. He tuned them out, trying not to eavesdrop.

A few words of "Yes" and "Right" from Eleanor. A few nods. Then, "I'll be careful, I promise. Love you, girl."

Vivi said she loved her back.

The call ended.

His lips pulled up at the corner. "Told your roommate about me, hmm?"

She tutted. "Just that you ruined my favorite shirt."

"Me? I seem to recall someone wasn't paying attention—?"

"If you hadn't been there, *stalking me*. I bet you orchestrated that entire thing, didn't you?" she accused. He kept his lips pressed together because, yes, in fact, he had. He'd purposefully placed himself in her path. Hadn't moved out of the way when she barreled right into him. Had used his magic to ensure the coffee wasn't scalding so it wouldn't burn her skin when she bumped the mug.

"I knew it," she hissed. "You owe me a new shirt."

"Fine."

She hesitated, perhaps not expecting him to agree so readily. "Thanks."

Silence fell for several moments until he said, "So, Vivi is your roommate?"

"Vivian, yeah. She's gone. Flew back home yesterday, thank God. I can't imagine…"

He glanced at her. "No point in stressing over what might have been, sugar. Let it go."

"Right." She folded her hands in her lap, fidgeting with her fingers. "So, what now?"

"Now? I'm going to get you home and settled. Can't stay for long. I got some stuff to take care of. You'll be safe at the house."

"Okay."

He glanced over his shoulder. "That cat is house trained, correct?"

She made a sound of disgust. "*Yes, Bastian*. What do you think? That he was shitting and peeing all over Peter's apartment? Coughing up fur-balls all over the couches?" He winced at the thought—his designer furniture ruined. "I've house-sat for Teddy plenty. He's an absolute sweetheart. Trust me, by tomorrow, you'll be cuddling him."

"No, I fucking won't."

"Not a cat person, huh?"

"Not an anything person," he snapped.

He didn't bother admitting that he volunteered several times a year at Walton City Animal Shelter. Not to mention the shelter's annual holiday party. He dropped a cool five grand, sometimes more, in financial donations to that place on a yearly basis.

"Well that's unfortunate for you," she tsked. "You're completely missing out on the unconditional love animals have to offer."

"Guess so."

They fell silent for the remainder of the ride. He retreated into his thoughts, going back through all the information they'd gathered, tying it together. He needed to visit the coroner's office again, have another look at Professor Miller's body now that he'd seen Peter's. There were too many similarities. He also needed to have a nice, long talk with Eleanor about the Luke-issue. He had a bad feeling everything was connected. And yet, that almost felt *too* coincidental. He'd been involved in plenty of investigations where the most obvious suspect turned out to be innocent.

His house loomed before them. Yesterday, Eleanor had seemed both surprised and impressed by it. That both pleased him and royally pissed him off. She probably thought he'd hired a decorator, but in truth he had enjoyed doing it all himself.

He didn't park in the garage, putting them right at the porch. "I'll get the cat," he said, shutting off the ignition and climbing out of the truck. He keyed in the code, gave it his fingerprint, and opened the door. She followed him inside where he deposited the cat carrier. "I'm serious, sugar. Make sure that thing behaves."

"He's not a *thing*," she whined, bending to release Teddy, who crawled straight into her arms. "I know you miss him," she cooed. He stared at her, studying the gentle way she coddled the animal. Warmth spread through his chest. Her lips pulled into a cute little pucker and a crease appeared between her brows as she said, "I know, baby. I know. It's going to be okay. I'm going to take care of you now. We're going to stay here for a bit, okay? In this *nice man's* house." She threw him a glare to emphasize her point, before turning back to Teddy. "You'll see. It will be just fine. You can even sleep in my bed tonight."

His lips parted at those words. *Sleep in my bed.* He inhaled, nice and slow, then let it go. "Make yourself at home," he said, mostly to distract himself. "Let me know if you need anything. There's food in the kitchen, if you're hungry. Feel free to use the TV, or whatever."

"Can I explore?" She asked, keeping her eyes on Teddy. A flash of heat coated his skin. It was just a fucking cat. It shouldn't have irritated him to see her pay it so much attention. And yet, she hadn't looked at him once since walking in.

He hesitated. "Fine. Explore wherever you want. Just… stay out of my room."

"Sure." She glanced up. The tightness in his chest eased the moment her eyes fell on him. "Is the house still…locked or whatever?"

"Yes. It's got a solid security system—a hybrid form of witch tech. You won't be able to get in or out without me. We can fix that once I know you're safe. But until then…"

"Right. I guess that's fine, since I'm going to nest."

"Nest?"

"Yes, it's what you do when—"

"I know what fucking nesting is, sugar."

"Okay, then why are you so surprised?"

Because his goblin brain seized on that word like a drug—nesting, claiming, *staying*. A female making herself at home in *his* space, arranging *his* things to her liking, settling in for the long haul. Every possessive instinct he possessed was purring with dangerous satisfaction. He blew out a breath, trying to get his shit together.

She'd had a bad night, seen her dead professor's house this morning, and discovered her apartment destroyed, her neighbor murdered. He needed to stop being such an asshole. "Fine. Do whatever you need. Like I said, make yourself at home. It's your house too, for the time being." Tingles spread through his limbs at those words. He ignored them. "Let me know if you need anything."

"Sure."

He turned to the stairs, climbing them.

"Bastian?" Her voice was soft. He stopped and looked over his shoulder at her.

She licked her lips, drawing his gaze there briefly. His fist clenched.

"Thank you. I know I called you an asshole. And I mean, you kind of are." He huffed. "But it's really nice that you're letting me stay here when you don't even know me. I'm sure it's purely professional—can't have your business partner getting murdered—but..." The sarcasm dropped, sincerity bleeding through her next words. "I appreciate it."

His chest tightened at the way she'd dropped her walls and shown him her soft vulnerability underneath all that fire. He swallowed, hard. "No problem, sugar." Then he turned and fled up the stairs before he did something stupid. Like tell her that what his body was feeling for her wasn't professional at all.

12

Most of my day passed in a blur. I got Teddy settled, finding a place in the laundry room for his litter box, putting the majority of his things in my own room. Then I showered and unpacked, taking advantage of the dresser and empty closet in the guest suite. I didn't know how long I'd be stuck here, but I had to admit, it was a big step up from my apartment in terms of amenities.

Not only was there a jetted tub in my guest suite, with a separate, giant shower, there was a pool and a hot tub out in the back yard equipped with a deck perfect for entertaining. Not that I could enjoy it, since I was stuck in the house. When I explored the rest of the house, it only got better. Besides two bedrooms on the second floor, one of which was Bastian's, there was a game room in the third floor attic. He had a collection of old arcade games, an air hockey table, and a pool table. The far side had a small wet bar. I stood in there and gawked for a good five minutes.

The finished basement had been turned into a giant gym. Not your run of the mill home gym. It was packed with equipment, sure, but it also housed an entire section of weapons, punching bags, and everything else a mixed martial arts student like myself might fawn over.

At least while I was here, I wouldn't get rusty. Maybe Bastian could teach me a thing or two. With a gym like this, and given what he was, he was highly skilled. I'd seen how quickly the knife had appeared, how deftly it sank into Luke's chest. I wondered how often he practiced down here.

That pulled certain images to the front of my mind. Images of him shirtless, fists taped up, throwing his body into punches. My eyes darted to the punching bag and my cheeks flushed. Because I could practically see him there, covered in a sheen of sweat.

Heat rushed through me and pooled in my core. Ugh. I should have packed my vibrator. Something to take the edge off all this…tension, or whatever it was building between us.

Turning my back on the room, I trudged up the stairs.

Bastian had left earlier. I knew because I'd heard him shout his goodbye while I was freshening up in the bathroom. I wasn't sure how long he'd be gone, and I didn't have his phone number, which was probably a good thing.

I wandered around the house, looking at things in more detail. My mind kept jumping back to my apartment. I didn't want to think about it, but each time I pictured the devastation, a sinking sense of helplessness washed over me. Assuming I was ever safe enough to return, what the hell was I going to do about the mess? How much was it going to cost to replace everything? Mattresses, furniture, my freaking TV?! It would run somewhere in the thousands. I didn't know if Vivi had this sort of thing covered under her renter's insurance, but I had a feeling we wouldn't see a penny of reimbursement.

I forced my attention elsewhere, taking a seat at the kitchen island where I opened my notes app and spent some time making the list Bastian had requested. My phone was in airplane mode, just to be safe. I mentally confronted everything I remembered about Professor Miller's artifact collection, and then I started listing everything out. I put a couple of details about what I remembered about each artifact, and then a note for all the ones that were missing, which had been nearly all of them. As I'd told Bastian, I really didn't know if she'd gotten rid of them over the years.

Artifacts were powerful objects. While they could only be made by humans, they could be used and controlled by anyone. That's why my necklaces worked so well for me. One had been a gift from my father during my childhood, the charm that allowed me to see through glamor. The other was a protection medallion that Professor Miller had come across long before she'd met me. She'd found it accidentally, after seeing it worn by a female subject in a famous art piece. It was what was supposed to keep me hidden after the *Luke Incident*.

My fingers drifted to my neck and I brushed both pendants. Artifacts didn't fail. Something had happened that allowed Luke to find me, after two years of remaining hidden. I'd stopped leaving a paper trail, gotten rid of my credit cards, used a burner phone, and relied on Vivi to maintain the paperwork for our apartment. I guess it was naive to think I'd hide from him forever. I suppose I hoped he'd forget his threats, forget about me completely and move on.

Dragging my hands over my face, I squeezed my eyes shut and exhaled.

What I needed was a good distraction. I put my phone away and located Teddy. We curled up on the couch, him in my lap, a heap of pillows and blankets around us. I could get used to this, I decided. I unlocked my e-reader, diving into the spicy romance I was reading.

Teddy kneaded my leg while I petted him, whiling away the hours. My cheeks were already flushed when I heard the familiar buzz of a bike engine, listening as it grew louder. The mechanical jolt of a garage door gently shook the house, and then silence.

I closed out of my book and powered off my device. Bastian found me with an innocent look on my face, waiting for him. He stalked into the living room, tossed his leather jacket on the couch, and sank down onto the sectional, the same spot he'd occupied last night.

Unbothered by my presence, he released a tiny groan that had my nipples tightening. His arms stretched across the back, his legs splayed wide, like he'd just come home from a grueling day at work. His eyes lifted to meet mine. "Hey, sugar. Got plans tonight?"

A laugh burst from my chest. "You're joking right?" I was dressed in pajama pants and a tank top. His eyes snagged on my chest. The thin camisole did little to hide my peaked nipples or the fact I wasn't wearing a bra. There was a flare of black around his irises, but it was there and gone in an instant.

"How's Ted settling in?" he asked, turning his focus to the cat in my lap.

"*Teddy*, is settling in fine. He's always been adaptable. Already got up and used the litter box like a proper gentleman."

"Good. There's a cordless vacuum in the closet there, for when he sheds all over the couch."

My jaw dropped. "Can't you like, magic it away or whatever?"

He grinned, and for the second time, that dimple on his cheek appeared. "I *could*, sugar, but I'd hate to deprive you of your new cat-mom duties."

"And here I thought you were trying to be nice, asking about him."

"I was." He stood up and moved over to the liquor cabinet. "Want one?" I shook my head. He sat back down with a glass of dark amber liquid in hand. "Anyway, I was serious. You got plans tonight?"

I tutted. "You really think I have plans after I was A. Practically attacked last night—"

"You *were* attacked—"

"B. Saw my murdered professor's house this morning—"

"Speaking of, you make that list yet?"

"C. Had my apartment broken into. D. Saw my neighbor's dead body. And E. Adopted a cat?"

He shrugged a shoulder before shooting back his drink.

"Just trying to be polite. Anyway, you don't have a shift at Vortex tonight?"

"No. I'm off."

"Good. We're going out."

"We're—*what*?!"

"Going out. I need your help with something. I'll cook us dinner, then we can get going. Unless you'd rather eat out?"

I gaped at him. "Wait, excuse me. You need *my* help? Is this something to do with the case?"

"Nope."

"Okay then, no." It was a rapid reaction response, because I really *was* curious. As much as I wanted to hide, an entire afternoon indoors left me antsy.

"Come on, sugar. It'll be fun, I promise."

I scoffed, but secretly, I perked up at the word *fun* because, what did goblins consider fun, anyway?

"What, exactly do you need my help with?"

"I'm meeting an…acquaintance. Distant cousin, technically. I suppose you could consider him a rival, of sorts. You're going to be my plus one."

My eyebrows drew together. "I'll need more than that."

"Fair enough. Let's just say Aramis and I have a long-standing history of fucking with each other. He's a pain in my ass and I like to return the favor. I haven't seen him in a while. Last time, he got one up on me. I'd like to have the upper hand. Anyway, he's called me in to help with something. Not sure what, but it must be important. Aramis doesn't ask for help, especially not from me." A dark grumble sounded in his chest. "I can't wait to lord this over him."

"Oh…*kay*? So, what does this have to do with *me*?"

Now I was *definitely* curious, a little intrigued, and even flattered. I crossed my arms, shifting. Teddy didn't complain, just kept on snoozing.

"The less you know, the better. Look at it this way, we're going to play a game. Don't worry, I'll walk you through it as we go along, but you'll have to let me lead."

"That seems like a big ask. Pretty one-sided. What do I get out of it?"

"You help me tonight, and I'll help you put your apartment back together."

My brows lowered. "What does that entail, exactly? Like, you'll help me clean up?"

"Nah. I'll just use my magic to fix all the broken shit. Should save you quite a bit of time and money."

My jaw dropped. "You… You can do all that?"

The corner of his mouth twitched. Smug asshole. "It will take a lot of magic—trust me when I say, I'm offering you a very valuable service."

I hummed. "Well, *goblin*, you certainly know how to entice a girl." I pretended to contemplate his offer, but my mind was already made up. "I just have to…follow your lead?"

"There'll be a bit more to it than that, but essentially, yes. I won't ask you to do anything…illegal."

"Uhhh…"

"How about this? At any point, if I ask you to do something that makes you uncomfortable, or something you're not okay with, just use the code word 'Teddy' and I'll recalibrate, no questions asked."

"So… like an escape clause?" I leaned back against the couch. That did make me feel safer, especially since he wasn't forthcoming.

"Sure, if that's how you want to think about it."

"Fine. Deal. Where are we going? What do I need to wear?"

A mischievous grin stretched over his lips, one that had eager chills racing down my spine and butterflies exploding in my belly. "Something sexy, sugar. Something you can dance in. I need you to play a part. I want you to attract attention, but still look classy as fuck doing it. High heels if you can dance in them…and I know you can." His eyes heated, like he was remembering what I looked like at Vortex last night.

I leaned forward. "I can do that," I said, ready to play along.

"Good. Because we're going to *The Vault.*"

And then all my excitement slid right out of me and I reared back. "No."

"Too bad. You already agreed."

The Vault. I'd only ever heard rumors about it. "That was before you mentioned our destination."

"You'll be fine." He stood, taking his empty glass with him. "Now, I have some dinner to cook. Let's go, sugar. Clock's ticking and we don't want to be late."

All I could do was gape after him as I processed what was in store for me and wondered what kind of mess he was about to get us in tonight.

13

Bastian found me in my room twenty minutes later. I'd relaxed some. Had time to process what he was asking of me. I wasn't someone who reneged. But now I understood why he'd offered to fix my apartment.

The Vault. Just the name made my stomach clench with nerves. I'd heard whispers—stories about supernaturals who went in and never came out, about power plays and blood debts settled on the dance floor. Everyone knew humans weren't allowed in. Period. The few who'd tried... Well, those stories didn't have happy endings.

I assumed he had a plan.

"Picking your outfit?" he asked from the doorway, leaning against the frame.

"No," I lied, shuffling through the closet. I'd brought a wide variety of things. Comfortable clothes, like leggings and T-shirts, some jeans and blouses, and a slew of other items like dresses, shorts, and fancy tops. What did one wear to a place like The Vault?

"I'd recommend something you can dance in," he reiterated, as if reading my mind.

"Yes, yes. I heard you the first time. You want me looking classy as fuck."

"Exactly."

When he stood there for several more moments, watching me, I stopped what I was doing. "Did you need something?"

"Yeah. Wanted to know if you're good with chicken and rice for dinner? Got any dietary restrictions I should know about?"

The question caught me off guard in its thoughtfulness. "Yes and yes. But chicken and rice will be fine."

"What's the restriction?" He sounded genuinely curious.

"I've got a dairy intolerance," I admitted. "It's why I use heavy cream in my coffee. It's low in lactose. Tara always has my drinks made with either almond milk or heavy cream at Awake."

"Huh. I'll keep that in mind. So…you can't do milk at all then?"

"Oh, I can. Believe me, I'm an ice cream lover. I just… small amounts, you know?"

"Otherwise, I'll have to put caution tape around the bathroom?"

"Oh, my God!" I practically choked. "Can you *please* leave so I can get dressed?"

He grinned and walked out.

"Seriously," I mumbled to myself, hiding my smile. "What the hell?"

I slammed the bedroom door shut and locked it so he wouldn't drop in again, then planned my outfit. Bastian wanted me to dance, which meant tight dresses and skirts were out unless I wanted to show off my undies. I needed something I could move in.

I picked out a sassy skater skirt. It was made out of a flat black, leathery type material and came up to my belly button. It had built in spandex shorts beneath, perfect for what I needed. It made me feel like a cheerleader every time I wore it. Then I grabbed my shimmery silver tank top, relieved that I'd found it earlier among the mess of clothes in my apartment, unspoiled. It had a draping neckline in front, with a built in bra. Its spaghetti straps were embellished with clear beads, and the back scooped low like a ballerina top. The bottom half hugged my ribs and stomach, cutting off an inch above the skirt.

I finished everything off with a pair of black, studded booties, adding three inches to my height. In front of the mirror, I turned at different angles, ensuring I'd gotten it right. Yep, I understood the assignment. Black and silver were a perfect combination. Just enough to be eye catching and classy, but not too much. I didn't need flashy colors when I had pink hair. That would draw plenty of attention.

I spent the rest of my time on my hair and makeup. I put most of my hair up into a messy bun, leaving a few strands free. I added gold shimmer to my eyeshadow, making my hazel eyes pop. I did the contours of my makeup, highlighting my bone structure, then settled on a deep, maroon lipstick, which I'd apply after dinner.

One last look in the mirror and I was ready.

The scent of Bastian's cooking hit me as soon as I opened my door. I hesitated, inhaling. How did someone make chicken and rice smell so good? I strode through the house, my boot heels clomping on the wood floor, announcing my arrival.

I found him in the kitchen. He froze, frying pan and spatula in hand, hovering over two dinner plates. His lips parted as he made a slow perusal of my body. It sent tingles straight to my fingertips. I felt his eyes like a caress, gently gliding across my skin, hesitating on the low neckline of my top, snagging on the strip of exposed stomach, then faltering on the leather of my skirt, the length of leg on display, the boots that tied everything together. He worked his way up just as slowly. When his eyes met mine, they were nearly black.

"It's perfect."

My stomach exploded into flutters. I exhaled, running my hands down the fabric of the top. "You're sure?" Hesitance crept into my voice. This was *The Vault* we were talking about.

"Positive, sugar. One look and you'll bring them to their knees. Only reason I'm not on the floor is I didn't want to ruin our dinner." He winked, hefting the frying pan before finishing his work, loading a smothered chicken breast onto each plate.

"Uhm…is that what you want, though?"

"It's exactly what I want. Don't worry. I won't let you out of my sight. You'll be safe. Come, eat."

He set both plates on the island. I moved over to one and sat down. My mouth watered. The chicken was smothered in sauce, paired with long grain wild rice and sautéed carrots that gave off a hint of brown sugar. He'd garnished everything with fresh rosemary.

"Dig in," he said, adding a glass of ice water beside my plate.

I grabbed my fork and knife, cutting into the food. He took a seat beside me, head angled toward me as if waiting for my response. I didn't care that a tiny groan escaped as I bit into the chicken, chewed, and swallowed. "I don't think I've ever tasted chicken this good," I breathed, glancing at him. "I didn't think it could be anything but plain and boring."

"First for everything," he said, his lips twitching before starting in on his.

"Where'd you learn to cook like this, anyway?"

He swallowed and said, "Just time and practice. I've always loved food. I eat a lot of it. Need it for storing up energy and such."

Huh. Interesting.

We fell silent until our plates were nearly cleared. "So how exactly are you planning to get me into a supernatural-only club?"

"Right, about that. I'm going to send you in wearing a glamor—a good one. You should be fine. Which reminds me —" He fished around in his pocket, pulling out a thin band of gold. A ring. "Put this on, it should fit."

Heat flooded my cheeks. "You're not—we're not

pretending to be, like, a married couple or something, are we?"

He chuckled. "No, sugar. Here—"

He took my hand. I didn't fight him. Taking my pointer finger, he slipped the gold band into place. It was too large, but as I stared at it, it shrank into place until it was a perfect fit.

"Oh," I breathed, impressed. He was doing magic.

"I have an affinity for metals," he said by way of explanation. "I'll be able to send you signals with this."

"Like…what kind of signals?" I asked, lifting my hand, moving the ring about in the light. Despite being a simple band, it was elegant, and I rather liked it.

"Like this." The ring turned hot, but not hot enough to burn.

"Woah…" My eyes widened.

"If I want to get your attention or whatever, that's what I'll do. Got it?"

"Mmm-hmm," I managed, still staring at it. Then I dropped my hand. "Wait, a signal because we're not going to be together?"

"Not the whole time, no. Don't worry, I'll walk you through it. All finished?"

I glanced down and nodded. Despite how delicious the food was, I suddenly found I couldn't finish the rest of my plate. He got up and cleared them, fussing about in the kitchen for a few minutes before turning to face me. "All right. Let's get going."

I stood, then hesitated. "You're going to wear that?"

"Sure, why not?" It wasn't exactly *bad*. Black jeans and a black T-shirt like the one I'd first seen him in. "I'll probably carry a few weapons in, just to make a statement. But I can summon those once we get there."

Weapons…statement…his words began to register.

"I really don't know what I'm getting myself into, do I?" I

muttered, following him out of the kitchen and into the garage.

"Here, put these on." He handed over a leather jacket and the same helmet I'd used before. The garage door opened while I put them on. Then I was on the back of his bike, with him easing it outside.

Darkness greeted us. Bastian revved the bike's engine. A fluttery sensation planted itself in my stomach. We were really doing this. I hadn't processed much of my experience on his bike last night. I'd been too distraught over Luke. But now, I intended to enjoy every sensation, starting with the man in front of me.

I leaned closer to Bastian, tightening my hold around him. Instead of locking my hands together, I shamelessly splayed them across his torso. A rumble sounded in my helmet. "Hold on tight, sugar."

We shot forward, out of the driveway and onto the asphalt drive.

A squeal rushed from my lips. I tightened my hold, squeezing my thighs around him. Adrenaline dumped into my system and heat followed, pooling up in my core. My awareness zeroed in on all the places we connected.

Bastian's solid form handled the bike with ease.

It was hot.

"What made you choose Kentwood?" I asked as large properties sailed past us.

"I like the neighborhood."

"Right."

"Everyone keeps to themselves," he elaborated. "Most of them are supernaturals. They stay out of my business, and I stay out of theirs. But..." He fell silent. "Mostly it was the house."

"I like it," I admitted. "Your house, I mean. I thought it didn't suit you at first, but seeing you in it, now I get it."

A grumble was his only response.

The city rose up around us, suburbs first, then taller buildings, until we were drifting through traffic. He didn't drive like he had before. His maneuvering was smooth and leisurely. I paid careful attention to our path, curious as to the location of the infamous club. Admittedly, my mind raced ahead of me, trying to anticipate what happened next.

"When we arrive, I'll glamor you," Bastian said, his voice in my ear. "Having the ring will act as a conduit. On our way inside, we'll pass by the bouncers. You'll be on my arm, so you'll have nothing to worry about. I need not tell you to avoid acting nervous. Obviously."

"Right. Act cool. Got it."

He huffed. "We're going to head to the bar first. I'll order you a drink. You won't drink it—only pretend. After that, I'm going to leave you to go speak with Aramis. He has a VIP area exclusive to him and his clientele."

"Wait, Aramis owns the club? The guy you're meeting with?"

"Well…yeah. That's why I'm meeting him there."

"Oh. Shit." That was news. Clearly Bastian knew people.

"The VIP lounge sits right beside the dance floor—overlooking it, actually. Aramis likes dancing, enjoys watching. You'll be in sight the entire time. Even away from you, I'll still be keeping an eye on you. You'll be safe."

"But what if others try to talk to me?"

"The glamor I'm putting on you will dissuade them from it. They'll look at you, oh yes, stare, probably, but they will not try to approach you."

"Okay. So after you leave, then what?"

"Then you go dance while I'm talking with Aramis. I want you to make a scene. Clear the floor. I want all eyes on you. Let me worry about the rest, all right?"

"Okay. So, act cool, walk with you to the bar, get a drink but don't drink it, then you'll leave, and I'll go dance. And… that's it?"

"That's it. I'll manage the rest from there."

I blew out a breath. Didn't sound *too* difficult. I wasn't sure what his endgame was. He was bringing me because it had something to do with one-upping this Aramis person. But he'd said I needed to let him lead.

Well... At least I had a plan to work with.

I hadn't even realized we'd slowed down until he parked his bike on the sidewalk right outside a city building. I could hear music coming from the basement beneath it. I huffed. This was The Vault? Hidden beneath the Chrylon Building?

"Isn't this a national bank?" I asked. It had the words Chrylon on the top of the building, in glowing white letters that could be seen halfway across the city, and I'd seen plenty of the news stations pan across it when they did their aerial views.

"Yep. Funny right?"

"Yeah...absolutely *hilarious*," I deadpanned.

The city's most infamous club, exclusive to supernaturals only, was named The Vault and it was in the basement of one of the nation's biggest banks. *Ha ha.* Very original.

"All right, sugar. Time to rock and roll." He kicked the kickstand into place and we both climbed off. People milled around us, and I was sure that if I stared long enough and blinked a couple of times, I'd see them for what they were.

I felt a warmth radiating from the ring on my finger. "There, your glamor should be in place. You can remove your helmet."

I pulled it free and handed it over. He took it and it disappeared. His was already gone, too. I looked at my hands. They looked the same. Curious, I lifted them to my hair and—

"Oh my god, I have pointed ears?!"

"Yep. Fae."

"But aren't supernaturals supposed to be hiding? I've never seen anyone walk around with pointed ears before, like, out in the open."

"That's because generally, the glamor that supernaturals like the fae use only render them invisible to other humans," he said, a hint of impatience seeping into his tone.

"Wait so if other supernaturals look at you right this second, they will see gray skin, extra piercings, and all that?"

"Yup. Let's get a move on, sugar. Take off your jacket."

I shucked it off and handed it over. The second he touched it, it was gone. A slight chill caressed my skin, followed by heat as he looked me up and down. He grunted. "Huh. I think I prefer your ears rounded."

"Okay?"

"Much cuter that way. Let's go, *Dancing Queen*."

I chuckled, hooking my arm through his. There was a crowd gathered at the side entrance to the building, which, presumably led into the basement. "So, let me get this straight. Anyone here will look at me and see that I'm fae. But if humans are around, they'll only see my normal self?"

"I thought we'd already established that."

"Well, we did. But I'm just tripping because that's like… glamor inception. A human, who looks like a fae, who looks like a human, who looks like—"

"*Eleanor.*"

"Ohhhh. Pulling out the big guns. Okay, fine. I'll shut up now."

We were within earshot of other people now, so we needed to play the part. My heart leapt in my chest. "Uh, any way you can amp up my, you know, so that I can also see what everyone is?"

"I thought you could already do that."

"Well, yeah, but I have to stare at them kinda awkwardly first, and blink a little, and all that."

He suffered a long sigh but said, "There. How's that?"

"Holy…" I trailed off, blinking rapidly. Everyone around me was suddenly more defined. While I still saw humans for shifters, somehow, I could still sense what they were. A leopard shifter there, an eagle shifter beside her. Across the way there stood a group of mingling fae. I didn't see any elves, but I didn't expect to. They mostly kept to their forests. But what I really wanted to know is what their tensile silver hair looked like in person—

"Wait, aren't we going to get in line?" Bastian led me past it, straight up to the main door at the front.

"Well, fuck me," said a gravelly voice from one of the bouncers. "Aramis better be expecting you, Bastian. Cause if not, you ain't getting in."

"You know I wouldn't step foot in here if he wasn't."

"Well, shit. Good to see you, man. Business running okay?"

"Do you really care?"

"Only as long as you're not bringing it into this club."

"Fuck off, Ravi. I got shit to discuss with Aramis. And yes, he's expecting me."

Ravi nodded. The guy beside him, the other bouncer, turned away from the line, halting the flow of traffic as his eyes ran over me. "Cute little fae you got there."

"Fuck off, Caris."

Caris lifted a shoulder. "You're good man. Just don't make trouble. Last time you were here—"

"Yes, my memory is solid. Thanks," Bastian said, sounding like a real asshole as he cut off the bouncer and pulled me forward, right past them. I glanced over my shoulder, trying to offer an apology.

"Don't worry about them, sugar. You learn how to deal with people in the supernatural world."

"Well, now I know why you're so *rude*. Because apparently that's how you learned to deal with people, huh?"

He didn't answer. I didn't mind, because all of my attention shifted to the underground space that spread out beneath us. An industrial style design painted in dark colors, with muted lights and low, pulsing music. A giant vault was erected around the stage and DJ booth. There were piles of gold sitting out in plain sight, breaking up the perimeter of the dance floor, heaps of money on display. Not real, obviously, unless it was enchanted somehow, so that it couldn't be stolen. As far as names went, this one certainly lived up to its namesake. Size wise, it was smaller and more intimate than Vortex. And one look told me it was filled with nothing but supernaturals.

Bastian pulled me toward the wide staircase that led into the club. I spotted the bar at the far end. We'd have to cross the entire space to get there, putting us in full view of the VIP lounge beside the dance floor.

My eyes flicked over to it. It was nearly empty. A few bouncers stood, arms crossed, barring the way forward. Like a king holding court, sprawled on one of the plush couches sat one of the most commanding fae I'd ever seen.

"Is that him?" I asked. "Aramis."

The fae male's shrewd gaze was fixed directly on us. On me, actually. I swallowed.

"Yeah, that's him," Bastian said, his lips brushing my ear. "Don't worry. He won't fuck with us tonight." I huffed out a breath. I wasn't so sure he should be making promises like that.

"Well, sugar? Let's get this show on the road." He gave me a gentle tug and pulled me down the stairs, straight into the heart of The Vault.

14

Bastian left Eleanor standing at the bar as he made his way to the VIP area. She followed his directions to a T, innocently sipping her cocktail without actually swallowing any of it. They'd only lingered for two minutes, pretending to make small talk, before he'd dismissed himself. It was harder than he realized, turning his back on her, but his magic held. He could feel it channeling through the gold ring like a conduit, a steady siphon of power.

No one would bother her.

His fist clenched and unclenched, restless. The irrational part of him was spun tight, ready to pounce on anyone who got too close. He needed to leash himself, remind himself that she wasn't *his*. Aside from protecting her, everything else shouldn't matter.

He approached the four bouncers guarding Aramis's area.

"Boss's expecting you," Derek said, unclipping the red rope that acted as a barrier. He nodded, walking by. Through the conduit, he sent a flare of heat—Eleanor's signal.

"Bastian," Aramis growled, getting to his feet, greeting him like an old friend. He was several inches taller and built like a powerhouse. Most fae scorned half breeds, especially goblins, but Aramis had never been like that. Males like

Aramis couldn't afford to be like that, given who he was. "Almost expected you to ride in on your bike, like last time." The fae strode forward and clapped him on the back. "Don't think I'll ever forget the sight of you riding that thing down the stairs and scaring the shit out of my patrons."

"I brought something better this time," he said, returning the greeting.

"Oh? That pretty fae kitten you walked in with? Where is she? Afraid I might bite?"

"Something like that."

Aramis motioned him forward and they took their seats.

"Come now, I certainly hope you won't keep her hidden all night."

"I have no intention of that. Surely you know me better, Aramis." His gaze turned toward the dance floor. From where they sat, they had a direct line of sight. There she was, right on cue. The head of pink hair bobbed through the crowd, right toward the middle of the floor.

"What will you have to drink?" Aramis asked, not yet having noticed. He'd already downed his whiskey at the bar, so he requested another. Aramis gave the order to the server on call, who momentarily stepped away to fulfill it.

He hadn't taken his eyes from Eleanor. Aramis finally noticed and chuckled. "Ah. Not hidden at all. Excellent."

Eleanor started to dance. It happened gradually at first. The initial moments went unnoticed, but as she began to move, stretching and swaying, moving like a cat waking from a nap, a trance settled over those nearest to her. If he weren't absolutely certain she was human, he'd wonder if she might have siren blood, or something of the sort, the way she captured attention. Beside him, Aramis was silent, shrewd eyes missing nothing.

Good.

The crowd pushed further away, giving her room. Some continued dancing, while others stopped simply to watch. Her movements came faster, timed to the rhythm of the beat, growing more erotic.

His cock twitched. He inhaled, using the breath to steady him. The server appeared with his drink. He took it without looking up.

"My, my," Aramis purred. "Where have you been hiding her? Had I known, I'd have invited you back sooner."

His lungs expanded, eyes pinned to Eleanor's body. As he watched, everything else disappeared. She was magnificent.

His body reacted, blood pounding, dropping straight to his cock. His mind raced through scenarios, each more outrageous than the last. Licking up the column of her neck, tasting the pulse that raced there. Wrapping his hands around her hips, grinding her against him. Listening to her make those sweet sounds he'd heard earlier. If she sounded like that eating his food, what would she sound like riding his cock? His muscles twitched. He felt a strange urge to stand, to go to her, to wrap his body around hers and dance.

He blinked and the moment fractured. How was it possible that this little human could entrance him? However she did it, it wasn't good. His jaw clenched, irritation rising.

She was *human*. She didn't belong to him. Even if she wasn't part of an ongoing investigation, she could never be—would never be—more than a casual fuck. She deserved more than that—especially from him. So why did he want, so badly, to give her exactly what she deserved?

Eleanor held Aramis's attention. The spicy smell of arousal struck Bastian's nose. He ripped his gaze away, turning to look at Aramis, eyes widening as he made the realization.

Unusual. Very unusual…

A cruel smile pulled at his lips. Careful to keep her glamor intact for everyone around her, he removed it so that Aramis could see exactly what she was.

A hiss split the silence. Aramis jerked, then narrowed his eyes. "*Human?*" he spat. "You brought a fucking *human* into *my* club?"

Bastian's smile widened. "And yet she charmed you. *Aroused* you."

If he were anyone else to Aramis, the consequences might have been deadly. Instead—

"Well now," Aramis huffed, shaking his head. He knew he'd been beaten. "Well played Bas. Well played, indeed."

"Did you not tell me once, and I quote, '*No human will ever set foot in my club*'?"

"I did. And yet, you found a way to smuggle one in. Caris is going to have a field day with this. He really didn't see it?"

"No. I glamoured her."

"Damn. All right—I'll give you this one. We're even." Aramis chuckled, then shook his head, ripping his gaze from the pink-haired beauty to add, "Your abilities never cease to amaze me. Derek, Nils!" Two of the four bouncers walked over. "See that the woman with the pink hair is escorted over —*safely*, please."

They nodded and moved away.

Bastian started, frowning, but kept his mouth closed.

He watched as the bouncers parted the crowd. He hadn't expected Aramis to be so interested, interested enough to summon her. He sent a warning signal of heat to the ring. If Eleanor noticed, she didn't let on, just kept dancing. When the bouncers appeared before her, she stopped. One of them spoke, not getting too close. Her eyes darted over, and he nodded, letting her know it was okay, sending another flare of heat into the ring.

She allowed them to escort her over, climbing the short set of stairs. Aramis stood to greet her, Bastian did not. "You are a true gem," Aramis cooed, taking her hand, kissing her knuckles.

Heat flashed through Bastian. And anger, too, at the sight of another male touching her. He leaned forward. A quiet growl rose in his throat. Aramis hesitated, glancing over his shoulder. The jerk grinned, dropping her hand and spinning away. "What sort of friend would I be if I didn't rile you?"

"Sugar, come here." His voice came out rough, gravelly. He held out a hand for her, coaxing her over. Her eyes fixed on his. She walked over, mini skirt swishing. Everything around them disappeared at the sight of her before him. The warmth of her skin spread across his hand. He moved before thinking, pulling her into his lap, positioning her so they both faced Aramis, who had his back turned, speaking in a hushed voice to the server.

Eleanor went rigid against him, her muscles tight. He snaked his hands around her, splaying one over her bare thigh, the other over her stomach. "Relax, sweetheart. Remember what we discussed," he said, pitching his voice low. A shiver went through her. He let his lips linger, then brushed them over the shell of her ear, along the glamoured point, before nipping. She went rigid again and a small whimper fell from her mouth.

His cock twitched.

All of this was an excuse, a pathetic one, but an excuse nonetheless. It hadn't been part of his initial plan, which was simply that she would dance while they talked. The game had changed. Who was he to let a good opportunity go to waste? Besides, he wanted to make it very clear in front of Aramis, she belonged to him.

"Now, where were we?" Aramis asked, sitting.

"You were going tell me why I'm here," Bastian said. His thumb traced circles on Eleanor's thigh. She exhaled, relaxing into him with each brush of his thumb over her skin. The weight of her body against his tested his focus. Before he realized it, his thumb on her stomach was also moving back and forth, caressing that bare slip of skin. She was so...*soft*.

"Ah, yes. Well, I'll speak plainly, then."

The server rushed over with a tray—a glass of water. He offered it to Eleanor. "Oh," she said, breathless, reaching for it.

His hackles rose. He grabbed the glass before she could.

She leaned around to glare. He lifted it, sniffed, then handed it to her.

Aramis scoffed. "Come now, Bastian. You insult me. You think I'd give her anything but water? You are my guests. I've called you here for a favor. Fuck. I'm not a heartless asshole."

"Can't be too certain. Haven't survived this long by being careless."

Understanding dawned on Eleanor's face. Her glare slipped away. "It's okay?" she whispered, tentative, regarding him with wide, trusting, doe-eyes.

"It's safe, sugar." His voice came out more tender than he'd intended. Unable to stop himself, he reached up and brushed a strand of hair away from her face, tucking it behind the point of her ear. He still preferred them rounded.

She shivered against him—an effect of his touch that made his mouth go dry. When she shifted, righting herself again, the friction against his dick had him gritting his teeth.

"Carry on, Aramis," he said, forcing his focus away from Eleanor.

Aramis shook his head, incredulous. Like he saw exactly what the little female was doing to him. Like he couldn't believe it, but chose not to mention it.

"I've got something strange going on. Something I want your take on." Aramis shifted in his chair. "Few weeks back, one of my people was out on a patrol and…dropped to the ground right where he stood. No one suspected anything at first. Looked like he was sleeping. Took him to one of our fae healers, but she couldn't explain what had happened." Aramis crossed his arms, leaning back. "It reminds me of those human comas you hear about. Alive, but sleeping. Can't wake up. No one, not magic, not anything, has been able to wake him. Wouldn't have thought much more about it, except a few days later, three more fell into the same kind of sleep."

"Huh." Bastian had never heard of something like this happening to fae. Their kind didn't get sick. It would have to be magic related. Some sort of witch's curse, perhaps?

"I've got seven of my own people laying in some sort of coma," Aramis added. "Never in all my years seen such a thing."

Bastian leaned forward. "And no one knows what caused it?"

"Our healers can't explain it."

He resumed his caresses against Eleanor's skin, using the motions, the feel of her, to keep him calm. She softened against him, as if sensing his rising concern. His arms tightened, pulling her more firmly against his chest, her back flush to him.

"I called you because you've a knack for solving unsolvable problems, Bastian." To this, Bastian snorted. "I know this isn't like your usual job. I know we've had our differences, but this looks bad. Real bad. With Endorian's retirement, I've got the vote coming. Thadur and I are neck and neck. I know he'd do just about anything to get the position, including sully my name." Aramis sighed, running a hand through his dark locs. His hand dropped and he shook his head.

"I need your help."

Well, damn. Bastian wanted to gloat. He really did.

But this was serious, and not the time.

He exhaled, leaning in close to Eleanor's ear. "What do you think, sugar? Sound like a case for me?" She sucked in a surprised breath and he chuckled. "You don't need to answer that."

"But Bastian?" Aramis said in warning. "I think there is something—something even stranger going on."

"What's that?"

Aramis scrubbed a hand over his face. "Can't believe I'm even going to say this. It sounds insane. Two days ago, I got reports that someone saw a fae lurking around Thadur's property in Kentwood. A fae that fit Jamilla's description—she's one of the affected. Thing is, if she's been sleeping soundly in a heavily guarded facility. That's where I moved all the ones affected. So how the fuck was she seen moving around Thadur's property?"

Chills spread down Bastian's spine and Eleanor stiffened in his arms. He gave her a gentle, reassuring squeeze, even if the thought left him a little shaken.

"Anyway, I don't even know what I'm asking of you. Don't know how you're supposed to help with this. I don't even know where to start." Aramis leaned back against his sofa, letting his head fall back, eyes closed. When he looked up again, his expression was open. He looked exhausted. On closer inspection, there were dark circles marring his rich brown skin. Rare for a fae.

"I can ask around," Bastian said, taking pity on the male. "Can't promise much. I'd be interested to know if this was just happening to your people, or others, too. You haven't heard anything from the shifters? Vampires?"

"Nothing, man. But you've got connections with other supernaturals that I don't, being in my position and all."

Aramis held one of three fae positions on the Supernatural Council. Given Endorian's upcoming retirement, he was up for a potential promotion. Of the three positions, one always took point, the other two, support. Every supernatural faction had three representatives that held positions in the SC. The fae male was right to be worried. Something like this, a failure to keep his own people safe, wouldn't look good for him.

He'd lose the vote, for sure.

"You think anything like this is happening to Thadur's people, too?" He couldn't help but wonder if Aramis was the only one being targeted.

"I've got a few on the inside with Thadur. No. Nothing that I know of. But like me, perhaps he's trying to keep it quiet. This won't look good for the vote, Bastian."

"No. It won't," Bastian agreed. Eleanor shifted in his lap, sending a lick of heat up his thighs, straight to his balls. He needed to wrap this up. "I'll see what I can do, Aramis. Give me a few days. I'll get back to you."

"Good. Thank you." Aramis stood. It was their cue to do the same. He lifted Eleanor from his lap as if she weighed nothing, setting her upright. Aramis reached out to shake their hands. He kept an arm wrapped around Eleanor so she couldn't go far. "Feel free to linger, if you wish," Aramis added. "But if you do, keep her glamour intact. I'll never hear the end of it, otherwise."

He nodded, then swept from the VIP area, keeping a firm hold on his little female. He had no intention of freeing her. Not now. Perhaps *not ever,* said a voice in the back of his mind. But he ignored that voice, pushing it away.

15

"Dance with me, sugar," Bastian said, his lips close to my ear. A zing of adrenaline rushed to my fingertips. I was overly aware of his hand at the small of my back.

"Sure," I managed despite my suddenly dry mouth. Instead of heading toward the stairs that would take us out of here, I reached around and grabbed his hand. His rings were cold against my skin, a contrast to his warm palm. My stomach fluttered. I led us onto the dance floor, ignoring the erratic beat of my heart. I wasn't normally nervous about dancing. But this? Definitely.

The pulse of the music set a drum beating inside me, reverberating straight to my bones, making my skin hum. There was no denying my attraction toward Bastian Croft. Sitting on his lap had confirmed that, leaving me flushed and jittery.

I found a spot amid the crowd and turned to him, dropping his hand, taking a couple of playful steps away and then back, giving him a come-hither smile. His eyes darkened, pupils dilating. My arms lifted over my head. I swept my hips back and forth, laughing, giving in to the lightness blooming in my chest.

Our eyes locked.

I felt his stare burrow deep into me, latching on to something primal in my body, snaring me like I was his prey. He stalked forward, all predator, then wrapped his hands low around my hips, splaying them against my backside. His arms tightened, pulling me flush to him. I tilted my head back, maintaining our eye contact, moving my hips against his. We took small steps forward and backward.

The feel of him against me, his rock solid chest, the bulge in his jeans, the press of his thigh between the apex of mine, sent heat dumping into my core. My pulse kicked up, drumming heatedly against my clit. God, it felt good—too good.

I bit my lower lip, silencing the tiny noises I wanted to make.

I kept my movements loose, sensual. He showed me exactly how he might move against me if there weren't clothes between us. The length of him promised so much pleasure, hard as iron as I slid back and forth over him. I pushed a little harder, teasing. A growl rose from his throat. His hands crept up to my waist, circling around me, gripping me, possessive. The beat of the music intensified, matching his expression, the raw want blossoming over his features. His fingers tightened, guiding the flow of my torso side to side.

We moved like we'd been dancing together all our lives. I allowed him to lead, flowing like water where he guided me. A flash of something playful darted across his gaze as the music hitched. I knew what he planned before he moved. He kept our hips pressed tight, sweeping my upper body around and back in a circle, bending me backward at the waist. I arched. The world went upside down for a moment. I straightened, chest slamming against his as a laugh escaped my lips.

He rumbled a laugh of his own and said, "You're an absolute joy, sugar."

"Right back at you, goblin."

That brought a full smile to his lips—such a rare thing. I fixed my gaze on the dimple that appeared. Then, before thinking better of it, I inched up a little higher and kissed it. He stilled, just briefly, and then our dancing continued.

His eyes glittered, blackened with unmistakable desire. I was treading in dangerous territory here. My body didn't care, though. A dull ache built between my thighs, hot and wet. Could he feel it through the denim on his leg? Did I care if he did?

Our movements grew more erotic. I fisted the fabric of his shirt, all but groaning at the aching need that flooded me—

A scream split the air, rising up over the music. Suddenly, the crowd surged forward like a tidal wave, more shouts echoing. Bastian cursed.

I spun around, just in time to see a fist fly—wolf shifters. The world froze for a moment, and then the dance floor collapsed into chaos.

"Time to go," Bastian growled, wrapping his body around mine, enveloping me. Black shadows swirled around us. I had a single breath, then I was falling…falling…falling. My stomach lodged high up into my throat. I thought it might explode out of my mouth. *Ugh!*

"Bastian!" I screamed. I felt him wrapped around me, and yet, there was nothing.

Night air rushed in, and Bastian's arms fell away.

Everything tilted on its axis. My stomach lurched. My knees buckled and the ground rose up to meet me.

"Fuck." Sure hands caught me around the waist, just before my knees hit the asphalt, hauling me up from behind. This time, they remained firmly in place.

I doubled over, breathing hard, bracing my hands on my knees. "What…the…fuck?!" My vision swam, half tears, half dizziness. "I think I'm going to vomit."

"Deep breaths, sugar." A warm hand rubbed my back, the other keeping hold around my waist.

I held my position, gasping. Things began to settle. I gulped and swallowed. I took a slow breath through my nose and held it, counting to five, then released it. My nostrils flared as I took another, and another.

I finally began to calm down.

"You good?"

I straightened.

Bastian rotated me to face him, keeping an arm around my back, smoothing some hair back from my face. Green eyes darted between mine, his pupils still dilated.

"What the hell was that?!" I seethed, glancing around. "Are we… Did we just *teleport* or some shit?"

We were in his driveway, steps from the front porch of his beautiful craftsman home.

"Something like that." His jaw was tight. "I couldn't take any chances moving through the crowd. The Vault's the last place you want to be during a supernatural fight."

"That was *sickening*," I snapped, staring up at him. Glaring, really.

"Sorry, sugar." He didn't look sorry at all. "Why do you think I told you not to drink? Your stomach would be spilled on the pavement right now."

I made a hissing sound of disgust. Never mind that his arm was still wrapped around me, my body pressed tight to his. For stability purposes, of course. "You restricted my drinking, but didn't think to warn me as to *why*?"

"Didn't know it would be necessary—hoped it wouldn't be." But the twitch of his lips said otherwise. "Come on."

Ugh! Unbelievable.

My nausea subsided as he turned and led me up the porch stairs. The night air was a direct contrast to the loud music of the club. Crickets and cicadas chirped. A bullfrog croaked in the distance. Bats chittered. The trees surrounding his property were filled with life.

"How did you do that, anyway?" I managed, as we stepped into the house entryway. I bent to unzip my boots, placing a hand against the wall for support.

Still breathing harder than normal, I pressed my back flush to the wall as I watched him.

"Magic, obviously," he said, shucking off his boots, leaving them beside mine. He stood to his full height, regarding me with a lifted eyebrow. A perfectly fucking shaped pierced eyebrow.

"Yes, but how?" I demanded. "I didn't know goblins had magic like that. I thought you were fighters, warriors. And yet, I've seen you disappear things or whatever. You must be…"

Really powerful.

He heard the words even though I didn't speak them. Stalking over, he invaded my space, bracing his hands on either side of me. Everything I'd felt while dancing with him returned. All the heat and arousal. It came back tenfold.

His lips twitched in that infuriating way as he said, "Impressed, sugar?"

I snorted, rolling my eyes. But truthfully? I *was* impressed.

"Who *are* you?" I whispered, breathless, before I could help myself. His face was inches from mine. There were tiny gold flecks in his green eyes. The scent of musk and citrus soap wrapped around me, filling my nostrils.

"You really want to know?" His voice was open, honest, eyes darting between mine. I nodded, not sure I could speak.

"I'm a bastard fae, sugar. Lowest of the low. My mother's fae, father's a goblin. That's where I got my affinity for metals, the reason I was able to transport us like that."

"You use metal for magic?" My eyes darted to the piercings on his face, the one in his septum, the other in his eyebrow. I'd seen a flash of silver in his mouth, too, just now. Realization dawned on me. "Your piercings? That's why you have so many?"

"I use them to store energy." His low chuckle sent tingles skittering across my skin. "I don't punch pretty things into my skin for the hell of it. Though, I do dig the look. Apparently, chicks do too."

I huffed and said, "Right. It *is* kinda hot."

At my words, sparks crackled in the depths of his eyes.

I swallowed. "So…the more piercings and jewelry you have, the more energy you can store? And what, you use the energy for magic?"

"That's the simplest way to put it, sure."

"That sounds…"

"Extremely rare?" An arrogant smirk spread across his lips.

"I was going to say *interesting*. But yes, I guess it must be rare. Not that I'm an expert." I was highly aware of our proximity, how close his body was to mine. Not quite touching, but close enough that heat spread between us.

I cleared my throat. "What happens if all your jewelry is removed? You lose your power?" He made a thoughtful sound but didn't answer. I tried to keep a serious face and added, "I guess that's a secret you probably don't want to tell me?"

"I can do a little magic on my own. Not entirely helpless, sugar. Got my mother's fae magic. Like the healing." His eyes darted to my wrist. It hadn't bothered me since that first night. "But transporting us just now? That took a quarter of what I had stored in the jewelry."

His gaze swept over me, a slow perusal that had heat dropping low in my belly. I licked my lips and his eyes darted down at the movement.

"So…" I said, feeling the need to continue, if only to distract us from the inferno rising between us. "If someone were to remove everything, you'd be severely disadvantaged? We would have been stuck in the club?"

"I've got other back-ups." His words were almost distant, like he was focused entirely on something else and merely going through the motions of answering. Focused entirely on *me*.

"Oh?"

"My tattoos."

My eyes darted to his arms. Realization dawned. "The *ink*?"

"Mmm-hmm." The low sound he made had me squeezing my thighs together, desperate to ease the growing ache there.

Bastian inhaled, nostrils flaring, then glanced down, a small smile tugging at his lips.

My eyes widened. Was he *smelling* me?

"They aren't just for show," he explained. "Metal powder mixed into the ink. That's why they look silvery when they catch the light."

"Oh," I said, breathless. My chest was rising and falling faster. Thinking was becoming difficult.

"*Now* are you impressed, sugar?" His purring voice was pitched low.

Yes. So freaking impressed. Wait—no. What the fuck? Since when did I care? What the hell was going on here? I inched to the side, sliding along the wall. He took two steps with me, keeping me caged.

A flicker of predator filled his gaze, there and gone. "Where do you think you're going, little female?" A glint of silver flashed between his teeth, bringing my gaze to his lips. He noticed. That arrogant smile returned in full force, turning wicked.

"You…you have a tongue piercing?" I managed, stalling.

"Wanna find out?"

Shivers raced over my skin. I made a desperate noise, a needy noise. Neither yes nor no. He moved closer, bending slowly, until the fabric of his clothes brushed mine. His head dipped, but he held his face an inch from mine. When he exhaled, minty breath brushed my skin.

I whimpered, knees weakening. My palms were flush to the wall, fingers splayed wide, anchoring me to reality.

His gaze burrowed into mine and time froze. I didn't stop him, even though he gave me ample opportunity. His soft lips brushed mine, the barest of caresses. A request. My eyes fluttered closed. Desire drenched with promise spread through me. Everything else vanished—

Then it was gone, taken, just as quickly as it had come.

His lips disappeared.

A mewing protest broke the quiet. I realized it was me as I lifted my head from the wall, chasing after his lips. Lips I wanted so badly.

There was the barest of hesitation, and then his mouth crashed against mine, this time hungry, claiming. Roaring filled my head—my blood rushing past my ears. I met his kiss, eager in my own way, as if I could devour everything about him. He groaned, pressing his body against mine, his hard length making his arousal clear.

Heat exploded between us.

I gasped, opening my mouth to suck in a breath. His tongue swept in. A press of metal, almost invasive against me, and I moaned. He kissed the same way he handled his motor-cycle, with an expert, focused ease. A zing of eager pleasure shot straight down my spine, right to my core, curling my toes. I was caged, sandwiched between the wall and a powerful goblin-fae body.

Our kiss intensified. His fingers twisted into my hair at the nape of my neck. My hands lifted from the wall, tangling in the fabric of Bastian's shirt. His hips ground against mine. The feel of his hard length against the apex of my thighs brought a sound to my throat, a keening, needy noise. I should have been embarrassed, but I couldn't think.

He ripped his mouth away. "I thought you didn't *do* fuck boys," he bit out, chest heaving. He looked *frenzied*. Unhinged. "But your scent says otherwise."

Well. That answered that.

"I don't know what you're talking about," I lied, pathetically. "And—I don't."

His chuckle was more of a low grumble. "Well then, my apologies for kissing you." He pulled his hands from my hair and went to step back.

"No!" A pathetic sound of protest burst from me. My fists tightened in the fabric of his shirt.

He lifted an eyebrow. "No?"

I bit my bottom lip, contemplating. "I… Maybe I can make an exception?"

He huffed. "Oh?"

My eyes were wide, regarding him, giving everything away. Right now? I didn't care. Tomorrow? I might beat myself up over it.

"Then perhaps, so can I," he said.

I exhaled. "What's *that* supposed to mean?"

"It means, sugar, that I don't *do* humans."

I opened my mouth, then closed it. "Do, as in, *do*? Or…"

"*Do,* as in, *anything.* Your race—" He stopped himself, jaw clenching. Something passed over his features. Something that looked a lot like hatred, there and gone.

I frowned. The heated moment suddenly began to cool, right as my logic returned. What the *hell* was I doing? Perhaps this was a sign—I needed to slow down. I took a step to the side, attempting to get free of him. His arms returned to the wall, caging me. "We're *not* done here."

My eyes narrowed in irritation. I opened my mouth to say—

His lips crushed against mine, kissing, devouring. My stomach dropped straight to my thighs. I flexed my abdominals, trying not to give in to the rising pressure in my core. His tongue swept deep into my mouth, stroking along the roof, across my teeth. The metal ball of his piercing made me shudder. I made a tiny noise in response. He groaned, rocking his hips against mine, spreading my legs with his thigh.

A whimper fell from my chest when he pressed against my clit.

His fingers tangled into my hair again, this time, gently tugging. His other hand wrapped around my throat, until the feel of his warm palm had me caged right where he wanted. His tongue sank deeper. The hot metal of his piercing tickled the ridges on the roof of my mouth.

My desperation exploded—a mindless, rabid animal that wanted only one thing. Him.

What would his piercing feel like elsewhere? Between my legs? Wetness flooded my panties.

The hard length of him ground into me. The pressure of his cock had my core humming. A familiar desperation had me tightening. Oh, God. He was going to make me come—just like this.

"Fuck," Bastian growled, breaking our kiss but not our connection. He looked as if he was physically trying to restrain himself. His eyes darted between mine.

A blaring ringtone broke the tension. His pocket vibrated against my hip. Bastian cursed again, but his eyes didn't move. His phone stopped ringing. I never realized silence could be this loud. The ringing started right up again.

He made a sound of irritation, releasing my head, then fished his phone from his pocket, glancing at the screen. His brow furrowed. He slid the answer toggle and lifted it to his ear. "Bastian speaking."

I heard a voice on the other end. Male. But not enough to make out the words.

Bastian's frown deepened, his expression darkening. "I'll be right there." He hung up, slipping the phone back into his pocket.

"You're... You're joking, right?" I managed between my panting breaths. Was he *seriously* going to get me riled up and just...bail?

His throat bobbed, eyes fixed on mine.

"Well," I huffed, trying and failing to sound nonchalant. "I guess I'm no stranger to my own fingers. I'll just finish the job myself, then. Go...do whatever it is you do." I tried not to let my irritation show as I weakly pushed at him to get free.

His eyes darkened, but he didn't move. A second stretched into two, into three, emotion crackling between us. Indecision played out over his features. Then his mouth fell against mine, yet again, another growl rumbling deep in his chest. I huffed out a breath, trying not to get lost in his taste. This time, his hands explored my body. He pawed me everywhere, like he couldn't decide where to touch first, like he wanted to touch every inch of me simultaneously. At last, he palmed my breast with one hand, brushing his thumb over my peaked nipple, through the fabric, while his other traced circles across the exposed skin of my tummy.

My breathing turned erratic. Every angry thought slid right out of my mind. He had me right where he wanted.

Keeping hold of my breast, he slid his other hand down, wedging it between his thigh and my apex, gripping my pussy with possessive intent. A zing of desperation had me clenching against the pressure. Fuck, I was tightening.

"See now, sugar? I'm not sure I'm okay with the idea of you using your fingers on yourself," he gritted out. "What's a few more minutes, hmm?"

The pressure disappeared and his fingers swept beneath the waistband of my skirt, toying with the seam of my panties. He hesitated, waiting for permission. Waiting for *me* I realized. I sucked in a deep breath. Lost. I was so lost. Lost to the heat of desperation dragging me under.

Don't do something you'll regret, that voice in the back of my mind taunted. I knew it was probably right, and yet...

I nodded.

16

She was aching for him. Bastian could smell it, sense it in the sounds she made, so much better than the ones she'd made eating his food. Then, she nodded and his restraint faltered. He cupped her breast, gripping, pushing, while his other hand swept into her panties.

His fingers slid into the folds of her cunt and he hissed. "So wet for me, sugar? Did I do this to you?" She whimpered, pushing her hips against his hand. Answer enough.

He dragged his fingers back and forth along her slit, spreading her arousal around, then circled her clit. She felt like a fucking *sin*, a forbidden fruit, smooth and warm. His cock throbbed, pressed tight in the confines of his jeans, desperate to bury in deep where his fingers played. She groaned again, head falling back against the wall, pink wisps of hair framing her face, eyelids fluttering, struggling to remain open.

His gaze stayed fixed on her face, feasting on every expression that flashed over her features. So fucking beautiful. So fucking *perfect*.

Humans weren't supposed to appeal to his senses, not after everything in his past. He was crossing so many lines, and for once, he didn't give a single fuck. After he had time to process, he'd likely regret this.

But not now, not in this moment.

Desperate to see what she felt like inside, he slipped a finger in. She sucked in a breath, clenching around him. Her eyes opened, locked on his. That look had his balls tightening, stealing his breath. He wanted to rip her leather mini skirt right off, turn her against the wall, smack her ass for being such a fucking brat. Spank her hard enough to see the outline of his hand. Then fuck her until she screamed his name over and over.

No. He wouldn't go that far. This was where it stopped. His hand—nothing more. It was better this way. He'd make her come, then leave, get control over himself, and move the fuck on.

She'd be too much of a distraction, otherwise. And too much of everything else. Everything he couldn't have and didn't want.

"Bastian," she gasped. That one word had those thoughts sliding right out of his mind.

"Say it again, baby girl," he begged.

"Bastian," she whimpered, grinding against his finger, showing him exactly how she'd move those gorgeous hips if it was his cock instead. He pulled out and replaced the one with two, dipping in and out, fast and then slow, scissoring them inside her.

"Oh, fuck!" she moaned.

"You're drenched, sugar. So fucking wet. This pussy has been desperate for me all night, hasn't it? Desperate since you first laid eyes on me?"

"Mmm…"

"Answer me, baby girl. Let me hear you say it."

"Yes. All night—since yesterday."

He groaned and didn't care that he did.

He clenched his teeth until they ached. Little good it did, because it didn't keep him from grinding against her, grinding to the rhythm of his fingers just to relieve the ache in his cock. He pressed his palm into her clit with just the right amount of pressure.

"Oh, God, I'm going to—"

He halted, stopping the orgasm that nearly swept her over the top. *"Don't* say, God," he admonished. "God doesn't have his fingers in you right now. I do. God isn't making you feel good. I am. You got that, sugar?"

Her eyes struggled to focus on him. He expected her to argue. Instead she begged, "Please don't stop, Bastian."

And those words?

He could deny her *nothing*. His fingers moved again, sliding back in, fucking her harder than before. The wet sounds were erotic. Left him panting.

"Yes," she whined, grinding against him, against his thigh. She tightened around him, little kitten mews slipping from her throat.

He crushed his mouth against hers, eager to swallow every sound. His free hand slipped beneath her top and found her bare breast. The feel of her nipple against his thumb, soft to the roughness of his finger, made him shiver. He gently pinched it and she jerked against him, so he did it again.

All while his tongue claimed her, memorizing the feel of her mouth.

Her hands clenched him tighter, fingers digging into his shoulders. A strangled cry built in her throat. He couldn't decide what he wanted. Kiss her to orgasm, or watch her expression as she came apart for him? Both. Everything. All of it.

Which was when he realized this single orgasm would never be enough. He'd been stupid to think it might be.

Kiss her, he realized, mostly because he couldn't pull his mouth away, couldn't give up the taste of her. She tightened around his fingers, tighter and tighter, then jerked and cried out against his lips. He kissed harder, swallowing up the sound of his efforts, imagining it was his cock she was milking instead. Heated desperation seared him straight to his center, followed by a sense of success, and then…*pride.* Of all things.

He'd had many victories over the years, but damn, this one felt better than most.

Their heavy breathing punctuated the quiet. He pulled his lips away just enough, but kept his fingers buried. She was unusually tight around him, as if holding on, keeping him there. "This tight little pussy needed that. You needed that, didn't you, sugar?" he managed.

She made a little sound.

"I wonder. Do you taste like sugar, too?"

Her mouth opened, then closed, brows knitting as a cute little crease formed between them. He'd seen it before, when he'd said something particularly shocking. He freed his fingers, loathe to do it, then lifted them to his lips.

Her scent from the arousal on his fingers perfumed the air beautifully, and he inhaled, just to savor it. It made his magic falter. His glamor slipped for the barest of moments as he lost control. He leashed himself tightly, then slipped his fingers, covered in her, into his mouth.

She sucked in a breath. The taste of her exploded across his tongue. Just enough to make him regret not using his mouth on her. Fucking poor decision making—that. He should have tasted her orgasm in full. "Just like sugar," he growled, licking his fingers clean.

"Bastian!" she hissed.

His phone chimed, ringing in his pocket. He froze, then dropped his hand, letting a smirk cross his features. Then he stole a quick glance at the clock and said, "Well, sugar, that's my cue. But first, you got that list I asked for?"

He stepped back, shedding his arousal, making his voice sound tame and professional. The facade was necessary. He needed to put some space between them.

She scoffed. "Seriously? You just—"

"No time for complaints. I need the list. Where's your phone? You can text it to me." Her jaw clenched. Hazel eyes darted toward her room down the hall. "Well? Go and grab it." He motioned with his head.

"You're unbelievable," she muttered, stalking away. There was no bite to her tone, but incredulity, perhaps.

He tutted, waiting until her back was turned to exhale, to relax. Tension eased from his shoulders. Just her mere presence wound him up tight. He adjusted his pants, willing his dick to relax, though that proved harder than he'd hoped. His gaze tracked the sway of her skirt, her cute ass as she disappeared into her room before reappearing a moment later. Fuck, she'd been so wet and soft for him. So ready—

"Here. It's in airplane mode."

"No need for that. As long as we're in here—" he motioned, indicating the house "—no one can track you. Keep it on in case I need to get ahold of you, or vice versa."

So what? Maybe he was curious to see if she'd text him.

Taking her phone, he programmed it with his number, then sent himself a text. His phone binged. "There. You've got my number. Send me the list."

She took her phone and clicked around. He took his out, looking over his notifications. Christian could wait. His phone binged again. He glanced at the text, quickly programming her number before scanning through the contents of the message.

"I shared it from my notes app," she explained.

He frowned as he scrolled. "Avon's Cup. Keeps the drinker awake. Berrick's Belt. Makes the wearer invisible. Fatima's Dagger—"

"Yes, yes," she snapped. "I don't need you to read them to me. I know what I wrote."

He glanced up at her, reading the irritation on her face.

He surged toward her, invading her space. Her breath hitched at the change in proximity. She rapidly backed up until her back was against the wall again. "Don't worry, sugar," he growled. "We'll have some more fun another time."

He silently cursed the moment those words came out. A lie. He absolutely did *not* intend to have any more interactions like this one. Couldn't afford to. And yet, her expression, the annoyance there, drove him to make the promise.

She tutted. "Whatever. That's everything—on the list I mean. I don't know if it will have any significance. If it will help to locate her killer, I mean. Like I said, she could have gotten rid of any or all of them over the years. Or they could have been stolen by her killer just because they were pretty trinkets—"

His lips were on hers before he realized what he was doing. It was just, she was so damn sexy when she was talking about shit like this. He could picture her with her hair in a messy bun atop her head, textbooks spread before her, chewing on a pencil as she studied for her exams.

She was probably the world's sexiest student.

He told himself that's why he was kissing her again. That he just wanted one more taste. He needed to cement her kiss into his memory so that he could start fresh tomorrow, put this behind him. He swept his tongue through her mouth, then pulled away, giving her bottom lip a nibble. "It's fine," he said, reassuring her about the list. "I'll see if I can make anything of it. Let you know if I have questions."

He backed the fuck up before he did anything else utterly stupid. Like carting her up the stairs to his bed. Seeing her hair fanned out on his pillows. Telling Christian to go fuck himself so that he could fuck her instead.

No.

He strode over to the mat by the door and slipped back into his boots, then shucked on his jacket. "I'll be back later, sugar. Behave yourself. Get some sleep. Don't go outside the house. Got it?"

She nodded, watching him.

He didn't take the front door. Instead, he walked toward the garage, leaving Eleanor gaping after him in the entryway. With each step, her scent grew fainter, but it didn't disappear entirely. As he rounded the corner, he didn't look back over his shoulder, either. Couldn't. If he did, he'd never leave her. He had work to do. So, he left her standing there, smelling like sin and sex and everything he wanted to devour, and told himself that he'd have better control next time. Only because he had to.

17

The roar of a motorcycle filled my ears, breaking the spell Bastian had over me. I'd let him...*fuck*! I groaned, banging my head against the wall, squeezing my eyes shut, then opening them and blinking, like it would change anything. I couldn't believe I'd allowed that— couldn't believe I wasn't more *angry* at myself for it. If anything, my frustration stemmed from him running off, more than anything.

It was better this way. Better that I didn't have to face him. That I didn't have to talk to him or act like things had changed.

A goblin had just given me the best orgasm of my life, and he hadn't even used his dick—or his freaking tongue, for that matter. Ugh. How was I supposed to put myself back together after something like that? How?!

The reverberations of his bike drifted through the walls from the garage, followed by the rumble of the house as the automatic garage door closed. I frowned, logic kicking in. Bastian's motorcycle? But—

I huffed and shook my head. I wasn't sure why I was surprised. Sure, we'd left it back at the club. Now it was here, in his garage. *Freaking magic*. Somehow, he'd moved it through space, right back home.

Why did I find that so…appealing?

Ugh. I needed to go to bed. Get some sleep so that I could process everything that had happened in the last several hours.

I pushed off the wall and glanced at my phone, at his name in my contacts list. *Bastian Croft*. Posh as hell. Yeah, he looked like a Bastian Croft. I shivered, walking to my room. Teddy was curled on my bed, a divot in the middle of the comforter surrounding him, right where he'd been all evening. He looked up and gave a quiet meow.

"Hey cutie," I managed, walking straight for my bathroom. I turned on the faucet, dampened a cloth, used my makeup remover to clean my face, then set about the rest of my bedtime routine. A few minutes later, I was in my PJs, pulling Teddy to my chest like a stuffed animal. He gave a loud purr and cuddled up against me.

"*You* won't run off, will you?" I cooed, rubbing my face against his soft kitty fur. "No, of course you won't. You're a *proper* gentleman. Not like *some* people. I'd rather cuddle with you, anyway." His purrs grew louder, then settled into silence.

In the dark of the room, I let my mind wander, listening to the sounds of the house, the creak of the wood as the temperatures outside changed. I tried not to flinch each time I heard a noise, letting my breaths deepen. I was safe in here, safe behind Bastian's magical security system, safe from people like… *No*—I pushed Luke from my mind, forcing myself to think of Bastian, instead.

Bastian had handled me in a way Luke never had. Possessive, assertive, confident, and yet, he'd never once made me feel used or uncomfortable. The opposite, actually. Aside from grinding against me, he'd taken off before I could return the favor. He'd made my pleasure his priority, then vanished.

"*Just like sugar…*" Those words echoed in my head, paired with the sinuous smile while he said it, the hungry gleam in his goblin eyes. He'd promised there would be more, but there couldn't be—shouldn't be. I needed this to be a one-time thing, which I had no experience with. But I couldn't make the same mistake twice. I'd let someone else get close to me, and they'd used that against me, waited until I let my guard down to hurt me.

I wasn't ready to go through that again.

I brought my fingers to my lips. They were swollen, the skin around them mildly chafed from Bastian's stubble. I squeezed my thighs together, then smiled. The minor ache there reminded me of just how good it had been. All passion and heat, no room for thought or logic. Maybe I could do this for a little while, keep things casual, enjoy Bastian as a fling, then move on once this case was solved.

Yet, a nagging feeling warned that once Bastian was done with me, I'd never be the same.

———

My phone chirped. I rolled over, groaning as the room came in and out of focus. My phone chirped again, another text. I glanced at the bedside clock. It was nearly 10:00am. Teddy had left the confines of my arms at some point during the night, getting comfortable on the other pillow. He meowed when he saw me awake.

"Hello to you, too," I teased. Having him around meant I had someone to talk to. It made me feel less alone, too.

I rolled over and snatched my phone, quickly scrolling through notifications. Nothing from Bastian, but a handful of texts from Vivi, two from Tara, one from Eaden, one from Kaylee, and another from my freaking mother—which I promptly ignored.

I focused on Vivi's first, which had come in a few hours after we talked on the phone yesterday.

I sighed. The last four had been sent this morning. I'd slept through two of them. She was probably frantic.

I considered calling her, but I didn't feel like talking. Quickly punching out a series of responses, I sent them and moved on to Tara and then Kaylee.

Then finally, Eaden. He'd texted me two nights ago, but I was only opening it now.

Another had come in yesterday afternoon.

And then, later last night, after I'd fallen asleep.

I wasn't going to call him. It would give him ample opportunity to ask too many questions, so I shot him a quick text telling him that something went down, and I was okay.

A few moments later, the beeping began. The screen began to flash with incoming messages. Vivi, Kaylee, Tara. One from Eaden. Then another from Vivi. I grumbled. I didn't have patience for any of this.

Tossing my phone over on the bed, I climbed to my feet and slipped into the bathroom. After that, I crept into the kitchen. I half hoped to find Bastian standing there shirtless, cooking breakfast, but everything was quiet. The coffee maker hadn't been cleaned out from yesterday, so I went about rinsing it out, then making coffee.

"Woooowwww…" I whispered, finding the stash of expensive coffee in the cabinet. Small batch beans in bags labeled with different flavors. A smile pulled at the corner of my lips. How very *Bastian Croft* of him. I grabbed the one that was labeled *Oatmeal Cookie* and poured some into the grinder.

The smell that wafted through the air had me groaning in delight.

Once the coffee was brewing, I set about doing the dishes from last night's dinner. Bastian was neat, and there was only the small stack in the sink. He mostly cleaned up as he went.

My mind went to him. Had he gotten back late? Was he still sleeping? I wasn't exactly quiet while I loaded and began the dishwasher. Perhaps I should have been, postponing the inevitable confrontation that was coming. The thought of facing him after what had happened last night left my cheeks burning.

Perhaps the best thing to do was pretend it *hadn't* happened.

I crept upstairs, pausing to listen on the landing. At his door, I gave it a quiet tapping knock. "Bastian?" I called. No response. I tried again, but still nothing.

I tried the knob—unlocked. I opened the door, cautious. He'd told me to stay out of his room, so I wouldn't walk in, but I did peek my head in, bracing myself. My gaze feasted on the space that was so obviously *him*. The room was set up like a suite, with a small sofa arrangement near the window, and a bed framed by two nightstands. An acoustic guitar stood on a stand in the corner next to a small chair. He played? I pictured him sitting there, shirtless, tattoos and piercings on full display, strumming. He used those same expert fingers that had worked on me last night. The muscles low in my belly tightened, heat spreading to the apex of my thighs.

My eyes darted to the bed, still made. Bastian hadn't come home last night. That flaring heat turned ice cold. I closed the door and darted upstairs, just to be sure. The game room was empty. What about the gym downstairs? Perhaps he liked working out early? It was empty too.

"Fuck," I hissed, striding to my room. I grabbed my phone and opened the texting app, then stopped. It was only 10:30am. I didn't want to seem… *What?* Worried? Desperate? Clingy?

He was a grown man, after all. A grown *goblin*.

A darker, nagging thought seeped into my mind. He had never told me what his plans were, just that he had something that required his attention. An appointment of some sort. What kind of an appointment? The date kind? What if he'd stayed out with another woman?

A sickening sensation burrowed into my stomach.

No, that was ridiculous. He might give off bad boy vibes, but he didn't strike me as the type to shove his fingers in me, then go find another woman afterward. That meant that something else had kept him away.

From the kitchen, the coffee maker beeped. I decided to let it rest for a few minutes. I'd have my shower first. Then, if I didn't hear from him soon, I'd go have my coffee and text him.

When I made my way back into the kitchen, dressed in a pair of leggings and wide-necked shirt that hung off my shoulder, I still hadn't heard anything.

Don't panic. It's too early to panic, I said, coaching myself through it. *He's allowed to stay out all night and doesn't owe you answers or explanations.*

Calmly, I poured myself a cup of coffee, added some sugar and cream, then sat down at the island. I took a long sip, sighed, and smiled. It was so yummy. I took another sip, willing myself to be calm. But… I couldn't do it. I caved.

> Where are you? Is everything okay?

I pressed send before I could cringe at how clingy it sounded.

I was halfway through my cup of coffee when my phone sounded. I exhaled at the sight of the bubble notification with Bastian's name and opened the text.

> **BASTIAN**
>
> I'm fine, sugar. Seen the news yet?

I jumped to my feet. An ache formed in the back of my throat as I sprinted into the living room. I hesitated in the doorway, then walked in.

Meow—

"Jesus, Teddy!" I cried, jumping backwards. I put a calming hand to my chest, then exhaled, looking down at him. "Did you have your breakfast?" I asked. He had an automatic machine type feeder that kept his food and water bowls full with a sensor. He'd never been an over-eater so Peter hadn't worried too much. Teddy meowed again, blue eyes tracking my movements.

I found the remote and turned on the television, searching through the channels until I landed on one of the news stations. "…authorities are still searching for the suspects, but several faces have been identified and rendered, believed to be responsible for the attacks that left twelve dead and four in critical condition." Sketches appeared on the screen. "This was an exclusive dinner, with strict rules and an even stricter invite list. No photos have surfaced, as cell phones were prohibited. Some speculate the culprits infiltrated the mayoral dinner under false identities. The guest list is under scrutiny. The mayor's security team is facing heat for the incident. We spoke with witnesses in attendance, including Marsh Thadur."

An interview clip flashed onto the screen. The name was vaguely familiar, and it took a moment before I realized it was one of the names Aramis had mentioned the night before.

"There is no excuse for what happened tonight," Thadur said, his tone grave. I blinked, my eyes focusing on the face. Even though I was seeing him through a screen, his glamor wavered. His human face morphed—pointed ears and angular fae features.

So. He was fae.

"It is imperative that we keep our city safe. The events of tonight are a prime example of the growing crime throughout Walton. We should be putting more money into the police force, greater scrutiny into those hired to serve. We lost some good people tonight. I, for one, question the mayor's security team. Those criminals shouldn't have gotten in here."

The clip vanished, flipping back to the newscaster.

I didn't hear the rest. Instead, I sank onto the couch, picking up Teddy and plopping him into my lap. My hand stroked him absentmindedly as I watched the footage, most of it replaying over and over again. I had a feeling if I changed to other local news stations, they'd be playing much the same thing.

My phone chirped. I looked down at the screen. *Bastian Croft.* His name lit up in a bubble, showing a preview of his text. I sighed, turning off the television, removing Teddy from my lap, and padded back into the kitchen. I needed more coffee to process whatever he said.

BASTIAN

Did you see the news?

Yes. Is that Marsh Thadur the same one Aramis mentioned?

BASTIAN

Same guy. Did you notice the sketches? All four are of the sleeping fae Aramis told us about.

The sleeping bodies?! How is that possible?

BASTIAN

That's what I'm trying to figure out. Stay inside. I'll be home later.

Fine...

Dots appeared, then disappeared. They didn't reappear again.

I didn't want to admit how much I liked his protective words. *Stay inside. I'll be home later.*

I liked Bastian's house. I could get used to living in a place like this, slightly removed from the city. In fact, I had every intention of taking advantage of it until we fixed my apartment.

So I finished off my coffee, and raided the pantry. Whatever I attempted wouldn't compare to Bastian's pancakes yesterday, so I settled on a banana. Then I went and changed in to a pair of shorts and headed downstairs to the gym.

Which was exactly where Bastian found me two hours later.

18

I had my fists wrapped, taking my frustrations out on the punching bag in Bastian's gym, when he appeared. I paid him a sidelong glance as he got comfortable against the wall, leaning against it with a shoulder, arms crossed.

One look at his smug smile had me faltering.

I lifted my eyebrows, barely an acknowledgement, then turned back to the bag, throwing my body into every punch. It helped. All the guilt I felt surrounding Professor Miller's death, all the frustration over my choices, like letting Luke into my life, sacrificing my dreams, my trashed apartment, my dead neighbor, faded into the background. I didn't want to face any of it, but I couldn't run forever.

Luke was like a festering sore, bleeding and infected. He'd burrowed so far into my life, that disappearing hadn't been enough. I should have known better—

"You hungry, sugar?" Bastian's voice pulled me from my spiral and my movements slowed to a stop. I was panting, my chest rising and falling in bursts. I blew a lock of pink hair out of my face.

Bastian's eyes darted over my sweat-slicked body, over the sports bra and stretchy, barely-there shorts. There was heavy heat in that gaze, words unspoken, pleasures left untested. My cheeks flushed.

"I could eat," I said, stepping away from the bag.

He glanced at it, smile tugging at the corner of his lips. "You throw a mean punch. Something tells me there's a story there?" I shrugged. "All right, then. Keep your secrets—for now. Up for a little sparring later?"

I opened my mouth, then frowned. That was *not* a good idea. Getting so close to him after last night…

"Come on, it'll be fun," he teased.

I scowled. *Fun?* Right. Assuming that by fun he meant, ending up on the floor with our clothes off, tangled up in each other, yeah, sure, *fun*. I didn't respond.

"I'll let you think about it. Meantime, I got sandwiches from the deli. Come and eat. We can talk." He nodded with his head toward the stairs. I swallowed, hesitating.

"Here—" He stepped forward and took one of my hands before I could stop him, then began unwrapping my fists. I winced. "Sugar…" he scolded, eyes darting up to meet mine. "Is there a reason you got blood seeping into your wraps?"

I took a deep, slow inhale. "No…" I said at last. He lifted a brow.

"You know I can smell a lie," he warned. I snorted. "All right. I won't push. Come on." He led me up the stairs and into the kitchen, only dropping my hand when we got there. "Grab the bag there, and I'll get the rest."

I hesitated, watching him move around past the island. He pulled a couple of bottled waters from the fridge, a bag of chips from the cabinet, napkins, and paper plates. Then he moved to the French doors, opened them, and walked outside. "You coming?" he called over his shoulder.

I rushed to grab the bag of sandwiches and chased after him. He set us up beneath the umbrella on the patio, over-looking the pool and hot tub. Trees shaded the perimeter of the backyard. It was late spring, warming up to summer. The weather was perfect.

"It's beautiful back here," I found myself saying.

"You like it?" he asked, gaze searching my expression.

I nodded. "It's like a little slice of paradise."

"I had the pool put in after acquiring the property. Most goblins don't like water, but my mother…" He trailed off. "Anyway, got it from my fae side, I guess."

I hummed, avoiding his gaze, taking a seat and shuffling things around before unwrapping my sub. I could see him out here swimming. Alone. The thought of him in a pair of swim trunks, water droplets dripping down his skin, over his tattoos, had my heart rate spiking.

Bastian inhaled through his nose, sniffing. My eyes shot to his face in time to see his pupils dilate. "What are you thinking about, sugar?" His voice pitched low.

My body betrayed me, heating.

"That's not fair," I snapped. "*And* it's intrusion into my privacy."

He chuckled. "Is that what it is? Not like I can just turn it off. Can't help what I am."

"Well, it's not like I can—" I stopped myself before I said anything embarrassing.

"—control what you feel for me?" He finished, lifting an annoyingly perfect eyebrow.

God. Sometimes I hated that stupid dumb face of his. Hated how perfect and handsome and…ugh.

"You're unbelievable," I muttered, grabbing my sub and shoving it into my mouth, taking a bite. I chewed slowly so I wouldn't have to speak, wouldn't have to admit that he was right.

At last, he did the same. A long silence stretched out between us. It wasn't until we nearly finished that the conversation picked up again.

"What happened last night?" I asked after swallowing. "The mayor's thing? Is that why you got the phone call?"

Bastian sighed, leaning back in his chair. He picked up a

chip, regarded it with interest, then tossed it into his mouth, chewed, and swallowed. "More or less, yes."

"You work for WBI, don't you? That's why everyone knew you at my apartment."

"Sort of—yes."

"Sort of?"

"I work for a special branch of WBI, the Supernaturals Affairs office. It's…a subset. SA for short, since we all love our acronyms."

"The SA?" I frowned. "Never heard of it."

"You wouldn't have and you're going to pretend you haven't. Surely you don't think the world is ignorant of super-naturals?"

"Well, I mean, I figured the few people who *do* know about them keep it quiet."

"They do, mostly. It's better that way. Less dangerous. Can you imagine if the world… Well, never mind. That's not the discussion we're having."

"So… What does the *SA* do?"

"Also not the conversation we're having," he said, holding a chip between his fingers, playing with it.

"Okay? Then, what *is* the conversation we're having?"

"Aramis isn't paying me for his favor."

I lifted a brow. "*Okayyy?* You mean, looking into the sleeping fae issue?" He nodded. "But you're going to do it anyway?"

"I don't have much choice. Not after last night. Professor Miller's case, while important, is getting shoved to the back burner."

I frowned, not sure how I felt about that, especially given my gut feelings about Luke. "So… You don't need me anymore?"

"Now, now, sugar," he said, his voice dropping to a low purr. "I didn't say *that*. I still have plans for you."

The promise of those words made my thighs squeeze

together. Green eyes darted to my lips and back. Wait… Were we still talking about the case? Or something else entirely?

I cleared my throat and groped for a topic change. "Those sketches on the news, the ones you mentioned—of the perpetrators—they were at the event?"

He sniffed, shoulders relaxing. "On the guest list, yes."

"*What?*" My eyes bulged. "But how is that possible? They showed up?"

"They did."

"But…" My eyebrows drew together. It didn't make sense.

"Aramis confirmed that they remain safely locked in his high security vault under constant surveillance. They're in hospital beds, closely monitored, with a fae healer on duty at all times."

"Then…how?!"

"That's what I'd like to know, sugar. That's what I'm looking into."

A long hesitation and then, "Where does this leave me?"

"Ah. Yes. Let's discuss that," he said. I shifted, crossing my legs. "Your apartment is in shambles. And if I'm not mistaken, it appears you're in some kind of danger? This Luke person, yes?"

I chewed on the inside of my cheek. "Yes," I managed.

"Then you'll understand why I cannot let you return home, even if we clean the place up and all that." He waved a hand.

I opened my mouth—

He lifted a finger. "I made a deal, Eleanor. I intend to uphold my end. The magic required to fix your apartment will take most of what I have stored, and that's fine. But I'd like your permission to hold off for a few days, given the state of everything else. I have no idea what I'm about to get myself into."

I frowned. That was unexpected, but refreshingly so. Thus far, he'd been a lot more honest with me than I expected. His magic, especially. Was it because he knew how much power he held over me? That I was no threat whatsoever?

I cleared my throat. "And…what…you expect me to just…stay here?"

"That's exactly what I expect, yes. Even if I fix everything today, I will not let you back into your apartment until I know the danger has passed." His tone was firm. I sighed. "Not the answer you were hoping for?"

"Actually…" I rolled my bottom lip between my teeth. "I… I'm not sure I'm ready to go back yet, anyway, given what happened with Peter." I said his name like a whisper, like I could barely acknowledge it. "And you're right. I don't think it's safe."

I'd once promised myself I wouldn't do this again—alone. That I wouldn't expose myself to danger and keep quiet. That I wouldn't sit back and let Luke destroy my life while staying silent about it. Plus, Bastian didn't seem to mind my presence in his home.

"I do like it here," I admitted. "It's peaceful, compared to the city."

He grinned and his dimple appeared. "Glad to hear that. I feel the same. And since you'll be sticking around a bit longer, that brings me to my next point."

"Oh?" I sat up straighter.

"I might need your assistance."

"Really?" The word came out breathy.

"Sure, why not? An extra set of eyes. An extra mind. Someone I can talk things through with." His words meant more than I cared to admit. "I know you've got a smart brain under that head of pink hair. Might as well earn your keep while you're here."

Then he winked.

My chest expanded, wider and wider. I shifted, trying not to preen, trying not to reveal exactly how his words made me feel. "Right. Fine. Deal," I said casually, like he hadn't just made my day. "What do you need to discuss?"

I didn't want to be a mooch. If I could help in any way, I would.

But it was more than that.

Something deep inside me coiled tight with eagerness. Staying at Bastian's might mean other things, too. Things I needed to be careful about. But since I was trying for casual. Trying to give myself room to have fun with no strings attached, maybe I didn't have to be too careful.

"Well, for starters," he said, "I read through your list of artifacts and it got me thinking…"

"Oh?" I perked up. "Do you think that what's going on could be artifact related?"

"Depends. I don't want to rule anything out. Magic is obviously involved. I trust Aramis. If he says his people are safeguarded, under constant surveillance, I believe him."

An idea struck and I leaned forward. "What if we're dealing with an artifact that allows someone to be in two places at once?"

A lazy grin spread across his lips and a blush crept up my neck. "I like the way you think, Eleanor. Might you know of any capable of that?"

"Hmm. Two places at once," I mused, my eyes going distant as I flipped through my mental library of artifacts, but nothing came to mind.

I'd encountered the mention of many artifacts during my studies. Professor Miller and I had only come into contact with a fraction of what existed in the world. Knowing what artifacts were capable of, the vast span of things they could be used for, I didn't doubt for a single second that this was possible.

Bastian rubbed his temples, leaning back, his eyes fluttering closed. I used this unguarded moment to study him. When I blinked, the transparent glimmer of his true form came into view. I tried to hold it in place, to better assess him, but like always, it quickly disappeared.

I liked his goblin form. I wanted to learn its intricacies when I shouldn't have.

What would it be like to kiss him that way? What would it feel like? What would *sex* be like?

My chest fluttered. Would he show me his true form, if we ever—

"Why don't you think on it, hmm?" Bastian said, grounding me. "I don't expect you to come up with something right this moment. I haven't slept for nearly…thirty-six hours? I need to build up some energy. I'm lagging." His eyes opened again, pinning me in place. "Let me have a quick nap, then we can blow off some steam downstairs."

My eyes widened and he laughed. "Sparring, sugar. In the basement. Unless… Well, we can certainly have fun in other ways, if that's what you're thinking."

I made a choking sound. He stood, all cocky exuberance, and began collecting our things from the table, sliding them into the bag to dispose of. "Come on inside. I'll feel better with you behind the security barrier."

I stood and followed him in, my eyes lingering on the pool. Going for a swim sounded kinda nice. Bastian caught my gaze and seemed to read my mind because he said, "How about later, sugar?"

"Are you *ever* going to call me by my actual name?"

"Eleanor?"

"Ugh, no, Rose."

"I like *sugar* better."

I shook my head, tossing my plate into the trash. He did the same with the rest of our stuff before heading for the stairs.

"Have a good nap, I guess."

"Yup," he said, throwing a hand over his shoulder in farewell before disappearing.

I retrieved my phone and saw the missed calls from Eaden. Great. I'd have to face him eventually. Exhaling, I braced myself and called him back.

"Rose? There you are. Is there a reason you've been ignoring my calls?"

"Not ignoring, no. Just… It's a long story." I sighed, pacing in my room.

There was a pause and then, "Everything okay? I'm kind of freaking out over here."

"You, freaking out?"

"Rose," he growled.

"Fine. I assume you saw the security feed?" I knew he kept cameras around the exterior of the club.

"Yeah, and heard about your apartment. Wanna explain what's going on?"

"Not at the moment, no." I had initially planned to tell him about Luke. To see if there was anything he could do. Now that I had Bastian… I was less inclined. "Look, I need a few days off to sort things out. Then I'll tell you what I can."

"Fine. Not a problem. Take whatever time you need. If anyone knows about dealing with personal shit—well, whatever. Take what you need. Just don't start avoiding my calls. You go silent, I get worried."

My chest warmed at his concern.

"Speaking of," I said, "did you ever get ahold of Micky?" There was a long silence. I glanced down at my phone but we weren't disconnected. "Eaden? You there?"

He sighed. "Yes. I got her."

"She's…okay?" Relief unspooled in my chest.

"Not so sure, actually. Probably shouldn't talk about it, especially on the phone. Some weird shit's been going down in Walton. You saw the news this morning?"

"Yes?" I frowned. What did Micky have to do with the mayor's gala?

"Right. Then you know that there's some strange stuff going on."

I hesitated. "Eaden, have…have any of your people been acting strange? Like, falling asleep and not waking up?" Another long silence. "Eaden?"

"Come to the club, Rose," he said at last. "Let's talk there, not on the phone."

My heart thudded. "Then you ha—?"

"Rose! Enough. Come to the club if you want to talk about this shit."

My mouth dropped open. I pulled my phone away, glancing at it, then put it back to my ear. He was right. Something like this should only be discussed in person.

"I… I can stop by tonight, if that's okay? I can't work though."

"Fine," he said after a long hesitation. "Come by and we'll talk. Until then, take care of your shit and do what you need to do."

"Thank—"

The line went dead. I huffed.

"What did he say?"

I yelped, whirling around.

"Bastian?!" I hissed. He stood in my doorway, leaning against the door frame. "What the actual fuck? You can't just…"

"It's my house, sugar. I *can*. With just about anything I want around here. What did he say?"

"He wants me to come by the club tonight—to talk. I think something might have happened with some of his people, too."

His jaw flexed, then he nodded. "Probably a good thing. I was hoping to talk to him anyway."

"You… You want to come with me?"

His eyes narrowed. "You really think I'd let you go alone? Yes, I'll be going with you. Maybe we can do a little more dancing while we're at it." His voice dropped suggestively and he smirked.

The reminder of everything that had happened last night flooded through me making my breath hitch. I pushed it away and stood up a little taller. "Weren't you, like, going to go nap or whatever?"

"Yep." He winked. "Night night, sugar." He disappeared again, out of my doorway and up the stairs. I rolled my eyes at the wall, then went in search of Teddy and my e-reader, cozying up on the couch to get a good dose of smut.

19

———

Bastian woke from his nap and inhaled. He smelled her, faintly. He'd smelled her earlier too, in the doorway of his room, but no further than that. A smile stretched across his face at the mere thought of her.

"Teddy, no!" Eleanor's voice drifted upstairs, scolding. He sat up, listening. "Bad kitty! Why would you *do* that? We're guests here!" He sat up and groaned. Great. The cat probably took a shit on his favorite rug or something. "Bastian's going to kill us," her voice hissed, quieter now.

He wouldn't have heard her, were it not for his supernatural senses. Taking a deep breath, he swung his legs off the bed and used the bathroom. Then he had a seat on the chaise in the corner of the room, forearms braced on his knees. He hung his head, closed his eyes, and set about pouring energy into his metals.

It was a tedious process, requiring focus and calm—

"No! Come back here!" Eleanor's voice again.

"Fucking hell," he muttered, eyes darting open. There was a clatter, followed by the slapping of bare feet on tile. Was she chasing the damned cat? A smile tugged at the corner of his mouth. He pushed away the thought of her running through his house and closed his eyes again, this time gathering his extra energy and channeling it into his metal jewelry, including the jewelry he kept hidden behind his glamor. He only showed off about half of what he wore. Most humans were already shocked by his number of piercings. Keeping the rest hidden avoided extra questions. Extra attention.

While the majority of his piercings were for magic, a couple were purely recreational. He chuckled, recalling Eleanor's surprise at his tongue piercing. If she knew about the other, the one at the base of his cock, she'd probably require a fainting couch.

His cock twitched and he adjusted his pants. She would like it, the way it teased her clit while he fucked her. What sorts of sounds might she make for him?

He shot to his feet, restless—

"See that?" Eleanor admonished. "Don't ever do it again, understand?"

He chuckled, striding from the room. It was a fucking cat. Not like her scolding would make a difference. He was more eager about what it might mean for *her*…

No. He pushed that thought away, disbanded the images of punishing her, putting her over his knee, and leaving hand-prints on her ass.

He found her in the living room, staring at the side of the couch. Right where—

"Your cat clawed my fucking couch?!" he hissed, sneaking up behind her. She jumped backwards and spun toward him, eyes widening.

"Bastian! Hi! Didn't know you were up." She inched over to try and hide the corner of the couch from view. He caught her up, wrapping his hands around her upper arms, pulling her flush against him, against his hardening cock.

Okay…perhaps he should have waited to calm down before coming downstairs.

"Uhm… It was an accident?" she squeaked, eyes darting over his expression.

"That so?" His hands drifted down and splayed open,

wrapping around her hips, pressing her more firmly against him. "I suppose I could use a bit of magic to fix it, unless you want to sew it up?"

She scoffed. "Yeah, sure, let me run to my room and get my handy little sewing kit. I take it everywhere with me."

He lifted his brows. "If I wanted your smart mouth, sugar, I'd have claimed it already."

"If I wanted an asshole, Bastian—"

He dove for her, capturing her lips before she could finish the sentence. She let out a squeak, pausing only momentarily before kissing him back. Her groan had his balls tightening. He ripped his lips away just as quickly, pushing her to arm's length, breathing hard. "That was for the couch," he explained. Then, just for the fuck of it, waved a hand dramatically and watched the cat's scratches stitch back together, like it had never even happened.

"Now, go change back into those sexy little shorts you were wearing earlier. I need to blow off some steam. Meet me downstairs in five."

She made a sound of complaint in the back of her throat. "I'm not sparring with you."

"You are. Want me to throw you over my shoulder? Rules of the house. You live here, you spar with me."

"That's bullshit. You made that up just now."

"So? Doesn't make it any less of a rule."

She squared her shoulders and planted her feet, crossing her arms. "And, what? You're just going to start making up rules whenever you want?"

"My house. I can make whatever rules I want. Now, go get dressed."

"I'm wearing this."

He arched an eyebrow. "Pajama pants and a tank top? Well, all right. I don't mind if your tits pop out. I certainly wouldn't mind seeing them after last night."

She growled—if it could be called that—and pushed past him, elbowing him as she went.

"Fine," she hissed. "I'll go change."

He fought the smile threatening his face. Fought, and lost. Then he adjusted his pants and headed downstairs.

———

The sight of Eleanor, sweaty and panting, did so many things to him. She shot forward, trying to land a punch to his side. He dodged, moving slowly like a human might, then spun around and put her in a chokehold. She grabbed his forearm and dropped her shoulder, pulling him forward, then elbowed him, freeing herself from the hold. "Good," he said, pleased. "You're already better than you were an hour ago."

She'd been taking MMA for a little over a year, and while it showed, she still needed work. Work he was happy to help her with. Especially if he got to watch her tight little ass in those little shorts.

"How long do we have to keep doing this?" she panted, bending over to plant her hands on her knees.

"'Till I get tired of touching you, sugar."

"You're a pig."

"Oh? Did you think so last night when I had my fingers inside you?"

"What the fuck?!" she sputtered. Her face turned a darker shade of red and she stalked away to the water dispenser. He watched her gulp down a full glass, watched the movement of her long throat before pulling his eyes away.

A quick glance in the mirrors showed him panting too, muscles corded from the increased blood flow. His long black hair was braided tightly down the side of his scalp. The shaved side was going to need attention in a couple of days.

His eyes flicked back to Eleanor. She was filling her glass again, probably stalling.

"What made you want to learn martial arts?" he asked, crossing his arms, watching her. He'd been curious but had refrained from voicing the question until now. She tensed, then shrugged. "In my experience, there's always a reason. Want me to start guessing?"

She threw him a glare. He already had a solid theory. There was a reason he was good at his job. Drawing conclusions was one of them.

"All right," he said, when she didn't respond. "You said that asshole—*Luke*—trashed your apartment? The one manhandling you inappropriately behind the club? You've got some history with him?"

Her face, red with exertion only minutes ago, went pale.

His jaw tightened as a new realization struck him. The blood pumping past his ears turned to a roar. He took a step forward and she flinched—fucking *flinched*. Just like she'd done in the coffee shop. Which confirmed his worst fears.

"Did he hurt you, sugar? Before?" His voice was sharp enough to cut.

Her throat bobbed. She shook her head, then kept on shaking it.

"Well?" His fists clenched.

"I don't want to talk about it," she whispered. Then she spun and turned her back to him, fussing with the dispenser.

"No, fuck this. We're talking about it." He swallowed the distance between them and lifted a hand to reach for her. She flinched again, as if sensing it. He froze, arm outstretched, but didn't lay a finger on her. He would never touch someone in such a state, never force his touch on anyone.

"Please, don't," she whispered as if reading his mind. His chest constricted.

"He fucking hurt you, didn't he? You think I can't tell what the aftermath of abuse looks like?"

He knew—all too well.

"I don't want to talk about it," she said again, lifting her voice, rounding on him. Her face was tight, eyes flashing with hurt, with fear.

"I will fucking *kill* him," he hissed. "I will hunt him down and I will rip out his entrails. And then I will fucking *strangle* him with them."

Her eyes rounded. She took a staggering step back, a new fear flashing in her gaze. "Stop," she whispered. "Please, just —stop!"

He froze, mouth opening, closing. His throat went dry and he swallowed. He was scaring her. "Fuck," he muttered. He ran a hand over his face. "I'm sorry, Eleanor. I didn't mean to get carried away. I'm sorry."

Her jaw clenched. "It's…"

It fucking *hurt*, seeing her like this. It woke a primal side of him—made him want to protect her. "We don't have to talk about it," he said, rushing through the words, hoping to calm her down. He didn't want to cause her pain, no matter how badly he wanted to know what had happened. It was his fault. No—it was that fucking *human's* fault. Another fucking human. Even without magical abilities, they could be as bad, if not worse, than supernaturals.

"I'm sorry," he said again. "I didn't mean to upset you."

It shouldn't have wrenched his insides to see her like this, but it did. It made him see red, made him want to smash someone's face to a pulp—Luke's. He leashed the goblin side of himself.

"I was hurt too," he said, the words catching in his throat, surprising even himself. But now that they were out, he couldn't seem to stop. "When I was younger—a long time ago now. I was betrayed by someone I loved."

She watched him, motionless, except for the tilting of her head.

"I told you yesterday that I draw the line with humans, and for good reason."

Her brows pulled together, a small line appearing. "They hurt you?" she asked, her voice tentative.

He exhaled, letting the memory wash over him. How long had it been since he'd thought of it? There was a time when it was *all* he could think of.

He walked over to the mats and sat down, crossing his legs, bracing his forearms on his knees. Eleanor stayed put. Her eyes were glued to him.

"I fell in love with a human once," he said. "And I thought she loved me back." He blew out a long breath, loathe to recall the dark days he'd been born into. "This was during a time when magic was feared. Witch trials and inquisitors and exorcists." Her eyes went wide. He'd expected that. He didn't look a day past thirty. "The world fears what it does not understand, and in those times, humans feared anything they could not explain. Now you have stories filled with boy wizards and magicians and vampires. Women read books about dominant wolf shifters and all the naughty things they do."

She blinked. Red crept up her neck. Hmm, interesting. He'd explore that later.

"Things have changed, sugar. The world has changed. Not so, when I was young—young and naive."

"What happened?" she whispered, inching closer.

Good.

"Come and sit. I'll tell you." His heart was racing.

She nodded, finally creeping over.

Once she was seated on the floor, he began again. "I fell in love with a human named Sara. She was bright and loud, the daughter of a well-loved magistrate in a large village in eastern Europe. I was born there in that region, you know, in Europe. Didn't move here to America until a hundred years ago.

"In those days, women were expected to be silent, but she would walk into a room and speak, and everyone would stop what they were doing and listen. Being the daughter of a magistrate, she had more freedom than most, even though religions were sweeping the European continent at the time. I should have known that kind of sway could be dangerous in the right circumstances." He pressed his teeth together, inhaling through his nose.

"I cannot say for sure, how she found out about me. I tried to determine the truth for years after. For a while, it ate me alive—became an unhealthy obsession. But I realized that to move on, I had to give it up. It was freeing. But, I digress.

"One afternoon, I ran into her in the market. We'd been courting for months. My mother and father had warned me against getting tangled up with humans. I didn't listen. I was going to marry this girl, and then perhaps eventually, tell her what I was—or not. I truly didn't mind if she never knew. What kind of love forces a person to keep secrets?"

"The kind that isn't really love," Eleanor managed, her eyes wide and understanding.

He nodded. "As I said, I was young and naive. But, back to the market." He smiled—or tried to at least. There was so much he remembered vividly about that day. The smell of autumn, crisp with the scent of decay. The screaming children playing tag. The farmers walking their livestock past the outskirts of the village center. "She was shopping with a friend. We caught sight of each other and she signaled to me, so we retreated around the corner of a building. After kissing her soundly—because it was hard to do much else in those days—she told me that her father had found out about us, that we couldn't be together because he didn't approve. I was..." He shook his head. "I thought I was heartbroken. But she told me she wanted to run away. Knowing she would give it all up for me, leave everything behind, cracked my heart wide open like an egg. I should have known, even then. Sara wasn't the kind of girl to forsake her family, her life. But all the daydreams I had, the promises, us owning our own farm, raising a family together—" He huffed. "We agreed to meet just after midnight that night, behind the blacksmith's forge. I was to get a couple of horses, pack up as much as we'd need to move a few towns over and resettle."

"Oh, Bastian," Eleanor whispered, blanching.

He swallowed. "I agonized all evening, packing and unpacking, just to make sure I got it right. I lived by myself at the time. Though I was young, I wasn't young enough to cling to my parents. But I had no problem leaving everything behind—all I'd built for myself. I'd done it before."

"How old were you?" Eleanor asked, breaking his trance.

"I looked, perhaps twenty? But I was already approaching fifty."

"And you considered yourself *young*?!"

"For a goblin-fae, yes."

She nodded. "Fine. What happened after? Did she meet you?"

"No. I was ambushed at our meeting place. Taken by surprise. What little magic I had was useless. I could have defended myself against a couple of humans, not a mob. I was taken into the blacksmith's forge. They were ready for me. Turns out, I was in league with the devil, or some such nonsense."

"Did someone see you doing magic?"

He snorted. "I had little magic in those days. Magic matures with age. By my people's standards, I was little more than an adolescent. That was before I truly learned how to use metals." She nodded. "But it didn't take much for them to figure out their theories were true. You see, like all other supernaturals, I don't die as easily as a human." He summoned a knife, slid the blade down his forearm, and opened a gash along the length of it. His blood swelled.

"Bastian! What are you...?!" Eleanor's words died as the cut healed.

"So, you see? You can imagine their surprise when it came time to force my confession."

Her eyes widened and she gasped, covering her mouth. Those hazel orbs filled with tears. It wasn't exactly the reaction he was hoping for. To distract her, yes. Not to make her cry. And yet, seeing her emotion over something that had once torn him apart was somehow...gratifying. It told him that what he'd felt was warranted.

"That was the day I learned *exactly* what humans are

capable of. And since that day, I have never allowed myself to forget it." Which was why he needed to remember it, even now. Eleanor wasn't like any human he'd met, but he'd once believed the same about Sara. Even if they were different in so many ways, it was a risk he couldn't take. That wasn't going to stop him from fulfilling every dark desire he'd dreamt up. He was what he was, and he would never apologize for it. But when the time came, he would have to let her go.

20

My stomach churned listening to Bastian's words. "They tortured you?" I managed. As a student of history, I was well acquainted with the troubled times surrounding the witch hunts and Inquisition. It had spanned most of the known world. To know he'd been tangled up in it...

Bastian nodded.

"For how long? How did you get free? Was it really Sara's doing? What if...?" I bit the skin on my lower lip. "What if her father simply found out and circumvented her?"

A dark laugh burst from his chest. "Believe me, sugar. I thought that for days, as they cut me open, experimented. I couldn't believe otherwise, couldn't fathom a world where she would betray me. Amidst my screams, I kept telling myself that as soon as she found out, she'd find a way to stop it."

Bile rose in my throat. I swallowed, trying to dampen the acidity, to rid myself of the sour taste. "She sold you out?"

He scoffed. "She came to see me. I won't repeat what she said, but essentially, yes. I told her what they were doing was wrong. That everything we'd shared was real. She claimed we were a lie because I'd never told her who I really was. But... It was never a lie for me. She said that I deserved my punishment because I wasn't human."

"She… She said that?"

Bastian gave a jerk of a nod. I felt a tear slip from my eyes and hastily wiped it away.

"She claimed I couldn't *feel* in the same way humans feel. But I can assure you, Eleanor, I felt every bite of the knife, every slash of the whip, every bone break and reform, every flame, every brand. I felt it all, and it was excruciating. Though, not as excruciating as the pain of betrayal."

"Oh, my God." I couldn't stop myself. My heart felt like it was shattering, breaking into tiny pieces, all for a supernatural I'd only met days ago. Did he think I was the same way? That because I was human, I'd be like the ones who had hurt him?

"I… Bastian, I would never hurt you like that. Never betray you, no matter the circumstances. I know we…" I swallowed. "I know we don't really know each other, but I could never subject *anyone* to that."

His eyes darted away. "Never make promises like that, sugar. Things are different. Times are different. Perhaps not now, but who knows what might have been, hundreds of years ago?"

"I mean it," I said through gritted teeth, squaring my shoulders. "Even if you don't believe me."

He didn't answer. The silence that stretched between us made my stomach squirm. I knew what I had to do—knew and dreaded it, but I did it anyway.

"Luke and I had sociology together," I managed. My pulse accelerated. Perhaps this had been his intention all along—tell me about his past so I'd tell him about mine. It was obvious that his truth wasn't often shared, if at all. That he trusted me with it, that he'd trusted me with so much, was a weighty privilege I wouldn't squander.

His head snapped in my direction, eyes wary.

"He started sitting next to me during lecture. At first, we were study partners. It turned into something more. He made me feel special, bragged to his friends about how smart I was. He'd always been popular among our classmates. I became popular by association. We dated for a year before I realized something was...off. Everything seemed fine, and maybe it was just the honeymoon phase. But the bragging stopped shortly after we became official, and he would say things, little jabs about the way I did stuff, about how his way was the *only* way, the *right* way."

My jaw clenched as I was forced to remember those times, even though they'd never been the worst of it. "It didn't get bad until I started my master's program. The first time he hit me was because we'd gone out to dinner and another man had bought me a drink at the bar. He'd slipped away to the bathroom and hadn't come back for ten minutes, maybe? I didn't know the man, and he'd purchased the drink before I could decline. Luke chose that time to appear. It wasn't until...well, we got home, and he was furious. I told him it was nothing, that he should be flattered another man found me attractive. Instead, he backhanded me."

Bastian went rigid. I kept my gaze fixed on the mat, it was easier to talk this way, to avoid his gaze. "It went downhill from there. He started taking a keen interest in my studies. I was... I don't know, flattered? Desperate to please him? Desperate to make things normal between us? So, I told him whatever he wanted to know. When I started going out on trips with Professor Miller to track down artifacts, things got especially bad. He got suspicious, thought I was seeing other men, so I had no choice but to tell him what I was doing.

"Then one day, he asked me about a particular artifact, Foust's Drum. It's famous, on display in a small art house here in Walton. I told him what it did—"

"What does it do?" Bastian asked, his words measured.

"It..." I swallowed. "It freezes time for a short period, when it's struck. The information varies, but...about ten seconds."

"Huh."

"He wanted it—Luke, I mean. It shocked me at first. He'd always taken a keen interest, but for him to talk about wanting something like that. He'd gathered a band of friends and began planning a heist, to break into the art house and steal it. The humans displaying it had no idea what it did, so security was lax."

I hesitated, cleared my throat, then continued, "The day before the heist, I tried to talk him out of it. He got so angry…"

Bastian sat frozen. I wasn't sure he was breathing. It was like he was spun up, holding on by a thread. "Keep going, sugar. I'm right here. It's all right." The calm in his voice spurred me on, encouraged me to get this off my chest.

"He beat me first. Then he raped me and beat me while he did it. I could barely walk the next day." My eyes filled, and everything turned blurry. *Not again,* my thoughts whispered. I didn't want to think about it *again.*

A low growl spread through the room. The hairs on my arms rose. I glanced about, momentarily shocked by the sound of it, only to realize it was coming from the goblin in front of me. Bastian didn't move.

If I didn't keep going, I wouldn't be able to finish the story. "That morning, when I was supposed to be surveying the perimeter of the art house, I contacted the authorities in secret. I revealed his plans. I… I betrayed him," I said, gasping at the last words.

"You did nothing of the sort," Bastian said.

I shrugged. "The cops showed up and most of his team was apprehended, but Luke got away. He found me the next day and he… He *attacked* me. Dislocated my shoulder, did…a lot of other things." Heat filled my face, embarrassment, shame. "The only reason he stopped was because Professor Miller showed up."

I slumped, hiding my trembling hands beneath my thighs. I felt the relief in that moment like it was happening all over again. That profound moment when Jane appeared, while I was lying there in my own blood and pain. Hearing her voice dragging me back from the dark pit I'd fallen into.

"I think he would have killed me—no, I know he would have, for what I'd done." I started shaking, trembling with the memory.

"Fuck," Bastian whispered, scooting closer, pulling me into his lap. "I'm right here, Elle baby. It's all right. I'm here."

Hearing my real name from his lips brought another piece of my old self back to life. It gave me the courage to keep going. To keep speaking.

"She found me and he fled. But right before he left, he told me that the next time he found me, he'd make sure I wished I'd never been born." A sob rose in my chest. "When I saw him at Vortex, everything came rushing back. I panicked. It's… It's been two years."

Silence fell.

I exhaled, and with that fleeing breath, a weight lifted. My chest lightened, and yet, I still felt a lingering ominous press of tension.

"You're safe here," Bastian urged, voice low. "Nothing will happen, I'll make sure of it. He'll never hurt you again."

I nodded, swallowing back a lump of tears. Why was I so desperate to believe him? Could I?

"You started martial arts training after that?" he asked, distracting me.

I nodded again.

"Good girl." The satisfaction in his voice sent warmth blasting through me. Pride. I was proud that I hadn't allowed Luke to completely ruin me. From the sound of it, Bastian was too. I could hear it in the way he spoke, as he said, "That was the right thing to do. It takes courage to face harsh realities. You made a decision that you were going to learn the tools needed to protect yourself." A hand stroked my hair, petting me. I went limp in his arms, wanting more than anything to stay like this, in his warmth, wanting to be held.

"I got the pendant from Professor Miller," I admitted, my

voice thick with unshed tears. I'd never told anyone but Vivi about it. But I needed him to understand the rest of my story, to understand my relationship with Jane and why things had happened the way they had. "It's an artifact. She stole it from the university collection."

"The university collection?"

"Yes, WU has a collection of sorts. They display a number of old objects throughout the library, historical artifacts, most of them donated. This one is an amulet of protection. Miller thought feeding it Luke's blood would make it nearly impossible for him to find me. And I couldn't leave Walton completely. Vivi was my only support system, the only person who knew the truth. Starting over in a strange city, completely alone? That felt more dangerous than hiding in plain sight in a place this big.

"When she showed up, I was a bloody mess, but some of Luke's blood had gotten on me when I'd tried to fight back. That's what we used."

"Good girl," he breathed against my hair, continuing to pet me.

There was something different about the way he touched me—gentle, asking permission with every movement. Even now, his arms held me like I was precious, not trapped. Like I could pull away at any moment and he'd let me go. After Luke's demanding hands, this felt like a revelation.

"I think Miller knew what was going on long before and was hoping I'd say something. But I… I never did. I was too scared."

"Damn," Bastian said. "I wish I could thank her."

I nodded and my throat closed up tight. "Me too. I mean, I thanked her at the time. But she told me to disappear, that she'd help me do it, that I needed to leave, or Luke would never stop. I didn't even realize she'd tampered with school records until you mentioned it." I shook my head. "She must have sensed something more in him that I'd missed, a bigger monster. He knew I'd blown his heist and he was going to get

his revenge. I couldn't stay at the university and feel safe. So…
I gave it all up. You asked why, the other night. That's why. I
let it go. A small price to pay for safety, I suppose. But I will
always love it—artifacts, their history, it's… It's in my blood."

"Oh, Elle. Baby." The rumble of his deep voice sent warm
shudders through me. "The world is so fucking unfair
sometimes."

"I know." I swiped at another tear before it had the chance
to fall.

"You should never be forced to abandon your dreams."
He rocked me back and forth, the scent of his musk and citrus
wrapping around me. I'd never expected goblins to be gentle,
they had violent reputations. But they were also hoarders, and
fiercely protective of their treasure. Was that what this was?
He considered me his? His treasure?

I should have felt alarmed. I wasn't willing to get close to
anyone after everything with Luke. And yet, a profound sense
of desire spread through me at the thought of being his.

"It's…okay," I managed, pushing my deep desires down
even deeper. "I was willing to do whatever was necessary to be
safe. Whatever I needed to escape him. I was still friends with
Vivian, at least, even though we'd mostly stopped talking
because of Luke." I made a sound in the back of my throat.
"She warned me against him, you know. When we first started
dating. Somehow she sensed something in him, too. Bad
vibes."

Two of the most important people in my life had known,
and I'd been a fucking idiot. Such a fucking idiot. That was
the most embarrassing part of all this. They'd seen what I'd
been too blind to notice.

"I couldn't go to any of my other friends because they
were all Luke's friends. So, I went to Vivian—she'd already
landed her job at the museum. She took me in that night, sat
with me at the hospital as I lied through my teeth to the nurses
about what had happened, then made me move in with her
immediately. We came up with a plan, changing my name,

dying my hair. Moving to West Cross. The medallion was supposed to do most of the work, keeping Luke from finding me. But I wasn't going to take any chances."

Bastian exhaled. "And yet, somehow, he managed to find you."

I swallowed. "I don't know how that happened. Maybe the magic only works for a certain amount of time?"

"Hard to say, sweetheart."

"Do you think he killed her? Professor Miller, I mean? Maybe in killing her, the magic stopped working? Maybe since she was the one who gave the medallion his blood?"

"I wish I knew," he mused, arms tightening around me. His lips came to my temple, a long kiss, like he wanted to rest them there. Silence stretched between us, but at last, he said, "Let me cook you dinner, and then we can head to Vortex. I'll make sure you're safe."

There it was again—that word. *Safe*. Warmth exploded in my chest, radiating outward until my fingers tingled. We barely knew each other, but he wanted to protect me. Our stories, while not identical, were similar enough that a connection had formed, tying us together.

"Okay," I managed, not sure what else to say.

"Tomorrow, we'll practice more self-defense tactics," he added, "since today's got cut short."

I snorted. "Right."

He helped me to my feet, standing beside me. "Elle?" He took my hand, pulling me so that I faced him. "Thank you for sharing that. I... I know it wasn't easy." He licked his lips, holding the bottom one a moment. I saw a flash of silver from his tongue piercing.

"I couldn't not," I said, shrugging, trying to pass it off as less than what it was. "After you told me yours, it only seemed fair. I—" I exhaled. "I'm sorry for what happened to you, Bastian. People are assholes."

He huffed. "Didn't you call *me* an asshole? More than once, if I recall?"

I winced, then gave a nervous laugh. "Right. Sorry about that. I… I was wrong."

The corner of his lips quirked. "Don't worry about it. There are assholes, and then there are *assholes*. I'm hoping I fall in the first category and not the second."

I burst into laughter, the emotion so…freeing. "Honestly, you've graduated from asshole and moved right into the smart-ass category."

"Perfect." His eyes glittered. "Come on. I'm hungry."

He led me upstairs. "I suppose you want me to get all dressed up again?" I wasn't sure why I said it, maybe because I was kinda hoping he would? If only so I could see the way his eyes heated.

"It's your club, sugar. I'd be just fine if you walked in wearing those cute pajamas you keep flaunting. But…" His voice dropped. "I did enjoy your outfit last night. You wanna shower while I cook?"

"You're going to cook for me again?"

"Sure, why not?" He hesitated at the top of the landing, looking down at me.

"Fine, you cook," I agreed. "I'll do dishes after."

He hummed. His expression made me think he was going to argue. But he surprised me by shrugging. "Deal. Go get ready."

He took a step to walk away toward the kitchen, but I reached for him, lifting on my tiptoes. I planted a chaste kiss on his lips. I wasn't sure what possessed me to do it. Closure, for what we'd just been through together, maybe?

For a moment, he held still, then his arm snaked around my waist and he deepened the kiss, until his tongue was stroking mine. I stifled a groan, trying to ignore the tightening muscles in my core. When we pulled away, I was treated to a genuine Bastian smile, dimple and all, before he disappeared down the hall to the kitchen.

21

I walked into the kitchen and Bastian's low whistle greeted me.

"You like?" I asked, stopping to twirl in place. I'd gone for something simpler this time. A pair of light washed denim cutoffs that were frayed at the bottom, black boots, and a cropped rocker T-shirt that skimmed my waistband. Everything was paired with a black studded rocker belt. The T-shirt was mostly for Bastian's sake. I'd curled my hair and left it down.

"No fucking way. You're a fan of Maroon Rage?" He chuckled, shaking his head, his eyes dancing.

"Yup. Got this at their concert last year."

"Shit." He rubbed the back of his neck, eyes devouring me as they turned heated. "Come here, sugar."

I strutted over to him. His hands snaked around my waist, settling low as he dipped his head and kissed me, softly this time. I deepened our kiss, swiping through his mouth with my tongue, trying to memorize the feel of it, the taste of it. What might it be like when he removed the glamor? Would his teeth sharpen? Prick me? Draw blood?

Heat built in my gut. I wanted that—wanted it badly. The

idea of exploring him without his glamor left my fingers aching.

His hands crept lower, to the frayed hem of my shorts. Fingers swept beneath, feather light over my skin. I groaned, pressing my hips against him. With swift movements, he scooped me up and planted me on the countertop. My knees spread and he pressed into me, pulling me flush to him. My head was a little taller from this position. I used it to my advantage, wrapping my fingers around his neck, angling his chin where I wanted him. He growled, the sound vibrating against my mouth. I claimed him, licking his tongue ring, biting on his lower lip, my movements hungry.

I pulled away and said, "You don't have any lip piercings?"

"I do. Just hidden by the glamor."

"Right." I often didn't notice the extra details beyond his pointed ears, teeth, and skin color whenever the transparent overlay appeared.

He tilted my head and began planting kisses along my jaw, down the column of my throat. "I have the rest of the night off," he managed between open mouthed pecks. "After we get back from the club, it should be warm enough for a swim. I haven't forgotten the way you were eyeing the pool earlier."

My breath quickened. "I didn't bring a swimsuit."

He scoffed. "Who said anything about swim suits? This is my pool, sugar. No one comes on my property. We'll have the place to ourselves."

A shiver raced down my spine at the picture he painted.

His tongue darted out at the base of my throat, licking the divot and sweeping upward in a claiming gesture. I groaned. The brush of his piercing made my thigh muscles go tight, flexing against his hips.

His fingers slipped beneath my T-shirt, palms warm against my skin. "I bet you got a whole collection of these cute little tops, don't you?"

"I…" I couldn't breathe.

"Maybe you can model them for me sometime?" I chuckled.

His kisses stopped just below my ear lobe—

A timer beeped. He pulled away and grinned. "Stay right there," he warned, his voice a growl I didn't dare disobey.

Then he busied himself around the kitchen, finishing up our dinner. I watched him, tucking my hands beneath my thighs as he began plating food.

"Meatloaf? You made meatloaf?"

"Yeah, you got a problem with that?"

I laughed. "Not at all! God, it's *so* underrated."

He grunted in agreement, then grabbed a fork and broke off a piece. A tendril of steam rose into the air. He blew on it to cool it, then brought it over. "Open up, baby girl."

A swarm of butterflies broke out in my stomach.

I opened and his eyes fixed on my lips, lingering as he placed the fork on my tongue and slid it out. Flavor exploded in my mouth, with hints of sage and tomato. "Oh mah gah," I managed through the steaming bite. "Delicious!"

He chuckled. "Thought so. Had the recipe since…the fifties? Improved on it here and there."

"Shit, what's your secret?"

"Wouldn't be a secret if I told you…"

"Fine. But I need more of that." I caught my bottom lip between my teeth. "Are you going to hand feed me here, or can I get down and eat."

He laughed. The deep and rumbling sound had my heart fluttering. I stared at him, an infectious smile spreading over my lips. He lifted me down off the counter. In my stiletto heeled boots, I stood close to six feet tall and could have slipped down myself.

We settled at the island and I dug in. Meatloaf and sautéed green beans. My mouth remained too full to speak until I slowed down. "How do you decide what to cook?"

"Just whatever comes to me, I suppose? I do a grocery run twice a week, usually. Grab whatever I'm in the mood for."

"You don't just summon your ingredients out of thin air?"

"Doesn't quite work that way, sugar. They gotta come from somewhere." He took another bite, then swallowed. "I guess technically I could steal it all from the store. But I can easily afford it, so should I?"

"You mean, you've never been missing an ingredient? Like oregano? And just, you know, summoned it?" He threw me a wicked smirk. "Hah! I knew it. So naughty."

"Very naughty. Perhaps I need—"

"Don't you dare!" I warned, knowing exactly where this conversation was heading. I ate the rest of the food on my plate, glancing at the clock. It was 8:45pm.

"You cool with taking the bike again?"

"You mean, no fancy sports car?" I pouted, wondering when I was going to get to take that thing for a spin.

He lifted a shoulder. "We could, technically. You'd be more comfortable. The bike is easier to get through traffic, and if we have to leave like we did last night, I'm not wasting magic to summon a whole car back here. That thing's way too damn heavy to move around. All the horsepower and whatnot…"

"But you could?" I lifted my brows in challenge.

"Oh, I could, sugar. I could do a lot of things. I simply spend wisely."

I hummed. "Reckless motorcycle it is."

Truth was, I liked it more than I should have, especially getting to wrap myself around him.

He scoffed. "It's not reckless. You forget what I am? I won't let any harm come to you."

My stomach dipped. Yep. There he went again making me feel safe. I was finding it harder and harder to keep my emotions separate from whatever was happening between us. He just made it too…easy.

———

Thirty minutes later, after I'd insisted on doing the dishes and cleaning Teddy's litter box, we were racing through Kentwood toward the city. I wrapped my arms around Bastian's torso. Soon enough, my fingers were creeping beneath his black T-shirt. His only response was a low chuckle, heard through my helmet's audio. It made my insides drip with heat.

We arrived at Vortex to find a line snaking around the front. Bastian parked his bike on the sidewalk like he owned the place, and the next time I turned around, it was gone. "Won't someone notice you just did that?" I asked.

"Nope. People aren't too observant, and my magic makes sure they miss it."

"Huh." I pulled off my helmet and handed it over, running my fingers through my loose curls.

"Ready, sugar?"

"Yep."

Bastian took my hand and my chest fluttered. He laced our fingers together as we walked toward the line. My focus zeroed in on our hands as I led him to the front.

"Hey, Tony," I said, approaching the bouncer. Tony was another shifter, tall and broad shouldered, his head shaved, with darker skin and a couple of tattoos scattered around his body.

"Rose, baby girl, you ain't working tonight?"

Beside me, Bastian let out a low, warning growl. Almost as if he didn't like anyone else calling me *baby girl* but him.

Tony glanced at him, did a double take. "Fuck," he muttered, then turned his attention back to me.

"Not tonight," I said in answer to his question. "We're here to see Eaden."

His eyes darted back to Bastian and he swallowed. "You got it. Head on in."

Interesting. If I wasn't mistaken, Tony seemed a little wary of Bastian, afraid even. It made me wonder if Bastian had that effect on the rest of the supernatural community. I was usually too busy being hyper aware of him that I forgot to look at how everyone else around him reacted.

We stepped into Vortex and I kept a firm hold of Bastian's hand. His thumb stroked over mine, calm, reassuring. I couldn't help my eyes, darting back and forth as I searched for a head of blond hair. Would Luke be here, looking for me?

"He won't get close, if he shows," Bastian said, as if reading my mind.

I led him toward the back of the club, then up the stairs and to Eaden's office door, where I knocked. There was a long pause, and then Eaden's voice sounded. A lock clicked, and the door opened.

Eaden's eyes found me first, looking me up and down. "Nice shirt."

"Thanks." I grinned. He was the one who'd gotten me tickets to Maroon Rage as a bonus. He did a lot of little things like that for his employees. It made a huge difference to us.

Bastian's hand tightened on mine and Eaden's eyes snapped in his direction. My boss went rigid, glancing between us, then at our hands. "*Enforcer*," Eaden bit out, "didn't expect to see you in my club. Can't say I'm happy about it."

I frowned. Enforcer?

"Relax, Eaden. I'm not here on orders tonight."

Eaden's jaw flexed. A long silence stretched between them. Eaden was the first to break eye contact, looking down and away. "Well, come in then," he muttered.

I glanced between them. I knew enough about shifter hierarchies, especially with wolves. If Eaden looked away first, it's because he recognized Bastian as the dominant of the two. Interesting…

We entered and shut the door, taking seats at the sofa where Eaden indicated. "Still drinking that shit whiskey, Bas?" Eaden asked, his voice softening as he moved over to a heavily stocked cabinet. Despite the change in his voice, his shoulders were still tense, his posture guarded.

My eyes darted between them. *Bas?* Well, damn. People *did* call him by that nickname. I liked the sound of it.

Bastian let out a dismissive snort. "I stopped drinking that shit centuries ago, Eaden, and you know it." Eaden's eyes darted between us, curious. Bastian shrugged. "She knows what I am," he added. His words were lazy, unconcerned.

"Huh. Guess that explains why you were asking about Micky and some of the shit that's been going down?" Eaden clarified.

"Micky?" I perked up. "What happened to her? You said you weren't sure if she was okay. Does it have something to do with the weird sleeping coma thing?"

Eaden scrubbed a hand over his face, then turned to the cabinet and poured three drinks. He brought them over.

I left mine on the table. "Probably a good idea," Bastian said, noticing my intention to ignore it.

"I don't want to barf if we have to teleport back," I snapped.

"So… This is your personal business, then?" Eaden lifted his brows. Though his eyes softened the longer they rested on me, releasing some of the wariness brought on by Bastian's presence.

"Long story," I said.

"Not very long," Bastian amended, staring at Eaden. "She was attacked outside your club in the alley the other night."

Eaden winced. "Yes. I saw the footage on the cameras after she disappeared. Just didn't realize it was you who'd picked her up on that death trap. Didn't put the pieces together 'till just now. Should have known." He turned to me. "Rose, what the fuck were you thinking going out there in the middle of—?"

"Don't you dare," Bastian warned, his voice a low growl as he leaned forward.

Eaden flinched. He hesitated. "She's my employee and I—"

"*Don't* say another word about it," Bastian warned again, a lingering threat in his words.

Eaden's jaw tightened, but he nodded. I got the impression that no matter how powerful a shifter, he wouldn't dare cross Bastian. That created so, so many questions. I glanced between them. "How the hell do you two know each other?"

"Long fucking story, sugar. Let's discuss what we came to discuss."

I sighed. "Fine. Eaden, you said to come in and discuss Micky with you in person."

"Hmm…" Eaden hesitated, then looked at Bastian. "I take it you're looking into this *officially?*" Bastian nodded. "Right. Well then, I probably don't have much of a choice. A few of my shifters dropped into wakeless sleep earlier this week. And it's been happening since. One or two here and there. It's like they're in some kind of coma—I like that word for it, Rose. Hadn't thought of it that way. Micky is one of them."

"That's why she didn't show up to her shift the other night," I mused, a sick realization sinking in.

"My people didn't find her until yesterday morning. Thought she was passed out at home." Eaden scrubbed a hand over his face. Bastian sighed, leaning back. He kept ahold of my hand. "You going to tell me what fuck is going on?"

"Don't know much," Bastian said. "If Aramis was the only one having issues, I'd keep it quiet. But since you're having issues too—"

"Aramis is having issues?"

"He's the one who pulled me in."

"Fuck—should have known." Eaden shook his head. He'd relaxed a little, but not completely. I suspected it had something to do with having another powerful supernatural male in his space. "If one of our SC reps is involved, then it's more serious than I thought."

"Believe me, it's worse." Bastian stretched out his other

arm, resting it along the sofa. He looked perfectly at ease, unlike the shifter. "Several of Aramis's sleepers were seen at the gala last night, their faces are the ones in the sketches."

Eaden swore. "You're sure?"

"You asking if I'm mistaken?"

Eaden huffed and shook his head. He let out a long, defeated exhale. "I need to make a few calls, make sure I got our people at a secure location."

"Won't matter. Aramis's people are."

"Then how'd they get out?"

"They didn't," I said, jumping in. "They were in two places at once. Somehow."

"How is that possible?" Eaden frowned, glancing between us and his phone, as he began sending off a series of quick texts.

"That's what we're trying to figure out," I added. Bastian glanced at me, lifting an eyebrow. At the *we* part. Probably reminding me that this was *his* case, not mine. I was just along to bounce ideas off of.

"You might want to talk with Caden about it," Bastian advised.

"Yes, just set up a meeting with him." Eaden sent off another text.

"Who is Caden?" I asked, letting my curiosity get the better of me.

"Shifter SC rep," Bastian said at the same time Eaden said, "My older brother."

"Huh." I tangled my fingers in a pink curl, wrapping it around my pointer finger. "Didn't realize you had a brother, Eaden."

"Got two. I'm the middle child."

"And they're both wolf shifters?"

"About that," Eaden said, setting his phone on his thigh, crossing his arms and leaning back to regard me. "Sounds like you've got some explaining to do."

"About what?" I lifted my chin.

"About the fact that you are human, but you clearly know more than you should. How long have you known? Since you started working for me? And how did you find out? Did one of my people run their mouth? They know better."

Bastian released a long, audible sigh. I threw him a searing glare to *shut the fuck up*, turning to Eaden. "I've known all along. And I found out because I can see through glamor—"

"Humans don't have such an ability."

Bastian tensed. I glanced at him in warning before saying, "Trade secret." Then I grinned.

"Fine. Whatever. Keep your secrets." Eaden's gaze darted between us. "Didn't realize you and the *fae enforcer* were a thing. How long have you two—?"

"We're not," we said at the same time, then glanced at each other before looking away, like freaking teenagers. Heat flooded my cheeks. The denial stung more than it should have, and I couldn't ignore the hot disappointment that dripped into my stomach. Saying it didn't sound so bad, but coming from Bastian's mouth? That was a denial I didn't want to hear. I had no right to be upset. He didn't do relationships, especially not with humans. He'd made that clear. Me? I hadn't been in one since Luke, and since I didn't do casual sex, we weren't exactly compatible.

Despite that, I found myself desperate to make an exception. When I looked at Bastian, I wanted him in whatever way I could get him, and then I wanted him ten times more than that, a thousand times more than that. It scared the living daylights out of me. But it was also thrilling and unexpected in a way that made me feel like I was waking up after a long slumber. Like I was seeing my life clearly for the first time in two years.

I swallowed, clearing my throat.

"I think that's all we needed," Bastian said, standing and pulling me to my feet.

"So, just to be clear," Eaden said, looking at me, "I'll be

filling your shifts for the next several days? So that you can deal with…?" He waved a hand.

"Yes, please. I can't work right now."

"Did you *not* hear about her apartment?" Bastian asked, voice pitching low. As if that was explanation enough.

"I did. If there's anything I can do—"

"Don't worry about it," Bastian said, cutting him off. "I already got her taken care of. She'll let you know when she's ready to come back."

I bit my tongue, letting them hash it out. Better to pick my battles.

Eaden swallowed, then took a step back, probably to avoid the aggression pouring off Bastian. "Of course, Bas. Not a problem." Eaden and Bastian held each other's gazes for a long moment. Then they shook hands as we said our goodbyes.

As I walked out, Eaden looked at me, a warning in his expression. "Be careful, Rose."

I nodded, then followed Bastian out of the room. As we made our way down the hall, fingers still twined, I couldn't decide what Eaden's warning meant. Was he warning me about the stuff we'd gotten tangled up in? Or was he warning me away from Bastian? Either way, it felt ominous.

22

———

We didn't linger in Vortex, not even for a drink. For a brief moment, I *did* consider hitting the dance floor. The memory of our bodies moving together made me forget all about what Bastian and I had said in Eaden's office. About how we weren't a thing. Made me forget how disappointed I was hearing the sentiment voiced aloud.

The idea of his body rubbing mine had liquid desire dripping into my core. But then a new thought barged in. The thought of Luke lurking in the shadows, waiting for me to appear. That desire dried right up. I kept my hand in Bastian's as he led me out of the club.

His bike materialized in front of us. I studied it. The sleek build was perfect for navigating city streets. A symbol was etched into the side, up near the handlebars. My eyes narrowed, focusing on it. I hadn't noticed it before. A circle, topped with a crescent moon, and two crossed swords. Eaden's words came rushing back.

Enforcer, the symbol screamed.

I glanced at Bastian. He walked with a swagger that most didn't possess. It's what I found so sexy about him.

He dropped my hand and turned, helmet appearing. He fit it over my head and gave it a little tug. Then his hands drifted down my torso, lingering, leaving a trail of heat. Another helmet appeared and he slid it over his head.

"Let's go," he said.

We climbed on the bike and I wrapped myself around him, my mind immediately jumping ahead. We were going back to his place. He'd mentioned swimming, and the thought of being naked with him in the pool made my panties damp. Was I in over my head? Bastian should have scared me. Hell, he seemed to scare everyone else around him.

Bastian's motorcycle revved. "Hold on, sugar." A second later and we were off.

I wasn't naive. I knew enough about goblins, how the fae used them for their dirty work. Bastian seemed to know everyone. Or rather, everyone seemed to know Bastian. That probably wasn't a good thing. He moved like someone who was used to power, like he handled copious amounts of it.

My brow furrowed. Who *was* he to the fae? What kind of work did he do for them? Why had Eaden warned me to be careful?

These were the thoughts plaguing my mind for the entire trip back to Bastian's house. But when it came into sight, those thoughts slipped right out, replaced with new ones. Part of me hoped Bastian had forgotten his earlier words. The safe thing to do was turn in early for the night. It was nearing 11:00pm. But I was a night owl, used to sleeping late and rising late.

The garage door opened. We slowed to a stop inside. The engine died as the door closed behind us. I climbed off, handing my helmet to Bastian, shaking out my curls. He pulled his off too, and they disappeared. "Still up for a swim, sugar?"

My heart skipped.

"Uh, yeah, that sounds great."

"Great. I thought I'd open a bottle of wine. You game?" I nodded, not trusting my voice. "Awesome, I'll just grab a couple of things. Meet you out back?"

"Yep, sure."

He led me in and split away to the kitchen. I ducked into my room and closed the door, leaning against it, breathing harder than usual. Swimming—with Bastian. I glanced down at myself. My bra and panties were adequate. Maybe I'd just swim in that?

Slipping into the bathroom, I took a few minutes for myself, checking my reflection before heading back out. Bastian was already out back. Electric lanterns that looked gaslit lined the house's back facade, paired with decorative lights that lined the pool's perimeter. The place glowed with warmth.

A sound system trilled the electric guitar solo I knew from *Maroon Rage* in the background. I smiled. He'd done that on purpose. It wasn't too loud. I could still enjoy the crickets and other nighttime noise.

Bastian stood at the table where we had lunch, his back to me. He had a bottle of wine in hand, twisting the opener into its cork. I approached, watching the way his muscles bunched as he worked. A flare of boldness stole over me. I came up behind him, wrapping my arms around his torso, splaying my fingers over his rock-hard abdomen. Still in my boots, I was able to reach the back of his neck. I planted a kiss there.

He hummed, pleased.

"What did you pick?" I asked, leaning around to look at the bottle in his large, capable hands.

"Thought you'd like a pinot noir."

"I would. Good choice."

"You'll enjoy this one. Been holding on to it for a while. Snagged it at a wine auction."

"A... A wine auction? They have things like that?"

He chuckled, pulling the cork free with effortless grace. He didn't slosh any from the bottle like I did on occasion. I dropped my arms so that he could fill our glasses. The red liquid trickled out, pooling up. "They've got auctions for everything under the sun, sugar."

"Right." I swallowed, my throat suddenly parched. He

filled each glass with a perfect pour, not a single drop wasted as he turned the bottle to avoid dripping, setting it into the ice bucket on the table.

I smiled. He liked his pinot noir chilled like a white. So did I.

"Got this one for a steal, actually. It's a six-thousand-dollar bottle, but I practically stole it, for two."

I sputtered. "Two?! You mean, like, two hundred?"

"Two thousand. Told you, been holding on to it for a while."

I gawked, glancing between him and the bottle. This wine would be wasted on me. Well, not entirely. I treated myself to a fifty-dollar bottle occasionally. But I'd never had one that cost more than a hundred and fifty, and that had been a special occasion last year. A gift from Eaden on my birthday. I huffed and said, "I'm gonna to have to tell Eaden I feel short-changed."

He grinned, lifting the glasses, handing me one. "Cheers, sugar."

"What are we toasting to?"

"To forgetting the past and embracing the future. To making worthwhile exceptions." His eyes glittered with meaning.

"To worthwhile exceptions," I repeated, trying to ignore the sensation expanding in my chest as I clinked my glass against his.

I took a sip. Light, crisp flavor exploded on my tongue. I swished it around a moment before swallowing. Then I took another sip. Bastian eagerly watched me. "God, this is so *smooth!*"

"Good, yes?"

I took another sip. There was no chance I'd recognize any of the flavors. I wasn't anything close to a sommelier. But I could tell it was the best wine I'd ever had. "So freaking good. I could get in trouble with this."

"Glad you like it. Thought the occasion called for it, after the day we've had."

I nodded, setting my glass down to unzip my boots. I slipped out of them, discarded my socks, and grabbed my glass, going to sit at the side of the pool. Cool water met my skin and I sighed, swishing my legs through it, wiggling my toes. I could feel Bastian's gaze digging into my back.

After a moment, the sound of his glass plinked on the table. I turned to regard him and caught an eyeful of skin as he slipped out of his shirt. Next came his pants.

My lips parted. Maybe I should look away, but I couldn't. His briefs hit the ground and he straightened to his full height, eyes heatedly challenging me. I didn't stop myself from looking my fill. My gaze lingered on his hardening length. I swallowed, mouth suddenly dry. He was...*huge*. His cock stood proud, curving slightly. I wasn't close enough to make out the intimate details of it, but I saw enough.

For a brief moment, his glamor flashed, giving me an eyeful of his goblin form, which was—

I ripped my gaze away, turning toward the pool. His low rumble skittered over my skin, sending goosebumps in its wake. He knew exactly where my mind was. I refused to look at him. The splash of water was my only indication that he'd jumped in.

I watched him pop up. His wet hair slicked back, unbraided now. The ends fanned out around him in the water as he treaded in place. The pool rippled, but I could still see everything below the surface in a distorted way. Heat prickled my skin, set my toes curling.

My panties were dripping wet, an ache building between my legs. I wanted him—badly. I squeezed my thighs tightly together, as if that would make a difference.

Bastian swam in my direction, stopping several feet away. He made a show of inhaling before a smug smile spread across his face, enough to form a dimple. "Love that smell on you, baby girl."

"You're such a prying asshole," I muttered under my breath, positive that he'd heard my words with his goblin hearing, especially when he chuckled and ducked beneath the surface.

I took the moment of privacy to pull my hair up off my neck, to cool myself. It was no use. I was burning up, tiny beads of sweat forming at my temples. I buried my nose in my wine, taking several big gulps to distract myself. But nothing could distract me from the sight of him swimming around underwater. The tattoos that lined his body. There was one low on his hip that wrapped around to the back of his left buttock. Fucking hell, I was so, so lost.

He popped back up, grinning. "Why don't you join me, Elle? You shy?"

My answering laugh was brittle. He wanted me in the pool with him—naked. I could keep my underclothes on. He didn't have to see *everything*, which would make me look and feel like a total prude. Ugh. I knew he'd seen plenty of female bodies, possibly even males too, if he enjoyed that sort of thing. Someone as old as him probably did. But…

"Shall I turn around first, to allow you some privacy?"

I scoffed and stood, taking another gulp of wine, enjoying its warmth. Then I strode to the table and set it down before stripping. I kept my eyes locked with his as my shirt came off. Then I shimmied out of my shorts. Even at this distance, I could see his pupils dilate, swallowing up the green.

I reached for the clasp of my bra and paused, gauging his reaction. His lips were parted, breaths coming a little faster than normal. I snapped the clasp and let it fall down my arms and onto the pool deck. I was a modest B cup. I'd been a dancer much of my life, so my curves were lean. I was fine with that.

Apparently, Bastian was, too.

I knew the moment his eyes lost the battle, trailing down to my chest. His gaze was fixed there. I slipped my fingers beneath the band of my thong. As soon as it began sliding down my hips, he followed the motion downward with a muttered, "Fuck," that pierced the tense silence building between us. I slipped it off, letting it fall beside my bra, then I walked gracefully to the deep end of the pool.

His eyes branded every inch of my exposed skin. I welcomed the heat, knowing the water would douse the flames. I'd need it, especially between my thighs, to temper the ache there.

Gently bending my knees, I sprang from the ground and executed a perfect swan dive. I heard a distant, "Fucking hell," right before I plunged beneath the water's surface. Cold rushed in around me, tightening my nipples. I let myself sink all the way to the bottom, then gave a powerful kick, pushing up to the surface. When I broke free, I opened my eyes and found Bastian's hungry face, inches from mine.

23

"I think you delight in impressing me," Bastian rumbled. His hands darted out, wrapping around my waist and pulling our bodies flush together. He was tall enough to touch the bottom, but I was not. I practically groaned at the feel of him against me. The contrast of heat pouring off his skin against mine, surrounded by cold water. My nipples turned to painful points.

"Is it working?" My words were breathless. "Me impressing you?"

I tried to keep the mood light, despite the sparks crackling between us.

"I've been impressed since the moment you sassed me in the coffee shop."

"Oh? Not used to women mouthing off at you?"

"Depends on what you mean by *mouthing off*."

I choked and made a half-hearted attempt to push him away. His hands tightened. He backed up until I could just reach the bottom if I pointed my toes. Then his knee parted my thighs, leg pressing against my pussy. I whimpered.

Bastian's mouth found mine, swallowing the sound. I tried to touch him everywhere, desperate for the feel of him, desperate to explore. I wrapped my fingers in his wet hair, searched for purchase on his broad shoulders. When his hands gripped my ass, I brought my legs up and wrapped them around his waist. His cock nudged between my folds and we both groaned, breaking away from our kiss, panting.

"I want to see you without your glamor," I breathed, barely able to formulate thoughts. His hands on my hips pushed them far enough away that his length was no longer pressed so perilously close to me.

"Not sure I want to do that," he said, his voice a warning.

"Why not?"

"Isn't it obvious?"

"Not to me, no."

He sighed. "Sugar, the last thing I want is to frighten you."

"I've already seen your goblin form…sort of."

He hesitated. "It's not just the visible aspects. When I submit to my form, *that* side of me comes out to play."

"I want to play," I quipped, then felt my cheeks flame hot. Really? Had I just said that aloud?

His rumbling laugh resonated low in my belly. "That so? Well, don't say I didn't warn you."

His glamor fell away, like pulling a sheet off old furniture after sitting in wait. His ears sharpened to points, revealing twice as many piercings. His features turned more angular, sharp. A piercing appeared on his lower lip, near the corner of his mouth. His eyes turned entirely black, no white, no green iris. They were also a little wider. His hair, though wet, showed shiny strands of deep green. His skin turned a color of dark aluminum, stealing my breath at the sight of it. And where he held me, I felt the sharpening points of his nails.

I didn't dare pull my gaze from his as I said, "You're beautiful."

He made a sound in the back of his throat, more growl than anything. "I was hoping for dashing, or hot, or sexy…" In this form, his voice was lower, rougher. It sent chills across my skin, made my muscles quiver in anticipation. "*But,* beautiful works too."

I laughed, the sound bursting from my chest before I could help it. Bastian growled, his hands tightening on me, pulling me more firmly against him. The tips of his nails bit into my skin, but not enough to hurt.

"I like that sound," he purred, mouth moving against my ear. My laugh died, breath catching in my throat. "I must warn you now, Eleanor. Goblins are fiercely possessive creatures. We greedily hoard treasure without shame. We are not to be denied. We allow nothing to come between us and that which is ours. *I* will allow nothing to come between me and that which is *mine*."

The pulse between my legs pounded. "What are you saying?"

A long silence and then—"I'm not sure you know what you're getting into, little female."

The next words out of my mouth surprised me. "I trust you."

Bastian blinked, surprise morphing his features. "Hmm. Well, in that case—"

I yelped, as he moved with superhuman speed, wading the couple of steps to the edge of the pool, lifting me up and over. My bare ass came into contact with cement. My breasts on full display. Bastian parted my thighs. His face was suddenly so very close to my exposed pussy.

"Shit..." I breathed. That had escalated fast. He held inhumanly still, looking his fill. His black eyes darted over me, over my folds, like he was trying to memorize what he saw. He inhaled then, drawing in my scent, and heat spread up my neck.

"Now this—*this* is beautiful," he growled. A desperate mew escaped my throat. His eyes finally lifted to mine. "May I?"

My pulse thundered in my ears. I swallowed, then nodded, not trusting my voice. At my permission, his hands wrapped around my hips and slid them forward, slipping me across the wet cement. My thighs parted wider to accommodate his shoulders. A hand came to my stomach, fingers splaying wide as I was pushed back.

"Bastian!" I half yelped, half scolded. I tried to lift to my elbows, to see what he was doing, but the low growl and firmer press of his palm had me accepting. I laid back against the cement. It was still mildly warm from a day in the spring sun.

Fingers pressed at my opening, spreading me wide, immediately followed by the warmth of a wet tongue and—

"Oh!" I jerked as the ball of Bastian's tongue piercing sent a zing of pleasure straight to my core. His hand slid down my stomach, coming to rest low on my abdomen, pinning my hips. "That feels…so good," I moaned, still trying to squirm.

"You like that, baby girl? Makes your pussy come alive for me, hmm?"

A shocked gasp fell from my lips. His words made me blush more furiously than the mouth between my legs. I simply could not respond.

But he didn't expect a response.

His mouth lavished me, tongue licking in broad sweeps. An animalistic growl vibrated against my flesh, eager and possessive in nature. Occasionally it was fractured by words as he said naughty things, sometimes muttered to himself, and sometimes directly to me. A dart of his tongue slipping inside me, rubbing his metal piercing around my entrance, had me tightening. A pause and then—"You taste sweet enough to eat, sugar." My head jerked up to better see him. My muscles twitched, heat searing through my core. The points of his teeth connected with my clit, gently pulling. I cried out, letting my head fall back. Above me, the stars glittered, uninterrupted, blurring together as the pleasure inside me rose.

Bastian worked me until my thighs quivered. I glanced down when he lifted his hand, biting off the sharp tips of two nails. Then his fingers were slipping inside, plunging in and out to the speed of his tongue. "Such a perfect pussy," he purred against me, "I want you milking these fingers."

I squeezed around him.

"Good girl," he said, rewarding me with a long suck against my clit. My breathing turned to gasps, chest arching, fingers clawing at the cement with nothing to hold on to.

The intensity of his movements paused, the world frozen for just an instant. Then his pointed teeth nipped my clit again and I shattered over the edge. A strangled cry fell from my lips, my back arching up off the cement. His hand wrapped around my lower back, pulling me upright while his mouth continued to feast before slowing to a gentler pace.

I whined, my heart pounding, trying to catch my breath. My fingers wrapped around his head, pressing him more firmly to me, even though I'd just come. I didn't want it to stop.

But it did, his movements eventually ceased, fingers slipping out of me. He looked up, a smug expression curving his lips. The sight of them, moistened and swollen, had me tightening all over again. I glanced below the water's surface where I could just make out the gray head of his cock. My breath hitched.

A low, laughing grumble brought my eyes back to his. "Not tonight, sugar."

"What do you mean, not tonight?" I pouted. "You aren't going to let me return the favor?"

"It wasn't a favor. I just took what I wanted."

I gave a dismissive snort. "I seem to recall agreeing."

"Even still."

"That's not fair, and you know it."

His jaw tightened. "When I fuck you, Eleanor, it's going to be harsh and unrestrained."

"That's a bullshit excuse, Bastian. You think I don't want that?"

"You've been hurt before. I don't want to hurt you—"

"You *won't!*" There was something else. Something he wasn't telling me.

"I said not tonight, Eleanor. Do not push me on this—

please." The last word. The openness in his expression, the pleading I saw there, made my chest sink.

"All… All right. But you *will*, right? At some point in the future? Or was this it?" I hated how disappointed my voice sounded.

Bastian ran a hand over the shaved side of his head. "I'm not ready, Eleanor."

That wasn't an answer. I clenched my teeth, trying to ignore the unsettling flop of my stomach at being rejected. A piercing needle of anger hit me. "I thought you were all about casual sex, one-night stands and all that." The words were out before I could stop them.

Bastian flinched, the movement subtle, but I caught it. His mouth pressed into a line, eyes tightening. "There is absolutely nothing casual about us. If I take this further, a single step further, there will be no going back." I opened and closed my mouth. Damn it. He was right. He didn't *do* relationships, and I was too scared to allow myself to fall into another one. I knew even now, after only a few days with him, that if I gave myself to him entirely, it would break my heart to end things. And yet, if I stayed with him, my heart could break just as easily.

"You see now?" he prompted.

I swallowed. "I don't accept this—"

"You don't have a choice. I said I wasn't ready, and you need to respect that."

My stomach dropped. I wasn't trying to *force* him, was I? That wasn't what this was about. I just didn't understand…

"Is this because of the human thing? Does your mistrust of humans, your dislike for them, have something to do with this?"

He shook his head. "No, it's simply that I feel too much for you. If I have you, I will own you. If I own you, you will be mine. I warned you, did I not? I will not relinquish that which is mine."

"I'm not property, Bastian. I'm not a possession—"

"Which is exactly why we cannot go any further. I don't do relationships for a reason. I'm a possessive bastard. I know what I am, Eleanor."

"What about the things we can do that aren't sex? Things I can do. Why won't you let me touch you?"

He gave a frustrated growl, backing up several steps. "Because if you so much as lay a finger on my cock, Eleanor, then I'm going to bend you over the side of this pool and fuck your fucking brains out."

I swallowed. That's…exactly what I wanted. And maybe I didn't mind the possessive aspects that might come hand-in-hand with it. But I wasn't sure I could open myself up to the relationship that might follow. The heartbreak that would assuredly come. Clearly, he didn't want to either—or was afraid to, because of his tendencies.

Fuck, I was so confused.

"Come on. Let's just…swim. Enjoy our wine."

I hesitated, waiting for the ball to drop. He didn't say anything else, so I did instead. "Do you regret it?"

"Regret what I just did to you?" he asked. I lifted an eyebrow, challenging him. "Not at all, sugar. I'm quite pleased with myself for that."

I huffed, then slipped off the edge and into the water. "Fine. Let's swim." And that's exactly what we did.

24

Bastian pulled himself out of bed and spent a few minutes charging up his metals, dumping as much as he could into them before going about his morning routine. Entering the kitchen, he set about pulling things from the fridge and cupboards. He stared at the ingredients, trying to decide what to cook. Eleanor had been upset last night, angry that he'd been selfish. He'd given her the truth. If he slept with her, there'd be no going back.

Unlike the majority of women in his past, for which casual had always been an effortless thing, there was nothing casually effortless about Eleanor. She demanded his attention, pulled at a primal part of his brain that filled him with need, a desire to protect, to claim, even own. In mere days of knowing her, she brought out the worst of his goblin side and the best of his fae side. Of course the one species he'd avoided for centuries had to be the one that fucked with his head.

Waffles—he'd make waffles.

He pulled out the waffle iron and got to work. They'd eaten all the bacon. Breakfast sausage would be good. He glanced in the fridge, contemplating. His mind went back to Eleanor, to what she'd said about conjuring missing ingredients with his abilities. A package of breakfast sausage appeared, wrapped in plastic wrap. He siphoned ten bucks—likely more than what it cost—and put it in the cash register at his local grocery, which probably wasn't even open yet. He glanced at the clock, approaching 6:00am.

His phone went off with an incoming text. He frowned as he read it, sent an answering reply, then got to work. He would've made Eleanor breakfast no matter what had happened the night before, but his guilt drove him to make it extra special. It's exactly how he'd felt the other morning, too. Seemed to be an ongoing theme.

How many more guilty breakfasts would he feel obligated to cook? Not that he didn't enjoy it. He loved cooking. Loved even more seeing her obvious pleasure at eating the food he created. So, fuck it. If he had to make her apology breakfasts for the duration of her stay here, so be it.

Shuffling around in the cabinets, he picked out his favorite dark chocolate coffee, the one she'd had the first morning. It would pair perfectly with the flavors of their breakfast. He got it going.

He was pulling the first waffle out of the iron when the sound of a bedroom door opened, footsteps padding down the hallway. His senses came alert. Her smell hit him first, soft and floral, with hints of the vanilla moisturizer she used, and something else he hadn't been able to place. A lingering undertone of…coffee, perhaps? Whatever it was, drove him wild, and might possibly be the reason he felt more attracted to her than expected.

Speaking of coffee, he kept his back turned and grabbed a mug, preparing it exactly how she liked.

"Morning," she grumbled.

His eyes snapped in her direction at the sound of her sleepy voice. Heat instantly shot through him. "Nice shirt," he said over his shoulder to hide the things it did to him, seeing her in it.

"Oh? This old thing? Some goblin guy gave it to me the other day."

He chuckled, not bothering to hide his smile. She must have laundered it the other day and worn it to bed. Fuck, that made him feel even guiltier for last night.

"Apology waffles?" Eleanor asked, lifting an eyebrow before pulling up a chair at the island.

"Something like that," he grumbled, caught red-handed.

He set her coffee before her.

"For me?" Her face lit up, the sight of which made his stomach swoop. She took a sip and hummed in pleasure as a small smile formed on her lips around the rim of the mug. "It's so good."

He returned to his task, quietly working for a few minutes before he set a plate in front of her. Waffles, topped with powdered sugar and strawberries, syrup, and a side of sausage. Her eyes went round. "Wow, apology accepted," she said, lifting her gaze to meet his. "You're not looking for a permanent roommate are you? Vivi would totally understand. She's a sucker for food too."

Heat swelled between them, mostly because of her expression. He cleared his throat, then turned away to build himself a plate, avoiding her question—it'd been rhetorical anyway, right? They hadn't touched after last night, after the tension had grown between them. They'd simply swam around, finished the bottle of wine, then gone to bed. He hated that she had shut him out, without so much as a peck on the lips when they parted ways, especially when he couldn't get rid of the lingering taste of her in his mouth.

It was better this way, wasn't it? They could use the tension to build a wall between them, to set boundaries. There need not be anything else physical. There was a job to be done, and as soon as he did something about that scumbag Luke, she was free to return home.

His chest tightened. Why did he hate the sound of that? Why did he feel a rising panic at the thought of her leaving? Was it already too late? Had his goblin already added another treasure to his hoard?

His palms grew sweaty against the fork in his hand. She wasn't a possession, an object to be hoarded. She'd made that clear last night, and he agreed entirely, because she was so, so much more. But he couldn't help the way his goblin side felt about that—about her.

They ate in silence. He waited for her to finish the majority of her plate before saying, "Christian texted a little while ago. He said the WU library reported some missing items and wanted me to come take a look."

"Oh?" Her fork paused mid-bite.

"Apparently the staff noticed several items missing from one of the display collections. They didn't think much of it at first. They thought the items were checked out for cleaning or restoration. It wasn't until they couldn't find the extraction records that they filed the report with campus authorities."

Eleanor turned to face him, a crease pulling between her brows. His fingers twitched, desperate to smooth it away, to reach for her. He clenched his hand into a fist and held himself still.

"Also, Professor Miller's badge was scanned for entry after-hours," he added, getting to the crux of the matter, "right around the time the items went missing."

Her shoulders fell as she exhaled. "Do you think she went and picked them up? Before she died, I mean?"

"Nope. The time of the scan was after her death."

"Oh… No one thought to see if her security badge was in her purse when you searched the house?"

"I wasn't the one who did the searching, sugar. But I'm guessing the folks with WBI either missed it or didn't think it was all that important. Christian is looking into it. In the meantime, since I've got some free time this morning, thought we'd pop over and see the list, get an idea for what was taken, and perhaps put some clues together."

Eleanor pulled her lips between her teeth, looking thoughtful. "Most of the items on display in the library were historical artifacts."

"Of the magical variety?" he wondered.

"Yes."

"Interesting. Well then, we'd better look into it, don't you think?"

"I…" She sank lower into her chair. "Yes, I suppose we should."

He frowned. "What? What is it?"

"I haven't been back since…"

Ah. Of course. "Will you be able to handle it? I can check on it myself—"

"No. I need to be there. I agreed to help you."

He hesitated, studying her. "We'll try and make it quick."

"It'll be okay," she said. He wasn't sure if it was for his benefit, or hers.

Given that she'd abandoned her dreams. The fact that she was willing to go was admirable. But after what she'd been through, he knew she was a fighter, that she could handle this. A flare of pride wedged a nail into his heart, making cracks. If he wasn't careful, she'd break it wide open.

25

The Mueller Library was exactly as I remembered it. The familiar atrium buzzed with students. A massive cement stairway led us up to the reservations area. That was where Christian waited, standing with two library employees. They were wearing slacks and polos with the WU insignia on the breast.

"Took you long enough," Christian said, his eyes darting to me. "Rose, right?"

"Yep," I said weakly.

Christian's gaze lingered on Bastian, a question in his expression, but he didn't voice it. "This is Alex and Sarj," he said, instead. Student employees. Alex was heavy set, with pale skin and shaggy auburn hair. Sarj was gangly and darker skinned, a medium brown toffee, with black hair expertly styled. They both fidgeted, glancing nervously between Christian and Bastian.

"Alex and Sarj are going to show us to the glass displays that are missing their artifacts. Gentlemen?" Christian stepped aside, motioning with his hand.

We were taken to the third floor where the stacks began. This had always been my favorite floor. It was filled with academic texts from A to Z. A Mecca of learning. I'd spent countless hours on this floor, curled up on one of the many couches, or at the tables, studying. Now it was just a reminder of what I'd given up. A reminder of the past. Of Luke.

A shudder raced down my spine. Bastian's hand found my lower back, fingers stroking gently before dropping away.

The first glass case was medium sized, empty except for the artifact stand, and a plaque with a black and white image depicting the location it had been found along with information about the item. *The Cauldron of Illoch*, was written in calligraphic letters. Beneath it, a description of what it had been used for, to prepare meals, and the types of people that would have used it. I knew it as *Hayden's Cauldron*, which had been found amid the ruins of Illoch, the temple of rejuvenation. But it was certainly *not* used for eating, if the rumors of its magic were to be believed.

We moved on to several more displays, all of which were items believed to be simple artifacts, of nothing more than historical value, but I knew better. With each empty display, my belly sank lower. Ayla's Bag, Pybalt's Horn, Meera's Comb. The list went on. My limbs turned cold at the last, though. Gideon's Harp. I bit my lip, regarding the empty case, reading the description.

Professor Miller had acquired the harp on one of her archeological adventures long before I'd arrived at the university. I knew she had extensive records about it, had even mentioned it in a class or two, remaining within the limits of human belief.

Alone, she and I had discussed it more deeply.

This was it. It had to be. I didn't believe in coincidences this perfect. I caught Bastian eye. He must have noticed my expression. His gaze darted to the empty display, then back to me. I lifted my brows.

"Well, that's all of them," Sarj said, a nervous pitch to his voice. "Is… Was there anything else you'd like to see, sir? Anything else we can help with?"

Christian shook his head. "I think that's good for now. You

guys can head back to the front desk. We might hang around a bit, if that's fine with you." It wasn't a question.

"Of course," Sarj said, nodding vigorously. Alex elbowed him. They both turned and fled.

"Interesting development, don't you think?" Christian asked, giving Bastian a look.

"I suppose. Not sure how it all ties together."

"Me either." Christian rubbed the stubble along his jaw. Then his eyes darted my way, like perhaps he was too reluctant to be forthcoming in my presence.

I cleared my throat. "Actually, I wouldn't mind perusing the books while we're here. I'll leave you two to…talk."

It wasn't a lie, exactly. I *did* want to look through the books, for one in particular. I wasn't sure if it would still be here. Bastian nodded, said he'd come find me in a bit.

So I left them to it.

The stacks were long and deep. While the entire Mueller Library had been built in a modern style, with floor to ceiling windows, the stacks didn't get a whole lot of light, and a section of the third floor had study rooms that hogged the windows, making the area I prowled dimly lit, as it should be in any proper library. But that was just my own personal opinion.

I ran my fingers along the spines, inhaling. The smell was nostalgic—old paper, binding glue, wood. My grin was wide.

I found the section I wanted, then ran my fingers down the titles. I knew exactly what I was looking for—had studied from it often enough. High on the top shelf, I spotted the textbook with its black spine and gold lettering. *Music: The Art of Sound Through the Ages*. Musical instruments were notoriously favored for magic throughout history.

I reached up, standing on my tip toes—

"Here, allow me."

I gasped and jumped backward as long, pale fingers snatched the book. My hand went straight to my chest. "Sorry, you… You caught me by surprise."

"Ah, forgive me." The stranger turned to face me. I immediately recognized the dark shag of hair, so black it had hints of blue. My muscles tightened and I glanced toward the end of the stacks. The male held the book forward, waiting for me to take it.

"You… I saw you on the news. You're—"

"Oh, right! Forgive me. Marsh Thadur." He shifted the book and reached out a hand, smiling. I stared at his hand, then blinked. The transparent overlay revealing his glamor shifted his ears to points, sharpening his features into fae. *Handsome* fae. Swallowing, I reached out and shook his hand. His grip was firm, and he held on a moment longer than I was comfortable with.

When our hands dropped, he lifted the book and regarded the title. "Ah, interesting. A fan of music? What do you study?"

"I—"

Marsh Thadur's eyes lifted and his expression suddenly changed. There was a presence at my back. My shoulders immediately relaxed.

"Marsh."

"Bastian."

"I see you've met Rose."

"Ah, Rose. She failed to give me her name."

"Purposefully, I'd assume."

"No matter," Marsh said. "We were just discussing her book." He held it forward again. This time, I snatched it from his grasp, clutching it to my chest. His smile widened, the expression disarming, transforming his face into the kind of handsomeness that made me forget what I was doing here. I blinked.

"What are you doing here, Marsh?" Bastian's question made my thoughts sharpen. Helped me remember where I was. Unlike so many others, Marsh didn't appear intimidated by the goblin.

He waved a dismissive hand. "Board of trustees meeting

for the university. All-day thing. Thought I'd get some fresh air. I find libraries so…quiet. The perfect escape." His eyes met mine and held.

A shiver crawled down my spine.

"Well then, we'll leave you to it. Sugar, you ready?" I nodded and Bastian placed a palm at the base of my back, steering me around Marsh. He stayed silent until we reached an empty study room, closing the door behind us.

"Are you okay?" he asked, keeping his voice low.

"Fine, I suppose?" I exhaled, slumping into a couch near the window. "Something about him gave me the creeps."

"Yeah. The feeling is mutual. He's a royal pain in my arse."

"You seemed to know each other pretty well. He didn't look very afraid of you."

"Oh, he should be very afraid. In terms of power, I far surpass him, though we've never had the opportunity to face each other. He knows I'm a threat, but he's also a lot higher on the food chain in terms of status. Fae don't like the threat of low-borns, but they like bastard half-breeds even less."

"I only recognized him because of the news."

"Ah yes. He's a well-known public figure, politically. Supernaturally? He's one of three reps on the SC. He's also hoping to replace Endorian as pinnacle."

"Pinnacle?"

"Every supernatural creature race is represented by three delegates on the SC. Of those three, there is always a pinnacle, a point of power. The other two are supports. Being pinnacle comes with additional privileges. Even though the SC relies on a voting system, it's still a coveted position."

"Huh." I frowned. My gaze darted down to the book and I was reminded of why I'd wanted it. Fae politics were the least of my concern right now. Pushing my disarming encounter with Marsh Thadur out of my mind, I focused on the matter at hand.

Bastian plopped onto the couch beside me. "I take it this has something to do with the missing harp?"

"Yep." I began flipping through the pages. "Gabriel's Harp."

The pages had been combed through so many times, there were finger smudges, pencil marks, even passages highlighted and underlined. History of Music was a popular course in the art history track. Music was art, expressed through instruments, after all. And since my minor had been in anthropological archeology, this course had been one of my top choices.

I found the chapter on various instruments. There was an entire subsection on harps, specifically Gabriel's Harp. I cleared my throat and read the first few paragraphs out loud to Bastian.

While harps have always been iconic throughout music's history, there is none more so than Gabriel's Harp. His harp is believed to be the first "frame harp" ever constructed. Prior to this, harps were shaped like bows and couldn't handle significant string tension. By including variations of a straight forepillar, this allowed for increased tension and higher string counts. Given the early stages of evolution, Gabriel's Harp had only twelve strings. Historians have speculated over this number, in particular.

The invention of Gabriel's Harp came during a time of musical revolution in Europe. Minstrels become akin to celebrities. It was an honor to host one at large events and a luxury to play host for smaller, more intimate settings. Those who could afford to hold private concerts were considered of high status.

The historically famous painting, Harper in the Throne Room, *depicts a minstrel playing for the king and queen of Freyland. Records indicate that this was a recreation, a depiction of Gabriel showcasing his talents, given the portrayal of the harp in his hands. There is a myriad of controversy surrounding Freyland's history during this time period, and this painting is one of the only surviving pieces. Freyland was thrust into a time of upheaval during which, much of its art was destroyed...*

I stopped reading and looked up at Bastian. "I take it you weren't alive during those times?"

He grunted, rubbing his chin. "I'm old, sugar, but not that old."

Freyland was no longer a country—hadn't been for nearly a thousand years.

"But you know something of King Aloc and Queen Neris?"

"Heard of them, sure. Something of a troubled reign of terror?"

I bit my bottom lip. "Right. Yes, and no. After reading about the harp, I went back to the history books and looked up information about their reign. That's what prompted my questions to Professor Miller. As someone who learned to connect various events in certain time periods and bridge the connection with famous objects, I had an eye for that sort of thing."

"Well? What did you find?" He'd angled himself toward me on the sofa, with his arm slung over the back and his knee bent in front of him.

"The king and queen of Freyland didn't always have a troubled reign of terror—as you put it. There was a long period of prosperity, with a peaceful rule and happy citizens. Then… It was like a switch was flipped. Rumor has it they fell into a peaceful sleep for weeks, no one could wake them, and when they woke, they were…changed. Atrocities happened all across their country and within years, it fell, conquered. Then conquered again by neighboring rivals."

Bastian was quiet, thoughtful.

"This harp is known by other names," I finished. "You probably wouldn't have heard any of them. *The Sleeper's Harp* is one of its most prominent aliases. I'm sure you can imagine where it came from? There were others, more obscure names I've forgotten. But *The Sleeper's Harp* was always the one that stuck. I learned it from Professor Miller. She found it on one of her archeological expeditions into Europe. She never gave me the details, but it took a great deal of detective work to track it through history and locate it."

"The Sleeper's Harp," he mused, leaning back. "So, this is it? This is causing magical comas for supernatural creatures?"

"Maybe."

"It still doesn't explain how they can be in two places at once."

"No, perhaps not. But don't you think it's funny that King Aloc and Queen Neris *woke up changed?*" I used air quotes for the last part.

Bastian grunted.

A new thought hit me, one that made a chill bleed into my fingertips. "What if they never woke up at all?"

Bastian jerked forward. "Shit." He glanced down at the book in my hand, then stood. His hand found mine and he all but pulled me off the couch. "Time to go, sugar. And bring that book."

"But," I protested, "I can't take it with us. I don't have a library card. Only students can—"

"It's not stealing if you plan to return it." He snatched it from my hand and it disappeared. "It will be at home waiting for you. I'll drop you off. I've got some things I need to look into."

He kept a tight hold of my hand, practically pulling me through the library. We strode past clusters of studying students, their heads down, noses glued to the textbooks they studied. Those who glanced up and saw Bastian regarded him with wide eyes.

There was no sign of Marsh Thadur.

"You're not going to take me with you?" I whispered. "To these…things you need to look into? I want to be involved with whatever you find! Especially if this involves the harp."

"Sorry, sugar," he said, keeping his voice low. "If I discover anything you ought to know, I'll tell you. For now, I think I got what I need."

"Great," I snorted, rolling my eyes. "I'm so glad I could be of use. How convenient." He didn't answer. "We need to find that artifact, Bastian. Find it before more bad shit happens."

"That's exactly what I plan to do."

I scoffed but said nothing else. Of course that's what he planned. And he intended to do it without me. After all, this was his case, not mine. Given the involvement of a prized artifact, one that most humans had no idea about, I felt I had a right to be involved. I couldn't help the heaviness taking over my body at being denied, the disappointment eating away at the fringes of my mind.

We emerged into the parking lot adjacent to the library. Bastian dropped my hand. Only then did I feel the absence of its warmth, even out in the sun. His shiny sports car waited in the front spot. I smirked. "I told you that you needed a permit."

"That's great, sugar. And I told you that I didn't care." He plucked the parking ticket off the windshield, crumpled it in his fist, then opened his palm. It was gone.

"Nice magic trick, Mr. Magician. That won't make it disappear from their digital records. Trust me."

"Oh? Speaking from experience, are we?"

"Nope. Not once."

I couldn't help my pleased grin. Bastian Croft had gotten a parking ticket. Served him right for being a total ass.

26

Bastian dropped me off with a warning to stay inside, then sped off, leaving me alone with my thoughts. I checked Teddy's food, cleaned his litter box, then curled up with a book. A couple of hours passed before I was seeking out my phone. I had two missed calls from Vivi. I called her back.

"Jeez, Rose! Did you die?!" she asked, picking up on the first ring.

"Sorry!" I said a little sheepishly. "Been preoccupied."

"With that hot goblin guy, huh?" she teased. I rolled my lips between my teeth, contemplating what to say. The silence was telling enough. "Oh. My. God! You have been, haven't you?"

"I'm in way over my head," I admitted.

"All right, spill. I want all the details—wait, did you guys kiss?! Tell me you kissed."

"Ugh." I let a silence stretch out and then—"Yes, all right. We kissed, and…did some other stuff, too."

Her shriek was so loud I had to pull the phone away. "Okay, you owe me details. I want everything!"

So, I spent the next thirty minutes telling her what was going on with Bastian. I glossed over some of the stuff we'd done, since that felt private, even when she pushed me for more. I focused on what had happened during the pool incident, how he hadn't allowed me to reciprocate.

"Huh," she said at last. "It sounds like he's pretty conflicted."

"One minute he's all over me, the next he's all, 'If you lay a finger on my cock, I'm going to fuck you.' Actually… It was pretty hot, but still."

"Wait, he said that?"

I bit my lip before allowing a full blown smile to unfurl. "I think it was more like, 'I'm going to bend you over the side of the pool and fuck your fucking brains out.'"

"Oh, my God!" she breathed. "I don't think anyone has ever said anything that hot to me. Ever."

Muscles twitched low in my abdomen, just recalling how those words had made me feel.

"He clearly wants you, but he's afraid to have sex because he's afraid of getting too close and being all possessive and whatnot. But I gotta say, that's pretty hot. I'm all about possessive dominant men—shit, I mean, the kinds that don't hurt you. The sexy dominance, not like the…"

I winced. "Yes, yes, I know what you're trying to say." We both read plenty of werewolf smut. "Honestly, I thought I would never be into dominant guys after Luke. *But…*" My grip tightened on the phone. "Bastian is different."

"From the little I've heard, he sounds completely different. Rose… I don't think he'd ever hurt you, not like that. Not based on what you've told me."

"I don't think he would either." Somehow I'd known it from the moment I laid eyes on him. When my insides had turned hot at the sight of him. Which was why it was easier to be sassy around him, even during that first moment, covered in coffee. Yes, there'd been a few gut reactions when he'd gotten too close. But I'd pulled myself together.

I sighed and said, "The only problem is, my conscience keeps telling me that my judgment is compromised. That just because I *feel* like he won't hurt me, doesn't mean he won't."

"Well, maybe not in the same way," Vivi pointed out. And she was probably right. There were many ways to break a heart, and Bastian probably excelled at most of them. Sure, he wouldn't lay a finger on me, would never physically harm or demean me, but that wouldn't stop the pain when it came. There was no way things wouldn't end badly between us, me being human and him being…what he was.

"I'm like a moth with a flame." I groaned at the admission. "I know he's capable of burning me. I know it deep in my bones. And yet, I just don't fucking care. For once, I just don't."

"Then go for it," Vivi said. "What if… What if you don't and end up regretting it for the rest of your life? You don't want this to be something you look back on and wonder, *what if?* You know?"

"I know," I whispered.

She was right. I wanted to lean in to the attraction between me and Bastian. To explore it more. Even if he'd pushed me away yesterday.

We chatted for a few more minutes. She filled me in on her sister, and how she was doing post break-up. I warned her not to come home until I'd had a chance to fix the apartment and take care of the Luke situation, then we hung up.

In the wake of our conversation, the house felt too quiet. Too much of what we'd said spun through my mind. Sighing, I went to my room and changed into some workout gear, then took my phone downstairs and plugged it into the sound system.

———

When Bastian hadn't returned by dinner, I took matters into my own hands. I wasn't an outstanding cook by any means, but I could whip up fresh Alfredo sauce, which was by far my specialty. I mean, it was hard to screw up a cream and parmesan base. I prided myself in elevating it with red pepper flakes and fresh garlic. I also found several steamer bags of veggies in the freezer. I selected the peas, then grilled up some frozen chicken breast.

I found crusty sourdough in the pantry that would make a perfect pairing. For a single guy who shopped twice a week, he seemed to keep a stocked kitchen. He'd had everything I needed, and more.

Except, where did he keep the wine—?

The purr of an engine and rumble of the garage door made me freeze in the middle of buttering the bread. I glanced down at the two slices, then grabbed two more. I'd made enough pasta for leftovers, but I hadn't planned on him joining me. I popped them into the oven right as a door slammed.

"Damn, sugar. Look at you. Did you cook me dinner?"

I spun around and smiled, then my smile faltered. Bastian was spattered with mud and… "Is that blood?!"

I gaped at him.

He moved into the kitchen. "Not mine."

"Whose?!" I demanded, immediately thinking of Luke.

"Nothing you need to worry your pretty little face over." He inhaled before letting out a pleased groan. "You made me fresh Alfredo?"

"That depends…"

"On what?"

"Whether you answer my question."

He sighed, rubbing the back of his neck. "It was work stuff. No one you know or should worry about. In fact, someone you shouldn't spend an ounce of thought on."

"Work as in WBI? Or your other thing?"

"My other thing," he said, like it was no big deal.

I hesitated, looking him over from head to toe. "But… you're okay?" Besides the blood and dirt, there were rips in his jeans, like he'd gotten into a fight and someone had used a knife.

"Fine as ever. Even better once I eat."

I pulled my shoulders back. "You're not eating in that state. Go clean yourself up first, it will hold."

"Yes, ma'am." He gave me a two-finger salute, a grin pulling at the corners of his mouth, then disappeared.

I resumed my search, looking for where he might keep his bottles of wine. I hadn't spotted any kind of wine rack. I tried not to think about Bastian going head-to-head with someone dangerous. Tried, and failed.

My nipples tightened to points at the image in my mind. It was freaking hot, the thought of him wielding weapons and his fists.

"Whatcha doing in here, sugar?" I jumped, swearing under my breath as I spun around.

"I was looking for the wine," I squeaked, gaping at the sight of him. He'd cleaned up quickly, now dressed in a black button down, his sleeves rolled up to his elbows displaying his ropy forearms and the tattoos that covered them. He wore a fresh pair of denim jeans. My gaze snagged on his hair, braided back along his scalp.

God, it wasn't fair that he should be so hot.

"You won't find wine in the liquor cabinet."

"Okay, well, I looked everywhere else!"

He chuckled. "Come here, I'll show you. I keep my collection hidden, for obvious reasons."

"Let me guess, because of all the six-thousand-dollar bottles?"

"More like the fifty-thousand dollar bottles. But yes, that's exactly why," he said, throwing me a grin.

All I could do was gape at him.

"Come on." He led me to the hall and pressed his palm against a hidden panel. The wall slid away, revealing a dark staircase. A moment later, the stairwell illuminated with a soft yellow light. He disappeared and I followed after him, descending into an undercroft. "One of the selling points of the house," he said from the bottom of the stairs. "I made some modifications of my own, concealing the entrance and widening it into part of the basement."

I emerged into a wine cellar, but unlike any I'd ever seen. Not even in movies. The walls were lined with racks of wine, floor to ceiling. The shelves were broken up with ancient looking wall sconces that burned with gas flames. My mouth opened and closed as I turned in a wide circle. It was the size of my living room at home, and something akin to an old-fashioned setting. There was even a small dining set carved out of dark, richly varnished wood.

"You like?" he asked.

I jumped. He'd come up beside me. His gaze was assessing when I looked up.

"I love it," I breathed. "What's with the table?"

"Ah, for tastings and such."

An idea came to me. "Do you think we could have dinner down here?"

Perhaps it was a bit *too* romantic a setting, but with our pasta and a bottle of wine, this little slice of heaven would be transportive.

"I think that's a great idea. Why don't you explore while I plate everything up?"

"Okay," I managed. "Don't forget the bread in the oven. I don't want it to burn."

"You got it, sugar."

When I turned, he was already disappearing up the stairs.

I walked through the cellar examining the bottles. There was a glass door at the end. I slipped through—right into a cooler room. A shiver raced over my skin, welcome after the intensity of cooking in the kitchen. No, more like the intensity of being in Bastian's presence. The lights were sensor acti-vated. They clicked on and revealed another collection of chilled whites and dessert wines.

"My God," I whispered. He was a fucking wine collector. I should have caught the hint when he'd opened a bottle of wine last night, but somehow I'd overlooked it, too distracted by the naked goblin swimming around in the pool.

"This looks delicious," a voice called from the other side of the cellar. I turned in time to see Bastian depositing plates piled high with Alfredo, peas mixed in. There was a basket covered by a cloth holding our bread. He moved over to the side of the room and plucked a couple of wine glasses for us. "Any preference on wine?"

I made a sound between a laugh and a nervous chuckle. "Considering you're an expert, no. Something that pairs well with Alfredo?"

"I'll try not to disappoint."

There was no way that was possible.

I took a seat, watching as he walked along his collection, fingers stroking the bottles in the lightest caress. He slipped into the cold room and emerged seconds later with a bottle.

Over at the counter he made quick work of the cork, then poured us each a generous amount. A few moments later, my wine was placed in front of me. The sound of ice slushing and then a metal bucket appeared in front of me too, the bottle propped inside to stay cold.

A cloth napkin appeared in his hand. "Allow me," he said, leaning forward and spreading it over my lap before I could stop him.

He'd thought of everything. My heart fluttered as he took the seat opposite me.

He hesitated, his brows drawing low as if in thought, then he flourished his hand. Music started from somewhere above, the sounds drifting down to us. Classical, this time. "There. That's better."

Now he really *had* thought of everything.

I was in so much trouble.

Bastian inhaled. "Damn, this smells amazing. I'll have you know, I'm a bit of an Alfredo connoisseur."

"Crap," I muttered under my breath. "Knowing how you cook, I'd have cooked something else then."

"Why? Afraid I'll be a harsh critic?"

I snorted. "I'd rather you be harsh than tell me lies."

"Noted. Let's see then."

He twirled fettuccini around his fork. I held my breath as he took a bite. His face gave nothing away—absolutely nothing. He swallowed, then his eyes lifted to mine and a smile spread across his lips. "It's perfect."

My stomach swooped. He took another bite as I managed to find my voice. "I… You're just saying that."

"I told you I wouldn't lie to you."

Instead of answering, I picked up my fork and speared a piece of chicken, dragging it through the sauce and stuffing it into my mouth. I chewed and swallowed, then smiled. "Okay, in your defense, this might be the best Alfredo I've ever made."

"See? And I know my Alfredo. It happens to be one of my favorite comfort dishes."

"It is?"

"Yes, which is why I am so pleased you made it tonight. Thank you. That means a lot. Things got…a little out of hand earlier and I got home later than expected." Something flashed in his expression, there and gone.

I wanted to ask about it but didn't want to pry. Instead, I picked up my glass, now coated in condensation. I swirled it a couple of times before taking a sip. Crisp, light, buttery flavor spread across my tongue. The perfect palette cleanser.

"I love Chardonnay," I murmured, taking another sip. "This is good. Really good."

We ate in silence for several minutes. I devoured half my plate before slowing down. Bastian inhaled most of his. If I'd doubted him initially, the vigor with which he ate changed my mind. There was something indescribably satisfying seeing him eat my food. And not just eat it but *enjoy* it.

"Mmm…just the right amount of spice," he said, leaning back and stretching.

"The red pepper flakes."

"Right, I noticed that. Nice addition. I like adding it to mine, too."

I grinned, butterflies bursting through my stomach. He finished off his glass and refilled it, then topped mine off. Like the wine last night, this one went down so smoothly.

"So, what did you get up to today while I was out?"

"Oh. Not much." I gave him the abridged version of what I'd done, taking sips of wine between my words. He nodded, listening patiently. His eyes glittered with curiosity when I told him I'd talked with Vivi, but he didn't ask about the conversation. Maybe he didn't need to. He could probably tell just by my voice.

Another silence fell before he said, "I think Luke is behind Professor Miller's death."

I faltered, my breath stalling in my chest. I recovered and took a gulp of wine. Then another. It did little to calm my racing heart. "I had the same hunch."

"Tell me your theories and I'll see if they align with mine."

"Luke was always overly curious about artifacts. That's the first red flag—given what we've discovered. He shouldn't have had trouble tracking down Professor Miller. He knew we worked together—probably still held a grudge from that night, when she interfered."

Bastian listened patiently, taking a moment to refill our glasses while I spoke. The bottle was emptied. I watched him set it back in the buckct as I continued. "I wouldn't have suspected him, except that he found me not long after Jane's death, that night at Vortex. But then, with my apartment getting trashed and Peter's body." I shook my head, thoughtful. "That was too coincidental. I wasn't positive until that happened—like a gut feeling—that it was him. But the missing badge? The artifacts in the library. It's too suspicious."

Bastian nodded, his fingers drumming the table. He took a sip of wine before speaking. "So, you think Luke could be behind the sleepers too?"

Sleepers. It was a fitting name, given the name of the harp.

"I mean, I wouldn't have thought him capable of that much, but he always showed a hunger for power, which didn't become apparent until we'd been together for a while. He must be. He has to be." Dread formed in my gut. I clutched my arms against my chest like I could ward off the emotion.

"I hadn't believed the two might be intertwined," Bastian mused, "but you might be right. I received more intel this afternoon—from the vampires. A number of their people have suffered the same sleeping episodes."

Chills raced down my spine.

"How is he doing it?" I whispered. "I never learned how the harp worked. Does he need to play it in the vicinity of the person he wants to affect? Or what?"

"I was hoping you'd know."

I shook my head, a little mad at myself. Mad that I hadn't pushed Jane harder for details. Had Luke? That night when he'd invaded her home? Had he hurt her, forced the information out of her?

My stomach roiled. The pasta and wine turned into a hard ball. I took a deep, calming breath.

Bastian sat back in his chair. "If we don't know how it's used, we are at risk."

"You think he'd use it against us?"

A low growl rose in his chest. "He could have used it against you in the alley that night."

An ache formed at the back of my throat. "Thank you," I whispered. "For coming for me, I mean."

"You're welcome, sugar. I told you I'd keep you safe, and I intend to."

A ball of warmth dropped into my belly. The threat of Luke faded into the distance. Bastian had a way of making things feel less frightening with just his mere presence and reassurance.

He rocked back on his chair legs, rubbing the back of his neck. "We need to form a plan to catch Luke, but I think for now, we table it."

"We?"

"You heard me correctly." My eyes narrowed. "I have a feeling you'll be instrumental in catching this asshole. And anyway, if I could leave you out of it, I would. I want nothing more than to flay the skin from his bones. There's no guarantee I won't. My contractor never required me to keep him alive. So…no promises there." I made a choking sound, something tightening between my legs at the menace in his voice. It shouldn't have sounded so fucking hot—shouldn't have turned me on. "But if he wants you badly enough, then I'll need you."

"You're going to use me as bait?" My eyes widened, the realization sinking in.

"Possibly. Like I said, let me think on it. I've had a hell of a day. I need some sleep. We can discuss it in the morning."

He drained his wine and stood. My eyes roved over his body. He set the glass on the table, waved a hand, and our plates disappeared.

"Thanks for dinner, Eleanor. That was a treat."

"You're welcome." My voice was soft.

"Good night, sleep tight, and close the door on your way out," he added, winking. Then he headed for the stairs, leaving me alone surrounded by hundreds of thousands of dollars of wine.

27

Hours later, I finally crawled into bed with Teddy curled up beside me. I closed my eyes and let my mind drift. Dinner had been unexpectedly…nice.

Things with Bastian had been awkward after our sexual activities in the pool. But after his waffles and then our day at the library, we seemed to have reached a new normal.

Maybe…

Vivi's words played over and over in my mind. What if Bastian and I didn't take this chance? What if two years from now, I was stuck in a loop, always wondering what might have been? What if I regretted passing up the best sex of my life?

And I *would* regret it.

Something curled low in my abdomen, raking delicate claws over my insides. Bastian had already given me two orgasms, and they'd been beyond the best thing I'd ever felt. Better than anything I'd had with Luke times a million. I thought of Bastian in his goblin form, his head between my legs, his pointed ears peeking out. Heat sprang to the surface of my skin.

Not for the first time, I wondered what sex would be like with him in that form.

I knew without a doubt that it would *ruin* me. Utterly. Did I want to be ruined?

A faint sound came from outside my room's sliding glass door.

The back of my neck prickled and I went utterly still. My gaze darted out to the back yard patio. I stared into the dark, taking slow, deep breaths.

After a few moments, I closed my eyes again. But the sensation returned, stronger this time. It wasn't like when Bastian stared at me. It felt…invasive. I had half a mind to throw the covers over my face and sink deeper into bed.

Except, a shadow stirred just beyond the patio. My heart rate ratcheted up. I took a deep breath, gripping the top of the comforter. The shadow moved again. It was definitely too tall to be an animal.

"Fuck this," I whispered. Sliding out of bed on the opposite side, I raced from my room. My breaths came shallow as I sprinted silently up the stairs.

I tapped on Bastian's door before pushing it open. "Bastian!" I hissed.

Shadows swarmed around me and I yelped. They fell away instantly. "Fuck, Elle. What are you doing?!" I caught glimpses of darkness retreating along the walls.

"Don't turn on the light," I gasped out a second later.

Silence, and then he was beside me. I couldn't see much, but he was naked except for a pair of boxer briefs.

"What's the matter?" He hooked a finger under my chin, lifting my face.

"Someone's out there."

He went still. "Outside?"

"Near the patio," I clarified.

"What did you see, exactly?"

"A shadow? Like, a person-sized shadow. I thought I was just imagining things but…"

"But…?"

"It walked by my patio doors, Bastian," I hissed.

"You sure?"

"Sure enough that I'm not freaking sleeping down there tonight."

He exhaled. "Stay right here. I'll be back." A leather baldric appeared across his bare chest. He drew a sword from it and strode from the room.

I stared after him, mouth hanging open. "Wouldn't a gun be more efficient?!" I whispered, taking several steps after him.

"Too noisy. Stay there—the house is safe." I froze, mid-step, then retreated back into his room. I ran to the window and looked out, searching the yard. A moment later, I spotted Bastian prowling around his property. He froze, hesitated, then turned and started off in another direction. After a minute, he disappeared around the side of the house.

My chest pounded as I waited. What if it was Luke with the harp? What if this was a trap?

"*Fuuuuck*," I breathed, my skin prickling. I took a step away from the window, then waited.

It felt like an eternity, though in reality, it was probably only a few minutes. Bastian appeared in the room and flicked on the lights. I blinked, my eyes adjusting to the brightness. It took a moment to really sink in, that I was *in* his room. The sword—a freaking sword—was sheathed at his back. He was in a pair of sweatpants now, but no shirt. The leather baldric crossed his bare chest.

I swallowed hard.

His jaw was tight. His gaze settled on me and he seemed to relax. "You okay?"

"Me?" I all but squeaked. "You're the one who went out there. You didn't find anything? I swear I saw—"

"He was already gone."

"He?"

Bastian stalked across the room to the window, looking out before he turned to me. "I smelled him. That fucking asshole came onto *my* property. Left his fucking scent everywhere."

My limbs went cold. "Luke?"

He gave a jerk of a nod. "He walked right past your patio doors."

My stomach bottomed out. "He could have…"

"No, he couldn't have," Bastian snarled, turning to face me. "A measly fucking human can't break through the magic on those doors."

I opened and closed my mouth. "What if he'd been out there with the harp, Bastian. We need to be more careful. He has an entire arsenal of artifacts now."

"He's a fucking *human*, Elle."

"With powerful artifacts, *Bas*!" I all but shouted. "You need to be *careful*."

He took a slow, steady inhale. "I'm going to find this piece of trash, and I'm going—" He stopped himself, hand clenching into a fist. His chest rose and then fell. "Let's go to bed."

I hesitated, then nodded. As if I could sleep after a thing like this. "I'm not sleeping downstairs tonight."

He nodded, his expression softening. "There's another guest bedroom down the hall. No bathroom but—"

"I'm… I don't really want to be alone right now," I managed, my cheeks flushing red.

He sighed, ran a hand over the shaved side of his head, then jerked his chin in a nod. "You can sleep in here. I don't bite."

Heat shot through me, remembering how he'd made me come with those gentle bites. Poof. Just like that—my fear was replaced by reluctance. I licked my lips, glancing at the bed. It was just a bed—for sleeping, of course. "Uh. Yeah, sure. As long as you don't mind."

A slow smile spread across his face. "You can be my first."

"Your first? Human?"

"No, my first-*first*," he said. "I've never allowed other women into my bed, Elle." He'd been calling me Elle, I realized. "It seems you're full of firsts, for me."

What was *that* supposed to mean? I certainly wasn't the

first woman he'd touched or gone down on. And while I *was* the first human he'd indulged in after having sworn them off, I wasn't technically the first where that was concerned, either. So…first *what*?

Meow.

We both looked toward the doorway. Teddy sat there, watching us.

"No fucking way. That cat is not sleeping in my room."

"Oh, stop. He can come in."

"No, he can't."

"Bas," I whined. "It's Teddy. He doesn't have to sleep on the bed. But come on, he doesn't want to be alone either, *do you, Teddy*?" The words came out in a baby voice. Bastian made a groaning sound and I knew I was close. "Please?" I pouted and batted my eyelashes.

"Ugh. Unbelievable." He stalked across the room, throwing back the covers. "Fine. But no bed, Cat. You sleep on the floor."

I rolled my eyes and slipped beneath the covers. Bastian kept to his side. He propped himself up on an elbow, looking down at me. "You good?"

"Yep. Think so."

He plopped back onto his back and the lights went out. *Meow.*

"Teddy," we both said at the same time. I snickered. "Go lay down, Teddy," I added. Teddy was silent after that. But that didn't stop Bastian from muttering something about stupid cats under his breath. He probably wouldn't admit it—ever—but something told me Teddy was growing on him.

I turned onto my side facing Bastian, then closed my eyes. Sleep felt a long way off. I turned back onto my back, and then a few minutes later, my other side, facing away from Bastian. A soft groan sounded and then hands wrapped around my waist, pulling me against a firm body. "If you don't stop squirming, sugar, we're going to have problems. I can't get any sleep when you're flopping around like a fish out of water.

Stay put." To emphasize his point, a thigh wedged between mine, and his arms tightened, holding me in place.

"Are you… Are you *spooning* me?"

"That's what it looks like," he said.

Just to test him, I pressed my hips back against him. He growled in my ear. "Elle," he warned.

"What? I'm trying to get comfortable. You've got me in a vice grip."

"I've got you right where I want you. Now go to sleep."

I rolled my eyes, not that he could—

"I can feel you rolling your eyes. Stop. Go. To. Sleep."

I snickered. He was trying to sound forceful, but I felt the underlying tension in his words. If we didn't sleep, other things would happen, and he was trying hard to ensure that wasn't the case. Fine. I'd let him have this one. But… I couldn't promise I'd hold myself at bay for long. He'd gotten to have his way with me, and I had yet to have my turn.

I took a deep breath, trying to calm the emotions swirling through me. Bastian's arms were warm around me. Despite being nearly pinned, I felt safer than I had in…as long as I could remember. I might have had a fancy techy-magical security system around the house, but around my body, I had an even stronger protection. And in this moment, it felt like nothing could possibly touch me—not even Luke.

28

S oft sleek fur made Bastian's fingers twitch. He stroked, calmed by the feeling. A comforting scent flooded his nostrils. The muscles low in his abdomen clenched and unclenched, an ache building in his hardened cock.

His hand moved again, stroking—his eyes flew open. "Fucking Teddy," he hissed, jerking his hand back. A soft giggle wrapped around him, the most beautiful sound he'd heard in a long time. A sound he wouldn't mind waking up to on a daily basis. His cock twitched and he shifted to ease the ache, only to press it more firmly into a soft backside. Sensation erupted, skittering across his skin, straight to his fucking toes. He jerked his hand away from Teddy and pulled her in closer. Pressing himself to her everywhere.

"I think he's growing on you," said the feminine voice beside him. A woman. There was a woman in his bed. His goddamn bed!

Not just any woman, Eleanor.

A low, desperate growl built in his chest. He nuzzled against the soft skin in front of him, letting his lips brush across the back of her neck. Her breath hitched and warmth exploded across his chest at that sound—the effect he had on her.

It left him ravenous.

"Bastian," she gasped, shimmying her hips against his cock.

"Fuck," he breathed, meeting her movements with his own, grinding against her as he teased her neck with his teeth. His hand slipped beneath the blankets, finding its way beneath her pajama top. He palmed her breast then hesitated, waiting for her reaction. She pushed her chest forward into his hand so he continued, still grinding against her.

A low moan rose from her throat.

She sounded so *desperate* for him. A primal switch flipped in his brain and he lost control of his glamor. It melted away and the goblin side of him emerged in full force. He nipped along the skin of her neck, then opened his mouth and dragged his tongue over her, all the way to her hairline, an act of claiming, covering her in his scent. A cry fell from her mouth. He did it again, licking at her like a depraved animal.

The scent of her arousal—spicy with that amplified hint of coffee he went wild for—exploded around him. He groaned, his cock throbbing. With one arm wrapped around her shoulders, he made use of the other, slipping it down her stomach, to the waistband of her pajama pants. He hesitated, waiting.

She could very well deny him—especially after what had happened last time.

"Yes," she breathed, backing into him harder. "Yes, please," she begged. He lost it. His claws had grown back from the other night, so he put his hand to his mouth, biting down and ripping away the first two. Then he slipped his hand down between her thighs, right to her slick pussy.

"Fucking hell. Baby girl, you're so—"

"I know—I *know*. Please, Bastian. I need you."

"I know, sweetheart. I got you." And he did. He wanted to —have her, that was, and give her everything she needed. Everything she deserved. Specifically, he wanted to make her scream his name in the throes of passion. Over and over.

He pressed his palm against her clit, working in circles, careful not to scratch her with his remaining claws. She was so delicate, he wouldn't dare hurt her like that. She mewed in response, her hips rocking more chaotically. He sank a finger into her, and then a second. The sensation of her wet warmth made him imagine all sorts of wicked things. Particularly, exactly what that wet warmth would feel like tightening around his cock.

His mouth went for her ear. He latched on and pulled. She jerked and her muscles tightened. His name fell from her lips, garbled and breathless as she came, gripping his fingers, spasming around them. A whimper followed and her scent shifted, satisfaction mixing with the lingering spice of her arousal. It was fucking *intoxicating*.

Her hips stilled.

But this wasn't—he wasn't—it wasn't *enough*. Not even close. He needed more.

Teddy yowled, dislodged, as the blankets were ripped away. Bastian fumbled at Eleanore's waistband, dragging her pajamas and panties off in one swift movement. She gasped at the sight of his true form, her pupils dilating with want. She'd seen him like this before, but never *quite* like this—never wild with need. Never hovering over her with such raw hunger.

He could see all of her now, sleep tussled hair, flushed skin. Flushed for *him*. Her chest rose and fell in rapid bursts. The after-effects of her orgasm left her glowing. An orgasm *he'd* given her.

His goblin purred with satisfaction. *He could give her so, so much more. Worship her. Covet her. Keep her close. Never let her go—*

Pushing his possessive thoughts aside, he parted her thighs, eyes locked on her pussy, the beautiful sight of it glistening and bared for him. His restraint snapped and he dove between her legs. The taste of her flooded his mouth. He groaned, lapping at her. She would be especially sensitive right now.

"Oh, *fuck*," she cried. "Fuck, Bastian. I... Please. Please let me touch you. *Please…*" He stilled. "Please, I'll regret it forever if you don't let me."

An invisible fist wrapped around his heart, squeezing, clearing away some of the goblin haze. He didn't move, swallowing against the sudden dryness in his throat. Giving himself a moment to process the raw want in her voice, he pressed his face against her, but didn't speak.

"Please," she said again, this time softer.

Mine. His brain cried. *Mine.*

How could he deny her? How could he keep her from what she truly desired? She was his, and with that came certain…obligations, including that of her happiness. Ensuring she got everything she wanted.

With a frustrated growl, he pushed himself away from her pussy, scrambling from the bed. He removed his lounge pants before thinking better of it, letting them fall to the floor. A small, feminine gasp had him watching her, watching her reaction while she took him in. Her gaze lingered on the metal piercing at the base of his shaft, and her pupils dilated further. This was different from the other night in so many ways. Here, he was more exposed, caught in the heat of his arousal and desperation, unable to hide what he wanted—no, *needed.* His cock bobbed, almost beating out an accompanying rhythm to his heart.

She came up on her elbows, tongue darting out to wet her lips. Her eyes were fixed on his length, slightly widened and unblinking. "I… Can I taste you?" She asked. At last, she brought her gaze to his.

A shiver raced down his back, radiating straight to his extremities. The sound of her question, soft and tentative, unbound him. "Only if you're okay with me fucking your mouth the moment your lips wrap around me."

She nodded, the motion abrupt. The effect he had on this little female… *Fuck.* He felt powerful—more powerful than his magic made him. A profound sense of responsibility settled over his shoulders. She was his—no matter how much he tried to deny it. The way his chest—his whole *heart*—reached for her, desperate to latch on, to claim her, to own and keep her, to hoard her away like the precious jewel that she was, pink hair and all.

"I'm okay with that," she said at last. "I…" She exhaled, falling back onto the bed. "I haven't been properly fucked in a long time, Bastian."

His world crumbled away and he snapped.

With fluid movements, he bounded across the bed for her, took her mouth in a hungry kiss, his tongue moving against hers. She let out a surprised squeak before relaxing against him. His pointed teeth weren't so sharp as to cut her.

A gentle hand pushed at his shoulder, a request. He rolled onto his back, dragging her with him. She straddled his chest, leaning over to lay kisses along his throat. Every one made his heart beat faster. Made his breaths come faster.

Her hair tickled his skin, sent shivers racing over him.

He watched with heavy lids, one arm propped behind his head, as she made her way down his body. She used the same focus on him that she used while dancing, each movement sinuous and graceful, from the placement of her arms to the way she tilted her head, the slope of her neck.

She settled between his thighs and her warm palm found his length, wrapping around him. His abdomen clenched. Her fingers brushed over the metal piercing and she hummed in appreciation, eyes flicking up to meet his with curiosity and heat. His lips twitched before he pressed them into a tight line. Mostly to keep from crying out. He'd never been vocal in bed —it wasn't his thing. But damn, he was about ready to moan as she stroked him with a firmness that had his balls tightening.

He'd imagined this multiple times over the past few days, imagined it was her hand instead of his that he fucked in the shower. He thought he'd done a good job of it, but this? This was a thousand times better.

"Eleanor," he bit out—a warning.

A mischievous smile—so fucking mischievous—stretched across her lips. "What's the matter, *Goblin?* Can't control yourself?"

He tutted. "My control is unparalleled. Usually." His brain was short-circuiting, his thoughts fracturing.

She lifted an eyebrow, stroking him up and down again. "But not this time?"

"You difficult female," he growled, his voice a deep rumble. Her pupils blew wide and she caught her bottom lip between her teeth. She was so fucking sexy—and entirely his. "I know exactly what you're doing."

"Oh?" She bent forward and her tongue darted out, licking away the bead of precum seeping from his tip. His hips jerked upward, the sensation sending shivers through him. "Well then. Let's see how long it takes for that *unparalleled control* to snap, hmm?"

She fell upon him then, her mouth wrapping around his cock, swallowing him. His jaw wrenched open and a loud, uncontrolled cry burst free. Warmth and pleasure spread through his center, racing up his spine, up his neck, burrowing into his brain. His chest heaved and he tried—oh, yes, he tried so hard—not to slam his hips upward again. Tried and failed. His fingers found that beautiful cotton candy pink hair, tangling in her tresses.

He'd warned her, hadn't he? And she'd known what she was getting into. So…

He fucked her mouth, rolling his hips as she took him so well, swallowing him down against the back of her throat. His female was an absolute *pleasure.* Why had he withheld himself for so long? From this? From her?

Tiny sounds came from her throat, vibrating through his cock. Sounds of pleasure. She was enjoying this. He shuddered against her, overcome with sensation. His balls tightened. He tried to push back against that welling feeling. But her teeth gently grazed upwards along the length of him, biting, just rough enough that—

He came apart, his seed rising up, spilling out in hot waves as his cock spasmed. He groaned her name, no longer caring for the sounds that he made. She swallowed him down, his female. Heat spread through his chest, radiating outward like charges of electricity, traversing his veins, straight to his extremities. It swept over him, dousing him, *changing* him.

Something fundamental shifted in his brain—something he'd never felt.

Her tongue continued to lap at him, cleaning every last drop. Then she pulled away. The mess he'd made of her was sublime.

When her eyes found his, she wore a crooked smile on her face. A smile he'd never seen before. A smile just for him.

Seeing it, *feeling* it—everything clicked into place. He swallowed, mesmerized, unable to tear his gaze from her, this beautiful little female who had ensnared him so fully.

Fear pierced through his post-orgasm haze as the realization sank in. There was no question now, who she was, *what* she was to him. Which meant he also knew with absolute certainty there would be no turning back. Not now. Not ever.

29

I stared at Bastian, my chest swelling with smug satisfaction. He looked at me with wide eyes, his breaths coming in rapid bursts. I'd never felt so *worshiped* with that gaze. No one had ever looked at me like this.

"Well," I managed, running a finger around the edges of my lips like I was fixing lipstick, cleaning up the mess he'd made of me. "So much for your unparalleled control."

A low, warning growl lifted into the air, setting the hairs of my arms on end, sending shivers of delight down my spine. I backed up on my knees, unafraid, when I probably should have been. He tracked the motion, sitting up. I backed up a little further. He seemed to lean toward me, like a predator tracking prey, like he knew what I intended and was anticipating my movements.

He hadn't lied. He'd fucked me—thoroughly. My jaw would be sore. But none of that mattered. I ached for him, my arousal slicking my thighs. The orgasm he'd given me had done little to temper this fire. But instead of giving in, I had the sudden urge to see how far I could push him.

In a graceful sweep of motion, I slid off the bed and stood. His movements were inhumanly swift as he followed after me. "Eleanor," he warned, speaking through clenched teeth. "Where you going, baby girl?"

My pussy fluttered. The question, the way he said it, the animalistic wickedness that simmered beneath his surface unnerved me. This was Bastian at his basest level. If I ran from the room, he'd chase after me. He'd tackle me on the stairs and claim me entirely.

Anticipation and deep longing welled up inside me, all warring together into a potent cocktail of emotion—

A shrill chime fractured the silence. We both froze, our eyes locked. The ringing continued. His phone.

I lifted my eyebrows in question.

"You think I'd let you get away so easily, little female?"

Shivers raced across my skin. My eyes darted over the creature before me. How much was Bastian and how much of him was his goblin? I really wanted to find out.

My tongue darted out, licking my lips and his eyes traced the motion. The phone stopped and silence followed. Then it rang *again*. He growled, annoyance morphing his features as he glanced over at the nightstand. I used the brief distraction to dart away and slip through the door, closing it behind me before I raced down the stairs, slipped into my room, and locked the door.

I leaned against my door, nearly gasping for breath. I wasn't entirely sure why I ran. Yes, I liked teasing him. But…it was more than that. What we'd shared—I needed a moment to cool down. To process.

And yet, I also wanted him to *claim* me. I was ready for it, had been ready since last night, since seeing him race out of the bedroom with a massive sword in hand. But I was also overwhelmed. The way he'd looked at me after coming, like I was the only woman on the planet for him, like no one had ever given him what I had…

It left my heart swollen to near bursting.

I frowned, listening for any sound from upstairs. There was nothing but silence now. The phone had stopped ringing

—he must have answered it. As the minutes ticked by without any footsteps on the stairs, my stomach sank. Whatever that call was about, it had been important enough to pull him away from this. From us. I caught my lip between my teeth, chewing nervously. Maybe it was better this way? Maybe we both needed time to think about what had happened between us?

Yes, that was probably for the best. Nodding to myself, I strode across the room and closed myself in the bathroom.

I emerged clean and showered, dressed in yoga pants and a T-shirt that I knotted at my belly button, revealing a strip of exposed tummy. I hesitated, listening. There was activity in the kitchen, so I went there. Bastian was pouring coffee into a travel mug, capping it off. He was dressed in his usual attire of dark jeans and a black T-shirt that was tight enough to show every line of his muscular frame. He must have had a hundred of them.

No complaints here.

He turned. His eyes landed on me, sweeping me from head to toe. His pupils dilated, hand tightening around his cup, making his rings more stark against his tattooed fingers. "Gotta head into work, sugar. Need you to stay here and stay put. Don't leave the house."

"Oh." My lips pressed into a tight line.

"There's coffee and plenty else in the pantry. Toast, oatmeal, or whatever you feel like eating—"

"Is it Luke?" I asked. "Did something happen? The phone call…"

His body tightened. A dark expression crossed over his features at the mention of Luke. "Not quite sure. But I'll know soon enough. I gotta go."

Suddenly, my ribs felt too tight for my body, too tight to breathe. Was he keeping something from me? Why did this feel like he was shutting me out? Why, after what we'd shared?

"Right. Okay."

His brows drew together. He strode over and wrapped an

arm around my waist, pulling me close. My breath hitched, muscles immediately relaxing beneath his touch. "We're not done, sugar. Not even a little bit. This morning? It isn't over." Then he kissed me, his mouth hot and coffee flavored. I groaned, going limp in his arms. His tongue caressed mine, the bite of metal sending sparks straight to the back of my throat.

I was instantly wet again.

He inhaled and pulled away, then pressed his forehead to mine. "Fuck," he breathed. "I'll never tire of that scent on you."

I blew out a breath, my shoulders dropping.

"Gotta go." He said it like he was reminding himself, not me. Then he gave me a chaste kiss on the lips. "Stay here. I mean it."

I nodded, gazing after him as he retreated to the garage. His truck revved, followed by the rumble of the garage door, then silence. I took a deep, settling breath.

First things first. Coffee. I went to the coffee maker. Everything I needed was already sitting out. The extra large mug I loved, the cream and brown sugar. It was a thoughtful gesture I hadn't anticipated. One that made my eyes suddenly cloud with tears. Everything I was feeling for this male—it was intense. A small watery smile crept to my lips. I loved his thoughtfulness. It caught me off guard at the smallest moments.

I prepared my cup then went to sit at the island, staring at the kitchen, listening to the silence press in around me. Having this much time on my hands wasn't something I was used to. My normal routine kept me busy—working at Vortex into the early hours, sleeping away the mornings, filling afternoons with martial arts, drop-in dance classes, or chores. Books on my e-Reader when time allowed. Then back to work to do it all over again.

Here in Bastian's house, I felt almost…lost.

His downstairs gym was great, but it wasn't the same as

attending classes downtown. Perhaps I could do a little dancing downstairs too, work on my flexibility. But it still wasn't the same as dropping in for a class.

Taking a deep breath, I let it out slowly. There was also the matter of my apartment. Days had passed with everything sitting in disarray, broken and scattered—just like my life right now. As nice as Bastian's house was, nothing compared to my own things, my comfort, the freedom to come and go as I pleased.The little slice of paradise I'd made for myself. My bedroom with its neon pastels, beautiful art, and creature comforts.

Several gulps of coffee later, I sighed. Salted caramel. Regular coffee would never cut it again—once I moved back home, whenever that would be, an entire case of this brand was going on my shopping list. A small laugh escaped me. Bastian was such a coffee snob. *And* a wine snob. He was so many things I hadn't expected, just looking at him. The more I got to know him the better I liked him. The kind of like that was becoming dangerous. Because I knew he wasn't one for attachment, and if I let my heart latch on…this was going to become problematic.

I spent the entire day keeping busy, if only to stay out of my head. I checked my phone. I went downstairs to work out. Checked my phone again. Did some laundry and tidied whatever I could, mostly to avoid the fact that there was no word from Bastian. Then I settled in to read.

It was early evening. Teddy was curled on my lap, soundly sleeping, when the rumble of the garage announced Bastian's return. My heart hitched. I glanced down at myself, then back at my e-reader.

A door slammed. "Eleanor?"

"In here." My eyes fixed on the living room doorway.

He appeared. A sigh whooshed out of me as I checked him over. No blood today, but his expression was tight, his lips pinched. His shoulders relaxed a measure at the sight of me and I liked that, perhaps too much.

"Still here," I teased. "I didn't go anywhere, just like you asked."

He gave a jerk of a nod, then crossed the room and poured a drink, coming to sit at the couch. He swirled it, staring into it, but didn't lift it to his lips. My stomach hardened. "Long day at the office?"

"You could say that." He knocked it back, then leaned back against the couch. His muscles were rigid. "This cannot continue. It needs to end."

A sour taste filled my mouth. "End?"

"Yes. It's gone on long enough. We need to get this piece of shit. Quickly."

"*Oh.*" I set my e-reader aside and buried my fingers in Teddy's fur. It didn't stop their relieved trembling. "Right."

He cocked his head to the side. The corner of his mouth twitched.

"What'd you think I meant, sugar?" I didn't answer. "Ah. You thought I was talking about us. You and me." Still, I didn't answer. "No, there's no end for that—not at this point." He rubbed the back of his neck. "I haven't been able to escape the smell of you burned into my nostrils, the memory and taste of you on my tongue. My fucking cock has never ached so much. You've kept me in a constant state of frustration. If I don't pin you to the wall and fuck you soon, I'm going to lose my shit."

My lips parted. No one had every talked to me like this. This...dirty. This direct.

"I warned you, Eleanor," he said, voice dropping low. I couldn't tell if he was frustrated. It sounded like he was. "I warned you what would happen." There was a flicker as his glamor wavered, like he was fighting it. Fighting for control.

If he wanted me this badly, why was he holding back?

He groaned and shook his head. The tension in the room evaporated with that one sound. Setting his empty glass on the wooden tray, he crossed his arms and leaned back to regard me. "A handful of days—that's all it took."

"For what?"

"It's time for you to call Eaden," he said, side stepping my question. "Get yourself on the schedule. You're working every night for the foreseeable future until I can get my hands on Luke fucking Portman. We can go by your apartment tomorrow, clean things up. The sooner you're back at Vortex, pretending everything is normal, the easier it will be for me to catch him."

I went rigid. The whiplash had my mouth opening and closing. "You really want to use me as bait? You weren't kidding?"

"I wasn't. If Eaden has a problem, he can come to me. Get yourself on the schedule."

I swallowed. "This is your plan, then? I don't have a choice?"

"The mayor is severely wounded. He's in critical condition. Might not pull through."

I froze. "What?"

"Someone tried to murder him."

My eyes widened. "*What?!*"

"There's no proof that it was Luke, but…" He blew out a breath. "I don't think it was a coincidence, do you?"

"But… Luke's using the harp to put people to sleep, not to murder the mayor."

"And yet, he was capable of killing Professor Miller and your neighbor. Presumably, so that he could get his hands on the harp in the first place. And then we have the sleepers. Some of whom were seen at the mayor's gala the other day. They were used to kill a number of people. How do you think the mayor was handled?"

"I…" I pressed my fingers into my eyes, then rubbed at my temples, trying to make sense of this mess.

"Luke might be too weak to kill supernaturals, being human and all, but he can certainly use other supernaturals to kill for him."

"How… How many has he used the harp on?"

"Hard to say. From the intel I've gathered, he's got at least twenty people under his control now?" I made a choking sound. "This has to end, Eleanor."

"But..." My hands started to shake as my pulse thundered in my ears. I knew what Luke was capable of. I'd suffered through it firsthand. Now he didn't just have his fists. He had powerful supernaturals under his control. The thought of Bastian facing that—facing him...

"If you go after him, Bastian, he'll use it on you. You can't."

"I can, Eleanor. I'm decided on the matter. Now, go call Eaden. *Please*." He used the last word like an afterthought, to placate me.

I struggled to make my limbs move. I hated the truth, but Bastian was right. If this was Luke, he needed to be stopped. And no matter who went against him, there was risk. Maybe Bastian was the best person for the job—more equipped than most. So...why did I feel a crippling sense of dread at the thought?

30

Bastian led Eleanor into Vortex. He kept a hand against her lower back, his fingers itching to creep beneath the hemline of her top. "I'll be around, sugar. You do what you need to do. Business as usual, like we discussed."

"Right." She'd been tense all evening. Even now, her muscles were bunched beneath her uniform. She wore black slacks, a black button down, and a deep purple blazer tailored to fit her curves just right.

He leaned down, his lips brushing her ear. "He won't lay a finger on you, baby girl. Even if he's here. You'll be safe."

She bit her lip, obvious nerves pouring off her.

The soft waves of her pink hair tickled his cheek. "Do you trust me?" Part of him was afraid to know the answer.

"Yes." Her throat bobbed.

"Good." His shoulders relaxed. "Now, have a good shift." He let his hand slide down to the curve of her ass, gave it a gentle squeeze, then smiled at the sound of her hitching breath. She threw a sassy glare at him then sauntered off.

The gold ring he'd given her still circled her finger. He could use it to warn her, if necessary. The vantage point he selected up on one of the balconies made it easy to track her pink hair as she wove through the growing crowd, tray in hand, delivering drinks.

He watched, eyes transfixed, as she smiled and spoke to a group of customers. One of them, a tall male, said something. She threw her head back and laughed. His gut tightened and heat burst through him. He forced the jealous feelings aside, pushed them down deep, and did what he needed to do. His fucking job.

He knew the moment he'd decided on this plan, it wasn't going to be easy. If circumstances were different, he'd have tied Eleanor to his bed for the next week and claimed her thoroughly. Claimed her the way his instinct demanded. Instead, he was stuck watching her give her attention to others during the most volatile time in his life.

It was unlikely that Luke would show. Still, he needed to take the opportunity, just in case. If it wasn't tonight, eventually word would spread that Eleanor had returned to work. He'd come. Someone stupid enough to go traipsing around a goblin's property was stupid enough to come looking.

"Do I want to know why you're lurking in my club, *Enforcer?*" Eaden appeared beside him, keeping to the shadows. He offered a low, warning growl. His only answer. "Work business, then? Because you haven't taken your eyes off her."

"It's none of your concern, *Shifter.*"

"My employees are my concern, *Goblin.*"

"She's not yours," he bit out.

"Whether you like it or not, she's mine to—"

"No," he hissed, rounding on Eaden. "She is *mine*. She works for you—and probably not for too much longer, if I have any say. But she *belongs* to me." The words were out before he could stop them, and they revealed too much. This was what he'd tried to warn Eleanor about—this side of him.

Eaden wasn't slow. The shifter saw the words for what they were. He inhaled, nostrils flaring. Sudden realization passed over the shifter's features. He backed away a step and nodded.

"Keep her safe, then, Bas. And let me know if you need anything." With that, he was gone.

The next six hours passed painfully slowly. Bastian's muscles were aching and tense. Every new interaction between Eleanor and her customers had him fighting the urge to jump from the shadows and interfere. His eyes darted to every face, every head of shaggy blond hair, searching. Luke did not appear. He wasn't sure if he should be furious, or relieved.

When last call was announced, the club's patrons began filtering out. Then the music died down, and the remainder of lingerers were ushered from the building by Eaden's bouncers. They'd given him one look and steered clear, leaving him to the shadows where he waited as Eleanor did her closing duties and side work.

When she emerged from behind the bar, untying her apron and hanging it up, he crept out. She stood speaking to one of the other servers. Both their eyes fell on him and her co-worker's widened; she elbowed Eleanor.

"All done, sugar?" he said at the same time Eleanor whirled to face him.

"Oh. Bastian, this is Kaylee. Kaylee, Bastian. Kaylee is one of my friends," she added, by way of explanation.

"Nice to meet you, Kaylee." He held out a hand, which he didn't usually do around skittish females. Kaylee eyed it for several moments, swallowed, then tentatively reached forward. He gave her a gentle shake then turned back to Eleanor.

"Ready?"

"Right. Yes. See you around Kay?"

"You'll be here tomorrow?"

"Yup."

Kaylee nodded, then reached forward and pulled Eleanor into an embrace. "Take care of yourself, then. I'll see you tomorrow." She threw a glare at Bastian as she said it, as if he were some kind of liability to Eleanor.

He snorted and started walking away. Eleanor caught up a

moment later. He nodded at several lingering bouncers who waited around to walk the employees to their cars. Awareness crawled over his skin, and he glanced over his shoulder. He caught sight of Eaden in the shadows near the back hallway, his arms crossed. The club's owner watched him, then nodded. He gave one in return, then placed a protective hand at Eleanor's lower back and ushered her from the building.

"No Luke, I take it?" she asked, once they were out of hearing distance. The street was silent. His bike appeared and he pulled on a bit of magic to summon her helmet and then his. She fitted it onto her head. She always looked so damn sexy in that thing. He summoned his jacket next, even though there was no danger of crashing. She'd been worried about it the first night. What he hadn't told her was that his magic was capable of protecting her if anything were to happen. So, technically, she didn't need the extra gear. The helmet was great simply for the com system. But the jacket? He just liked seeing her in his clothes. He made a point of helping her into it, knowing she could damn well put it on herself. It smelled like him, and the idea of her wrapped in his scent triggered something primal in his brain.

She huffed but didn't complain. After spending an entire evening watching her, he wanted to put his hands all over her —could hardly wait to get her home.

"All set?" he asked, his words strained. She nodded.

They sped through the city. He took the curves gently, even with her arms wrapped around him, he didn't want to make her uncomfortable. Every shift of her thighs against him, every time she tightened her arms, or rubbed her palms up and down his abdomen, he practically growled, tempted to pull over and rut her on the side of the road.

When her hand sank down and palmed his cock over his jeans, she discovered the truth. He was hard as iron; it was entirely her doing. "If you're trying to tease me on purpose," he bit out, "it's working. Obviously."

Her gentle giggle made him shiver with anticipation. He

revved the bike and accelerated. She squealed. A grin spread across his face.

They entered Kentwood and soon he was pulling up the tree lined drive, then into the garage. He hit the button to close the door behind them.

His heart kicked up a notch as they climbed off and he removed his helmet. She removed hers, shaking out her hair. His cock twitched. He studied the sensual movements of her neck, his mouth watering at the sight of her.

"I'll take that," he said, his voice gruff. The helmet disappeared, followed by the jacket, which he hadn't bothered giving her time to remove.

"Fancy trick for a fancy goblin," she cooed. "Are my clothes next?"

"Saucy female," he purred. The thought of removing her clothes with the sweep of a hand was too tempting. His glamor wavered. Before he could stop himself, he pulled energy from his metals and channeled it into magic.

She shrieked as her clothes melted into nothing. "Bastian! I was—*fuck*. I was joking!"

Her hands went to cover her breasts, and her legs crossed together, thighs pressing tight. A brief flash of regret overcame him. Had he gone too far? Damn it. "I'm... I shouldn't have done that. I can give them back."

She blinked a few times. Then a grin spread across her features. She dropped her arms and closed the distance, sauntering up to him. "No need."

The sight of her naked, standing beside a two-hundred-thousand-dollar car, made him groan. His glamor wavered for a final time before disappearing entirely.

"Oops," she pouted, looking him over, taking in the changes like his pointed ears and gray skin. "Did I do that?" She ran a hand down his chest lower and lower, her path obvious.

He slapped a hand over hers, halting her motions, pinning

her palm against his abdomen. "That's far enough," he managed.

Her eyes lifted to his and she caught her full bottom lip between her teeth, suddenly looking shy.

"You are so fucking *beautiful*," he whispered. "You know what happens next, I hope?"

She licked her lips and nodded. "I… Yes."

"I would warn you, but I'm not sure there's any stopping this."

The corner of her mouth twitched and she said, "You mean, now's not the time to run?"

"Running is the absolute worst thing you should do around me right now."

"Is that a dare?" Her words came out breathy.

"It—"

She ripped her hand from beneath his and darted around him, breaking into a sprint for the door leading into the house. For a split second, every coherent thought slid from his mind. A primal roar rose from his chest then burst free. He lunged for her, catching her just as she reached for the doorknob. His arms wrapped around her, dragging flush against him. The feel of her naked, soft skin beneath his palms short-circuited his brain.

A delighted giggle burst from her chest and she all but collapsed into him. He wanted to devour her, to possess her, to fuck her until he was imprinted between her pretty thighs, so that every time she saw him, her pussy tightened in memory of him.

"That, baby girl, was a very bad decision." He was already walking them forward, keeping a tight hold on her, until her body was pinned flush to the door, his chest pressing tight against her back. Her breathing turned to panting, and damn. He lifted her hair away, then licked up the column of her neck, covering her in his scent, tasting her skin, nuzzling against her.

"Are you wet for me, little female?" He already knew the answer. His voice was pitched lower, a goblin's voice.

"Maybe," she whispered, half-heartedly squirming against him, as if she were going anywhere. No, he wasn't letting her go.

Not now.

Not ever.

He blinked, regaining a modicum of rational thought. What the fuck was he doing?! Was he going to fuck her right here against a door in the garage? Growling, he wrenched himself backwards. He hauled her from the door, keeping her firmly tucked against his chest, and opened the door, walking her in, guiding her through the house and up the stairs, then into his bedroom.

She kept giggling the whole way, tiny bursts of delight escaping her. She hadn't been drinking—he'd watched her closely. No, these little giggles… They were because of him. Heat radiated from his chest. She was happy *because of him.*

He turned her to face him. Using more restraint than he thought possible, he said, "I won't make you do anything you don't want to do. I would never. So if you don't want this, you need to tell me now, because the moment I get started…"

"You won't stop?"

He ran a hand over the shaved side of his scalp. "I would never hurt you, Elle, baby. If you tell me to stop, I'll stop. I'm not that much of a beast."

"Well, you look like one, and I'm completely here for it," she said. "I'm serious, it's freaking hot. You know that right? Like—" She twirled her pointer finger in circles. "This whole goblin thing. It makes me wet."

He groaned. "Not helping, baby girl. Just answer my question before my control snaps. And no talking of—that. Not until I can unleash myself."

She huffed, reigning in a smug smile. "I didn't lie this morning when I told you I haven't been properly fucked in a while. In case you're wondering, a while translates to *years.*

Like, zero sex at all. So, I don't know why you're still standing there when I'm dripping onto my thighs—"

He was on her in a blink, his mouth fitted over hers, silencing her, turning her words to gentle mews and sighs as his tongue claimed hers. His arms wrapped around her body, lifting her to bring her closer, until she wrapped her legs around his hips. The warm heat of her bared pussy pressed against his jeans, left him cursing under his breath. He carried her to the bed and gently deposited her.

She was naked, and flushed, and entirely his.

His movements turned urgent as he jerked out of his shirt and shucked off his jeans. He stood motionless, letting her look her fill. This little female had no fucking idea what she was in for. But she was about to find out.

y mouth went dry at the sight of Bastian's gloriously naked body. Naturally, my eyes went straight to that damn piercing at the base of his shaft. I'd be lying if I said I *hadn't* thought about it since my mouth had explored him.

I had.

The bar was bent to shape, and capped with metal balls on each end, sized perfectly to massage my clit while he was inside of me. What would it feel like? A little whimper fled my lips at the thought.

"I'd tell you there's still time to change your mind, but I'd be lying." His eyes darted over my naked body sprawled on his bed. I glanced down and immediately snapped my thighs together. They'd been obscenely splayed. Just for him.

"Oh no, Elle, baby. Open wide for me."

I sucked in a breath.

"Now," he ordered. "I won't ask again."

Heat raced through me. I should have balked at his command, but my body betrayed me, legs falling wide. I was completely exposed, just as I'd been when we'd gone swimming.

"That's my good girl."

He was over me in an instant, fitting his body to mine, arms braced on either side of my shoulders. His skin, though inhuman, was covered in the same kind of hair humans had. Dark and coarse, it grew along his arms and legs, tickling my skin. There was a little across his chest, and bit of it trailed down his navel to his cock, now hidden where our bodies touched, hard and hot between us.

Our eyes locked. I saw myself reflected in his black orbs. Unlike his human form, there was no green to be had. Just inky blackness, almost demonic.

I wanted this more than I'd wanted anything in a long time. Knowing he'd wrestled with indecision over the past few days, it was a thrill that he'd finally given in. Like he couldn't resist me, just as I could no longer resist him.

He dipped his head and found my throat, licking in broad strokes. His tongue was flat and hot against me. Wet. I'd never been…licked like this, with this kind of intention. It felt animalistic, like he was trying to cover me in himself. My core clenched.

I reached for him, relishing in the feel of his warm skin beneath my palms. I explored his torso, anywhere I could touch. Squeezing. Loving the feel of his dense muscle.

His licks turned to nips, and then he was working his way down my body, pausing to circle his tongue around my pebbled nipples. He took one into his mouth and sucked. I felt a zing straight to my clit. The ache between my legs pulsed. I tried to squeeze my thighs together, only to squeeze his hips instead. He continued downward. Each press of his sharp, pointed teeth sent jolts of electricity straight to my core. My body worked itself into a desperate frenzy and my breaths turned heavy.

The wet sensation of his tongue found my folds and he began lapping at me, letting out tiny growls that vibrated against my skin, against my opening.

"This pussy is my undoing, sugar."

I stifled a gasp. Lips latched onto my clit, then sucked. My hips arched off the bed. A series of mews fell from my mouth as he worked me, as I rose higher and higher. His tongue sank inside and swirled. I cried out, jerking against him.

Pressure built, expanding outward. Leaving me incensed.

"Bas… Bastian…" I chanted. "Please, I'm…so close. *Please!*"

His movements slowed, doing the exact opposite of what I was begging for.

"Bastian," I hissed, releasing the bunches of comforter and tangling my fingers in his long hair. My other hand cupped the shaved side of his scalp, the short hairs velvety soft against my palm.

He lifted his head and growled, his eyes locking with mine for a brief instant. My stomach swooped at what I saw. A predator, claiming his prize. Like a starving wolf tearing at a fresh kill, guarding it with his life. The thought should have disgusted me, but it did the opposite. My chest burst with something I'd never felt.

He dipped his head again and continued. I pressed his face more firmly against my pussy, hips rolling to meet each swipe of his tongue. My abdomen tightened. "Come for me, Elle," he ordered. "I want to taste you coming on my tongue."

He was, every inch of him, pure male. It had never been like this with anyone. *Never.* For all Bastian's intimidating experience, his confidence, his possessiveness, there was still a vulnerable quality about him. I felt sexy, worshiped, adored… powerful.

So fucking powerful.

"Yes," I breathed, my hips bucking. "Yes!"

A hand came around and pinned me in place, his ringed fingers splayed wide over my abdomen. Another broad sweep of his tongue, then a final suck on my clit. I cried out, back arching off the bed as my orgasm washed over me, drenching me in unguarded pleasure, dragging me away with it.

I collapsed onto the bed, gasping for breath, tiny stars

exploding in my vision. A low growl, laced with satisfaction, punctuated my noisy breathing. I blinked up at the ceiling, still floating in bliss, when strong hands found my hips. Before I could process what was happening, Bastian flipped me onto my front. I half gasped, half giggled, drunk on pleasure. Then my hips were being lifted into position.

"Oh, fuck," I managed, quickly bracing my elbows on the bed. His knees nudged my legs apart until I was fully bared.

"Good girl," Bastian purred, that goblin voice so low, so sinful, I couldn't help but shiver at his praise. I wanted every *good girl* he was willing to give. Something about him made me want to be on my knees before him. Made me want to submit.

Lips kissed my left buttock, feather light, then my right. Heat erupted on my face. The thought of Bastian Croft, a goblin bounty hunter, seeing me like this, completely bared to him, with his face so close, made me fluttery. It was in incredibly vulnerable position. Yet, I still felt safe.

There was a long pause, then a hot tongue at the base of my spine, licking upwards. "You are *mine*," he uttered. The power of those words settled over me like a blanket, and for a split second, I wondered if there was magic in them.

Then he loomed over me, pressing his chest to my back. He used his hands to pin mine in place. The move was so erotic. He was claiming me, as if he thought I'd escape. His thick arms braced mine, chin tucked in the crook between my shoulder and neck.

"You on the pill?" he asked, his breath tickling my ear.

"Mmm," I managed.

"Answer me."

"Yes. And I've been checked."

"Wouldn't matter—I'm a supernatural. Don't get sick."

Oh, right. Well, that was convenient.

"But I can get a condom—"

"No," I cried. I wanted to feel him. All of him.

"Thank fuck." The head of him pushed at my entrance. I gasped as he filled me slowly, in and then out. It was a gentleness I hadn't expected. Halfway there, that changed. He pulled out and then slammed into me with one final sweep, burying himself to the hilt. My eyes widened and I gasped at the intrusive feel of his piercing. From this position, it wasn't hitting my clit like I'd expected, but pressing against somewhere else entirely.

"Oh, God," I groaned.

A feral growl sounded against my ear, sending shivers racing down my spine, straight to my core. My walls fluttered around him, stretched tight. He was bigger than I was used to, big enough to create a sense of invasion. I took a deep breath, attempting to steady myself. With each passing moment, the uncomfortable stretch turned to liquid heat.

A dull ache began to build. I tightened around him, wanting more. Wanting him to move.

"Fuck," he groaned. "You take me well—so well. So *tight*. Damn it, Elle. I need to move, baby girl. I need… Are you okay? No pain?"

"What? I… No. It's…" I tried to catch my breath. "You feel good." It was an understatement.

"Mmm." He moved slowly at first, pulling out to the tip. It felt like he took all of me with him as he did that. There was a slight hesitation, then he snapped his hips forward, surging back in. My stomach fluttered, sparking with sensation. I cried out, the sound of it mixing with Bastian's hiss. His fingers around my wrists tightened. Again, he retreated then advanced, pistoning his hips until I was bucking wildly beneath him. The ache between my legs turned to molten lava. The piercing at the base of his shaft created a whole set of sensations I was embarrassed to consider, because I loved the feel of it so much.

A set of teeth found the base of my neck and clamped down.

My head lowered and a whimpering cry fell from my mouth. A numbing tingle spread over my body, trickling to my extremities, curling my toes. I could do nothing but fall into my pleasure, like being swept away in the current, as my body reached its peak, clenching and unclenching around him.

Our movements were erotic, *indecent*. The sound of our mingled breaths. The wet slap of his skin against mine.

He swelled inside me, growing even larger. My impending orgasm rose higher in response to the tightness of him. He made sounds I'd never heard from him, swallowed up by my skin where his teeth remained latched, pinning me in place, moving with me. Claiming me—

I erupted. My entire body went rigid, then exploded with the pulse between my legs, slamming into me and radiating outward. Bastian's mouth released me and he roared, burying himself a final time before grinding against me.

I couldn't breathe, couldn't hold myself up any longer, couldn't move. My arms collapsed, right as Bastian released my wrists and braced me in place, then gently lowered me to the bed, his body lined along mine, still buried deep. I pressed my face into the comforter, practically moaning with each breath I exhaled.

A long silence stretched between us and then—

"Elle? Baby? Was I too rough?" His voice held a measure of hesitance, uncertainty I hadn't expected. "I should have been gentler."

"No," I whispered, trying to find my voice. "*No.* I wanted that. Just like that."

We lay panting as minutes slipped by. Our orgasm haze began to clear, replaced by something softer, more intimate. This was the part I'd never experienced before. The quiet aftermath, the gentle touching, the way he looked at me like I was precious.

At long last, he pulled himself free of my body. I could feel the evidence of what we'd done, warm and intimate between my thighs. He nestled me against him, turning me so that we lay with our foreheads pressed together. His hand splayed over my backside, thumb stroking.

"Your eyes are so pretty," I murmured. "Like onyx. I never realized goblins didn't have irises or anything."

He hummed in response. "I don't frighten you? My appearance?"

"No." I tried to shake my head and found I was too bone-limp to move.

"Fascinating."

"Why?" I managed.

"You're the first who's ever wanted to see me like this." The words were a quiet admission. "Most prefer the human version."

He'd never fucked anyone in his goblin form? "Why wouldn't they like that? You're so—"

"I'm a goblin, Elle." He was reminding me of what the supernatural community thought of goblins.

"Well, *I* find you beautiful."

"So you've said." I didn't miss the small smile that pulled at the corner of his lips. I lifted a finger to trace it. His felt just like normal lips, but they were also metallic in color, several shades darker than his aluminum skin. He caught my hand and slipped my pointer finger into his mouth, the one wearing his gold ring. He gently bit down. I squealed, then laughed at the sensation of his pointed teeth.

A low noise sounded in the back of his throat. "I love that laugh. Love hearing you happy."

I sucked my lower lip between my teeth. I was, wasn't I? Happy? The sensation had sort of...crept up on me. But I liked being here in Bastian's house with him, enjoying him, and that was saying a lot, considering the world was going to shit around us.

A hand came up, fingers caressing my collarbones, catching beneath my gold necklaces. "Professor Miller gave you this one?" He asked, lifting the medallion.

"Mmm-hmm."

"And what about this one? It's an artifact too, yes?"

I nodded, then hesitated. "It the one I use to see through glamor."

He frowned. "Where did you get it?"

I paused, then decided to give him the truth. "My father made it for me."

His head pulled back to get a better look at me, as if seeing something entirely new. "Your father. He was an artificer. That's why you studied artifacts. Fuck. This is a surprise—you surprise me at every turn."

I nodded, trying to hide my pleased smile. "I've always been fascinated by magical objects because of him. He made this for me before…before he died."

Bastian's face softened. "I'm sorry, baby girl. What about your mom?" He stroked his fingers down my cheek. I closed my eyes, practically purring from his touch.

"We… Our relationship was never the best. She… She wasn't a fan of his work, of the danger that it posed."

"But she married him?"

"She didn't know much about it until they were married. She scorned supernaturals when she discovered their existence. He couldn't exactly hide it, considering it was such a large part of his work."

He hummed. "That's too bad. It must have been really hard for both of them. For you as well."

I blinked, looking at him. "It—yes, it was. He died a couple of years before I went to college. I lived on campus, mostly to get away from my mom, from her bitterness. It felt toxic in a way that I couldn't handle. Like she was mad at everyone and everything and I was the closest thing available to take it out on."

Bastian nodded.

"To her, I was always my father's favorite and she resented that. Resented that he shared his work with me. He would have done the same with her, but she scorned it." I shook my head and sighed. "Things got a lot worse when I told her what I was studying in school. I don't think she ever forgave me for wanting to do something that made me feel closer to my dad."

"That makes sense." He hesitated. "Would you go back to school, if you could? If the threat of Luke didn't exist? Would you finish what you started? Complete your master's degree?"

My chest squeezed and a burst of longing settled over me. "I guess I've never allowed myself to think about the possibility."

It had been too painful.

I thought about it now, in the safety of his arms. I thought about what would happen if Luke didn't exist anymore, if he was no longer a threat. There wouldn't be any remaining fear of him finding me, hurting me, using me to plan heists and steal valuable historical objects. But Professor Miller was gone. I'd have to do it without her. That left a different kind of ache in my chest. And yet…

"Yes, I think I would." The admission felt bright and hopeful. I knew why he asked. If all this worked out, if Luke really *was* the one responsible, if we brought him to justice, then he wouldn't be my concern anymore.

"I owe it to myself," I added. "It's what I wanted, and I was good at it, passionate about it. I wouldn't have quit if things were different."

"What would you do with it? A degree like that? I assume that unlike your father, you're not interested in making artifacts, just studying them, studying history? Art?"

"All of it," I said, my heart kicking up a notch. "Minus the artifact making. I love looking into the past, reflecting on the way it shaped our world. Vivi works in a museum now, did you know? I'm not sure that's the path for me, though. Maybe I could follow in Professor Miller's footsteps. At least, that's what I thought I'd end up doing, working at the university with her, teaching lectures, all of that. But now she's gone, so I don't know…"

Bastian's features softened. He held my gaze for a moment, then leaned in and kissed me, slowly, gently. Like he was telling me it was okay—everything would be okay. Heat spread through my core. His thigh nudged between my legs, pressing against my pussy. I groaned and flexed my hips, grinding against him. Already, I wanted him again. I deepened our kiss, pulling at his bottom lip, biting harder than I would have with a human. A brazen challenge, a show of dominance.

He growled, and in one fluid motion, rolled us over and pulled me on top of him. I settled against his chest, then pushed myself up, pinning his shoulders. "I need you again," I admitted. "Need to feel that fancy piercing of yours."

His lips tipped up and a challenging gleam lit his eyes. "Take me," he commanded, his gaze darting between my face and breasts.

I didn't need any further prompting.

His hands tightened on my hips as I found his hard length, guiding it to my entrance. I delighted in the hiss of pleasure that broke from his lips as I sank down on him.

My lips parted, a cry of delight breaking free at the feel of him filling me. At the feel of his piercing. It hit right where I wanted it. With the pressure of sitting on his cock, it was even better. It was bliss, absolute bliss, having him this way. Lifting my hips and snapping them back down, I rode him, and just like he'd commanded, I took him.

32

A snore sounded next to my ear, pulling me from sleep. I woke with the weight of a body atop mine. Bastian. I tried to shift and found myself entirely trapped, so I lay there, blinking up at the ceiling in his room. My legs were parted, and he'd found a way between them, his entire body aligned to mine, sleeping on top of me. His face was nuzzled into the pillow beside mine, his breath fanning against my cheek.

I swallowed. We were naked and he was hard. His length pressed obscenely between the apex of my thighs, *so close* to where I wanted it. If I shifted, I could probably work him in.

Heat flushed my cheeks as memories from last night came rushing back, the way he'd fucked me from behind, the way I'd ridden him. We'd collapsed after that, at nearly five in the morning, and passed out. I hadn't even gone through my bedtime routine, which was why my face felt gross with day-old makeup.

Annnnd, I had to pee.

Groaning, I finally pushed him aside. He gave another little snore and readjusted, grabbing the closest pillow and pulling it toward him, wrapping his arms around it. My shoulders shook with silent giggles, taking in the sight of him, all six foot something, layered with muscle, half his body covered in tattoos and piercings, rings on his fingers, beautiful gray skin, pointed ears, and black hair laced with deep green fanning out around him.

I was in so much trouble with this male.

I shook my head, forcing my gaze away. Otherwise I'd stand here all day. I slipped from his room, leaving him with Teddy curled up at the foot of the bed. I went to my bathroom. Standing in front of the mirror, my mouth dropped open. My hand jumped to the crook of my neck to rub the bite mark there. He'd bitten me! It had been *so damn hot.* His teeth hadn't broken the skin, but there'd be a nice bruise and the outline of his pointed teeth. I leaned closer for a better look. Except, the longer I stared, the fainter it grew, until it disappeared completely. Like I'd imagined it.

Weird.

I rubbed my temples then set about cleaning myself up. I washed off yesterday's makeup and brushed my teeth—

"Running from me, sugar?" Bastian's gravelly voice nearly made me jump from my skin.

I sprayed toothpaste on the mirror as I rounded on him, brandishing my toothbrush. He was back in his human form, propped in the doorway with his arms crossed, amusement dancing on his features. He was still completely naked—as was I. I rushed to spit and clean my mouth.

"Thanks for that," I said, then grabbed a towel and wiped the toothpaste off the mirror. He chuckled, sauntering into the bathroom. My heart kicked up as he stalked toward me. He took me by the hips and lifted me onto the counter, coming to stand between my legs. His lips found mine, sweet at first before a hand slipped into my hair and tightened, tilting my head back for better access.

A moan escaped me as his tongue swept in.

"Good morning," he teased, pulling back slightly to look at me. "Think I might be lucky enough to get you in the shower?"

"That depends," I managed, trying to look annoyed about the toothpaste.

"On?"

"Whether you'll make me breakfast?" I batted my eyelashes.

He laughed, full bodied and uninhibited. The sound sent shivers across my skin. Something told me he didn't let just anyone see him unguarded like this. Which made me feel immensely special.

"How are you so fucking cute, even when you scowl at me?" He pressed his finger into the crease that had formed between my eyebrows. "I love this. But anyway, I was already planning on making omelets, so…"

"Omelets?" I sat up straighter. I loved a good omelet, and I was certain his would be amazing.

"Omelets."

"Then yes! I'm all yours." He wasted no time. His hands came under my hips, scooping me up. I squealed, trying to wrap myself around him, clinging to him for dear life. "Bastian!" I pinched his hard muscle. He didn't even flinch.

He walked us into the shower, turning me away from the spray as water came cascading out. Goosebumps prickled my skin and I shivered against him. He set me back on my feet, letting my body slide down his, over his hard cock. Then moved me into the stream of hot water.

My eager groan was answered with a low rumble of a chuckle. His fingers found my hair, working it back, getting it wet. I rolled my lips between my teeth before saying, "Are you going to wash me?"

"You're mine to care for, so yeah."

There was that word again. *Mine*. I let it sink in, trying to ignore the thrill of it. Did he really mean it? I cleared my throat. "Uhm, Bas?"

"Hmm?" He set about lathering up my loofa. "You don't exactly do relationships, do you?"

"Not usually, no." His focus was absolute as he prepared to

wash me. His long fingers, the way he worked my body wash into a lather, was distracting as hell.

I cleared my throat. "Right. So, relationships. When, exactly, was your last one?"

He shrugged. "Couple centuries ago, give or take"

Which confirmed my suspicions. He hadn't had one—not since he'd had his heart broken by Sara. The human who'd given him his distrust for humans. For relationships in general.

The loofa was well and truly lathered. "Turn around, Elle. Let me get your back."

I sighed, complying. A hand wrapped around the front of my shoulder, gently holding me in place while the other began to clean me. I waited in silence for several minutes before saying, "So. You don't do relationships at all then?"

"Nope."

"I… I see." A horrible ache welled in my chest. I'd known this about him. And yet, I'd jumped in head first.

"After Sara," he finally said, breaking my tortured silence, "I wasn't interested in getting close to anyone. At first it was out of bitterness and fear. But then I realized that it was just… easier."

I held my breath, waiting.

"Given what I am, what I do for the fae, it's just…easier. No expectations, no complications. I can disappear for days tracking a charge and not have to explain myself. Never have to meet the parents or friends. Don't have to plan date nights or buy flowers and chocolates—"

My body was rigid beneath his touch. These were all things I wanted to have with someone someday. Call me a hopeless romantic, but I wanted my significant other to spoil me with little surprises. I didn't need them to spend an exorbitant amount of money on me. Just…little things, thoughtful things to show they cared.

Bastian's movements slowed.

I cleared my throat, trying to inject levity into my tone. "I suppose it's good to know I shouldn't expect any roses, then?"

I was so disappointed. In myself, mostly, for getting my hopes up.

Bastian's hand tightened, gently pulling me back. His mouth came to my ear. "Baby girl. I will buy you a hundred roses if that will make you happy. Or even a thousand. What's your favorite color?"

My stomach bottomed out. "My… My favorite color?"

"Mmm-hmm"

"You can't guess?" A hot feeling that felt a lot like hope rekindled in my chest.

"Pink?" I nodded. "I thought so."

I sucked in a sharp breath because—

"There. It's not a *thousand*, but I'm not sure that would be a good idea."

My vision blurred with tears. I was surrounded by roses. They lay strewn across every surface in the bathroom, even littered over the floor, clustered in vases, everywhere. Countless long stemmed pink roses in various shades. "You… How… What… Did you just…?"

"Don't worry." He lips brushed my ear with a gentle kiss. "I paid for them. I keep loose cash around for all those *missing ingredients* you mentioned. The stuff I might need on occasion."

A giddy laugh burst free of my chest. "I can't even… That's a lot of loose cash for missing ingredients," I managed. Because this many roses must have cost a fortune.

I took it all in, my chest burning. A few tears slipped free, mingling with the water slipping down my skin. Their sweet scent filled the room, mixing with the heavy steam of the shower. I inhaled, my shoulders immediately relaxing.

"Now," he said, "what else would you like, since we're at it? Chocolate? Diamonds? Both?"

"You," I gasped, spinning to face him. "Just you. On your knees for me."

His smile was pure wickedness. He complied, erasing any doubt that he wouldn't be good at this sort of thing—whatever it was we were doing. I still had a lot to get off my chest regarding what we were—because I wanted an answer to that —but for now, the gesture was enough.

When his tongue found the heat between my legs, I braced my back against the shower's tile. I wrapped my hands around his head to anchor myself, draping my right leg over his shoulder. He lapped at me, running his tongue along my opening, circling my clit. His piercing sent zings of pleasure straight to my core.

Soon enough, my legs began to tremble as my orgasm built.

My head fell back against the wall. I closed my eyes, letting the steam and the scent of roses wash over me. "Fuck, Bastian," I whispered, my body tightening.

A low chuckle sent tingles shooting straight to my pussy. Pleasure raked its sinuous claws over me. I rocked my hips against his mouth, moaning. "More," I begged, growing desperate, aching. Bastian's fingers slipped inside me. First one, and then two. They curled, hitting my inner walls just right. I came apart. A cry wrenched from my lips, hips bucking against his mouth. His movements slowed, growing gentle as he finished licking me.

When I dropped my gaze to his, all I saw were hot green sparks. He licked his lips and his glamor flashed in and out, a sign he was losing control. When he smiled, all I saw were the points of his goblin teeth, ready to devour me whole.

I wasn't sure there was a single thing Bastian *couldn't* cook. I shoveled a combination of diced mushrooms, tomatoes, basil, cheddar cheese, and egg into my mouth, like I couldn't eat fast enough. "Hungry much?" Bastian chuckled beside me, watching me eat for several beats, his eyes dancing.

I moaned. "It's so frigging good."

"Good, eat up. You'll need your strength today."

Hot fire dropped into my belly. "I…will?"

Because we'd be having so much sex, right? Yes. Good. I was ready for it. It didn't matter that he'd fucked me thoroughly in the shower after I'd finished coming on his tongue. I could take so much more.

It was funny, because I thought I would be sore. Yet, everything felt fine. Perhaps my prolonged celibacy hadn't been so detrimental after all. I could go at least another five, maybe six rounds? It depended on how many breaks we took—

"Whatever your thinking, I can smell it." My lips parted. "We're going to your apartment this afternoon, sugar. We had a deal, remember? I'm going to magic your apartment back to normal. It needs to appear as if you've gone back to your everyday life, just in case Luke comes looking."

My mind came to a screeching halt. Luke. Apartment. Bait…

I set my fork down, stomach clenching into a tight ball. "I suddenly find I'm not all that hungry."

"Elle." Bastian's voice was gentle. "Eat your breakfast—lunch—whatever. You'll be fine, I promise."

"But you're not going to make me stay there, right? While he's still on the loose?"

Bastian's body went rigid. "You will stay where I can keep you safe." His words came out as a menacing growl. "With me."

I nodded and relaxed, glancing down at my plate. It really was a freaking good omelet. I lifted my fork again, taking another bite.

Around us, vases of pink roses littered the kitchen. He'd cleaned up his grand gesture in the bathroom by summoning additional vases to house the loose roses. Now they were everywhere—a reminder. My cheeks washed with heat.

"Still thinking naughty thoughts about me?"

"Will you just—eat your food!" I snapped, even though there wasn't any bite to my voice. "God!"

He chuckled, then returned to his omelet. My stomach

relaxed and I managed to devour the rest of my food—not hard, considering it was incredibly delicious—and finish my second cup of coffee. Then we were headed out the door to my apartment.

Our drive through the city was quiet. Bastian didn't appear talkative, and I didn't want to push. Instead, my mind replayed our words, our actions, everything. It would be silly to think I was somehow special—that after he'd had his pick of partners over the years—correction, centuries—I was the one he'd make an exception for. And yet, his actions spoke otherwise.

Bastian found a spot along the curb and parallel parked his truck. I punched in the code on the building and we took the elevator to my floor. My heart lurched at the sight of Peter's closed door. There was no longer caution tape lining the entry. It wasn't swarming with police. Everything looked as it ought, as if he might pop his head out and say, "Eh, Rose? All right, girl?" And I'd nod and say, "Yep, thanks, Peter. How's Teddy?" And he'd chuckle, regaling me with Teddy's latest antics while I unlocked my door, then we'd bid each other goodbye. Only to do it all over again the next time I came home.

"You okay, Elle baby?" Bastian's hand tightened on mine, sending butterflies fluttering through my chest. I nodded, pulling my gaze from Peter's door, focusing on mine instead. "I had the landlord replace the locks," he said by way of explanation, pulling a set of keys from his pocket and handing them over. "Hope you don't mind."

"I… Thank you for doing that."

He nodded, motioning me forward with his head.

I took a deep breath, fitting the key in the lock, trying to keep my hand from shaking. When the door swung open, I felt the same shock lurch through me at the disaster. It was just as it had been days ago, completely trashed, everything broken. I stood in the doorway, blinking.

Where was I supposed to start?

Fingers trailed down my arm, then a hand snaked around my front as Bastian pressed himself in behind me. He lowered his mouth to my ear. "I'll handle the big repairs. You can put things back where you want them. Something tells me you'll want it *juuust* right."

I huffed. "Yeah…probably. That… That sounds good."

I entered the main living area, reaching for the bowl to deposit my keys, only to find it was on the ground. That was the first thing I picked up, the first thing I put back into place. The first step to rebuilding my life—again—after Luke had upended it. Then with Bastian's help, we began moving around the room.

I watched him work for a few minutes, unable to tear my gaze away. He went to the television and pulled some black smoky tendrils of…something…from his metals. They settled over the screen, mending the shattered cracks. A couple of blinks later he was lifting it upright, back into place.

"Wow…" I shook my head, trying to clear away my surprise. "You really just…did that."

"Doubted me, did you?" He grinned, letting his dimple out. That freaking dimple.

My mouth opened and closed. Then I smiled. "Not even for a minute."

He winked and got busy with other things. As soon as the shelves and television cabinet was set to rights, I began grabbing objects, books mostly, and setting them back where they belonged. The items that were broken were set aside for Bastian's attention.

We moved through the living space into the dining room and kitchen. When I spotted the broken shards of the pasta bowl and spoiled lasagna, I began cleaning it up. That fateful night felt like ages ago. "I can't believe that I found out about Professor Miller's death from the news," I muttered, using a wad of paper towels to pick up the glass and spoiled food.

Bastian looked up from where he repaired a set of broken drawers. The bottoms had been punched out. The silverware and cookware were scattered everywhere, because Luke was anything if not thorough.

"I mean, I guess I deserved it for not keeping up with her. But still." He hummed, continuing to work. I grabbed a rag to clean the remainder of spoiled food from the floor, then paused. "You never told me who hired you to find her murderer. You mentioned the will and her family. Was it them?"

Bastian hesitated. "For the record, Elle, that kind of information is confidential." I gave him my best glare. "Yes, it was her family."

I nodded, then set about scrubbing the floor. Except—

"How did her family know to hire you?"

"What do you mean?" His words were slow, measured.

"I *mean*… You're a goblin who works for the fae. They wouldn't have hired you through the WBI. How would they have known who you are? What you do? Where to find you?" I fumbled with the rag, then let it fall, standing to face him. Something wasn't adding up.

He set the drawer on the countertop, arms hanging limp at his sides. "You didn't know, did you? I wondered when you never mentioned it."

"Didn't know what?"

He ran a hand over the shaved side of his scalp and swore. "Professor Miller was…she was a witch, sugar." I blinked back at him. "Not a very powerful one, from what I understand. But she did come from a semi-prominent witch family—the Millers, on her father's side."

"You're joking, right? This is just a joke. She wasn't a witch, Bastian. I'd have known."

He took a step back, crossing his arms. "Oh? That necklace lets you see a witch's glamor, does it? What, exactly does a witch's glamor look like?"

A sinking sensation filled my belly because…

"They don't," I whispered. "Witches are one of the few supernaturals who don't have or need glamor. They can hide in plain sight." The realization was a punch to the gut. "I knew that. I've always known that. But I never suspected Jane because I trusted her completely. I never even looked for signs because…why would I have reason to?"

That Jane had never mentioned such a monumental thing to me felt… Well, it felt a little like a betrayal.

Bastian's face softened. "I'm sorry, sugar." He came over and wrapped me in a bear hug, propping his chin on top of my head. For a moment, I let him. I took a deep breath, then another, but I couldn't fight the tears filling my eyes. My emotions morphed into anger. I roughly pushed against Bastian, slipping out of his embrace.

"You've known for days and you didn't think to tell me? Didn't think to mention it as part of the case? You knew what my relationship was with her and you, what, thought I shouldn't know? If you had a feeling I didn't know, you should have told me, brought it up. Something!"

"Sugar…"

"No! Don't—*sugar* me." I backed up a step. "You should have told me, Bastian."

I scrubbed my hands over my face, then wrapped them around the back of my neck, lacing my fingers together, looking up at the ceiling.

"At first, I assumed you knew. Then I figured if you didn't know, there was a reason she didn't tell you. And then I just sort of…didn't think about it again."

Pain filled the back of my throat. "Well, great! I'm glad you just forgot."

Bastian's jaw tightened. "I'm sorry, Elle."

My breath whooshed out of me. This… This wasn't how things were supposed to go between us. I was messing this up. I shook my head.

"No. I…" I let out a frustrated groan. "No. It's… You don't owe me an apology. Not really. It's not your fault she didn't tell me. I'm just…"

Looking for someone to blame. That wasn't very fair of

me. And for someone who had avoided relationships, I wasn't giving him a good reason to enjoy being in one by taking my anger out on him and blaming him for this. I dropped my hands.

"You're angry. I get it. I'm angry for you—that she didn't share this with you. That you had to find out this way. And I'm sorry that I had to be the one to break it to you." He took a deep breath, his chest expanding.

I nodded, then closed the distance between us. "I just—I don't want you to keep things from me, okay? If you think it's something I should know, tell me. I just… I hate that feeling, you know? Luke did it all the time, actually. Intentionally kept things from me."

"Fuck," he muttered, and his arms closed around me, pulling me close. "I'm sorry, baby girl. I know you and Professor Miller were close. Her family knows of me through the fae. That's why they hired me. Given that she had witch blood, they wanted someone supernatural involved, didn't trust the normie government to do an adequate job."

"That makes sense, I guess. I'm… I'm sorry for snapping at you."

"It's all forgiven." He tilted my chin up with a finger.

I nodded, then bridged the distance between us, bringing our lips together in a gentle kiss. I let everything about Professor Miller's betrayal fade into the distance—for now— and set about fixing the rest of my apartment.

33

Being in Eleanor's room was like being surrounded by her. Her scent saturated Bastian's nostrils, making his cock twitch in his pants. Everywhere he looked, he saw parts of her. Admittedly, it wasn't much to see at first. There'd been no floor space when they first entered. This room was the worst in the house.

A flash of fury had his mind jumping to Luke, to all the ways he wanted to make that human piece of filth *suffer*. He pushed that aside, because that wasn't what Eleanor needed right now, and set about mending broken furniture. Ever so slowly, her room reformed.

He hadn't meant for things to happen the way they had earlier. It was his fault. He should've mentioned Professor Miller's family sooner, especially given the way things were changing between them. Rapidly changing. It's like everything was slipping out of his control and he was simply dragged along, trying to breathe, trying to function. Her presence made that almost impossible, made him forget things that mattered, made him want to do nothing but fuck her brains out.

He'd lost control. That scared the shit out of him.

He lifted a photo frame off the floor and fixed the broken

glass. It was of a younger version of her, standing with her arms wrapped around the waist of a middle-aged man. They shared the same nose, the same eye shape. "Your father?" he asked, unable to look away. Her smile was brilliant, happy, blissfully ignorant of the future.

She appeared beside him, brushing a hand down his arm. "Oh, yes. I love that picture. We took it hiking. One of the rare times he pulled himself away from his work. He was a bit…obsessive."

Bastian chuckled and handed it over. She gazed at it a moment longer before setting it on her dresser. His eyes lingered over her, over the graceful way she carried herself as she went back to the pile of clothes she was sorting.

He helped where he could, fixing anything else broken, then he took a seat on her chaise lounge, continuing to watch. Every so often, a small frown drew her eyebrows together. He constantly fought the urge to jump up and press his thumb to the crease, to smooth away whatever worries she wasn't voicing. "Did you hike a lot with your father—when he could pull himself away, that is?"

She glanced up, clothing hanging limp in her hand. A strand of pink hair fell into her face and she tucked it behind her ear. Fuck, she was *exquisite*. His chest pulled tight, knowing she was his—entirely his.

It had never occurred to him—until this very moment—that he could simply sit and watch her like this, in her element, all day without growing bored. He'd certainly never wanted to do that with anyone else. Actually it was a wonder she hadn't noticed how much staring he'd done since yesterday. Since—

His insides went cold. He needed to tell her, especially after what she'd said. He shifted, trying to get comfortable.

He was about to say something when she spoke.

"My dad and I loved hiking together. I haven't gone at all, actually, since he died."

"We should go together," he blurted. "I haven't been in a

while either, but there are a few great places just outside the city."

"Penrose mountain?"

"Yep, that's one of my favorites."

"Mine too," she breathed, a small smile settling on her lips.

His eyes dropped to her mouth and he cleared his throat. "How about next Saturday?"

"I… Yeah, let's do it. That would be fun. And we haven't exactly been on any dates. Not that—I wouldn't want you to feel pressured about dates, given what you said earlier about—"

"It's a date. I'd like to go on a date with you, Eleanor."

He hadn't meant for her to take his words so personally. His fault, entirely his fault. If she wanted it, he'd become the most hopeless fucking romantic to ever hopelessly romance her. Just for her. All for her.

Her throat bobbed and she nodded. "Perfect. I'd like that."

Her eager response spoke to the primal side of him and drove him to his feet. He stalked over to her, his fingers all but aching to feel her. "Now, how about we christen your bed," he said. He tilted her head back and pressed his mouth to hers. The taste of her on his tongue had his glamor flickering. He'd never had this issue with another, but given what she was to him, it shouldn't have surprised him.

She mewed, dropping the clothing she'd been folding to reach for him, clinging to his shoulders. Their kiss turned frantic as his hands splayed over the curve of her ass, pressing her against his hardening cock. He tried and failed, to stifle a groan at the feel of her. It had been hours, and yet, her fucking pussy was all he could think about. He knew this desperate need would ease eventually, but fuck if he could think past wanting her *right now.*

He reached for the hem of her top, then slid it up, letting his knuckles graze her skin. With their fingers fumbling, it became a race of who could get the other undressed faster.

She reached for the button on his jeans. His hips pressed forward, eager.

When she slipped his boxer briefs down over his hips, she moved to her knees. He kicked his clothes away. She wrapped an arm around his thigh, pulling herself close to him, her hard nipples grazing his thighs, sending eager tremors through his muscles.

"Sugar…" he warned. Her gaze darted up to his, open and trusting. The sight of her like this, on her knees for him…

His breath hitched. "Damn, baby girl," he breathed. "You going to fuck me with that pretty mouth of yours?"

He reached for her, ran his fingers through her silky tresses, letting the waves caress his skin.

"Yes," she breathed, taking his cock into her warm palm. Pumping it once, twice. A zing of pleasure shot straight to his balls. Then her tongue flicked out and teased the slit of his cock, lapping up the precum that pooled there before taking him more fully into her mouth. A growl built in his chest and his head fell back toward the ceiling. Every thought in his mind fractured—it was just *so fucking good.*

His hands tightened in her hair, holding her to him. He used the pads of his fingers to massage at her scalp, rolling his hips against her as she worked him.

"You're going to kill me," he bit out. His goblin side roared to the surface, breaking through his glamor, settling over him. Eleanor's breath caught, but she didn't stop. "I want to own that mouth," he growled, his voice deepening to a low pitch. "Want to fucking *dominate* you." She whimpered. "What are you doing to me, Eleanor?!"

More—he needed more. *Now!* Reaching down, he pulled her to her feet. Her mouth came away with a *pop*, a mischievous smile on her lips. Like she knew exactly how she was driving him mad.

He carried her to her bed and settled beside her. They lay on their sides, gazing at each other. Their legs tangled together, one of hers between his, one of his between hers.

His arm wrapped around her shoulders, pulling her close. He gazed at her, taking in the fluttering pulse at the base of her throat, the rise and fall of her chest, her peaked breasts, perfect dusty pink nipples, the sleek lines of her body, the small tuft of hair above her pussy.

His—entirely his. He lifted his hand to his mouth, biting off the sharp goblin nails on his first two fingers. It was annoying how quickly they grew back. Then reached for her dark curls, running his fingers over the area, sliding down further between her legs until he reached her wet folds.

An ache built in his body.

She moaned and tried to squeeze her legs together.

"Don't fight me, baby girl. Let me claim this." He cupped her mound and a whimper fell from her lips. Obediently, she lifted her leg, keeping the other firmly pressed between his. The movement put her pussy on display for him. He swirled his fingers around her opening, working her. Every touch, every press of his palm, brought a satisfying reaction. A whimper here, a widening of her eyes, a hitch in her breath. Her body responded beautifully to his touch, muscles quivering. He wanted her to come like this, come from his touch alone.

"Bastian," she gasped, eyes widening. She tightened around his fingers, then her pussy fluttered, spasming as she cried out, eyelids falling closed. He growled in response, a smile spreading across his lips. Nothing had ever made him feel so satisfied. He kept his fingers in place, relishing in the way she milked him, knowing exactly how it felt when she did it to his cock. Then he leaned forward and kissed one eyelid, and then the other.

"Need your cock," she breathed. "Please."

"As if I could deny you," he scoffed, licking his fingers clean, letting the taste of her send him deeper into a frenzy. He rolled them over and positioned himself between her legs. Then he took himself in hand, working his tip into her. She was more than ready for him. He slid in to the hilt and immediately relaxed. Tension fled from his body, his muscles loosening. This was how it should always be, his cock buried deep inside her to relieve the nonstop need.

"You feel so good," she panted.

"That's because that tight little pussy was made for me," he managed, bracing both elbows, then pulling out, slamming back in. Her eyes widened. He did it again, forgetting about his own pleasure and enjoying hers.

Soon his hips were pumping steadily and hers were rising to meet him. Her hands wrapped around his waist, holding onto him while her legs wrapped around his thighs, twining them together. He lowered until their chests were flush, pinning her right where he needed her.

The heat of her skin, the feel of her nipples pressing into him, sent his movements into a frenzy. His balls tightened. He had to slow down or he'd spill himself embarrassingly early.

Her skin was flushed, cheeks pink, eyes bright. "You like when I come inside you, Elle?"

"Ye—yes," she managed.

"Want me to fill you up, don't you?"

"Bastian!" she cried. "Are you always this dirty?"

"What's the matter? Does it make you blush, sweetheart?" It did. Her skin flushed a darker shade of pink. A smirk pulled at his lips. "I want to hear you say it." He slowed to a stop. Her hands tugged at him to keep going, but he didn't. "You want that, don't you? You want me to fill that pretty pussy to the brim?"

"Oh, my *God*. Yes. Yes—just—keep going."

"I'd rather it be my name on your lips. But... I still want to hear you say it, baby girl."

A laugh fell from her chest. "Yes, *Bastian*. I want you to fill me up. I... I like it." Her lip caught between her teeth, pinned there.

So damn sexy.

He growled. "Good girl. I know you do." He started again. Teasing her was the only way to keep from exploding too soon. But it also drove the primal side of him wild. Catching her mouth in his, he brought her to orgasm, crying out her name when his flooded through him, spilling every drop of his seed inside her the way he'd promised. Then he slowed, his kisses turning gentle.

"Don't think I can ever let you go," he admitted, voicing his fears, unable to keep them buried. There would be no releasing her. He'd known that, known what would happen if they went this far. His goblin side would never allow it.

But then her next words blindsided him—completely blindsided him.

"You don't have to," she managed, her eyelids fluttering open to look at him. Her proclamation made his throat ache. He kissed her more deeply and they stayed on that bed for the rest of the damn afternoon.

34

The next several days passed in a blur of lovemaking, eating, and Vortex. I showed up for every shift, worked until 3:00am, then collapsed into Bastian's bed where he'd wring every last bit of energy from my body before I drifted off. He kept me plied with pancakes in the mornings, then disappeared for work, leaving me alone for most of the day.

Those were the only moments I had to myself. I used them to read, to exercise in the basement, and even to simply catch my breath. I tried to make him dinner in the evenings, often having something finished by the time he came in. While he hadn't returned covered in blood, I couldn't help but hold my breath each night when I heard the garage door.

The hours before work usually passed in a jumble of carnal activities—sex, mostly. He sampled me on just about every surface in the house. Splayed me across the dining room table, let me ride him on the living room couch, took me against whatever wall was closest, bent me over his desk, clutched me to him in the pool, the bath, the sparring mats in the basement. He ruined me for anyone else. I wasn't sure how I could come back from something like this.

Maybe you don't have to, said a voice inside my head. And yet, in the quiet moments when I had time to catch my breath, I found myself wondering when the other shoe would drop. Expecting it, because good things didn't last, because someone like Bastian, a goblin bounty hunter for the fae, would never end up with a mundane human like me.

We just…couldn't be endgame.

"Ready to go, sugar?" Bastian's head popped into the doorway of my bathroom as I finished my makeup.

"Yep." I turned and grinned at him, recalling too acutely the way we'd fucked like animals on the sparring mats just earlier, before I'd come up to get ready for work. He'd shown me the secret button that opened an entire wall of weapons, which in turn, had made my panties flood with wetness. Mostly because I had immediately dredged up fantasies of him using said weapons, which resulted in me being pinned beneath him for the next hour.

A phantom ache lingered between my legs as I squeezed my thighs. Bastian's eyes darted there, and a smile pulled at the corner of his mouth.

"We can go back down there once we get back. I might even show you how I handle some of the more exotic pieces, if that's your thing."

"Or we could skip Vortex entirely," I suggested, lifting my brows. "Go back down *now*." Returning to normalcy had been his idea, after all. I'd worked five nights in a row and still no sign of Luke.

"Mmm." His hand tightened on the doorframe. Was he was considering it? He blinked, then dropped his hand. "I want to, but I also want you to be safe. As tempted as I am to keep you locked up here—preferably chained to my bed, which is something we absolutely need to explore—I know you want your life back, Eleanor."

"I do," I nodded, expelling a huge breath. Truth was, I missed it. I missed Vivi, missed our girls' nights, which I never thought possible. I missed all of it. But I especially ached for the fantasy he'd created—one where I might go back to school once Luke was gone. "You're right," I said at last. "Let's get this done."

"Good." He walked forward. "I got something for you." A narrow leather band appeared in his hand with a small dagger. It was the one he'd trained me with earlier. I'd never trained with weapons before, but he'd insisted. "Let me see your arm."

I frowned but complied. He fastened it around my bicep. "There. I think you earned it, after today."

"I can't exactly walk into the club with this thing on, Bas."

"Don't worry, no one will see it, not even you, but it's there." He waved a hand and it winked out of existence. Then he waved his hand again and it was back. "Not even the supernaturals will know it's there. But when you need it, reach for it and you'll feel it."

"Wow, that's pretty freaking cool. Your magic is really impressive." I reached for it, and even though I couldn't *see* it, my fingers wrapped around the handle. I blew out a breath, impressed. Really, *really* cool.

"Goblins are masters of glamor, more so than other races."

"Huh. Well, it definitely shows."

Twenty minutes later, we found ourselves driving to Vortex in his sports car. A comfortable silence fell between us, and I simply watched the tall buildings pass.

"Vivi is flying back tonight," I found myself saying.

"Oh? She's not staying in the apartment I hope? You warned her?"

"I did. She's staying with one of my coworkers until we get things sorted out."

He nodded. "She seems like a good friend. I'm glad you have her."

"She's pretty much the best. I think you guys would get along. Maybe the two of you can meet now that she's back?" The words came out before I realized what I'd said. Suddenly, I wished I could take them back. Why the hell would he want to meet *any* of my friends? Hadn't that been on his list of reasons for not wanting a relationship? I glanced sidelong at him, bracing for his reaction.

His eyes flicked in my direction before finding the road again. "I'd like that."

All I could do was blink at the windshield. Because his tone mirrored his words. He was genuinely interested in meeting her.

We pulled into a parking lot a block from the club. Bastian escorted me inside, then did what he usually did and disappeared. I never saw him when he lurked. Somehow, he manage to find the shadows. I could always feel him though, that penetrating gaze between my shoulder blades. I'd come to feel safe knowing it was there, knowing he was watching out for me. It was also a confidence booster, knowing he stared at me so much. I wasn't sure he even realized how much and how often he did it. I certainly wasn't going to say anything about it. I liked the attention—no, I liked *his* attention.

Two hours into my shift, Kaylee came to me, breathless. "Rose, please please, please, do me the hugest favor and take my spot in the cage tonight."

"What?!" I frowned. "Eaden has you dancing?"

He rarely had her dancing. She hated that kind of attention. Her hands covered her face and she groaned. "Apparently two of his dancers didn't show tonight and he's *insisting* I go out there. I'll buy you that Ferris purse you wanted. You know, the cute white designer one you have pinned to your vision board. I'll seriously buy it for you if you do this for me. *Pleeeease*," she whined.

"God, Kay. You really hate dancing that badly?"

I glanced at the two empty cages in the middle of the floor, my heart kicking up a notch. It had been a while since I'd danced. Truthfully, if it weren't for the money, I'd do it all the time. "All right. And you don't need to buy me that purse. I want to buy it myself when I can afford it. But maybe dinner sometime?"

"Deal." She threw her arms around me, pulling me into a brief hug before saying, "I'll handle the rest of your tables." Then she scampered away.

I glanced around, not sure where Bastian was hiding, then headed to the locker room to get changed. I left my dagger on my arm since no one would see it. I wasn't sure if it would hamper my dancing, feeling it there, but I couldn't bring myself to remove it. Then I stretched out a little, warmed up my muscles, and left the room. I wore the signature Vortex outfit we danced in, the metallic gold crop top and thong.

I crossed the floor, nodding to Tanner before climbing into one of the empty cages. It gave a gentle lurch and started lifting. When the current song faded, a new one came on. I prowled around my cage, then reached for the bar and swung myself into the air.

A grin stretched across my face. It had been a little over a week since I'd danced. Soon my heart was pumping and my blood racing. I moved my body, letting the music flow around me, molding myself to it, becoming a part of it.

The gold ring on my finger gave a burst of warmth and I thought of Bastian. I could *feel* his gaze. I remained alert, not blatantly looking for him, but simply keeping an eye out, then I spotted him in the shadows of the farthest VIP balcony. He stood against the wall with his arms crossed, eyes glued to me. My ring gave another flare when he saw me looking, as if to say hello. He didn't look too worried, but I could tell even in the shadows that he was tense.

I swung my body around, climbing up the pole, then sliding down, moving along it, arching my back. The crowd was a blur around me. They'd all but disappeared with Bastian's presence. Knowing he watched, knowing I was dancing *for him*, sent butterflies fluttering in my stomach. I couldn't help but feel everything had come full circle. We were here again, where everything had started.

It wasn't until I felt my ring flare hot—hotter than before —that my stomach jolted. I looked toward where I'd last seen

Bastian, but he was gone. Then I found a frighteningly familiar pair of blue eyes latched onto me, and I understood.

Bastian had moved to intercept Luke.

I exhaled a shaky breath. My ex watched from one of the balconies, standing near the edge, forearms braced on the railing. When our eyes met, he gave me a salute. The grin on his face turned my blood cold.

Nausea pooled in my stomach. I pulled my gaze away, pretending like his presence didn't affect me, and kept dancing. A few minutes later, I spotted Bastian. He'd moved, gotten a better vantage point to keep an eye on Luke.

I blew out a breath.

Bastian and I had gone over the plan a thousand times. Knowing what I had to do, I finished my current song, then gave the signal for my cage to be lowered. I caught Luke's eye and gave him a nod of my head, angling it toward the back of the club. I couldn't be sure if he interpreted it how I intended.

A few minutes later, I strode across the floor to the locker room. When I entered, I let out a breath and leaned against the door. This was it—now or never. Preferably never, but if I didn't act, we might not get another chance.

My stomach roiled. I wasn't ready to face Luke, wasn't sure if I'd ever be. I felt braver here in the quiet locker room. But as soon as I faced him, what then? Would I turn into a scared little mouse?

No. I'd managed to fight back last time. *Only to be captured anyway,* said the voice in the back of my mind. If Bastian hadn't showed up, I'd be dead.

My breathing kicked up a notch. I hated that someone so awful could have this effect on me. I needed to be angry, not fearful. I needed to master this, if I was ever going to move on. For years, he'd made me feel nothing but weak. After I'd escaped him, I spent years living in fear and paranoia. This needed to end once and for all.

My phone beeped. Bastian had allowed me to bring it to

Vortex. If Luke was tracking it, all the better to lure him here. I pulled it from my locker and saw Vivi's text.

VIVI

Just landed! It's so good to be back. Heading over to Kaylee's house in a few. She gave me the code. You okay?

I'm not sure.

Actually, there's something I've been wanting to ask you.

Do you think you could start calling me Elle again?

Three dots popped up, went away, then popped up again.

VIVI

Are you sure that's wise?

I've thought about it. I'm done hiding who I am.

VIVI

Does this have anything to do with your sexy goblin?

A little, yeah. He makes me feel safe.

VIVI

I'm happy for you...Elle. God, I didn't realize how good it would feel to use that name again.

Thank you.

VIVI

I take it things are going good with you guys?

Sort of? Actually...

I could use one of your cheesy pick-me-ups right now.

VIVI

They're never cheesy!

Uh-huh. Come on. Just one!

VIVI

Fine.

VIVI

Never let someone treat you like yellow
Skittles. You're a badass bitch. Pink Skittles
all the way, girl.

A giggle burst from my lips and I glanced around the locker room.

Let me guess, you found that one online?

VIVI

Yeah, was it too obvious? It was for Starburst,
but I like Skittles better, and since I changed a
few words, it's my creation now.

God, I love you way too much.

VIVI

Love you too!

Talk to you soon!

VIVI

Xoxo

If things went south tonight, at least I got to share a few words with her.

There definitely weren't pink Skittles. Unless you counted Valentine's Day candy. "God, Vivi, you're such a weirdo," I muttered. But knowing that only made me love her more.

Changing back into my official uniform, I rolled my shoulders back and lifted my chin. My hands trembled slightly, but I clenched them into fists. Pink Skittles—I could do this. I slipped through the back security door and outside. I held my breath, glancing around. A shadow materialized and my heart punched a wild rhythm in my chest.

"Hello, Elle." My stomach clenched. I backed up a step, faltering, forgetting all about the bravado I'd had moments before. Luke held up his hands, like he was calming a frightened animal. He hesitated, watching me, his head tilting to the side. "Where's your goblin friend?"

I glanced around, blinking. "I…don't know."

"No matter. You can't run from me anymore, Elle. Give it up. I know where you live, where you work. Did you like the little warning I sent?" My stomach hardened at the reminder of what he'd done to my apartment. "I'm not the same person you knew. I've…acquired some advantages since then."

A deranged laugh burst from my chest. "If you're trying to scare me, it isn't working. Where's the harp, Luke?"

He blinked, genuine surprise flickering across his features before settling into cruel amusement. "Well, well. Look at you. Putting all the pieces together. Been doing your research, have you?" His smile turned razor-sharp, condescending. "I'm almost impressed. Tell me, what else do you think you've figured out?"

"That you're still the same pathetic coward you always were. Just with fancier toys now."

His face twisted with rage. "Enough talk, Elle. I'm done playing your games. I told you I would make you wish you were dead, remember? Do I look like someone who goes back on my word?"

Ice slid into my chest. Luke darted forward. I froze like a deer in the headlights. He grabbed me, fingers going for my throat, driving me backwards. *Oof.* I grunted, slamming against the wall. His fingers squeezed and I choked, heart pounding, body completely unresponsive. He'd moved too quickly. I wasn't ready.

A manic laugh slipped from his lips. He brought them close to my ear and my stomach turned rock hard. "If you think I'm going to kill you right here, right now, then you don't know what I meant when I said you'd wish you were dead."

I blinked, and my sluggish mind started screaming at me.

Fight back! This isn't you anymore! Do something!

His grip tightened around my throat and he lifted me, until my feet were dangling. Stars burst in my eyes. "Nice trick, huh?" He said through clenched teeth. "I'm a lot stronger now, thanks to a nice little trinket I acquired."

An artifact. Of course. Which meant he'd have others. That thought brought more clarity to my mind. Lifting my left arm, I reached for my right bicep. My fingers closed around the dagger strapped there. Bastian's gift. I pulled it free.

A frown stole over Luke's face. Since he couldn't see it, my arm motions probably looked weird. I moved, plunging it forward, right into his side where Bastian had showed me.

He grunted and doubled over as the hand at my throat fell away.

I sank to my knees, gasping. Coughing. My eyes watered and I could barely see anything. But none of that mattered. Warmth spread through my body. I had done what I'd struggled to do in the past. I'd pulled myself free of fear and acted.

"You fucking bitch," he hissed, examining his side. I heard the clank of metal, a dagger clattering to the ground. I clambered to my feet, ready to finish this. Time was up. I'd had enough of Luke fucking Portman.

35

Aflash of movement caught the corner of my eye. Bastian collided with Luke's body, and I stumbled backwards, finding the wall again. My legs wobbled, and I leaned my weight against it, trembling. A fist flew, followed by a crunch. He had Luke on the ground in seconds, holding him down with one hand, punching him in the face over and over with the other.

My expression went slack, eyes growing wide at the sheer brutality of it.

"You hurt her," Bastian ground out. "You hurt my fucking *mate*. How does that feel, hm? Taste of your own medicine? I should rip your fucking innards out," he growled. "String you up with them. Peel your skin from your bones and fucking *feed* it to you, you piece of shit. How would you like that?"

Luke managed to get a grip on Bastian's biceps and roll him over, probably with his added strength, but the victory was short-lived. He was still human, after all. Bastian had him pinned once more.

"Bastian," I hissed, my skin prickling. His fist didn't stop—like he didn't even hear me. *Crunch. Crunch. Crunch.* The sound made my stomach roil. Luke had it coming, and yet, I couldn't stand to watch. I couldn't look away, either. Soon, Luke's pathetic gurgling whimper filled the air.

"Do you know what goblins do when their mates are threatened?" His voice was an inhuman growl.

Crunch. Crunch. Crunch.

The breath fled my lungs. I shook my head like I was trying to rattle free the thoughts that stuck together.

Mate?

The word clanged around in my head. Everything else crumbled away, even the sickening sounds. A point found my throat—the point of a blade. I was dragged away from the wall. I didn't fight it, barely registered that there were several other people filling in around us.

"Tell him to back off," a voice growled in my ear, "Or I'll slice your pretty neck right open." A couple of people had filled in around us. Luke's people.

"I…"

Mate.

No. I'd misheard.

"Tell him to back off or I'll kill you," the voice repeated.

Bastian froze. When his head turned, eerily slowly, his eyes fixed on the person behind me. There was nothing of the man I knew. Only pure, undiluted monster. Though his glamor held, his eyes were entirely black. The expression on his face when he saw the blade at my throat. The way he looked at my captor. It would have turned anyone's bowels watery.

"I mean it," my captor said, shakier this time. "I'll kill—"

The blaring whine of a siren erupted around us. Another joined it.

"We gotta get out of here, Tony," a new voice said. Someone swore. The knife pressed more firmly against my throat. A bead of blood rolled down my skin.

Bastian's black eyes darted to it, tracking it, then back to my captor's face. "I will kill you for that." His voice was a low promise.

"Boss won't be too happy if we leave him," Tony snapped, addressing whoever had suggested they leave Luke behind.

"I ain't getting nabbed by the cops," someone else hissed.

Blue and red flashing lights filled the alley behind me. Tony cursed and the knife disappeared. I blinked. Then they were gone, darting toward the far side and disappearing.

Bastian's eyes darted in the direction they'd fled. I could see the indecision playing out on his face—chase them down or stay with me. His jaw clenched, hands fisting at his sides, but he stayed put. A second later and his eyes turned green.

"Elle, baby," he took a series of hurried steps toward me, rushing over—

"Hands above your head!" An authoritative voice filled the air. Spotlights fell on us. Bastian froze. "Hands where I can see them."

My eyes were glued to Bastian. His chest rose and fell, heaving. But his eyes stayed on me, darting over my body, assessing. He lifted his hands, planted them behind his head, like he knew exactly where to put them. I, however, didn't feel quite so confident. Limbs shaking, I lifted my hands too, but more in a half-hearted, awkward, upright position.

I looked down at Luke, unsure if I was relieved to see him still breathing. Part of me wished he was dead. And yet, what kind of person would that make me?

Feet pounded the pavement. A breath later and my hands were gently pulled into someone's grasp, cuffs placed around my wrists. Wait… What?!

"That's the guy," I managed, shaken and confused. "The guy on the ground. Luke Portman. He's the one responsible for the mayor's gala."

My words didn't seem to have any effect. Wait… Why were they taking *me* when it was *him* they wanted?

Bastian growled and surged forward. "Take your fucking hands off her, Floyd, or I'll remove your fingers."

"Ahh… If it isn't Bastian Croft," Floyd said, turning to him. Someone else was already putting cuffs around Bastian's wrists. A couple of other officers were crouched around Luke's bloodied body. One of them whistled and said, "Damn, Croft, was this you?"

Clearly Bastian's reputation went beyond the supernatural community.

"How about you two hang tight right here where we can see you," Floyd said, "while we sort this out."

A presence appeared at my side. Eaden. "You okay, Rose?"

"I—yes."

"I had to call it in," he explained, looking over Luke's unconscious body. Cops were cuffing Luke's wrists as paramedics rushed onto the scene. "I wouldn't have bothered to get involved at all, if some of his guys hadn't shown up."

"You should have kept your fucking nose out of it, Eaden," Bastian growled.

"Should he have?" I snapped, my patience thinning as I rounded on Bastian. My goblin's gaze was still locked on Luke, death lurking in his green eyes. "You probably would have killed him."

"I intended to—yes."

"You *intended…* Are you fucking insane, Bastian?! We need the harp. You were, what, going to kill him first and ask for its location second? Or were you not that concerned that a powerful—" I stopped myself and lowered my voice. "A powerful artifact is just floating around, putting supernaturals to sleep."

A couple of officers rushed by, helping the paramedics as they lifted Luke onto the stretcher.

"Well then," Eaden said conversationally. "I think I'll leave you two to it."

"I had everything under control, baby girl." Bastian turned back to me.

My breaths came faster and deeper. "Don't… Don't *call* me that. What the fuck was that back there?! *Mate?* Are you going to explain that? Something tells me you didn't mean girlfriend. Is this some kind of mate shit I read about in my werewolf books? Like, where we're tied together for the rest of our lives?"

My chest heaved. Somehow, I knew it was. There were too many signs. The possessiveness. His willingness to be something with me he hadn't been with anyone else. The fucking *roses*. "When were you planning to tell me this *super-fucking-important* piece of information?"

My anger was better than the sense of disillusionment lurking deeper. Here I'd been waiting for the other shoe to drop. Drop it fucking did.

"Elle…" His voice softened. Some of the frenzy melted away. "It's… I was planning to tell you. I intended to. Shit's just been… There didn't seem a right time—"

"Well, sorry about all this," came a familiar voice. Christian appeared, keys in hand, and began undoing my cuffs. Freed, my hand went to my throat where I'd felt the skin break from the blade. It must have been my imagination. The skin was flawless, even though I felt the smear of blood.

Bastian's eyes zeroed in on my movements. Christian fumbled with his cuffs. As soon as he was free, Bastian rushed over to me, his hands reaching for me. I stepped out of his reach and didn't miss the flash of hurt, there and gone, in his expression.

"I'd like to know what happened here," Christian interrupted, "but something tells me the two of you need a minute alone." We both shot him a *go-the-fuck-away* glare and he disappeared to speak with some of the officers.

"How could you not—?" I took a sharp inhale and shook my head. I should have expected this, should have known that things were too perfect. That there was something deeper going on. "I *told* you I didn't want you keeping things from me. You *knew* that."

"Fuck," Bastian breathed, raking his palms over his face. The knuckles on his right hand were covered in blood—Luke's blood.

My stomach churned.

"Baby girl, let me explain—"

"No. No… I don't want to hear it." And I didn't. My adrenaline was plummeting. I could barely hold myself up. My mind was filled with confusing thoughts. My heart felt like it was cracking wide open with the shock of the revelation, the hurt of betrayal. I was struggling to know what I should feel, beyond anger. Bastian reached for me again and I backed away. His expression crumbled.

"Here's what's going to happen," I said, managing to keep my voice steady. "We're going to do whatever we need to here. Give statements and whatnot. Then you're going to take me back to your place and I'm going to pack my things. After that, you're going to take me home. I don't want to talk to you right now—not about this. I'm so…" I sighed, taking a steadying breath. "I'm so fucking angry with you right now, Bastian. Like, peel your skin off your gorgeous stupid dumb goblin face kind of angry."

"I'm not taking you to your apartment—"

"Yes," I hissed. "You are."

His mouth opened—

"In case you missed it, Luke is in the back of an ambulance on the way to…wherever. He's in custody now. I'm going back to my apartment. I need… I need some space right now."

And to be with Vivi.

Bastian's shoulders fell. He watched me, nostrils flaring, like he was trying to get a read on me from my scent alone. "Fine," He bit out. "That's fine… Whatever you need, baby girl."

Knowing what I was to him, I understood that he was exerting a great deal of effort to give me the independence I demanded. Did that win him any bonus points? No. Instead, I scoffed at the pet name, then blew out a breath. Some things weren't worth my energy.

Everything afterward happened in a blur. He stood with

me while I gave my statement, spoke with several people who came and went. At some point, we were free to go. We drove back to his place in absolute silence. He opened his mouth several times, then shut it, shaking his head. I didn't care. Whatever he wanted to say, he could keep it to himself.

Mates?!

I thought back through everything in greater detail, trying to figure out what had happened. Maybe I'd been blind. Maybe I should have put the pieces together and come to this conclusion. In hindsight, it was all there, in bold lettering.

My fingers clenched and unclenched between my thighs, where I'd wedged them to keep them still. How long had he known? This entire time? Since spotting me in the coffee shop? I bet he'd had a nice laugh about it, knowing we were tied together in some way, and knowing what it meant for him —that he'd be tethered to me, a human, part of the race he hated so much for what they'd done to him.

When we entered his house, I rushed to my room, closing the door. I refused to cry. Not here. Not where he could smell it. So instead, I threw my things together, filling my suitcase. I was too incensed to check if I'd packed everything, but fuck it. Part of me thought this wouldn't be forever, the other part, the frightened part, didn't want to face any of this ever.

I emerged into the main part of the house.

"I packed up Teddy's things already," he said, his voice flat. His eyes darted over me, searching. When I passed him, I noticed the way his hand lifted to reach for me before clenching into a fist and dropping.

I ignored it.

He stopped in the doorway to the garage, Teddy's cat carrier in his hand. "Baby girl, isn't, can't…can't we just talk about this? I'm sorry. I should have told—"

"No!" I rounded on him, holding up a hand. "I told you I didn't want to discuss this right now, and I don't. I need… Fuck! I don't even know what I need, except that I need to be away from you right now."

"And you think I'll let you go so easily?" His voice pitched low, some of the goblin bleeding through as his eyes blackened. Then he froze, horror flashing across his features, like he realized what he'd just said. His eyes shifted back to green. "Fuck. Elle, I didn't mean—that's not—" He ran a hand through his hair looking stricken. "I'm sorry. That's not who I want to be."

"Good." My shoulders relaxed.

He gave a stiff nod and deposited Teddy in the back seat before climbing into his truck.

I shot Vivi a quick series of texts on our way back into the city. When he parallel parked, she was already at the apartment, standing outside on the sidewalk. Bastian reached for the door.

"No," I said. "I've got it. Vivi will help. You don't need to get out."

His expression faltered. It was brief, but I saw the pain there, the uncertainty. A spear of guilt shot straight for my heart, but I ignored it. I was resolved in this. Bastian had kept something *monumental* from me, something I deserved to know. The professor Miller incident was one thing, but this?

I opened the door without another look, grabbed my suitcase, and passed it off to Vivi. Then I got Teddy's things, gave Bastian a final resigned look, and slammed the door to his truck.

Vivi's own things were waiting in the atrium. She didn't have the new key to our apartment, so she followed me up, carrying Teddy's things and a few of her own. We managed to get everything into the elevator with minimal words.

I unlocked the door.

The apartment was flawless. My insides squeezed. The last time I'd been here, days ago, was with Bastian. I looked at the television he'd fixed, remembering how I'd watched him work, unable to pull my gaze away. The memory brought tears to my eyes. I was losing it, seconds from imploding.

As soon as I stepped inside and set my things down, I

crumpled to the floor, sobbing. Most of it was because of Bastian's dishonesty, but not all of it. Some of it came from my drained adrenaline, from Luke's manhandling, from the fear I'd felt when he'd had his fingers wrapped around my throat, from the blade that had been moments from slicing my neck wide open. It all crashed down in a torrent of tears.

"Oh, Elle!" Vivi dropped her things and came to her knees beside me, wrapping me in her arms. We'd been in a similar position two years ago, when she'd brought me home from the hospital. When I'd cried for hours on end, and we'd curled up in her bed to watch sitcom reruns.

"He—he *lied* to me," I managed between gasps. "I thought… I'm just… Why would he do that?!"

She made shushing sounds and rocked me back and forth, letting me cry, offering low, comforting words.

Meowwwwww.

Teddy made his presence known. Vivi crawled away and let him out of his carrier, before coming back and pulling me into her arms again. He darted off to scope out his new territory.

I loved Vivi. It was hard to imagine what my life would be like without her friendship. She'd seen me at my worst over the past few years, knew me better than anyone. We were sisters in everything but blood.

Ever so slowly, my crying slowed. When I could speak, I managed to tell her the whole story. She'd known some of it from our phone calls, but I gave her greater details, especially where Bastian was concerned.

"Damn," she whispered. "Mates? Really?"

I nodded.

"And you're sure it's like that possessive alpha-hole mates shit, that super hot kind? Like, bend you over the table and claim you kind?"

My stomach lurched because that's exactly what he'd done. "Yes," I managed. "He didn't say it explicitly, but looking back, I'd be stupid to believe otherwise."

"And that asshole didn't say a word?!"

"Not a peep," I groused.

"Well, fuck him!"

"Exactly," I said, a weak smile pulling at my lips. "Fuck him."

She sighed. "What are you going to do? Kick him to the curb? You know I've got your back no matter what you decide."

"I don't *knowww*," I whined, covering my face with my hands, squeezing my eyes tight. "He lied to me, Vivi. I mean, he kept this from me, but that's practically the same as lying. But I… Fuck. I'm so conflicted. He's nothing like Luke. He's never physically or mentally hurt me. He's never made me question my worth. He's never played mind games. It's the opposite, actually. He makes me feel so fucking beautiful, stares at me all the time. I mean, he cooks me freaking *pancakes* and plies me with thousand-dollar bottles of wine."

"Okay, if you don't want him, I'll take your leftovers," she teased.

I groaned and bumped her with my shoulder. "Too soon. Not funny."

"I know, I know. Sorry. It sounds like you need to think about what you really want. I can't tell you what to do. Not with this."

"I know," I whispered. She was right.

What *did* I want? I'd known him just under two weeks and I was already falling for him. Falling hard. Was that because we were mates?

"What if this is one of those mate things where I'm not allowed to be with anyone else, like…ever? Like, what if I won't be able to love anyone else? What if I'm *forced* to be with him," I managed. "When I was with Luke, I was trapped. I… I'm afraid, Vivi. I don't want to feel trapped like that again. Maybe that's why I ran tonight. Why I wouldn't let him explain."

"Girl, Luke Portman fucked you over. That kind of shit

doesn't just go away immediately. You gotta work for it. There's nothing wrong with being afraid of things that happened in your past."

I sighed. "I think I just need time to think about all this."

"That's probably a good idea," she said. "And I'm always here to bounce ideas around." She hesitated, then said, "You know what you need?"

"Hmm?"

"A girls night. We're canceling work, life, everything. We're getting our girls together, no excuses."

I managed a watery chuckle. "Maybe that's exactly what I need."

"But for now," she amended, "you need your bed, and a good Teddy cuddle. I was going to steal him tonight, but you need him more than I do."

I smiled, my first genuine smile since the start of this entire discussion. "Have I told you how much I love you, Vivs?"

"Yep. But you're always welcome to say it again." Her eyes crinkled as she smiled. "And for the record, I love you too."

We hugged. Then I stood and grabbed my things, heading down the hall and disappearing into my room. I tried not to think about the bed. Tried not to think about what I'd done on it the last time I'd been here. Instead, I went about my bedtime routine, put some of my things away, found Teddy, and collapsed beneath the sheets.

astian kicked the door frame and listened to the house shudder, then walked into his living room. His hands were locked behind his neck as he began to pace. "*Fuuuck*," he growled, feeling his glamor waver.

He went to the liquor cabinet and pulled out his most expensive bottle of whisky. Then he downed a third of it in one go before slamming it on the cabinet surface. He needed something to tie him down. If he didn't get his shit together, things would take a turn for the worse. He was seconds away from grabbing his bike and storming Eleanor's apartment building and throwing her over his shoulder. Bringing her home, here, where she belonged.

With him.

Because she was *his* and he wasn't letting her go. He'd warned her. Goblins didn't relinquish their prizes. And a mate? No.

He picked up the bottle and took another long swig. He'd fucked up. He'd known what was happening to him—to them. He'd known they were mates since the morning she went down on him, when his orgasm rocked him and everything clicked into place. But he'd been a fucking coward. Afraid to tell her how deep this thing between them was, afraid to say aloud what it would mean for them.

Mated pairs were common among most supernatural races, but it was rare to see pairs cross-species. His parents had been a rare pairing, fae and goblin. Goblins were said to be a sub race of fae, but as far as he was concerned, they were their own race. The fae just liked to make shitty claims to feel superior. How fucking unsurprising, then, that something similar had happened to him.

Elle's face flashed before his eyes, her pink hair and flushed skin. He growled, letting his fist fly. It slammed into the wall and the house shuddered again.

"Motherfucker," he hissed, looking at the damage. Pulling energy from his metals and turning it into magic, he fixed the damage.

Yes, he needed to get his fucking shit together.

He headed for the garage, then stopped himself. He could *not* go back for her. He'd seen her face, her expression. If he pushed, it would make things worse. He would not be like Luke. Not even a little. He would not force her to be with him —would not take her choice away from her.

"I don't want you to keep things from me," she'd said. *"I hate that feeling, you know? Luke did it all the time, actually. Intentionally kept things from me."*

This was his fucking mess to fix. He deserved this for being so damn stupid. Deserved to feel this way, because he'd hurt her.

His chest caved in. He'd *hurt* her, when she was his to protect, his to care for, to cherish and worship. "Fuck, fuck, *fuck*." He went back to the living room and resumed his pacing. She was probably crying in Vivi's arms right this second. His stomach turned into a hard knot. She should be crying in *his* arms. He deserved to see the tears, to be tormented with them.

Or maybe she's not crying at all, a little voice taunted. *Maybe you fucked up so badly, that she's done with you. What makes you think you're so special? What makes you think she wouldn't just abandon you the same way Sara did?*

He opened his mouth and roared. The sound shook the walls. He needed to break something, a lot of things. Instead, he stalked through the house to her room. It smelled like her. For a second, it was like she'd never left. Exhaustion pulled at him.

He sank onto the bed, bracing his forearms on his thighs. His head hung low. He closed his eyes. Right now, there wasn't much he could do, except grow some fucking balls and deal with the aftermath. Deal with his feelings.

He thought about everything else that had happened. Luke was in critical condition at the hospital, under tight watch. He needed to go there and get some answers. It'd felt damned good breaking that asshole's face—too good.

He sighed and went into Eleanor's bathroom, stripping off his clothes, climbing into the shower…the shower he'd fucked her in. After that, he climbed naked into her bed, pulling the covers over his face, closing his eyes, letting her smell surround him.

When it was clear he wouldn't get much sleep, he got up. Putting his time to good use, he began digging around in Luke's background. Looking for pressure points. Anything he could use as leverage for what came next.

When he had everything he needed, he formulated a plan.

———

The following morning, he made pancakes—Eleanor's favorite—with bacon and coffee. He cut up strawberries and made fresh whipped cream. He shouldn't have, it was probably overstepping, and she might hate him for it, but she was still *his* to care for. So he'd make sure she was fed. And…

He was good at this sort of thing.

He plated everything, covered it with a metal plate cover to keep it warm, and paired it with a large mug of coffee prepared exactly how she liked it. He summoned a bit of creamy cardstock and a pen, then scrawled '*I'm sorry.*' If he had to apologize for the rest of his life to make this right, he would.

He sent her breakfast, the card, and a single red rose to her apartment, to the desk in her bedroom.

There was no guarantee she'd be in her room to see it. No guarantee she'd even touch it after what he'd done. But he felt better knowing he'd done what he could—for now. Then he downed a cup of coffee and set off for the city. He didn't bother eating, since he couldn't stomach the thought of food, but he did take comfort in the hope that Eleanor might be eating his pancakes right this second, dousing them with the mini carafe of syrup he'd included.

Luke Portman was being held under high security at the hospital. He took a certain satisfaction seeing how fucked up his face looked. Christian sat in a chair, waiting.

"He said anything useful yet?"

"Hasn't said shit," Christian confirmed, sitting with his arms crossed. "But we did confiscate a couple of interesting items from his pockets, ones that were missing from the WU library displays. Strangely enough, one of them must have kept him alive after your beating."

"Damn. Too bad." Bastian eyed Christian and the other officers in the room. Luke's eyelids fluttered, like he was waking up. "I want to talk to him. Alone."

"Not happening."

"Christian."

"You think I'll leave you alone with him after your actions last night?"

Bastian rolled his eyes. "I won't touch him. You have my word."

Christian watched him for a long moment then sighed. "Fine. Ten minutes."

"Thanks."

The others left the room while he pulled up a chair. "Not the best look for you, asshole."

A wheezing laugh was Luke's only answer. He didn't even open his eyes.

"Here's how this is going to go. You're going to give me answers, and I'm going to leave you alive. So, why don't you tell me where you hid the harp? Your answer won't make any difference on your record, but it might make your life a little less shitty, considering what I've got planned."

Luke laughed again, his eyes finally cracking open. "Did you fuck her? Did you get after that tight pussy? How'd you like the way she feels?"

Red flashed in Bastian's vision. He was snarling before the sound registered as his. He took a steadying breath. "Don't mention her. Don't even *think* about her."

"Your mate, huh? A little human mate. Does it bother you that I fucked her first?"

This time, every coherent thought slid right out of his mind. He was going to fucking *kill* this little piece of shit. He reached out, then closed his fist before it made contact. Keeping his voice lethally calm, he said, "You are so, *so* very lucky I promised not to touch you." Luke only huffed. "Tell. Me. What. You. Did. With. The. Fucking. Harp."

"I don't have it," Luke said, staring at the wall. A small smile pulled at his lips. The asshole was fucking enjoying this.

"What do you mean, *you don't have it*?" He hissed. "You used it. Where did you put it?"

"Oh. I didn't use it." Bastian blinked and Luke snickered. "You think I did all that? Pulled those specters from their bodies? Created a bunch of walking ghosts? Not so great at your job, huh?"

Luke was baiting him.

"*Where is it?*" He snarled.

"I'll tell you, but in return, I want a favor."

"You're not getting shit. How about this, instead? I might be bad at my job, but I found your father, found out what care facility he's located at, found out how much you've been paying to keep him there. He seems real nice and comfortable. Also saw that you visit several times a week. I promise you this. If you do not tell me exactly where the harp is, then Mr. Portman might not wake up tomorrow morning."

Luke's body went rigid.

"You hurt someone who means *everything* to me—my fucking mate. I am a goblin. If you think I possess a shred of decency where your father is concerned, you're wrong. Do not think I have qualms about hurting someone you love in return, for the way you hurt Eleanor."

Luke's throat bobbed. His eyes darted in Bastian's direction. "Fine," he rasped. "Get a piece of paper. I'll give you the address."

Game. Over.

37

"He made you pancakes?!" Vivi cried as I carried the plate and coffee into the kitchen, setting it on the small table.

"Yes," I grumbled, trying to be bitter about it. Key word, *trying*. I'd already peeked under the plate cover, then quickly covered it again so that I didn't have to witness the full force of what was hiding beneath.

"You're going to eat them, right? Are they still hot?"

"Warm, yeah." I lifted the mug and took a sip, then groaned. "Oatmeal cookie," I whispered.

"You're joking right?! Flavored coffee?"

"Vivi," I snapped. "You're supposed to be on my side."

"Girl, I am on your side. I'm also freaking starving for pancakes."

A small smile pulled at the corner of my mouth. "Wanna split them?"

"Tcha! Yes. You bet your freaking life I do."

We pulled up chairs and forks. Beneath the plate cover, we found four fluffy, perfectly formed pancakes topped with expertly arranged sliced strawberries, a generous side of bacon, and syrup.

"Aww, he arranged the strawberries like flowers!"

"Vivi!" I snapped. "Not. Helping."

"Right. Sorry. Fuck him! Who plates food like this? We should mess it up." With that, she grabbed the syrup, doused the pancakes, then cut into them. I snickered, waiting. Her groan made me grin. "Oh. My. Fuck!" She said through a mouthful, then swallowed. "Is that…vanilla? And almond extract? And cinnamon too? What the fuck are these?!"

I sighed, sinking low into my chair. "The best pancakes in the world. That's what. *Ugh.*"

"You should demand a thousand of them, in penance for what he did. Pancakes every single day—for the rest of your life. And…don't forget about your friends."

I rolled my eyes, then took a forkful and shoved it in my mouth. I didn't bother hiding my own groan of delight. These were especially good, like he'd really pulled out all the stops to make them perfect.

"I fucking hate him," I groused. "For being so goddamn perfect, and then being an asshole at the same time."

We spent the rest of our meal talking shit about how amazing Bastian's pancakes were and how much we hated him for it. Turns out, that was exactly what my heart needed. Damn that goblin!

Vivi insisted that I do everything as normally as possible, so that's how I found myself at my martial arts studio later that afternoon, and then at Awake Coffee, grabbing drinks. I was waiting in line when I felt a tug at my abdomen. The sensation jolted through me, like someone was pulling out my insides. I gasped and placed a hand over my stomach.

I glanced at my phone. Bastian hadn't texted me all day. Shouldn't he have?

In a moment of weakness I wasn't proud of, I opened my texts and fired one off.

> Thanks for the pancakes. They were amazing. I'm still mad at you. Don't think this fixes anything.

There. That would set matters straight. I considered adding something about how, maybe, if he sent me pancakes every morning, it might help me figure things out faster. But at last, I decided not to push it. I stared at the screen for a moment, but nothing came in response. I slipped it into my pocket and stepped up to the counter, placing my order with Tara.

"Excited for girls night tonight?" Vivi had let it slip that she'd invited her.

"Yes! Should I bring anything?"

I grinned. "Just yourself. Well, and maybe a bottle of wine."

"Vivi told me you were having boy trouble."

I snorted. "Of course she did."

"So… Maybe I should bring two bottles of wine?"

"One is fine. If I have too much, I'll end up drunk dialing him in the middle of the night."

"Been there, done that," she joked.

I paid for my order and went to wait for our drinks. Vivi, bless her, had sent out the call. Those of us who were scheduled to work, (Kaylee, *cough-cough*) decided to make various excuses about being ill so that we could all be together.

Admittedly, I was looking forward to it. As much as I wanted to mope around, eat ice cream out of a container, wear PJs, leave my makeup a mess, and lounge in bed watching TV for the foreseeable future, this would be good for me.

———

The door bell rang later that evening and Vivi began buzzing people up. Soon, the couch was filled. Amira, Kaylee, Mikka, Tara, Yvonne, and Vivi gathered around me. Three bottles of open wine sat on the coffee table, along with one of Vivi's famous charcuterie boards. I took a sip of Chardonnay, trying not to think of Bastian. He still hadn't responded to my text.

Vivi had music playing in the background while we all caught up on each other's lives. Amira worked with Vivi at the museum. She'd moved to Walton after college. She and Vivi had immediately hit it off, despite being polar opposites of each other. Where Vivi was easy going, Amira was tight laced and extremely organized. They'd bonded over their love of books and the rest was history.

Kaylee worked with me, but also held a day job as a receptionist in a dental office. I'd seen her in her usual pencil skirt and cute little blouses. Mikka was Tara's best friend, someone she'd known since childhood, who worked in the engineering sector. She beat everyone for brains and beauty, with a Ph.D in mechanical engineering and a delicate bone structure. But it was her big cartoon-ish eyes that made me weep with jealousy.

Tara didn't just work the front counter at Awake Coffee, she was the co-owner. She'd opened the shop with her mom. They were a power team, with her mom baking in the back while Tara managed most of the scheduling, finances, and front counter. Talk about a boss bitch!

Lastly, there was Yvonne. She was a dark-skinned beauty who worked in hospitality, though she used to serve drinks with me at Vortex. She had moved on, now managing staff at one of Walton's premier hotels, The Wisteria. Her sharp tongue, good listening skills, and attention to detail made it easy to see why she'd been promoted so quickly.

I had to admit, every woman in this room was pretty badass. We were all human, and none of us had been born wealthy. But we'd managed to make good lives for ourselves… except, perhaps, me. There were definitely times where I felt like the weakest link. I probably made less than all of them and didn't feel like my career was as impressive as theirs. But I tried not to let that bother me. And they never once made me feel inferior.

To everyone here, I was Rose. I'd met all of them, except for Vivi, after my life with Luke had shattered into a billion pieces. Vivi had been careful to keep up the ruse when we were all together, but I was growing tired of it. So when it was my turn to speak, I said, "There's something I need to tell you guys."

And because they were all so freaking amazing—and I was so damn lucky to have them—they all sat quietly while I told them exactly what had happened with Luke (the abridged version), and why I'd changed my name.

"Girl, if you think we didn't already suspect you'd changed your name," Yvonne said, throwing her arms around me, "you're delusional." She sat on my right and was the first to react. "The way you hesitate sometimes when people call you Rose? We noticed."

I nervous-laughed into her shoulder and hugged her back.

"Does this mean we can't call you Rose anymore," Mikka said, pouting. Her huge eyes narrowed. "I liked Rose. It goes with that amazing rosy hair."

I burst out laughing. "Yes," I managed, a weight lifting from my chest. "If you want."

"You look like an Elle to me," Amira said. "It suits you. But I'll probably still accidentally call you Rose."

"You guys are so amazing," I breathed. "You're not… mad?"

Kaylee scoffed. "You think we'd be mad about you trying to protect yourself?"

I opened and closed my mouth, relaxing into the couch. Vivi sat on my left and leaned in, resting her chin on my shoulder for a second. "See? Told you they'd take it well." I simply lifted my eyebrows and grinned. We'd briefly discussed it before they had come over, the potential of me finally coming clean. Now that Luke had been apprehended, I felt safer about my best friends knowing.

"And they really caught the scumbag that hurt you?" Tara asked. She sat on the fourth couch cushion, on Vivi's left. I didn't miss the way their hands were creeping closer and closer. Every time I glanced over, they were a centimeter nearer. I wasn't the only one to notice. I didn't miss Mikka's knowing glances, nor the gleam in her eyes. Now, their fingers were practically touching. I watched Tara's pinky twitch, like she was working up the courage to make contact, while Vivi seemed completely oblivious—or was pretending to be.

Part of my heart was soaring to see it, because I wanted them to happen so-freaking-bad. The other part of my heart was squeezing tight, because as much as I didn't want to admit it, I was already missing Bastian. Missing my mate.

Fuck, that would take some getting used to. I pushed aside my thoughts of him and nodded, answering Tara's question. "He was apprehended last night. Cops got him."

"Damn. Thank goodness," Tara breathed, her eyes darting between mine and Vivi's. "That asshole deserves to rot in jail."

I hadn't told them all the details. Far from it. All they knew was he'd hurt me badly and was now suspected of murdering both Professor Miller and Peter. Oh, and also that he'd trashed our apartment. They falsely believed that we'd managed to put it back together. I didn't reveal how badly it had been destroyed.

"So…" Yvonne said, "tell us about this Bastian guy." Her eyes danced. I knew it was coming, but that didn't stop my stomach from dropping at the sound of his name. None of us were in serious relationships, but they all dated around. And if things went well tonight, maybe Tara and Vivi would become an item.

"Oh," Vivi jumped in. "You have no idea what he did this morning. He—"

"—brought me apology pancakes," I said, cutting her off. Vivi's eyes widened, probably realizing what she'd been about to blurt. That he'd used magic to deliver said pancakes.

"Yes, right," she said, recovering. "And they were the best fucking pancakes I've ever tasted. Like, restaurant quality. Better, even. You know, something you get at those bougie places with the strawberries arranged all fancy and such."

"So he can cook?" Mikka asked.

"You have *noooo* idea." I felt a pang of longing but forced myself to smile.

They wanted details, so I gave them as much as I could, shamelessly revealing a few of the naughty things he'd said. But I kept most of our sex life to myself. It felt private. Something Bastian and I had shared, something I wanted to keep between us.

As the night wore on, we moved to other topics. I found myself grinning nonstop. It helped that I'd consumed several glasses of wine and enough cheese to give me a cheese-high. Maybe this wouldn't be so bad, this time away from Bastian. Being without him would allow me the space to think, to really figure out what I wanted. Whether I wanted a mate. A freaking *mate*.

Perhaps it was time to hear him out about the bond—what it meant and why he hadn't told me. Did I want forever with him? My chest tightened, but for the first time, it wasn't from fear. It was from hope.

38

I spent the majority of the next day in my PJs in bed, even though I'd said I wouldn't be that person. Mostly because of my awful hangover. But also because when the morning hours ticked by and no pancakes appeared, no return text from Bastian, my mood took a turn for the worse.

And here I'd thought I might reach out to talk things over, despite my gut telling me I needed to wait for him to come to me. So instead, I got angry and mopey and took a couple of painkillers to rid myself of my headache. Vivi got us takeout for lunch, and left mine at my bedroom door when I refused to let her in. The high from our girls night had worn off.

After lunch, I napped, cuddled Teddy, and binged sitcoms. When that didn't work, I scrolled videos on social media. But that still didn't work. I couldn't stop thinking about him, about the way his hands touched me, the way he kissed me, fucked me.

I lifted my phone and checked it for the umpteenth time. Still nothing.

"Ugh. Freaking, *ugh*." I threw it across the room and groaned, collapsing back onto my bed.

That was when my phone rang.

I jumped up so quickly that Teddy went tumbling. He gave me an angry meow.

"Sorry, Teddy! Sorry!" I glanced apologetically at him before rushing across my room and plucking up my phone.

I frowned. It was a local area code, but one I didn't recognize. I almost didn't answer it, considering how few people had this number. "Hello?"

"Rose?" It was a voice I recognized.

"Christian?"

"Yes, this is Christian Wells. Sorry for reaching out like this. Have you heard from Bastian?"

I sank onto my bed. "Uhm… No? Why?"

There was a heavy sigh on his end. "I've been trying to get ahold of him. He hasn't been returning my calls. Been MIA since yesterday afternoon. He came by to talk to Luke Portman in the morning, then left in a hurry and didn't say anything."

"Maybe he just needs some space? We kinda had a little… disagreement."

That was putting it mildly.

"Hmm." There was a hesitation. "That's not like him. It's not like him to ignore work calls."

Chills spread down my arms, lifting my hairs on end. It was probably nothing to worry about, but I could hear the concern in Christian's voice. "Well, did you go to his house and check on him?"

"Yep. Did that. Can't get inside. The security system isn't dialed in to me. I knocked though, and there was no answer."

"Are you a supernatural?" I blurted.

He grunted. "No. Technically, for bureaucracy purposes, I'm just his boss."

"Of the SA?"

"Of the SA," he repeated. Which meant he knew all about supernaturals. Knew what Bastian was.

"Huh." I chewed on the inside of my cheek, trying to ignore my rising worry. "Well, I haven't heard from him. Not since yesterday morning." I didn't need to give him the details about Bastian's apology pancakes, or that my version of *hearing from him* was merely in the form of two words scrawled on a piece of cardstock.

"All right. Well if you do, this is my cell. Would you mind letting me know?"

"Is… Is everything okay? Did something happen with Luke?"

Another long hesitation. "Portman's transfer from the hospital was scheduled for later this week. Only problem is, he's dead."

"What?!" I gripped my phone until my fingers ached. "Dead?"

"This is confidential, but I think you have a right to know, seeing as you helped bring him in. I can't explain how it happened. He was under high security. None of his guards can explain what happened, either. He was slated to make a full recovery, but a nurse came in to check his vitals this morning and everything was unplugged. He wasn't breathing. Looks like he might have been strangled, but considering all the damage to his face and neck, it's hard to tell if those are just left over from…before."

"Right." From Bastian's fists, is what he didn't say aloud. I blew out a breath. "I'll let you know if I hear from him. I promise."

"Thanks, Rose. Take care."

The line went dead.

My thoughts spiraled. I let them for several minutes, until things began to crystalize. I couldn't just ignore the way I felt, the worry that something bad had happened. I scrolled to Bastian's number and pressed the call button. It rang four times, then went to voicemail. I tried twice more, both times the same. I looked at the last text I'd sent him, about the pancakes. I texted again anyway.

I stared at the screen, waiting. Nothing came through. I chewed on my bottom lip, the knots in my stomach tightening. Something was wrong. It wasn't like him to ignore me. If we *were* mates, which apparently we were, he should have been desperate to answer. I'd seen the look on his face the other night, knew he was reluctant to let me go.

Fuck.

My hands started shaking. I typed out another text, then deleted it. If he wasn't responding, sending him another wouldn't make a difference. I needed to make sure he was okay.

Jumping from the bed, I changed clothes, throwing on a pair of leggings and a T-shirt. I pulled my hair back, washed my face, brushed my teeth, and grabbed my purse. "Vivi?" I shouted down the hall, walking toward the living room.

Her head popped out of her doorway. "Yes—oh." She looked at me. "Something wrong?"

"I don't know. I just have this…feeling. I'm going to Bastian's house. Going to check that he's okay."

"Did something happen?" She frowned.

"I… I don't know." My eyes started to fill as I blinked back the tears. "Christian called—that's Bastian's boss—and said he couldn't get ahold of him. I'm… I'm really worried. What if…"

My hand flew to my stomach. Yesterday I'd felt something. A weird swooping sensation, like someone was pulling on my insides. And for a second, it had been difficult to breathe.

I hadn't thought anything of it until now.

"What if he was so angry that he did something? Something stupid? Like, you know how in some of those mates stories—like, mates get all possessive and emotional and dramatic and whatnot?"

"You don't think he would have done something extreme, do you?"

What if he thought he'd lost me for good? What if he thought I was completely done with *us*, to the point where he didn't want to live without me? It seemed extreme, but right now, my mind was entirely irrational.

"I don't fucking know, Vivi," I whispered.

"Okay, let me grab my purse. I'll come with—"

"No. I need to do this alone. If he is there, I… I want to be alone with him."

"But what if something happened and—"

"I'll call you. I promise. If something else is going on, I'll call you and send you his address."

She bit her lower lip, then nodded. "Fine, just be careful, okay?" Her arms came around me and she pulled me into a hug. "Don't do anything stupid. And if he is there, give him hell for making you worry like this."

"I will," I managed. Then I opened my phone and ordered a ride.

———

I breathed a relieved sigh when Bastian's house came into view. My fingers tapped my thigh impatiently as we drove up into the driveway. My driver stopped in front of his craftsman home, and I emerged, looking up at the porch, trying to determine if anything was amiss. Everything looked completely fine. "Thanks," I told the driver and shut the door. I walked up the steps, opening my phone and giving the driver a tip before sliding it into my pocket.

I made sure he drove off before pounding on the door. "Bastian?" I called. "It's me. Come on. Open up."

Still no answer.

Sighing, I went for the keypad and punched in the code, a string of ten numbers and my fingerprint, because he didn't fuck around. The magical tech system gave a zap and I saw a veil of blue waver around the house, long enough for me to open the door and slip in. As soon as the door closed behind me, it armed itself again.

Standing in the foyer, I listened. Everything was silent except for the ticking clock in the living room.

"Bastian?" I called. My eyes darted to the wall beside me, the one he'd pinned me against, the one where everything had started. Memories came flooding back. I swallowed. "Bas?" My voice shook. Still no answer.

My stomach lifted into my throat. I forced my legs to move. I didn't have proof that something was wrong. And yet, I could feel it in my bones. Perhaps some additional sense that came with being mates.

I popped my head in the living room. There was an emptied whisky bottle sitting out on the liquor cabinet, but no sign of Bastian. I ran up the stairs to his bedroom. It was empty, the bed made. My stomach dropped. I went back downstairs and checked in my room. The bed was rumpled, even though I'd left it made. He'd slept there.

My chest fluttered. "Freaking *fuck*," I muttered. Warmth spread through me at the thought of him lying there, missing me, trying to be closer to me. I trudged into the kitchen and shrieked.

"Oh my, God! Bastian!" My heart dropped to the floor as I ran forward. He sat at the island, slumped over a plate of food. All my worst fears exploded in my mind. Did he ingest the entire bottle of alcohol? Take some pain killers? How could he be dead, when we were only starting our lives together as mates?!

"Oh my, God!" I breathed, trying to see through the tears springing to my eyes. "Oh my fucking God!" My hands trembled. I couldn't *breathe*. The world tilted on its axis and I reached out to grip his chair, to steady myself. Each inhale was a sharp knife. I wrapped my arms around him and hauled him upright, leaning him against me. His head flopped against my shoulder. Tears began dripping down my cheeks. I looked for evidence to explain his death.

"No. No, no, no, no. Bas!"

How could this have happened? Was it my fault? Did he think I was done with him? Did he not—

A light breath tickled my skin near the base of my neck. Bastian's exhale. I sucked in a breath, looking for a pulse, then groaned. Alive—he was alive. His heartbeat was steady, eyes chaotically darting beneath his closed lids.

"Wake up, Bastian." I gently smacked his cheeks. "Wake up, baby. Come on. Wake up." The roaring pulse in my ears grew louder. I slid the plate with a half-eaten sandwich and chips aside, brushed his face clean, and leaned down, kissed his lips. He didn't kiss me back. His lips were warm, but they were unresponsive. I kissed him harder, willing him to wake up. His breath hitched, like somewhere deep inside, he recognized me. But that was it.

"Wake up, baby, please," I whined.

Nothing.

"Fuck-fuck-fuck." How was it possible? Had he turned into a sleeper? But… Luke was dead. Christian had confirmed it earlier. If Luke was dead…

My heart jumped in my chest, putting the pieces together. Luke didn't have the harp when we'd found him. It was never him. We were wrong. Claws scraped against my insides. I caressed Bastian, petting him, trying to think as my fingers brushed the velvety hair on the shaved side of his head.

My eyes fell to his phone on the breakfast bar. Next to it, a slip of paper with something scrawled in Bastian's handwriting. It had been torn from a notepad with Memorial Hospital's logo on the bottom corner. I reached for it. An address in the city.

I frowned.

The address was on Sepula Industrial Boulevard, which housed distribution centers and manufacturing plants. Why would he have this?

I pulled out my phone and punched the address into my maps app. It popped up as a big warehouse, but didn't have any kind of company name associated. The street photo made it look like an abandoned building.

My skin crawled. I thought back to what Christian had said. Bastian had gone to talk with Luke at the hospital yesterday. At some point last night, someone had killed Luke. Why? To silence him? Tie up loose ends?

If so, what did Luke know? Did it have something to do with the address on the paper? I rolled my lips between my teeth—thinking.

If *I* were Bastian, I'd have gone looking for the harp. Luke would have been my best lead. That's the first question I would have asked. It was doubtful that Luke would simply tell Bastian the harp's location. But maybe he'd convinced Luke to talk.

I touched him again, kissing his forehead.

"Did you leave this for me to find?" I wasn't sure if Bastian could even hear me in his current state. But I hoped so. "I'll figure it out, baby. I'll fix whatever happened to you. I promise."

If the harp had done this to him, if someone was still out there using it, this wouldn't stop. More sleepers would succumb. I needed to act.

I glanced at my phone. Christian had asked me to call as soon as I heard from Bastian. I almost dialed his number, then hesitated. He wasn't a supernatural. If Bastian had gotten this address and didn't tell him, brought it home, sat here with it, was there a reason? Maybe supernatural politics I didn't understand. And if this was connected to magical artifacts, what could Christian actually do?

My cheeks puffed up, blowing out a breath. Maybe I'd just pop over and give it a look. Maybe it was some kind of storage facility and Luke had hidden the harp there, along with the other artifacts he'd stolen. The idea of reclaiming all those items for the university made my pulse speed up. It certainly wasn't the first time I'd gone on an artifact hunting mission. I'd been on several.

I could pop over, have a look around the premises, then give Christian a call if anything looked suspicious. Or even if it didn't. He should at least know that Bastian—in physical form—was home, alive and breathing.

I glanced around the kitchen. I wanted to make Bastian comfortable, but he was the size of a brute and there was no way I could move him. I gently eased him back onto the island, ran to the living room and grabbed a pillow, then came back and wedged it beneath his face.

Poor thing. I ran my hand down his back as a final good-bye. Thundering down the stairs into the basement, I went to the wall he'd shown me and found the hidden switch, revealing his massive weapons collection.

I looked it over. I couldn't cover myself in weapons. Actually, I couldn't even use most of what was here. I'd probably just end up injuring myself. I spotted a couple of black back-packs. I grabbed one, unzipped it, and threw in several daggers, one of the cool smoke bombs he'd shown me, and a 9mm handgun. I'd gone to the shooting range with my father but hadn't shot anything in at least five years. Still, I would be stupid not to take one, even if I only planned to scope this place out.

Zipping the bag closed, I returned to the main floor. Bastian was exactly where I'd left him, not that I was surprised. It just felt so…surreal. He was always full of life. Seeing him like this, lifeless, made my stomach churn.

I turned away, heading for the door. Entering the code on the inner security pad, I stepped outside and took a seat on the porch. Then I ordered a rideshare. While I waited, I texted Vivi, trying to control my trembling fingers.

I'm heading into the city. If you don't hear
from me in two hours, contact this number.
His name is Christian. Give him this address.
If you don't hear back, or if he gives you any
reason to be suspicious, contact the police.

I took a photo of the memo paper and sent it, then copied Christian's cell and pasted that, sending it afterward. I crumbled the memo paper and stuffed it into my pocket.

VIVI

What the hell is going on, Elle? Did you find
Bastian?

I sighed.

I found him but…it's a long story. Just,
promise you'll do it, okay? Two hours. If I
don't text you in two hours…

Dots appeared and her message came through.

VIVI

Then I'll send that photo to Christian and tell
him…what?

My rideshare app binged, giving me a two minute warning.

Tell him that I'm in trouble and need him to
come get me.

It took ten seconds before my phone started ringing with Vivi's name. I didn't answer. If I did, she'd talk me out of this. I ignored her call and texted.

Just do it, Vivs, please.

VIVI

Fine. Two hours. If I don't hear from you, I'll
contact that number. But I can't promise I
won't come looking for you myself.

                    Don't you dare! Promise me you won't.

VIVI

You're fucking insane. If something happens
to you I won't forgive myself.

                    Nothing is going to happen! Just do it. Please.

VIVI

Fine.

VIVI

I love you.

                    I love you too.

My ride share pulled into the driveway—a four-door
sedan—and I climbed in. My driver confirmed my name and
address and then silence fell. I tried not to think about what
had happened. My hands hadn't stopped trembling. Instead, I
scrolled through social media, trying to distract myself.

The industrial side of the city was opposite of Kentwood.
Surprise, surprise. So, it took nearly thirty minutes to get to
the address. The driver pulled up and parked, then turned
back to look at me. "You sure you want me to drop you off
here?" she said.

"Yep. Meeting a friend. Thanks."

She hesitated, then nodded. I climbed out and tipped her
on my phone, adjusting the backpack. The sun had nearly set,
so I was running out of time. The air smelled of diesel fumes
and something metallic, with an underlying staleness that
made my nose wrinkle.

I listened as the sedan drove away, peering through the
fence. It was chain link, but there wasn't any barbed wire. I
walked along it. The parking lot was empty. The occasional
semi drove past, churning up the air along the road. Otherwise, everything was silent.

I found a delivery driver entry point with a gate arm. I
walked over and slipped beneath. Goosebumps crawled across

my skin and I glanced around the parking lot. The asphalt was cracked; weeds grew up between. There were small trees in the planters, but they looked neglected.

There weren't any cameras on the outer walls of the building. I breathed a relieved sigh and walked closer. It was an industrial style, so I didn't expect many windows. Metal doors were spaced every hundred feet. I walked around to the back side where I found the loading bays. One of them was open, and several cars were parked nearby.

A scuffing shoe made me whirl around. I froze. A tall female walked toward me, perhaps twenty feet away, looking in my direction, coming straight for me. I went rigid. "Shit," I breathed, glancing around. I could run. Instead, I opened my mouth to formulate an excuse——

She didn't slow, didn't even stop. In fact, she gave no sign that she even saw me. Instead, she walked right through me and continued on through the open bay door. And that's when I knew I was in deep trouble.

39

My heart raced as I spun, looking after the ghost-thing that had just walked through me. That *had* happened, right?

I should have run in the opposite direction, but instead I crept close to the wall, then looked in through the open bay. I could not help myself. What if Bastian was in there? Or…his ghost. I couldn't just leave him here, not if I could help him, speak to him, and perhaps figure out how to fix all this.

The lighting was dim, but I could see that the warehouse was filled with racks of boxes. Perhaps some kind of distribution center. I hadn't planned to break in, just have a look around. But now?

I pulled my backpack off and removed the handgun. I also tucked the sheathed dagger in the waistband of my pants, wishing for all the world I hadn't lost the one Bastian had glamoured for me in the alley. I slipped around the opening and kept to the shadows, walking along the nearest rack. I heard voices farther into the building. None of the boxes were labeled, and I didn't want to make any noise by pulling them down and checking their contents. Any one of them could have hidden the harp.

A figure appeared at the end of the aisle. I froze, backing

against the rack. There was nowhere to hide. A male, I realized, as it grew larger. He walked with his face forward, carrying a large box. Like the other, he didn't even look at me. I reached out as he passed, and my hand went right through him.

Otherwise? He looked completely solid. Real.

"What the fuck?!" I whispered. Some weird ghost shit was going on, and I was not cool with it. I crept along after it, sticking to the shadows. More of these strange ghosts appeared—or, I assumed that was what they were—moving boxes, working together as they created stacks of them.

"Eleanor Rose Kennedy. My, my." I went rigid, heart nearly bursting in my chest. I recognized that voice. "Did you come looking for your boyfriend?"

I whirled around, coming face to face with—

"Marsh Thadur?" I lifted my handgun, pointing it at him. His eyes darted to it before finding mine again.

He smiled. "You seem surprised to see me."

"What did you do to Bastian?" I punched the gun forward so he'd get my point.

"The same thing I did to all of them." He lifted a shoulder as if no big deal. "Barbara!"

A woman, the one I'd seen earlier, walked over. "Take her. Cuff her to the rail over there."

Adrenaline flooded me and I whirled toward the ghost approaching. Barbara wore the same blank look as earlier. My breaths turned shallow and I pulled the trigger on my handgun. Shots rang out and went right through Barbara's ghost.

She came straight to me, not stopping, and pulled the gun from my hand, flinging it away. Her fingers wrapped around my wrist and dragged me through the central open area of the warehouse. I kicked at her, and my foot went right through her.

"What the fuck?!" I hissed.

It made no sense. I couldn't touch her but she could touch me?

I tried to get free, punching her in the face with my free hand. That went through her too. She dragged me to a set of racks and ripped my backpack free, flinging it away. Pulling a zip tie from the tool belt at her waist, she snapped it around my wrist, tying me to the bars. She put a second in place, just to be thorough.

I struggled against her the whole time, but nothing I tried worked.

"She's a specter, Elle darling. You're wasting your time."

My head whipped around to Marsh. He walked toward us, his steps unhurried. The expression he wore was amused.

"I don't understand," I managed.

He laughed. "And here I was told you were an artifact *aficionado*. What aren't you understanding? The Sleeper's Harp pulls the specters from their bodies, putting them into a deep sleep. I control them, as the harp's owner. They do as I say. Anything beyond that and they are untouchable. If whatever you try is outside the description of their job, it will have no effect whatsoever."

My brows pulled together.

"Think of it this way, Elle. They can touch you when I command them to. But you can't do anything about it."

My stomach dropped. I tested the zip tie, tugging as it cut into my wrist. My other hand was free. But there was nothing I could do without something to cut my binding.

"Don't bother," Marsh said, noting my movements. "In fact, how about I send someone to keep you company? Bastian!"

I sucked in a breath, my heart dropping. From the cluster of bodies hauling boxes, Bastian appeared. My mouth fell open.

"Bas?" He didn't acknowledge me, didn't even look at me. Instead, he walked right up to us, a blank look on his face. Everything about him was completely normal, aside from the fact that he seemed unresponsive, his expression and eyes empty.

"Guard her," Marsh barked. "If she tries to break free, knock her unconscious."

With that, he walked away.

Bastian walked over, took up a wide stance five feet from me, facing me, and stared off into the distance. Like I wasn't even here.

"Bas!" I hissed, trying to get his attention. I waved my hand in front of his face, snapping my fingers. He didn't flinch, didn't respond. He was just out of reach, and I knew if I tried to touch him, my hand would go right through.

"Marsh's gone," I said, keeping my voice low. "Help me get this zip tie off." Bastian *still* didn't move, looking through me.

"Bas, *please*! It's me! Your *mate*. Remember?" I pulled at the zip tie while I said this, trying to put enough force behind my movements that it might snap.

"Stop doing that." His voice was a low command, eyes flicking to the motion I made as I pulled. When I stopped, his gaze went distant again. The back of my neck prickled. This wasn't Bastian. Marsh was right. Whatever fell within his orders was all he was programmed for.

I deflated and leaned against the shelving rack, studying the rest of the activity taking place. Minutes ticked by, and boxes were carried out. A roar of an engine sounded as a semi-truck pulled up. The back was opened, and the boxes were loaded.

How much time had passed? Had it been two hours yet? I thought of my instructions to Vivi. Soon, she'd be calling Christian. The cops would come and this whole mess would be sorted.

Hopefully.

The semi left and Marsh appeared, walking toward the open space in the middle of the warehouse.

"Bastian, remove the zip tie and bring her here."

I glanced between them, then saw what Marsh held. My heart leapt. The harp! He held it casually, like it was little more than a regular object and not some ancient thing of power. I was vaguely aware of the zip tie snapping with magic —Bastian must have retained his magical abilities in this form —and a hand wrapping around my wrist. He didn't pull me the way Barbara had.

"Come," he said, when I hesitated. There was something gentle in his voice. Was… Was part of him still in there? Fighting?

I licked my lips, but complied. He led me to Marsh. My eyes zeroed in on the harp in his hands. If I could just get it, could I find a way to reverse this?

Marsh chuckled. "It's rather a work of art, wouldn't you agree?" He asked, as if reading my mind.

"How does it work?" I found myself asking, curious, yes, but also eager to distract him.

"Ah, I thought you'd want to know. The trick is in the strings. There are twelve total. The first five, put a person to sleep, depending on what type of supernatural they are. You must be within hearing distance when the chord is struck. So, you see, it was rather annoying, but I managed to sneak onto Bastian's back patio yesterday. He has quite the security system, but alas, it isn't soundproof."

My muscles tightened.

"Oh, don't worry. It won't work on you. It doesn't work on humans, unfortunately."

I cleared my throat. "What… What do the other strings do?"

"Ah. The next set of five pulls the specter from the body. The last two are…" He hesitated, contemplating, then said with a shrug, "simply ornamental."

I snorted. "You don't expect me to believe that do you? Like, what about waking up the bodies? Controlling them?"

He grinned. "Now, why would I tell you that?"

I rolled my eyes, trying to appear nonchalant. "Because you're probably just going to kill me?"

"True. Very well. As far as commands, if you're the one to

wield the harp and summon the specter, they follow your commands automatically. The eleventh freezes them in place. And to put them back in their bodies? Simply stroke the twelfth." He shrugged.

I tutted. "I thought it would be more complex than that. Seems kinda underwhelming."

He barked a laugh. "Yes, it does, doesn't it? Anyway, I have places to be, and unfortunately, I don't wish to spare any of my specters to guard you. Unfortunate casualty, I'm afraid. Bastian? Kill her."

"What?" I cried. "No."

I jerked against Bastian's grasp. A knife appeared in his free hand. He lifted it.

"Bas, no!"

I knew that if this happened, if he killed me and lived afterward, he would never forgive himself. It would ruin him. I pulled, trying to put distance between us.

The hold on my wrist disappeared and I staggered backward.

"Kill her!" Marsh barked.

I backed up. My foot caught on something and I slipped, arms flailing before landing hard on my ass. Bastian bore down on me, his knife raised. He lunged forward. The knife swung wide, slamming into the cement. I couldn't be positive, but I knew Bastian's aim was perfect, so he must have intentionally missed. A small, low growl escaped his lips as he grabbed me again, taking aim.

"Bastian, please don't do this," I implored, needing him to snap out of it. What else could I say? "Bas, please. I'm not mad at you anymore. We can be together. I... I *love* you."

He froze, blinking down at me. Something flashed across his face.

"How are you doing that?" Marsh barked. "Stop it. Bastian, follow your orders." Bastian didn't move. He just stood there, blinking down at me.

Seeing me.

"You can't control him," Marsh hissed, anger creeping into his voice. "Never mind. Barbara, kill her."

My breath caught. I scrambled to my feet and moved toward Bastian. He stepped back, coming upright. His blade disappeared, but he didn't move.

Barbara walked toward me, carrying a long blade. "Bas?" I glanced toward him, but he didn't move.

"If you think he'll protect you, you're mistaken. The magic of the harp will not allow him to do anything beyond his orders."

"Well, I managed to get him to stop, didn't I?" I spat. "And maybe if you weren't such a coward, you'd kill me yourself instead of making a bunch of specters do your dirty work."

Barbara lunged toward me. I dodged. She came at me again. I'd never imagined fighting someone I couldn't actually connect with. She moved with inhuman speed. When I focused on her, breaking through her glamor, I noticed her fae ears.

"Fuck," I muttered. I was up against a fae specter with magic. I didn't stand a chance.

Dodging another thrust, my foot connected with a box and I stumbled. A hand fisted the back of my T-shirt and I was pulled backwards. White hot pain pierced me through my lower back, into my abdomen. I looked down in time to see the tip of Barbara's blade protruding from my front. I blinked, then screamed as the white-hot pain flooded my system. The blade retreated and I crumbled to the floor, gasping. Blood spilled from my body. I gazed at it, wide-eyed. Every muscle began trembling.

"No!" A voice roared, laced with anguish. Bastian's voice.

I whimpered, turning to face him, my eyes locked on him. He stood rooted in place, chest heaving, watching me, his face screwed up with pain. His expression was more present than I'd seen so far.

"Bas," I breathed. Heat spread around the wound, tingling. Perhaps I was numb with pain. Or perhaps...

A wild notion took hold. But there wasn't time to contemplate it. Barbara was bearing down at me, blade poised for the killing blow—

"Hands where we can see them!" The loud command split the silence of the impending moment. "Hands in the air! Move. Move. Move!" Voices erupted, shouting commands that echoed through the warehouse. I had just enough time to roll away as Barbara's blade came down on me. The pain from the movement made me scream, but I rolled three times to get far enough away from her that I'd be safe. Then I blinked, my eyes darting around. The crash of several doors sounded next, being kicked in. People poured into the warehouse in vests, guns drawn, the letters S.W.A.T written on their backs.

Marsh swore, glancing around. More and more bodies filed in, quickly outnumbering the number of specters gathered around Marsh. He lifted his arms, summoning shadows around him, his fae magic. My eyes widened.

Gunshots split the air. The harp clattered to the ground. I gasped, then glanced down at my abdomen, my brows pulling together. My shirt was ripped and covered with blood, but the wound wasn't weeping.

Lurching into motion, I scrambled across the floor, speed-crawling toward the harp. No one else seemed to notice. The shots stopped and the shadows cleared. Marsh lay on the ground, chest heaving. He was fae, after all, so the gunshots wouldn't kill him, but they would keep him down.

I snatched the harp.

Everything was chaotic. I didn't know if it would work, didn't know if Marsh had to be the one to do it, or if anyone could pluck the strings. He lay there blinking. I took hold of his wrist, dragging his fingers across the twelfth string. He hissed and snatched his hand away. The specters filling the warehouse vanished.

40

I collapsed to my hands and knees, letting the harp lay where I left it, struggling to get air. Fumbling with my T-shirt, I pulled it up, baring my abdomen. All I found was a red line where the blade had driven through my body. I touched it and winced, still tender.

Again, a strange theory floated through my mind. I was Bastian's mate. And Bastian was some kind of immortal fae supernatural. Did that tie us together in…other ways?

"Rose Kennedy? Elle? Eleanor!" Christian's voice cut through the chaos. Voices weren't yelling commands anymore. Several people rushed in around Marsh, cursing when they saw who he was. They put cuffs on him, keeping their guns drawn.

"Christian," I warned, "it's Marsh. Marsh Thadur. He's fae."

Christian fell to his knees beside me, saw my blood, and cursed under his breath. "You're okay?" he asked. I nodded. He turned to the others who were lifting Marsh off the ground. "Keep him well guarded. He's supernatural. Fuck. We need Bastian for this shit—"

"WHERE IS SHE?!" A voice roared, shaking the walls. Bastian. It had worked. He must have transported himself straight here once I'd freed his specter, using a decent portion of whatever magic he'd saved.

I spotted him then, his eyes glued to me, sprinting across the warehouse, pushing people aside to get to me. Christian stood up, took a step back—smart man. Bastian fell to his knees, pulling me into his arms, eyes wide as he took in the blood. His mouth crashed over my lips, kissing me, holding me tight to him. I whimpered. The tightness fled my muscles and I burst into tears. He was here. He was okay.

We were okay.

"Shh. Shh. Baby girl, it's okay. Fuck. You were so brave. So fucking brave." He held me, rocking me back and forth. He fumbled with my shirt, pulling it up and checking the wound. His eyes darted back and forth before settling on my face. "The mate bond," he said. "I didn't realize. Fuck." He dragged a hand over his face. "Thank fuck."

I'd never heard him so relieved.

The supposed bond had saved my life. Whatever connected us had allowed me to heal, had given me his magic. I was too overwhelmed to think about it right now.

"I thought… I thought you were dead." The words came out choked as more tears fell. "When I found you."

"Shhh." He stood, moving me around until I was wrapped around him spider-monkey style.

"Bastian, we need—"

"No, Christian." His head snapped to the side. "Have Phillip handle this shit. I'm taking care of my girl." Christian's mouth opened and closed, but Bastian strode off without waiting for him to respond. I burrowed my face in his shoulder as he walked me to a more secluded area back in the racks. He set me on one of the shelves, pushing boxes out of the way.

His hands roamed over me, checking every inch of my skin. I shivered against him, pawing my eyes.

"You'll be expected to give a statement, sugar. But I want your story before you give it to them, hmm?"

I nodded, then told him exactly what had happened. How I'd found him. The slip of paper. I reached into my pocket and fished it out. He took it and simply tossed it away, lifting my hand and kissing my palm.

"Did you mean what you said?"

"What?" My voice was still thick with tears.

"Did you mean what you said earlier, when I was fighting Marsh's compulsion." I hesitated. "Say it, Elle. I need to hear it again."

"I love you, Bastian. It's only been two weeks and yet, I've fallen deeply in love with you."

He leaned forward, his mouth molding to mine. I groaned, kissing him back, sweeping my tongue along his.

Eventually, I pulled away. "I didn't know if you'd be able to hear me. Didn't know if it would work."

"That fucking—" He stopped himself and took a deep breath. "He tried to make me kill you."

I felt the tremor that went through him, felt him shudder against me.

"You didn't," I whispered. "You fought it. I saw you fighting it."

His forehead came to rest against mine. "You made all the difference. I don't fucking deserve you. Elle, baby, I'm so fucking sorry. I should have told you when I realized what we were. I should have—"

I kissed him, locking my hands around his neck and pulling him close. I wanted to talk about these things, but I wanted his body more. I needed to feel him inside me.

"When can you take me home?" I demanded. "Sex now, talking later."

He chuckled, fussing over me, making sure every inch of my skin was unscathed. "You'll need to give your statement to Christian or one of the others, then I can get you out of here."

He brushed a strand of hair from my face as I nodded, doing exactly that.

When we were done, he didn't fuss with human transportation. Shadows wrapped around us and that awful falling sensation returned. I pushed out of his arms as soon as the night air kissed my skin, stepping away. I bent over and he lifted my hair as I took deep breaths, felt the bile rise, then vomited. "You're all right," he murmured, his hand rubbing my back. I vomited again, completely emptying my guts. When I finished, I stood up and wiped my mouth on my arm before looking around. We were outside my apartment building.

I frowned. This wasn't…

"I thought you might like to get your stuff if you're going to spend the night."

"Oh. Yes, I suppose that would be good."

"And Vivi? She's probably worried about you?"

"Shit." I turned on my heel and raced into the building. I'd recovered my phone when I'd given the WBI my statement. But things had been too chaotic to call her. I punched in the code and raced inside. Bastian was close on my heels. In the elevator, he kept his hand on the back of my neck. My stomach fluttered at the clear possessiveness in his touch. He wasn't going to let me go anytime soon.

The elevator dinged and I strode to the apartment door, banging my fist on it. Rustling and cursing sounded from the other side. And then Vivi flung it open, her wide eyes darting between us.

"Motherfucking fuck!" She threw her arms around me. "If you ever make me worry like that again, I'm going to kill you!"

I hugged her back and breathed her in, the smell of her shampoo comforting me. "I'm okay. I'm okay."

"You better be." She pulled back to look at me, then her eyes widened at my disheveled appearance. "Oh my, God!"

"I'm fine. Seriously."

Her eyes darted to Bastian. "Did *you* do this?!"

"It's a long story," I said before he could answer. "I'll tell you everything later. Right now, I want my clothes. I'm staying at Bastian's tonight."

Her lips pulled downward.

I made a sound and said, "I need to fuck his brains out, Vivi. Unless you want to hear us in my room—"

"Okay! Okay. Fine! No. Get your stuff and go." She stepped out of the way and I rushed in, dashing around my room, grabbing my things. I made a quick stop in the bathroom and brushed my teeth, getting rid of the vomit taste.

When I came back into the living room, Vivi was staring at Bastian with cautious curiosity. The room was absolutely silent. He held Teddy in his arms, petting the cat's head. I faltered, watching those large hands stroke Teddy's fur. Wanting those large hands all over *my* body. Warmth curled in my core.

"I see you've had time to bond," I said.

"Who?" he snapped, his eyes darting toward Vivi. "Me and the cat? Or your friend who keeps giving me the death glare?"

"Both?" I grinned.

Vivi huffed, rolling her eyes. "You put my best friend in danger, *Bastian*. Excuse me if I feel inclined to glare."

Bastian lifted an eyebrow at me, as if saying *see?* without turning toward her. "She *does* make a good point."

"I put *myself* in danger," I clarified, adjusting the strap on my shoulder.

"Only because you felt inclined to play hero and rescue me, which, mind you, was very dangerous. We'll be having a chat about that later, by the way." And something in the promise of his voice sent shivers over my skin. We'd do more than chat about it, I was certain.

"The harp can't be used on humans." Not that I'd known this before setting out. "Far as I'm concerned, I was the best woman for the job."

"I won't argue with that." His eyes heated with the admission. He set Teddy on the floor then came over to me, hooking an arm around my waist. "Now, didn't you say something about sex?"

A choking sound came from across the room. "Can you please not?!"

I barely had time to shoot Vivi a grin.

"Sorry about this, sugar." Black shadows wrapped around us again, taking both of us and the duffle bag slung over my shoulder. I was falling...falling...falling. When my feet were on solid ground, I didn't feel as nauseous as I had before. I took a deep, steadying breath.

"You good?" Bastian studied me and I nodded. "Good."

He pulled my bag from my shoulder and scooped me up into his arms, carrying me up the porch stairs. At the door, he punched in the code and temporarily disarmed the system, then carried me inside, kicking the door closed behind us.

"Want a drink?" he asked.

"Later," I breathed.

He carried me to my room, then tossed my bag aside and walked me into the bathroom. My stomach bottomed out as he lifted my bloodied shirt from my body, then slid my leggings down. I stood and watched as he stripped away his own clothes, tossing them aside. Then he lifted me by my buttocks, forcing my legs around him, and carried me into the shower stall. He turned on the water, shielding me from the cold as it sprayed out and heated.

His lips found mine as he pressed me against the tile, grinding his cock against the apex of my thighs. I groaned, my hands slipping over him, looking for purchase. I pulled his long hair back behind him, then tangled my fingers in it. He growled, pressing his cock more firmly against me.

Sparks erupted at the contact.

"Mate," he breathed. "*Mine*."

Possessive words. The words of a goblin.

The muscles in my core clenched. I tightened my legs around him, rocking my hips. A hand slipped between my legs, fingers toying with me. My breaths came out shaky.

"So wet already, baby girl?" He massaged me, spreading my wetness around, coating me entirely before dipping a finger inside, pushing it deep. My hips bucked against him.

"More," I whined, needing all of him. One finger became two. My hips continued to rock, desperately needing release.

His hands went to my thighs, and he moved me into position. The head of his cock was at my opening, then pushing in. Then he backed out and gave a single thrust, sheathing himself fully. We both groaned at the feel of it, our mouths meeting, tongues dueling in a mess of lips and teeth. His body flickered and his glamor fell away. Pointed teeth nipped at my lower lip. I felt the metal of his piercing against my clit and a shiver wracked me.

"Yes!" I breathed, clenching around him. "Yes. More."

"So demanding, little female. I would never deny you." He pulled out, then slammed back in, sending a tremor through my body, a zing from the piercing. My body went molten, erupting with heat as I sucked in a breath. He did it again, and again, until his hips rolled powerfully against mine.

My panting turned to gasps as the ache between my legs built. As I trembled in his arms.

I'd almost lost him—almost lost *this*. Things could have gone very differently today. If the authorities hadn't shown up in time. If Bastian hadn't overpowered Marsh's compulsion. If the mate bond didn't have the power to heal me. So many *ifs*. But I'd succeeded, and we were here now, and I intended to make the most of it. There were still things to discuss between us, but for now, here in this moment, our bodies and the primal thing between us was all that mattered.

41

Bastian carried his naked mate to her bed. It smelled like her, and that's exactly where he wanted to be, bathed in her scent, surrounded by it, buried in her cunt. He'd come so close—so fucking close—to losing her. He'd been there the whole time, deep within the recesses of his mind, a slave to the compulsion. When she'd appeared in that warehouse, he'd felt a fear he'd never known. The fear of profound loss.

It had taken every ounce of his strength to fight Marsh Thadur's order. Had they not been mates, had she been anyone else, he would not have hesitated. Unlike Barbara, his blade was lethal. He knew how to kill, knew how to remove a head with a single, efficient swipe. Hers would have rolled. Instead, by some grace, Barbara had stabbed her and the mate bond between them had kept her alive, had healed her.

He would have followed her to the grave. This fierce female with pink hair had *changed* him. Now that he'd had a taste, in no life, in no world, could he give her up.

He crushed his mouth to hers, dragging the covers up and around their bodies, still damp from the shower, cocooning her in, making her comfortable in this nest of a bed. He planned to take pristine care of her, starting with fulfilling her every desire. How many orgasms were too many? And how long could she sustain the onslaught of his tongue, his cock? He planned to find out.

She kissed him back, dragging her tongue along his, groaning and grinding against him.

She'd professed her love earlier. It was the key that allowed him to rally his strength. That had been what finally snapped him out of the artifact's haze, bringing his consciousness to the forefront. Hearing those words on her lips, so desperate, hearing the truth in them.

Had anyone ever loved him this way before? No, not really. Sara's love had been false. His parents' love had been paternal. But Eleanor? She loved him, and it was a precious thing he didn't deserve.

Pulling away, he placed open mouthed kisses along her neck, nipping at her earlobe. Her breath caught. His hands ached with the need to explore every inch of her soft skin. The sight of his against hers, silvery-gray to lightly tanned, felt erotic. She was so different from him, and it was that difference that he cherished.

He slid down her body, laying kisses along her flushed skin, pausing to worship her breasts, kneading and licking, flicking her nipple with his tongue before moving on. When he reached her pussy, he removed a few sharp claws, parted the folds with his fingers, and gave a long, broad sweep of his tongue. The ball of his piercing caught on her clit and her hips jerked against him. A small smile toyed with his lips.

He looked up and said, "You are my mate, Eleanor. You understand what that means, yes?"

"I... Yes? I think so? I was hoping we might discuss it."

He hesitated. As much as he wanted to dive right in, bury his face in her, this probably shouldn't wait. "What would you like to know?"

She hesitated, looking down the length of her body, studying the way he sat between her legs, everything on full display. She pulled her thighs together, or tried to, but he was sitting between them.

"Oh no, baby girl. No hiding from your mate. Like the rest of you, this pussy belongs to me. I may look my fill whenever I wish." His hands parted her thighs wider and she blushed. "That is, assuming you will have me."

A frown pulled her brows together. "I have a choice?"

"Of course you have a choice, sugar. I would never force you to be with me, force you to love me, or be mated to me."

"But hasn't that ship sailed?"

He sighed. "In a way, yes."

"How long—when did you know? The whole time?"

"No. When you put your lips on my cock and blew me. When I came. When I looked at you in that moment, the bond clicked into place."

"Oh." She was likely recalling that moment the way he was.

"But as I said, if you do not wish for this, you may reject the bond. You have that power. All mates have that power."

She came up onto her elbows to better see him. "I do? And you do?" He nodded. "But…you won't, right? You won't reject me?" Her voice dropped low, and she licked her lips.

The vulnerability of her question split his heart wide open. The world around him had suddenly become so fucking beautiful with her in it. His pulse started to race. He looked at her, really looked at her, spread before him, beautiful both inside and out. Pure perfection.

"Elle, baby, I fucking love you. I'm so fucking in love with you. I am so deep in over my goddamn head that I'm drowning in it. No, I won't reject you. Not now, not ever. I meant what I said about goblins, do you remember?"

She pulled her bottom lip between her teeth and nodded. "That you're all filthy hoarders?"

A laugh burst from his chest, making him feel like a feather drifting in the breeze. "Something like that. *You*, sweetheart, are my most precious jewel. A thing to be worshiped and cherished, to be polished and shined, to be cared for and attended to, nourished and loved. If you want pancakes for breakfast every morning? Done. Ten orgasms a day? Twenty? More? Done. You want to go back to school and chase your dreams? Done. I'll support you through every minute of it. You want to keep shaking this fucking gorgeous ass in front of a crowd of people… Well, I'll have to restrain myself from ripping the throat out of everyone who watches you, but I'll manage."

A sobbing laugh burst from her lips. She fell back on the bed and covered her face with her hands. His chest tightened. Wait, wait, wait. Was she…*crying*?

He crawled atop her, laying his body over hers, wrapping gentle fingers around her wrists and tugging them away from her face.

"Look at me, sugar."

She turned teary eyes on him. "Do you really mean all that?"

"Every fucking word. I'm yours, baby girl. I… My lifestyle isn't the most kosher. You know what I do. If you want me to change career paths, then I will—"

"No! I mean, I could never ask that of you. But… You aren't going to get hurt, right?"

He chuckled. "I'd be more worried about the people I bring in." She nodded. "But no, I don't plan to die on you."

"I couldn't ask you to change for me, Bas. I love you how you are. I mean, maybe try not to come home covered in blood, but otherwise…" Something solidified in her expression. "I accept you, Bastian Croft, exactly the way you are."

His chest exploded with heat. The need to show her, to worship her, to claim her as thoroughly as she'd just claimed him, overpowered every other thought in his mind. He peppered her face with kisses until her tears turned to giggles and she was squirming beneath him. His fingers, still aching to worship her, moved down her body and slipped between her legs. As he played with her pussy, he carefully studied her face, soaking up every minute change in her expression. He pressed one finger, and then two, inside her, stretching her, working her. She tried to buck beneath his bulk, but he had her pinned.

When she was dripping from his efforts, he took his cock, guiding it to her entrance. Slowly, so as to not miss a single sensation, he eased inside. The warmth of her wrapped around him and a shiver worked up the length of his spine, short circuiting his brain at the base of his skull.

"I love it when you make love to me like this," she breathed, her eyes wide and filled with pleasure—pleasure from *his* efforts. Because she was his mate, only his. "In your beautiful goblin form."

Those words made his heart ache with so much emotion.

They hadn't really made love prior to this. It had been a lot of fucking, sometimes slow and languid, other times fast and frenzied. But this? He wanted to make this time different.

He kept his movements slow, holding her gaze, letting her see everything he felt. Letting himself be vulnerable for her. Allowing himself to moan when he moved in a way that felt particularly good.

Letting her see *all* of him.

"Yes," she breathed, pulling his long hair back with one hand in a tight fist, using the other to wrap around his neck.

Anchoring them together.

He wouldn't rush this. Each slow stroke was a true test to his patience. Soon she was whimpering beneath him, face glowing, eyes glazed with pleasure. It was impossible to stop himself from dragging the backs of his knuckles along her cheekbone, caressing her face, brushing strands of her pink hair back.

Fussing over her because she was precious to him.

"I love you, Bastian," she breathed. His heart fluttered as tingles spread through his body. He snaked his arms beneath her, wrapping them around her body, pulling her tightly to him, burying his face in her neck. He inhaled, letting her coffee scent soak into him, calm him.

His balls tightened, his seed rising. Eleanor's muscles went taught, hands moving over his back. When her blunt little nails scraped his skin, sending shivers through him, he combusted. Her body jerked at the same time as she cried out, "Bastian!" Her pussy clenched around him, milking him as he spilled every drop of his seed inside her. The sound of his name on her lips, and his entire fucking world just stopped, swallowed up by the wave of pleasure pounding in his center.

He pressed in deeper, grinding his hips against her, groaning out her name. Never wanting it to end. His orgasm disoriented him, brought a wave of blackness that rushed in at the fringes of his mind before receding. He tightened his arms around her, holding on to the only lifeline he'd ever need, and let it sweep him away.

42

Bastian pulled his truck in front of Eleanor's apartment building, shutting off the ignition. Nearly a week had passed since the events with Marsh Thadur. The WBI had found itself in an uproar. His department had worked day and night fixing things. Memory wipes for the humans involved, reuniting sleepers with their friends and families, restoring artifacts, and electing a new Fae in Marsh Thadur's place.

The WBI had argued over custody of Thadur, but in the end, the Fae stepped in—Endorian, specifically—and Thadur was moved into Carrok, the Fae's high security prison on the outskirts of Walton. No human prison would keep a Fae like Thadur. As far as he knew, the Supernatural Council hadn't yet finalized the male's punishment. That would be coming soon enough.

Giggles erupted outside his truck, pulling him back into the moment. Eleanor was arm in arm with Tara, the coffee house woman. Vivi trailed behind them, her eyes on her phone, frowning. The tight knot in his chest loosened, seeing the familiar head of cotton candy pink hair. He'd been so caught up in work that they'd only gotten in a couple of phone calls over the last three days.

This brief getaway was much needed. It was also technically their first date. The girls climbed into the truck, Tara and Vivi taking the back seat. Elle's scent hit him and he further relaxed. She settled in and slammed the door, belting herself in. He absentmindedly reached over and gave it a tug at the latch—a reflex, more than anything, to ensure she was safe. Always. Then he rested his arm on the center console, leaning in as he looked her up and down.

"Morning, sugar," he purred. "You sure you don't want a jacket?"

She was dressed in a pair of yoga pants and loose-fitting workout top. Her hair was pulled into a ponytail, loose curls bobbing, a few wispy strands framing her delicate features. He tried not to think about how it felt to wrap that ponytail around his fist. Yeah, his mind went there anyway.

"Once we get moving, it'll be hot." She shrugged. "I don't want to cart it around the whole time."

He sighed before rotating toward the back seat. "You ladies ready?"

"Yes," they chorused. "Let's do this!"

His mouth twitched, but he turned to face forward, starting the truck's engine and pulling out into traffic. A rustle beside him had him glancing over. Elle was already getting comfortable. She'd shed her shoes, placed her sock-clad feet up on his dashboard. She was peeling the wrapper off a granola bar.

"You didn't have breakfast?" he growled. She threw him a pout. "Fucking hell, Eleanor."

The thought of her hungry made him immediately consider how best to feed her. There was the coffee shop down the street—

"Bastian, stop scowling. This will be plenty. Besides, if I grow faint, I have you to carry me down the trail."

Giggles erupted from the back seat. God help him, this was going to be a day. They were finally having that date they'd talked about—going hiking. Except, Elle had wanted it to be a *double date* with Tara and Vivi. He hadn't objected. Oh, he'd wanted to protest. Alone, he could have found a secluded place along the trail and fucked her brains out.

He had days of steam to burn off.

But no. Not now. He would have to mind his manners. Besides, he couldn't say no, not when she'd asked him so sweetly over the phone. A hint of hesitance in her voice. Like she worried about his answer.

"Thanks again for letting us tag along," Tara said from the back, as if reading his mind.

He merely hummed in response.

"I made a playlist," Elle announced, fiddling with the truck's dials and her phone. He knew better than to say a damned word as pop music filled the cab. It was all he could do to keep his eyes on the road as the three women erupted into song. He caught glimpses of his mate from the corner of his eye. She glowed with happiness, exactly as she deserved to be. Exactly as he planned to make her for the rest of her life.

An hour later, they reached the trailhead, piling out and strapping on backpacks. Elle stood beside him, inhaling deeply. He watched her, a smile tugging at the corner of his lips. Her eyes were closed, a look of contentment on her features. "It smells so good out here, so clean."

"Come on, slowpokes!" Vivi shouted, already taking off down the trail, Tara on her heels.

He ignored them, pulling Elle against him, leaning down to kiss her, letting his lips linger. He nipped her bottom lip, then grazed his mouth along her jaw. "I want you in front of me, so I can stare at that tight ass the whole way."

She giggled as he spun her around and gave her a gentle push before slapping her ass. She yelped and darted forward, throwing him a teasing glare as they caught up with the others. One look at her backside and he suddenly regretted his decision.

Around them, the trees were thick, walling off the dirt path they followed. It was a cooler than usual spring morning, but the day would warm. Birds were already busy, and squirrels darted across their trail. He was careful to avoid rocks and other debris littering the way. The girls set the pace, far slower than he would have gone. He merely meandered behind, making sure they stayed safe.

His eyes rarely left Eleanor. The way she moved with easy confidence along the uneven trail, her ponytail swaying with each step. It had his chest tightening with pride. She belonged out here in nature, away from the chaos of the city and the horrors they'd faced.

When she paused to point out wildflowers to Vivi, or when she laughed at something Tara said, the sound carried back to him and made his heart race. His mate was happy—truly, genuinely happy—and knowing he'd played a part in that, knowing that he'd get to witness these moments for the rest of their very long lives together, left him feeling drunk on possibility. Because he had every intention of ensuring they lived long lives.

Just like the ability to heal, her life span would be tied to his. She wouldn't age. Wouldn't grow old without him.

He knew because he'd dug into records. Aramis had helped. Turned out, Elle wasn't the only human pairing that had happened in history. Aramis had put him into contact with a shifter couple—lion female, human male. The male was now approaching his three hundred and forty third birthday. He hadn't aged a day since accepting their bond.

Which meant Elle would live as long as Bastian did.

Every so often, Elle glanced back at him and caught him staring. Her soft smile made his goblin side purr with satisfaction. She was his. Forever.

Starting with today.

He'd cleared his schedule for the entire weekend, making it plenty clear to his boss that he'd be unreachable. He'd also made it clear to Eleanor that she belonged to him for the entirety of that time. Well, she belonged to him regardless, but she'd also cleared her schedule. There was an overnight bag in the back of his truck for later, after they dropped Tara and Vivi off.

It was thoughts of the night to come that occupied most of his mind while they hiked. Tara and Vivi chatted for the first hour, but soon enough, they were too winded to speak.

He liked hiking in silence, listening to the wildlife, letting his thoughts wander. He'd answered their questions readily enough as Vivi grilled him, but only because she was Elle's best friend.

Elle was lucky—damned lucky—to have her. Vivi was a protector, the one who'd been there for her during the hardest time in her life. He'd never forget that, never forget the way she'd taken care of his girl, his mate.

Mate.

Every time he thought about it, the world grew quiet.

As if sensing his thoughts, Elle threw him a glance over her shoulder. He winked, and perhaps there was plenty in his expression, because she blushed. He wanted that. He wanted her to look at him and never forget how thoroughly he pleased her, how good he made her feel. Her head snapped forward again as they made the final ascent to the trail's lookout point.

The forest opened up around them.

"It's gorgeous!" Vivi cried. The three women were breathing hard, their skin coated in a sheen of sweat. His heart rate hadn't even increased. He came to stop behind Elle, leaning in close enough to graze her body, keeping his hands to himself. Her skin erupted into goosebumps and he hid a satisfied smile.

"Wow," she sighed, taking it in. "I forgot how much I love this hike."

"I hope you didn't forget how much you love *me?*" he murmured against her ear. Tara and Vivi were already wandering off, looking for a spot to have their picnic.

"Does that cockiness of yours ever go away?" She leaned backwards into him. Her backpack was crushed against his chest. His hands came around her front.

"Hard to shed the habit when I have you worshiping my cock every night," he rumbled, not that he'd gotten much of that in the past couple days. But tonight…

"Oh, my God," she hissed, giggling. "That mouth of yours knows no boundaries."

"Course not. Especially not when its busy licking your—"

"Okay, who is ready for lunch?!" Elle blurted so loudly that he couldn't finish the sentence. He chuckled, releasing her so they could settle down and eat their sandwiches.

He ate as he watched the three of them, observed how comfortable Elle was with her friends. How much she laughed. How much her eyes twinkled. He hadn't even realized he was smiling until his cheeks started to hurt.

———

"Are those pancakes for *me*?" came a sleepy voice, laced with feigned innocence. Bastian huffed, hiding his grin. He set his spatula on the counter and turned to find his girl in the doorway. She was wearing one of his T-shirts, which had become a habit of hers when she slept over. His eyes narrowed. He was almost certain she'd confiscated it from his room before coming into the kitchen. It was clean, and he distinctly remembered folding it and tucking it away in his drawers after doing laundry the other day.

The sight of her in it made his chest swell with pride.

He wasn't even *slightly* covert as he traced her figure from head to toe, his eyes lingering on her bare legs. The satisfaction of her flushed skin left his cock twitching in his lounge pants. He needed to fuck her like this, with her dressed in his clothes.

After returning from their hike yesterday, they'd stayed up far too late making love. He'd let her sleep as long as he could physically manage, lying there beside her, watching her chest rise and fall, watching the beautifully calm expression on her face before slipping from bed to use the restroom and make breakfast. The desire to provide, to make her food, to see to her needs was too overpowering. His goblin side was already preening. Especially now. Seeing her there standing in the doorway with her sleep mussed hair.

It was so fucking *right*.

"I suppose that depends, sugar," he managed, finally finding his words.

A slow grin spread across her lips. "On?"

"On whether you've got any panties on under my shirt."

"Oh." She bit her lower lip, then her hand dipped between her legs, but she didn't lift the shirt, didn't give anything away. The sight of her touching herself sent fire roaring through his veins. He emitted a low, warning growl. "Hm… I'm not really sure I should answer that. Maybe you should find out for yourself."

His glamor broke. As usual, she had a way of tugging his basest form free. He took a step toward her, but she lifted her hands.

"Ah-ah-ah, your pancake is burning." And indeed, the scent of overdone pancake met his nose, mixed with the smell of her wetness now clinging to her fingers. Fuck, fuck, *fuck*. He growled, spun around and turned off the burner, then stalked over to her, snatching her up and setting her on the counter. He managed to get control of his form enough to ensure his claws wouldn't hurt her. His fingers slid up her legs, but he kept his eyes on hers, watched as they widened when he found her wet pussy.

"No panties," he concluded. "I'm not sure there'll be pancakes after all, sugar, since I'll be too busy fucking you on this counter."

"Bas!" she breathed as he slipped inside her. She clenched around his fingers. "Go wash your hands and finish my breakfast."

His mouth twitched. That bossy tone—he had plans for that. But, later. First, he needed to feed his female.

"Yes ma'am." He removed his hand and licked every drop of her off him. "There. All clean."

"Oh, my God. That's *not* what I meant."

"I know what you meant, sugar. You just sit right there where I can keep an eye on you. I'm going to finish your breakfast, and then I'm going to finish *you*. Understood?" Her lips parted, a tinge of pink creeping up her throat.

"Understood," she breathed. And that's exactly what he did, what he planned to do from this day forward, and every day thereafter. This new feeling, this completeness he'd found in her, it was something to be celebrated. He planned to embrace the shit out of it. Every. Fucking. Moment.

EPILOGUE

I walked up to the library building, standing beneath the overhang and looking out over Walton University's campus. Autumn was in full swing, the leaves changing to beautiful shades of red and orange. The air was crisp. I hugged my textbooks against my front, glad I'd worn a cardigan.

My phone chimed and I wrestled it from my pocket. It was from Bastian.

> **BASTIAN**
>
> Hope class went okay? I'm about ten minutes away.

I smiled and sent him a quick text in response.

A cluster of leaves blew across the cement in front of me, rustling my pink hair against my skin. I could have dyed it back to my natural color, but I'd grown fond of it. I didn't bother with tinted contacts anymore, either.

As a surprise, Bastian had enlisted the skills of a couple WBI friends to dig up my hidden records from the university database. Turned out I only had twelve units left to complete my master's degree, along with a thesis paper. Given my involvement in returning the library's missing artifacts, for which Bastian had insisted I receive *all* the credit, the university was practically begging to have me here.

They had no problem making an exception for my late enrollment at the end of the summer, giving me back my position in the program. They'd even noted on my records that I'd taken a two-year leave of absence for personal reasons. Normally, only a single semester was permitted.

I wasn't certain, but I had a mind to go for my Ph.D afterward. Possibly even take up Professor Miller's work here at the university. Bastian had already given me his full support on the matter, encouraging me to do exactly that. He'd admitted that it would be 'cool' if his mate was an 'artifact hunter.'

Of course, I'd snorted.

"Has a good ring to it," he'd claimed, a gleam in his eyes.

So, here I was, my first semester back at WU and already four weeks in. I was doing it—I was going after my dreams. I was reclaiming the life Luke Portman had stolen from me. And this time, I had someone so much better supporting me along the way. Bastian had shown me what a healthy relationship looked like, and now I couldn't believe I'd ever fallen for Luke's bullshit. But that's how destructive relationships worked. Sometimes, after getting stuck in a pot of water, it was impossible to sense the temperature rising around you. I was just glad I had people in my life to pull me from the pot if things got too bad. Not that they would. Not this time.

I walked toward parking lot when I spotted Bastian's sleek sports car pulling into a spot. I studied his muscled body as he emerged, broad shoulders, trim hips, gorgeous face. He walked over to one of the permit boxes and punched in a few numbers, grabbing the temporary permit to avoid another ticket. It was hard not to drool over the sight of him. He slipped the pass into the windshield of his car before slamming the door and heading my way.

A couple girls passing by, their arms laden with books, paused to watch him. *Sorry ladies*, I wanted to say. *He's taken.*

My eyes locked on Bastian's as he walked toward me. Heat

simmered between us. Even four months later, and not an ounce of desire had disappeared. In fact, it was the opposite. Everything just kept getting better.

That's not to say it was always easy, moving through our lives together. We argued. Bickered. Sometimes fought.

A month after the incident with Marsh Thadur, he convinced me to move in. It wasn't a difficult decision, considering I spent most of my nights with him anyway. Plus, Tara and Vivi had turned into a serious thing and they were eager to move in together, too. That had definitely been an adjustment for us, growing pains and all.

Vivi and I shared custody of Teddy, alternating each week. Teddy didn't mind, and neither did Bastian, considering he cuddled Teddy more than I did. Yeah, the cat had definitely grown on him.

"Hey, baby girl." Bastian hooked an elbow around my neck, leaning in to plant a sloppy kiss on my lips. Didn't matter that we were standing in public in broad daylight. Then he took my books from my arms and made them disappear. "You ready?"

"I think so." I had to swallow against my suddenly dry throat.

We walked across campus to the health and wellness building. I checked in and he sat with me in the waiting room. A few minutes later, an attendant appeared with a clipboard. "Eleanor Kennedy? Dr. Rosmond will see you now."

I stood, wiping my sweaty palms on my jeans. Bastian stood too, taking my hand and kissing my palm. "I'll be right here, waiting. You'll do fine."

I nodded, not sure I trusted my voice, then followed the attendant into the hallway. She asked for my date of birth, checking a couple things off her clipboard for admin purposes, then stopped outside an office door, knocking.

A soft voice called for us from within, and I was ushered inside.

"Ahh. Elle, welcome."

"Hi Dr. Rosmond." I tried to keep my voice from wavering as I shook her hand.

"Oh, please, call me Kelly." I nodded. "Have a seat and tell me what I can help you with."

I sat down across from her. Her desk was littered with papers, a laptop, and several family photos. I cleared my throat. "I saw online that there were several open positions for mentors? For the domestic abuse prevention and rehabilitation programs offered through health services?"

"Ah. Yes. Of course."

"I'd… I'd like to speak with you about becoming a mentor. Like, what it might entail? And see if I would be a good fit." My heart pounded in my chest. When I'd come across the listings on the health and wellness site, I'd shown Bastian and he'd encouraged me to seek it out.

"Fantastic," Dr. Rosmond said, her soft expression melting into a smile. I liked her voice, it was calming. "We are looking to help those who are currently suffering or have suffered various forms of abuse—both mental and physical. It's one of the new programs we're getting off the ground, but as you can imagine, there haven't been many people eager to come out and volunteer for the positions. So our need is rather dire."

"Right. I can see that as being a challenge."

"Why don't you tell me a little about yourself and why you feel you'd be a good fit for this position. As you can imagine, personal experience will play a large role in fitment. However, if there is anything you are uncomfortable sharing, do not force yourself outside your comfort zone. We take those things very seriously and would never ask you to talk about something you don't wish to share."

I nodded, tucking a strand of hair behind my ear, then launched into my tale. Something about Dr. Rosmond put me at ease. There were very few people in my life who knew all the details of what I'd suffered at Luke's hand, but I wanted her to be one of them. We spent the next hour in a deep discussion before she dismissed me from her office. I felt so light, and there was an added spring in my step.

I found Bastian in the waiting room, his ankle propped up on his knee, scrolling on his phone. For a moment, I just stared at him. All I could think was how damn lucky I was to have him. How thankful I was that we'd been brought together under unfortunate circumstances. I hated that Professor Miller's death had done it, but I sent a silent prayer to her, wherever she was, for being the reason we'd discovered each other.

Sensing my entry, Bastian looked up. Our eyes connected and I grinned. A smile tugged at his lips. He stood, coming over, wrapping his arm around my waist as he pulled me against his side.

"Well?" He guided me from the building, back out into the cool autumn air. Feeling the chill, he tugged the corner of my cardigan more tightly over my chest, as if he worried I might be cold. "Looks like things went okay?"

"I got it!" I breathed, excitement billowing out of me. My heart hadn't stopped hammering and my cheeks hurt. "Dr. Rosmond said that she's got a number of candidates looking for mentorship, that depending on what my schedule allows, she's got two or three she can team me up with."

"Baby girl..." Bastian's low growl sent warmth bursting through my chest. "That's fucking fantastic. I'm so proud of you for doing this, for being brave like this, for facing your fears, for being so selfless and giving. You're going to make a difference in these peoples' lives in a big way." My throat tightened and I nodded, blinking back tears.

He was right. That was exactly what I wanted.

"When do you start?" There was genuine curiosity in his voice.

"She said she'll call me next week to set up the first meeting." I sucked in a breath. "I... I really want to help, you know? Not everyone has someone like Vivi. Not everyone is lucky like that. I don't know what I would have done without her. I… I might have done something…drastic." He went rigid against me. "I guess I'm just hoping my experiences might help other people."

He blew out a breath, relaxing. "They will. I know they will." Then he bent down and kissed my forehead, his lips lingering. I wrapped my arms around his middle as we made the walk back to the library parking lot.

Months ago, I never imagined that spilling this goblin's coffee down the front of my shirt would bring us here, to this moment. I never imagined that someone could so thoroughly disrupt my life in the best way. That someone could give me a reason to work past my wounds, to stitch them up, let them heal, and be okay with seeing the scars. That was Bastian. He didn't mind a few scars. After all, he had some himself. He was okay with me in any form. My mate was…everything. And for that, I felt like the luckiest girl alive.

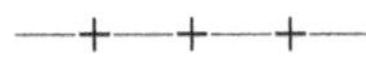

Want more Bastian and Elle? Read the free Bonus Epilogue by subscribing to my mailing list where you can access my Reader Vault of growing bonus content:

https://www.authormelissamitchell.com/newslettersignup

If you enjoyed this book, please make my day by leaving a rating / review. Reviews help get indie authors like me noticed.

The Arcane Artifacts continues with Lily and Laurent's story in Trapped by the Blood Ruby

Vampires don't exist. It's a mathematical certainty. But the mathematical reality? I'm trapped in a gothic mansion filled with them.

Get their story here: https://a.co/d/0dbd8ruw

THE ARCANE ARTIFACTS CONTINUES WITH... TRAPPED BY THE BLOOD RUBY

Lily and Laurent's story…

Vampires don't exist. It's a mathematical certainty. But the mathematical reality? I'm trapped in a gothic mansion filled with them.

Get their story here: https://a.co/d/0dbd8ruw

ABOUT THE AUTHOR

Melissa Mitchell is a fantasy romance author and creator of the seven-book *Dragonwall* series. Her love of fantasy began with *The Dragonriders of Pern*, and she now writes stories full of dragons, magic, hidden royalty, and slow-burn romance. She holds a PhD in physics and lives in Atlanta, Georgia with her husband, a husky, and four very spoiled bunnies. When she's not writing, she enjoys baking cookies, bullet journaling, and figure skating—usually while plotting her next book.

Visit her online at: authormelissamitchell.com

ALSO BY MELISSA MITCHELL

The Dragonwall Series

Talon the Black

Reyr the Gold

Verath the Red

Koldis the Green

Bedelth the Orange

Jovari the Blue

Dallin the Violet

The Lady Witch Series

Wielder's Prize

Wielder's Bond

Wielder's Might

Witch's Ruin

Witch's Heart

Witch's Crown

Royals of Dragonwall Series

For the Crown

Stand Alone Titles

Blood and Ballet

www.ingramcontent.com/pod-product-compliance
Lightning Source LLC
Chambersburg PA
CBHW021438310726

48971CB00005B/1409